Praise for Jen DeLuca

"*Well Traveled* is a true comfort read. Jen DeLuca is at the top of her game with this delightfully charming romance that will wrap cozily around your heart and warm it through. Lovable characters and the marvelously rendered world of the Renaissance Faire make the novel feel so real, and so very enjoyable. I recommend it highly."

—India Holton, national bestselling author of
The League of Gentlewomen Witches

"Lulu may live to work, but she didn't have to work for me to love her. Jen DeLuca has done it again [in *Well Traveled*], crafting another heartfelt rom-com that will make the dreamers in all of us squeal with delight!"

—Kosoko Jackson, author of *I'm So Not Over You*

"Charming, compassionate, and romantic, *Well Traveled* is a rich return to the Renaissance Faire, full of the delightful details De-Luca delivers in every wonderful installment. We loved every lyrical moment of Lulu and Dex's journey—a full-hearted story of following the song in your heart and finding your own path."

—Emily Wibberley and Austin Siegemund-Broka, authors of
The Roughest Draft

"A great comfort read. Warm, sweet, and hopeful, *Well Matched* is about daring to come out of your shell and building the life you always wanted."

—Helen Hoang, *New York Times* bestselling author of
The Heart Principle

T0262611

"This series is one of my ultimate comfort reads. I knew I'd adore April and Mitch together, but I didn't realize how deeply obsessed with them I'd be. *Well Matched* is for anyone whose life hasn't gone according to plan, and about all the joys that come with veering off course. Warm and witty, sweet and sexy—this tender hug of a book is Jen DeLuca at her best."

—Rachel Lynn Solomon, *New York Times* bestselling author of
Weather Girl

"Jen DeLuca writes with exceptional warmth. *Well Matched* is cozy, sweet, and brimming with charm. It's such a joy to go back to the Faire with Mitch and April!"

—Rosie Danan, national bestselling author of *The Intimacy Experiment*

"*Well Matched* is completely charming and delightfully touching. DeLuca delivers a love story that leaves you feeling as warm and fuzzy as you are hot and bothered. April's vulnerability and humor are endearing, and Mitch is book-boyfriend goals in a kilt—I couldn't put it down."

—Denise Williams, author of *Do You Take This Man*

"With well-drawn characters and laugh-out-loud scenes, *Well Matched* is a perfect opposites-attract romance." —Shelf Awareness

"This sexy, witty, fast-paced romantic comedy has surprising emotional depth." —*Library Journal*

"DeLuca's enchanting tale of unsought love developing over home improvement tasks and making family members happy, cheerfully set against the charming backdrop of a Renaissance Faire, is a joy to read." —*Booklist*

ALSO BY JEN DeLUCA

Well Met
Well Played
Well Matched
Well Traveled

Haunted Ever After

JEN DeLUCA

BERKLEY ROMANCE

NEW YORK

BERKLEY ROMANCE
Published by Berkley
An imprint of Penguin Random House LLC
penguinrandomhouse.com

Library of Congress Cataloging-in-Publication Data

Names: DeLuca, Jen, author.
Title: Haunted ever after / Jen DeLuca.
Description: First Edition. | New York: Berkley Romance, 2024.
Identifiers: LCCN 2024002997 (print) | LCCN 2024002998 (ebook) |
ISBN 9780593641217 (trade paperback) | ISBN 9780593641224 (ebook)
Subjects: LCGFT: Romance fiction. | Ghost stories. | Novels.
Classification: LCC PS3604.E44757 H38 2024 (print) | LCC PS3604.E44757 (ebook) |
DDC 813/.6—dc23/eng/20240125
LC record available at https://lccn.loc.gov/2024002997
LC ebook record available at https://lccn.loc.gov/2024002998

First Edition: August 2024

Printed in the United States of America
1st Printing

Book design by Nancy Resnick
Title page illustration by magic pictures/Shutterstock.com

For Amanda and Julie.
Y'all are what I miss most about Florida.

Haunted
     Ever
After

One

That meeting could've been an email.

Cassie Rutherford clicked "LEAVE MEETING" and took out her earbuds. Once she'd confirmed that her camera was off, the bright smile slipped from her face and she let her forehead thunk to the table with a moan.

What a week. And it was only Monday. She'd made a lot of mistakes in her thirty-one years of life, and of them all, this one was . . . well, it wasn't the worst one. But it sure as hell was the most recent.

Her life was chaos. Cassie didn't like chaos. She liked checklists. She liked the satisfaction of a job well done. She didn't like moving boxes filling every room of her new house, turning her morning routine into an obstacle course. She didn't like having no idea where her saucepans were, since they weren't in the box labeled **KITCHEN**. And she really, really didn't like waking up a half hour before an all-hands meeting with a dead laptop.

Most small Florida tourist trap towns had a schtick, and her new town had apparently been dubbed the Most Haunted Small Town in Florida. At least that's what the sign outside of the Boneyard Key Chamber of Commerce said. How many towns had been competing for that title? That was Cassie's question.

They certainly leaned in to it hard around here. Flagpoles lined the historic downtown sidewalks, each one featuring a banner with a classic-looking Halloween ghost: white, vaguely blob shaped, big black eyes. They fluttered in the early-morning breeze in the world's laziest attempt to be spooky. T-shirts hung in the window of the I Scream Ice Cream Shop that she'd passed this morning. I had a spooky good time in Boneyard Key, Florida! proclaimed one of them. Boneyard Key, where the chills aren't just from the ice cream! said another one. Both were illustrated with cartoonishly ghoulish graphics: a skeletal hand poking out of a grave, ice-cream cone in hand.

And this was all in April. This place probably went apeshit for Halloween.

Cassie's newly purchased historic cottage had gingerbread trim, little balconies off the upstairs bedrooms, a backyard that ended in a seawall bordering the Gulf of Mexico, and unreliable electricity. She'd left her laptop plugged in on the kitchen table last night, but this morning it was drained of all juice, like an electricity vampire had stolen it during the night. Thank God for Hallowed Grounds (man, this town really leaned in to the ghost puns); she'd found this coffee shop down the street just in time.

Cassie's ears were sore from her earbuds, and she rubbed at one while she reviewed her notes from the meeting. Doodles, mostly. She'd spoken all of two times. Once to chime in on the Farnsworth account, confirming that she was aware of the deadline and that she was on track to reach it. The second time toward the end of the meeting when her work bestie, Mandy, had asked about her move. Yes, the move had gone great. Yes, her house was right on the water, and she could hear the waves when she went to sleep at night. But then she'd seen Roz's expression pucker, even through the laptop screen, and Cassie had cut the nonwork-related conversation short. She'd update everyone in the group chat later.

And say what, though? Everyone wanted to hear good things.

No one wanted to know what was really on her mind: that maybe she'd made the most expensive mistake of her life. One that was practically impossible to unwind.

God, she needed coffee.

Cassie closed her laptop and leveled a glare at what appeared to be the coffee shop's lone employee. Still on his goddamn phone, just like he had been when she'd walked in. He was tall and lean, slim hipped in faded jeans and a gray pocket tee. His hair was on the long side, falling in russet waves around his face and over his forehead, matching his close-trimmed beard. She couldn't see his eyes, as his head was bent over the phone in his hands, thumbs flying across the screen.

He looked too old to be a Gen Z, TikTok-addicted kid, but his attention had been on his phone when she'd come in. He hadn't even looked up as she'd come barreling through the door. Hadn't said a word as she beelined to a table in the back with a blessed outlet nearby. As much as she'd wanted to fuel up before the meeting, she had just enough time to hook up, access the Wi-Fi listed on the card on the table, and get logged in. Caffeine had to wait.

A glance down at her laptop showed that it was charged up, so she should really get home. Get some work done. Find her saucepans. Figure out what was wrong with her house. Probably something wrong with the wiring that the inspector had missed, which was way beyond her scope.

Too bad houses weren't like other retail purchases. No returning it for a refund, even though she had the receipt. She was locked into a mortgage now.

At this point, she could just go home and make coffee, but dammit, that was boring, and she'd promised herself a little treat after the shitty start to the day. She could get a coffee to go; she deserved it.

Coffee shop guy looked up with disdain as she approached the counter. "Oh. Are you actually gonna order something?" His voice was deeper than she'd expected, with an undertone of gravel. But all Cassie could see was blue. That clear crystal blue that made you think of Caribbean water. Of lab-created sapphires, because a blue that blue couldn't exist in nature. Damn, but this slacker barista had pretty eyes.

Then his words registered and she frowned, pretty eyes forgotten. "What do you mean?"

"I mean . . ." He jerked his head in a nod toward the table she'd just vacated. "You've been sitting there for almost an hour, using my Wi-Fi, without even so much as ordering a cup of coffee. This isn't a coworking space, you know. It's a business."

"Really? Damn." Cassie looked pointedly around the place. Empty. "Sorry to occupy your fanciest table."

His lips twitched, sending a thrill through her. She didn't like this guy; why did she care if he thought she was funny? "You want to order something or what?" Despite the almost-smile, his voice didn't sound much friendlier. Great.

"Iced latte, please. Hazelnut, if you have it."

"We have it." He sounded insulted that she implied otherwise. "Anything else?"

Her eyes strayed to the pastry case. It looked pretty picked over; this must be a popular breakfast spot. "Is that banana bread?"

"Yep." His voice was clipped as he moved to the espresso machine.

"And I was going to order when I got here, you know." She raised her voice over the hiss of the machine as he steamed the milk. "You had your face shoved in your phone. Maybe a little less time on Tinder and a little more time doing your job." The machine cut off, and she was suddenly yelling in the very empty café. The slacker barista didn't respond; he just shook his head, his back to her as he worked.

If Cassie didn't like chaos, she really didn't like being ignored. "I mean, what would your boss think . . ." There was a stack of business cards in a little plastic holder by the register, and she snatched one, reading from it. "What would Nick Royer think about your lack of service?"

"I dunno." He plonked the finished drink onto the counter in front of her, ice sloshing against the lid. "Why don't you ask him?"

His mouth did that almost-twitch thing again, and there was something in his eyes—those stunning blue eyes—that set off a warning bell in the back of Cassie's brain. But screw that—she was too annoyed to listen.

"Maybe I will!" she said to his back as he bagged a slice of banana bread from the pastry case. She grabbed a pen from the cup in front of her and flipped the business card over. "What's your name?"

"Nick." He tossed the banana bread onto the counter next to her iced latte. "Nick Royer."

Well. Shit.

Cassie looked down at her order. The iced latte was in a plastic cup, lid firmly on and a wrapped straw on top. The banana bread was in a little paper bag. He'd prepared her order to go without asking. He didn't want her there any more than she wanted to be there.

She looked back up at Nick. His arms were folded across his chest, biceps straining against the sleeves of his gray T-shirt. His mouth was set in a thin line, and his warm blue eyes now looked stone-cold. "That'll be seven fifty."

Her new life in her new town was off to a fantastic start.

Cassie reached for her drink while he ran her card, punching the straw in and taking a sip. She closed her eyes with a grateful sigh as caffeine sped through her bloodstream and her shoulders relaxed. The drink was perfect: just the right amount of hazelnut syrup, not too sweet, with enough bitter espresso to wake up her senses. This dickhead made a fantastic iced latte, which was unfortunate. She was going to have to keep coming back here, wasn't she?

She blinked her eyes open to see said dickhead holding her card out toward her. "Anything else?" The question was automatic; she was supposed to shake her head, take her stuff, and get the hell out.

But inspiration struck. "You don't happen to know a good electrician, do you?"

Nick stopped short, blinked at what had to be an unexpected question. "A what?"

"Electrician. Handyman. Someone who can tell me why half the outlets in the house don't seem to work."

He shook his head, baffled. "Can't you just message the owner?"

"The what?" Now it was Cassie's turn to be baffled.

"The owner," he repeated with exaggerated patience. This guy really didn't like her. "Through the app or whatever. You don't fix stuff yourself in a vacation rental. That's the owner's responsibility."

"I am the owner. It's my house. Wait." A horrible thought occurred to Cassie. "You think I'm a tourist?"

"Well, yeah." He rubbed at the back of his neck as his brow furrowed. "You have the look."

"The *look*?" She glanced down at herself. She'd been in such a hurry this morning that she'd thrown on the first thing she could find: denim cutoffs and the **Give me the Oxford comma or give me death** T-shirt she'd gotten from her Secret Santa at work last year. Her hair was up in a bun because styling it had been out of the question. At least she was wearing her nicer flip-flops.

"Sure," Nick said. "Lots of tourists come in here with their laptops, get some work done while they're on vacation." He waved a hand toward her laptop bag. "So I just figured . . ."

Cassie crossed her arms over her chest; she couldn't believe this.

This was worse than not getting carded at the liquor store. Worse than being called *ma'am*. "I haven't lived in Florida for my entire life to be called a tourist."

A laugh came out of Nick's chest like a bark, an involuntary reaction that seemed to startle even himself. "Point taken. Sorry about that." That almost-twitch thing his mouth had been doing gave way to an actual smile, crooked and even a little bit apologetic. Something in the air shifted between them, the animosity from the past few minutes dissolving like sugar in the rain.

That shift made her take a risk. "Any chance we can start over? I was caffeine deprived before, and this is the best coffee I've had in a long time." She stuck her hand across the counter. "I'm Cassie."

"Nick." His hand was warm around hers, his handshake a solid grip. "And I think I can help you out with that handyman thing. Here . . ."

Nick came out from behind the counter, walking—no, sauntering—toward the front door. Clearly this café was his domain, and he was at home here. What must that be like? To be at home somewhere? Cassie had a home, technically, but she didn't feel at home there. Not yet.

He stopped at the bulletin board to the left of the door that she must have rushed right by when she'd come in. It was covered in so many business cards and flyers that the cork of the board had practically disappeared. Some of the cards were yellowed with age, while others looked like they'd just been pinned there yesterday. Nick scanned the board, his hands resting on his slim hips, before finally selecting one of the older cards.

"Here you go." He stuck the pushpin back in the board and handed her the card. "Give Buster a call. If he can't fix it, it can't be fixed."

"Is that his slogan?" And was that his real name? She examined the card, and sure enough: BUSTER BRADSHAW, with a little graphic of a hammer and a phone number. Minimalist, this guy. She was honestly surprised not to see a little ghost peeking out from behind the hammer.

Nick chuckled. "It should be. So which house is yours, anyway?"

Cassie turned and peered out the window, pointing down the street. "Down that way a little. Yellow house, where the street bends to the right toward the pier?"

"Wait." Nick's eyebrows crawled up his forehead. "You're in the Hawkins House?"

"The what?" That name meant nothing to her. The seller had been a nebulous LLC, probably a flipper, and hadn't been named Hawkins. "No. It's the Rutherford house now." She tapped her own chest. "As of nine days ago anyway."

"No shit." He leaned in conspiratorially. "What's it like in there?"

"Um. Well, right now it's filled with boxes since I haven't un-packed yet. But otherwise it's fine."

"I mean, everything okay there? Since you've moved in?"

"Yes?" Her answer was more of a question. What was he getting at? "Is there a reason it wouldn't be?"

"No weird noises? Anything like that?"

"Nothing except the wonky electric. What else would there . . . oh." She bit back a sigh. "Is this because of the ghost thing that this town is all about? I told you, I'm not a tourist. You don't have to do . . ." She waved a hand. "All that."

He watched her for a second before nodding slowly. "Right. Anyway, give Buster a call." He gestured at the card. "He'll set you up right. And make sure you tell him you're at the Hawkins House. I bet he'll come running."

"Okaaay." She drew the word out slowly. There was something

Nick wasn't telling her about her house, but she wasn't going to look a gift horse in the mouth. Anything that would make her life easier at this point was welcome. "Thanks," she said instead.

"Anytime." There was that crooked smile again. "Welcome to Boneyard Key."

As Cassie pushed the heavy glass door open, she noticed three little neon ghosts escaping as steam from the neon coffee cup in the window. Yeah. He'd definitely been talking about the ghost thing.

But what did her house have to do with it?

Two

Living in a tourist town would be heaven on earth if it weren't for all the damn tourists.

"Do you have cashew milk?"

Nick clenched his jaw so hard his molars ached, but he forced a cleansing breath through his nose before he answered. "We've got soy milk," he said, his voice even. Almost pleasant. "We've got almond milk, oat milk, and regular old cow's milk. That's it." That should be plenty, shouldn't it? How many damn milks could one coffee shop offer? Any more and he'd have to rebrand as a dairy.

The woman across the counter wrinkled her nose and curled her lip, the only parts of her face visible behind the biggest pair of sunglasses Nick had ever seen. He ground down harder on his back teeth, waiting for her to decide already. He could have made three lattes in the time it took this woman to make up her mind.

She finally gave a dramatic sigh. "I guess I'll have the almond milk, if that's all you've got. Can you do an iced shaken espresso?"

This woman was really missing her Starbucks. Unfortunately for her, he was the closest thing to a Starbucks around here. And as proud as Nick was of this place, Hallowed Grounds was absolutely not a Starbucks. He didn't know the first thing about shaking an espresso, but he was able to bargain her down to an iced latte with her precious almond milk.

"So tell me . . ." Big Sunglasses leaned over the counter while Nick ran her payment. Her tank top was low cut, and Nick wasn't complaining about the view. "Is this town really haunted?"

"That's what the websites say," he answered cheerfully as he handed her back her card.

Of course it was; being haunted was what put Boneyard Key on the map. When you were a tourist town in Florida, you had to have something to set you apart, something to attract any tourist dollars left over from the theme parks. One of those travel magazines a few years back had called Boneyard Key the most haunted small town in Florida, which had definitely helped pick things up. The chamber of commerce across the street had commissioned this big-ass sign, and Sophie's ghost tour had been sold out for months after that article had come out.

These days you couldn't throw a rock in this town without hitting a T-shirt store or a souvenir shop selling all kinds of ghostly wares. Trucker hat, tie-dye sundress, shot glass—if you could slap a ghost on it, you could buy it in Boneyard Key.

Of course, it was different when you were a tourist. When you were just here for the weekend, you get the airbrushed T-shirt with a ghost on it and tell your friends you went to visit the spooky town on the Gulf. But you never quite take it seriously. You don't believe.

But it was different when you lived here. As if on cue, Nick's phone buzzed with a text from an unknown number. Of course. No matter how many times he'd added Elmer's number to his contacts, each new text showed up as an unknown number. Sure, it had been a little weird at first, but you learned to roll with things like that around here. He'd been doing it all his life.

> What did you do to the banana bread?

Nick frowned at the text. How did he know? Stupid question, he thought as he started tapping out his response. Elmer always knew.

> Just put some cinnamon in it, no big deal.

> Cinnamon doesn't go with bananas, what were you thinking?

Sure it does. Nick rolled his eyes as he typed. It just wasn't in your recipe. But last I checked, you don't own this place anymore. Like that was going to stop Elmer from having an opinion. Nothing in the world could stop that—not even death.

The bell above the door chimed—thank God, a reprieve. Despite the bouncing dots indicating an incoming response, Nick locked his screen and shoved his phone back in his jeans pocket.

"Hey, Libby." He nodded at the woman who'd just walked in. Libby Simpson was a Boneyard Key native from a long line of Boneyard Key natives, just like Nick. And while they'd both stuck around this town, she'd gone into the family business instead of striking out on her own like he had. But Nick had never been cut out to be a tax accountant, and besides, Libby's family business was a lot more interesting.

"Morning." Her blond ponytail swung over her shoulder as she examined the pastry case. "The largest coffee you can possibly make, please."

When Libby said *coffee*, she meant *latte*. And it sounded like she needed an extra shot. "You got it." The espresso machine hissed as he got to work. "Nan working today?" he asked as he set her extra-strong latte in front of her.

Libby nodded, and he reached for the coffee pot. Libby drank lattes, but her grandmother was a purist. Black coffee and nothing else. "May I have a banana bread too?"

"Of course." He wrapped it up for her and placed it on the counter next to Nan's coffee.

Libby sipped her latte, closing her eyes briefly in bliss before blinking them open again. "Oh, hey. Did you hear that someone bought the Hawkins House?"

"Sure did." Which wasn't a lie. He just hadn't heard it through the usual gossip channels.

"I don't mean when that out-of-state contractor or whatever bought it a couple years back. I mean sold to a new owner."

"Yeah," Nick said. "I guess they finished fixing it up." And it had needed a lot of fixing up. Ever since mean old Mrs. Hawkins had died, long before Nick was born, the two-story house at the edge of the historic district had sat empty. It was practically a landmark on the way to the pier. *The road bends around to the right, past the creepy old house on the corner . . .*

"Anyway." Libby broke off a piece of the banana bread slice and popped it into her mouth. "I saw a moving truck there the other day. Someone's actually going to live there."

"I know." Nick handed her back her card. "She came in yesterday."

Libby's eyes went wide. "No way. What's she like?"

Pushy. Opinionated. Big brown eyes. Legs for days. A pain in the ass. She'd bustled in yesterday like she owned the place, plopping her bag down on that table in the back corner, plugging in her laptop and setting herself up for what looked like a business meeting. Hadn't glanced at the menu or asked him for so much as a glass of water. Of course, Elmer had been giving him a running commentary on the morning breakfast rush, so it was possible Nick had missed something.

He'd written her off as a tourist. The type who ordered one singular coffee and then set up camp for the day. Probably here on vacation for "inspiration," whatever the hell that meant. Nick had seen plenty of people like that in his time owning the café. They took up all his outlets and mooched off his Wi-Fi, all for the price of the cheapest cup of coffee they could get.

Then she'd insulted him, and he'd insulted her right back, and for some reason that had cleared the air between them. And for the first time he really noticed her. Her eyes were the color of espresso, and her dark, blond-streaked hair was piled up on top of her head in that messy way women did that still managed to look put together. She'd huffed a breath, blowing a lock of hair out of her eyes, which only served to dislodge another. Something about that lock of hair, falling down to curve around her jaw, softened her face and made her look younger, more vulnerable. That lock of hair transformed her from a bitchy customer into someone having a bad morning.

Libby's eyebrows went up, because Nick still hadn't answered her question. He cleared his throat. "She was all right. From Orlando, I think." As he said that, he heard her voice echo in his head, bright and professional on her virtual meeting. *How's everything back in Orlando?*

"She's going to be living here? Not turning the place into a vacation rental?" She broke off another piece of banana bread; he should have just given it to her on a plate.

"She was talking about moving boxes, so I think she's here to stay."

"That's wild." Libby considered that. "No one's lived in that house since before Nan was born; she said she always remembers the place being empty." She took another sip from her latte. "What's in the banana bread today? It tastes different." She said *different* the way a less polite person would say *shitty*.

Nick sighed. Maybe Elmer was right after all. "Cinnamon."

"Hmm." She took another bite. "It's not bad," she said finally. "It's just . . ."

"Different," he said. "I know."

"I bet Elmer had things to say about the cinnamon," she said with a wry smile.

Nick snorted. "He has things to say about everything. You sure your grandma can't talk to him?"

"She did, remember?" Libby shrugged. "Elmer said he's good where he is."

"I bet he did."

She clucked her tongue at him. "He likes you. Said you're his favorite."

Nick growled under his breath, but it was half-hearted. Elmer hadn't owned the café for a couple decades now, and Nick was the only one since who could put up with him. The last owner of the place had been happy to sell the business to Nick for a song, just to get away from Elmer's constant meddling.

After Libby left, the true morning rush began. Well, it wasn't so much a rush as it was a trickle: Theo dropped by for a large coffee and blueberry muffin on the way to open the bookstore a couple doors down next to a T-shirt shop. Two tourists consulted the novelty map while he made their vanilla lattes, denying their requests for extra foam and half caff or whatever the hell. (How is a coffee made extra hot anyway? If it's hot coffee, it's hot coffee.) Eventually he pointed them in the direction of the kayak rental and bait shack by the pier and tried to sell them on Sophie's ghost tour if they were still around on Friday. They made noncommittal noises in response, so that was a bust.

The end of the morning rush was punctuated, as always, by Josephine, running late to open the consignment shop down the street that she helped her parents run. Nick reached for the box of herbal tea before the door-opening chime had faded. Jo hated coffee, but she still came by for a morning cup of hot water with tasteless leaves. (Nick was not a fan of herbal tea, but he was a fan of the money Jo gave him for it.)

Jo dunked her tea bag a couple times before leaving the cup on the counter and taking a card out of her back pocket. "You mind if I . . . ?" She pointed to the corkboard by the door, and Nick nodded.

"Of course."

"That time of year again." She stabbed a pushpin into the middle of the card, securing it to the board. The words **HELP WANTED** were scrawled across the top in stark black marker, and he nodded knowingly. School would be out soon, and kids home from college for the summer would be looking for part-time gigs. Just in time for tourist season, when almost everyone around here would need the extra help.

Boneyard Key was too small to have a newspaper of its own. The best way to get the word out about something was by leaving word with whoever was volunteering at the chamber of commerce that day, or by sticking an index card on the corkboard here at Hallowed Grounds.

Of course, the other way to get the word out around here was an even more old-fashioned way: gossip. Had Jo heard the latest? "Did you hear someone's moved into the Hawkins House?"

"No shit?" Jo's eyebrows jumped up her forehead as she retrieved her cup of tea. She dunked her tea bag a couple more times before pitching it into the trash and adding way too much sugar. "Like, to live?"

"Yep."

"Man." She shook dark hair out of her eyes. "The number of times my brother dared me to go up and knock on that door during a full moon, see if a ghost would answer . . ." She gave a mock shudder and a crooked grin, then popped a to-go lid on her tea. "Can't wait to see who's gonna brave that place."

"Yeah, no kidding." He didn't need to tell Jo about Cassie's dark eyes and tousled hair. The gossip was really more about the house than about her. He could leave her out of it for now.

Jo shook down her wrist to look at her watch, a bracelet-like ornamental thing that was at least three generations older than she was. "Ah, crap. I'm late." Jo was always late. But then again, not a lot of people were hammering on the door of a consignment shop in a tourist town at nine fifteen in the morning.

She turned back at the door. "Oh, if you see Vince before I do, tell him Dad got a couple guitars from an antiques fair in Tampa. If he wants to come by, we'd love his help figuring out what they're worth."

"Oh, man. He's gonna be all over that."

"I know." She rolled her eyes good-naturedly. "I'll have to listen to 'Stairway to Heaven' at least twelve times, but he knows his shit."

Jo threw a wave over her shoulder on the way out, the bell above the door echoing in the ensuing silence. That silence would remain, mostly unbroken, until Ramon showed up a little after ten thirty to help with the lunch crowd. (This time of year, "crowd" was relative, but Ramon had been hired by the previous owner and was better in the kitchen than Nick, so it was easier to just keep him around.)

Nick liked the quiet. He liked that time to catch up on dishes and reset the coffee counter, which was in almost-constant disarray. He liked that moment of running a rag across the pristine countertops. He liked the peace of this time of the morning. The routine of it.

Of course, part of that routine was yet another text from Elmer. Told ya. Cinnamon is shit in banana bread.

Yeah, I know. There was easily a loaf and a half of the stuff left today. This town did not take well to change. But Nick was not going to admit defeat, especially not to Elmer. What if I tried chocolate chips? He pressed his lips together to hide his smile as he typed, knowing that would set Elmer off.

It did. What is wrong with you?

He was contemplating the many ways he could reply to that when the bell above the front door chimed. At first he groaned inwardly; he'd cleaned up from breakfast and had already mentally turned over to lunchtime. But then he glanced up. Tousled hair, dark eyes. Laptop bag over her shoulder.

"You're back." The words fell out of his mouth before he could think them, abrupt and unwelcoming. It really was amazing that he worked in the service industry. He tried to sound friendly, but it usually came out as gruff. Nick Royer was an acquired taste, his sister Courtney liked to say. Come to think of it, his ex-girlfriend had said that too. And most of his friends. Huh.

But this woman didn't know him, so she hadn't acquired anything.

"Sure am." She sounded about as happy as he did as she slung her laptop bag onto that same table in the back corner. The one near the outlet. "Don't worry," she said. "No meetings today. I just need to charge up my computer and maybe get a little work done."

Nick nodded. "Hazelnut latte?"

"Please." She smiled. "Iced." She uncoiled the charging cord and plugged it in. Nick narrowed his eyes at that.

"So what's up with your computer?"

"I wish I knew." She sighed and shook her head, sending that lock of hair that Nick couldn't stop thinking about tumbling down to curve around her cheek again. She tucked it behind her ear absently. "I leave it plugged in all night, and it's dead by morning. I've even switched outlets, but it's the same no matter what. It doesn't make any sense; if I plug a lamp in it works fine. But my laptop? No joy."

"Did you call Buster yet?" Nick was already reaching for his phone. There was a string of texts from Elmer, still waxing philosophical on the virtues of his banana bread recipe. He fired off a quick response to shut him up. Gotta go. Got busy again.

"No," Cassie said. "I didn't get a chance yesterday. I'll call him this afternoon."

"Nah, I got it." But before he could bring up Buster's number, another text from Elmer popped up.

Oh please. There's like one person.

"That's okay." Cassie frowned at her computer screen, hit a couple keys. "I'll get around to it soon."

"What are you going to do until then? Just keep coming here?" He fired off another text to Elmer (She's requiring a lot of attention) and was about to hit the Call button under Buster's name when a response came.

Damn, she's cute. Who's that?

"Wow. You make me feel so welcome."

"What?" His gaze flew up from his phone. Cassie had her elbows on the table, cradling her chin in her hands, looking at him with her eyebrows raised and a sarcastic smile. He'd said something wrong. He knew it. But having two conversations at once, while planning a third, was too much for his brain today.

So he stowed his phone back in his pocket. Elmer could wait. Hell, so could Buster. Cassie was a customer first and foremost. The rest could wait. "I'll get your coffee."

Her smile only widened as she turned back to her work, and Nick made himself stop watching his new customer and get started on her latte. But he was only human, and Elmer was right. She was cute.

Maybe he could pawn off some of this leftover banana bread on her. Did she like cinnamon?

Three

When Nick brought Cassie's iced latte to her table, he'd left a little plate of banana bread beside it.

She looked up from her email, confused. "I didn't order banana bread."

"On the house," he said on the way back to the counter.

Well. She wasn't going to turn down a free treat. She wasn't a dummy.

Cassie hit Send and returned to her inbox. What was the point in answering all these emails if people were going to just reply to them, sending the ball immediately back into her court again? This was unfair. As she opened the next email, the next fire to put out, she popped a bite of banana bread in her mouth. Ooh. Cinnamon. Yum.

By the time she got to a stopping point, her laptop was charged again, the banana bread was long gone, and the first trickle of customers had started to come in for lunch. Not wanting to overstay her welcome, Cassie dragged the watery remains of her latte through the straw, trying to get every last molecule of caffeine before she brought her dishes up to the counter. Nick was on his phone again, but he put it down at her approach.

"Banana bread okay?"

"More than okay. I like the cinnamon."

"Yeah? You're about the only one today."

"Well, everyone else is wrong. You can make that every day as far as I'm concerned."

"You're on." There was something about his face when he smiled. Frown lines were replaced with crinkles in the corners of his eyes, and he didn't look younger so much as hopeful. He looked much better when he wasn't frowning down at his phone. Had anyone ever told him that?

"I called Buster," he said as she paid for her coffee. His voice had a tone of *you're welcome* in it, even though she hadn't asked him to do it. "He said he'd be by this afternoon."

"I said I was going to call him." Her skin prickled, and not in a fun way. She handled her own shit; she didn't need help.

"But you hadn't," he said. "So I did."

"And you just scheduled him for this afternoon? What if I wasn't going to be home?"

"Then I would have called him back and told him to come later. It's no big deal. Are you going to be home this afternoon?"

Of course she was going to be home. That wasn't the point. She opened her mouth to argue more, but something in his face stopped her. Maybe he really was just trying to help. She sighed. "This afternoon, huh? That quick?"

Nick nodded as he handed over her change, which she promptly dropped into the tip jar on the counter. "I told you. You need anything around here—a plumber, roofer, anything—tell 'em you're in the Hawkins House. They'll clear their schedule."

Nick wasn't wrong. After Cassie got home, she barely had time to have lunch and unpack the first box of the day when Buster Bradshaw knocked at her door at two on the dot. He was roughly Cassie's grandfather's age, and his weathered face lit up like a kid at

Christmas as he took a tentative step over the threshold, looking around in wonder. But the glee on his face faded almost immediately.

"What did they do to you, old girl?" The words were softly spoken, not directed toward Cassie, but she heard them anyway.

"What's wrong?" Cassie looked around the way he did, at the probably-not-original crown molding, her senses on high alert. The electric was already screwed up—what else had the inspector missed?

He shook his head in barely disguised contempt. "Nothing. I'm sure it's fine." The word *fine* dripped with loathing. "It's just . . . modern, you know? This house never used to be modern." He sighed and shook off his bad mood. "But that's a flip for you. Anyway. You said there was something wrong with the electric?"

He started out upstairs, testing the outlets, before moving downstairs to the living room, while Cassie opened another box marked KITCHEN. Dinnerware. Finally. It had been a long week of eating off paper plates and drinking from the exactly two mugs she'd been able to find.

Tucked in a corner of the box near the bubble-wrapped plates was a coffee tin, and Cassie let out a small "a-ha" sound when she took it out. Inside was her magnetic poetry collection. The little tin contained dozens of single words with a magnetic backing. It was a silly thing she'd started in college as a party game, but over the years she'd found that arranging random words on her refrigerator soothed her. Cleared her mind in a way that any other form of brainstorming couldn't. At her rental, her landlord had replaced the fridge about a year ago, a brand-new one with a door that magnets didn't stick to. She never thought she'd say it, but thank God for older appliances.

Cassie hummed under her breath as she peeled the words apart, sticking them one at a time onto the door of her refrigerator. Eventually she pulled a few toward the center.

yellow

sunshine

feels

like

morning

Not very original, but it was a start. She switched the first and last words. **morning sunshine feels like yellow**. A little better.

She was jolted out of her almost-meditative state by Buster behind her. "Nothing wrong with any of these outlets."

"Are you sure?" That couldn't be right. Frustration rose in a grumble in Cassie's chest. "My laptop won't charge. I keep having to go down to the coffee shop to get it to power up."

"Oh, you mean Elmer's place, just down the way?" Buster's eyes lit up.

"No. Nick. The one who called you?" Who the hell was Elmer?

Buster snapped his fingers. "That's right, it's Nick's now. I keep forgetting. Nick's a good kid. Here. Lemme see." He gestured, and Cassie handed him her laptop and cord from the kitchen table. She tried not to heave a sigh as he hooked up her laptop and moved to plug the cord in the outlet in the breakfast nook. He was a nice old guy, and sure, Nick said he was the best, but this felt like every time the guy in IT asked her if she'd tried turning her computer off and on again. Being mansplained to in her own home was a little much.

"That's the first one I tried." She attempted to sound patient. Of course it was the first one she'd tried; that breakfast nook was the perfect place to sit with her laptop. In fact, it was where Cassie had planned to spend the better part of her day. If, you know, the outlet worked. "It's not gonna . . ." Her voice cut off abruptly as she heard the telltale chime of her laptop connecting to power. She flipped it open, and sure enough, the battery symbol in the corner glowed green, indicating that it was plugged in and charging.

"See? There you go." Buster didn't sound condescending or mansplain-y. His voice held the simple satisfaction of a job well done.

"But . . ." This wasn't helping her frustration. Why had it worked now? What had he done differently? She peered at the wall, then back at her happily charging laptop. "I tried that outlet. I tried it so many times."

Buster waved a hand. "These old outlets. They're temperamental."

But Cassie's attention was still on her laptop. The damn thing practically looked smug. "I guess," she said absently. "I'm sorry I called you all the way out here for nothing, though."

His laugh was a creaky wheeze. "There's no 'all the way out here' around here, ma'am. It takes maybe ten minutes to get from one end of town to the other, and that's if you're not in a hurry." He waved Cassie off when she got her wallet out of her bag by the door. "No charge. It was worth it just to see inside this place."

"Really?" Sure, the beachside cottage was cute and all, but it wasn't all that grand. What was so exciting about seeing inside it?

"This place was empty for years. Decades, to be honest. Just kind of sitting here, starting to fall apart. Part of the background, no one really thought about it."

"Oh." Cassie looked around the living room with new eyes. With its fresh paint and polished floors, it was hard to imagine the place dark and empty, abandoned and alone. Was it possible to feel sorry for a house? Because she kind of knew how that felt.

"Then that flipper from Jacksonville or wherever bought it a couple years back." Buster's tone of voice told her exactly what he thought of *that flipper from Jacksonville.* "Everyone hoped to get a look inside, but he didn't use a single local on the renovation. A whole lot of out-of-towners, big temporary fence, 'No Trespassing' signs up all over the place. Next thing we know, we heard some city girl bought it."

"Guilty." Cassie tried to sound cheerful, but from what Buster was saying, they didn't take too kindly to outsiders around here. Just another reason why this move might have been a mistake.

But Buster didn't seem to have a torch or a pitchfork anywhere on his person. "For a city girl, you seem okay. Have to say, I'm glad to see you're actually planning to live here. I figured it was gonna become one of those vacation rentals or something, like everyone's doing these days."

"Nope, just me." Her words bounced off the bare walls and boxes, echoing back in her ears. *Just me. Lonely girl in the lonely house.*

"Well, welcome to town." He extended his hand and she shook it. "Keep an eye on things around here, you hear? Call me if anything comes up. I'd be glad to stop by anytime."

What was going to come up? The house had been renovated, it had passed inspection, wonky electric and all. But out loud she said "you got it" as Buster left.

Cassie fell into an easy routine for the rest of the week. Work at the breakfast nook during the day, then unpacking boxes in the evening. With each box she emptied, the more the cottage started to feel like hers. Her mugs, her plates in the cabinets. The prints she'd bought at local art shows unwrapped and ready to hang in the living room. In the evenings she switched on the lamps and tried not to think about the picture Buster had painted of the house being empty and abandoned. They had each other now. Maybe that would be enough.

By Friday evening she'd had enough of work *and* unpacking. As dusk darkened the sky, Cassie took a glass of red wine upstairs to the balcony off her bedroom. It faced the street, but there wasn't any traffic. No smell of hot blacktop and exhaust from busy Orlando roads, no bumper-to-bumper commutes out to the suburbs. Here in Boneyard Key, the sound of the ocean meeting the shore was a calming, rolling sound, punctuated by the early-evening breeze ruffling the Spanish moss that hung from the live oaks that lined the quiet downtown street.

That breeze did nothing to cool things off. Cassie plucked at her shirt, unsticking it from her back, where a film of sweat had already coated her skin. Florida was damp, no way around that. She took a good deep breath—this close to the ocean, it was mostly a lungful of salt air and humidity.

Had she made a mistake, buying this badly flipped house on the other side of the state? She'd made the decision in a weak moment. Several weak moments, in fact. One too many "big announcements" in the group text, followed by a photo of an engagement ring or one of those sonograms that was supposedly of a baby but just looked like a grainy potato.

Cassie never had any big announcements to share. Perpetually single and not pregnant, those texts, with the strings of squees and "welcome to the club" responses, just made Cassie feel more and more like she wasn't in the same club as her friends. Like all of her friends had moved on to a different one, and she was all alone.

Then her landlord had decided to sell her house. The market was crazy, he wanted to sell, and he'd dropped that bomb on her right when it was time to renew her lease. The news sparked a home-buying frenzy of her own; she put down offer after offer on houses, biting her nails while interest rates soared and fell like a roller coaster. One by one, her offers were rejected in favor of real estate investors with seemingly bottomless pockets.

The culmination of those weak moments, where she felt like she was being pushed not only out of her friend group but out of her cute College Park bungalow, was when she'd widened her house search from the Orlando area. Sure, her mom had complained; she was used to her only child living practically in her backyard. But Cassie was ready for a change, and there was nothing really keeping her there. Her copywriting job at a big advertising firm had been remote for a while now, since the first lockdown. She'd proven that she could work anywhere, so it stood to reason that she could also live anywhere. Maybe it was all a sign. She needed a new start.

When a quaint, recently renovated beachside cottage came on the market, she'd jumped on it almost automatically. She hadn't expected to get it. It was a pattern by now: see a house, fall in love. Offer, get rejected. Mourn, then move on to the next. When her real estate agent had called to tell her she'd gotten the house, Cassie had barely believed it. Suddenly she was in uncharted waters, under contract on a house she'd only seen on a video walk-through.

Now three months, a couple inspections, and about four thousand signatures later, she was a homeowner. Wanting something new, she'd ended up with something old instead, in this weird-ass tourist town.

Cassie picked up her phone and fired off a text to the group chat. Hope y'all are having a great Friday night! Can you believe I moved somewhere without DoorDash? She glanced at the time before putting her phone down. Would anyone answer? What would she be doing right now if she were back home in Orlando? Probably wrapping up happy hour, easily two margaritas in by now, debating whether to hit the Thai place around the corner or find a Tijuana Flats and load up on flautas and at least three selections from the hot sauce bar. Either one was a solid solution.

The sudden sense memory of biting into a crispy cheese roll at her favorite Thai place, the melty cheese and brittle egg roll wrapper shattering under her teeth, brought tears to her eyes. She missed those nights out. She missed her friends.

Of course, that was all B.K.—Before Kids. Their solid group of six had dwindled one by one until Cassie was the only one unattached and ready to go on a Friday night. The other five would have to ask their husbands before going out—the hell?—or would be too busy with kids at home. Cassie missed those nights out, but truth be told, those nights had been over for a while now.

It was one thing to feel left out of the friend group, but to have left a big city like Orlando, with its many nightlife options, in favor of a tiny tourist town in the offseason . . . what had she been thinking coming to Boneyard Key? Making new friends as an adult in a new town, without the easy in of things like church or children, was all but impossible.

Her phone rattled on the side table, and she scooped it up, eager—and maybe a little desperate—for human contact. New messages in the group chat! She pulled it up: a photo of Monika and Christine, taken at the exact Thai restaurant whose crispy cheese rolls she'd been craving. Mamas Night Out! Hope you ladies can make it next time!

Cassie read the message a second time to let the words really sink in, each one a little dart to the chest. "Mamas." "Make it next time." There was nothing about that text that was meant for Cassie. Meanwhile, her earlier message was just sitting there, read and unacknowledged. She may as well be invisible. She'd been missing them, and they didn't even notice she was gone.

She tossed the phone back to the table. Screw it. Maybe a change of scenery was good for her after all. Sure, Boneyard Key didn't have a Thai place. Or a taco place. But maybe soon she'd have the nerve to try out that seedy-looking oyster bar on the other side of the historic district, and she'd seen a pizza joint around here some-where. And of course there was Hallowed Grounds—and its very hot, only slightly grouchy barista—though it was just a breakfast and lunch place that closed at two. But it wasn't tourist season yet; it made sense to roll up the sidewalks in the late afternoon.

Cassie leaned back in her bistro chair, moodily sipping her wine as night fell. From behind the house, the Gulf lapped against the seawall like her own personal meditation app. The sound of the waves lulled her into a dreamy half sleep that had only a little to do with the large glass of wine in her hand.

Then the silence of the night was broken by a lilting feminine voice from across the street.

"And our next stop . . . This is the Hawkins House."

The voice was directly below her. Cassie straightened up in her chair and peered down. The sun had fully set while she'd been out here brooding, and the darkened balcony gave her a tactical advan-tage. She could see them, but they couldn't see her. A group of peo-ple stood on the sidewalk in front of her house—though "group" was being generous. Handful. A handful of people formed a rough semi-circle, looking up at her house. Looking up at her. One person stood in front of them, with her back to the front door, a tour guide lectur-ing her audience.

"The Hawkins House was built in 1899 by William Donnelly, shortly after Boneyard Key was established here after the Great Storm of 1897." The lilting voice belonged to the tour guide. Who did a sightseeing tour at night? The sights were significantly harder to see. "The house was later acquired by C.S. Hawkins, who lived here with his wife, Sarah, from the time they were married in 1904 until his death in 1911."

Then it clicked. Walking tour at night, history of a house . . . this was a ghost tour. Cassie should have guessed; it went with the rest of the ghost schtick in this town. She knew about ghost tours. Just about every tourist town had one, and it was a fun way to spend a couple hours. She had yet to see one that was actually spooky or told any stories that weren't just a spin on the classics. The sad girl hitchhiking on the side of the road, brought home to sadder parents mourning her death from years ago. Sometimes there was a twist where the driver of the car loaned her a jacket that turned up draped over a headstone placed conveniently in the backyard. Historic ghost stories usually involved a forbidden love between a rich wife and a pirate, because who didn't love a pirate?

Cassie found herself leaning forward a little more, as though those extra six inches would help her hear the tour guide better. What story was she telling about this house? Would it be the hitchhiking ghost? Or maybe the pirate, since they were by the ocean? It would be pretty neat to have a pirate ghost around.

But the tour guide didn't veer off into generic ghost story territory. "And that's when Mrs. Hawkins became . . ." The woman dropped her voice a couple of octaves, sounding less like a tour guide and more like someone telling stories around a campfire. Preferably about someone with a hook for a hand. "*Mean Mrs. Hawkins.*"

"What did she do?" one of the tourists asked. "She off her husband?" Everyone else in the group laughed. But Cassie didn't. Because she had to sleep in this house tonight. And she would prefer that this house not contain a murderer, thank you.

Thankfully, the tour guide shook her head. "There was speculation. He was much, much older than she was. C.S. Hawkins was known as a pillar of the community, while Sarah was a relative newcomer, here from up north. His death left a hole for sure. But Mrs. Hawkins, she didn't care about being part of the town anymore. As the years went by, her place became *that house*, you know?"

A couple people in the crowd didn't even glance up from their phones, their faces bathed in light emanating from their palms, while the rest looked up toward the house in trepidation. "That house?" one of them asked.

A chill swept up Cassie's arms, cooling the sweat on her skin and making her shiver. She wasn't sure how much more of this she wanted to hear, but the tour guide was deep into the spooky story-telling now. "Some said she'd chase kids out of her garden with sticks because she didn't like anyone too close to her house. Before long this was the house the kids skipped when trick-or-treating on Halloween. No Girl Scouts dropped by to sell cookies.

"Some would say that from down on the beach you could see her on her back balcony, staring out into the water. But other than that, no one saw her. She never had friends going in and out. No relatives. She was a recluse here in Boneyard Key, and she didn't want company. So she lived here alone until she died, sometime in the 1940s. Since she didn't have children, the ownership of the house went to the city. They've tried to sell it over the years, but something—or someone—always caused the sale to fall through. So the house has been sitting here, vacant, for decades. If you ask me, that's thanks to Mean Mrs. Hawkins. Still here, not wanting anyone else in her home."

"Sophie," one of the tourists called out. "There's a shadow moving! Up there!" He pointed up to the balcony, and Cassie jerked back into the shadows so fast she nearly toppled her chair over. She scrabbled at the wall for support while clapping her other hand over her mouth to hold back a maniacal giggle. She'd been leaning forward, listening intently, and had made herself part of the show. Whoops.

The tour guide, Sophie, followed the tourist's pointing finger. "I'm not surprised." Her sigh was theatrical. "Don't get too close, and whatever you do, don't go through the front gate. Unless you want a stick to the back of the legs."

"The house doesn't look vacant. There are lights on inside." Another tourist sounded skeptical. "I thought you said no one lives here."

Cassie looked over her shoulder into the house. She hadn't turned on any lights upstairs, but the living room and kitchen downstairs were probably lit up like a Christmas tree. Whoops again. Should she keep those lights off on Friday nights? Help Sophie sell the idea of this place being haunted?

Sophie seemed to be able to roll with it. "You're right. I guess it's time to revise that part of the story. The Hawkins House was bought a couple years ago and restored. It's a private residence now."

But the tourist's skepticism thickened. "Who's going to willingly live in a haunted house?"

Cassie couldn't agree more. The inspection report on this place had plenty to say about the minuscule crack in the foundation and that one loose shingle on the roof. Shouldn't they have mentioned somewhere in there that the place was haunted?

But Sophie shrugged, then turned back to her group with a sunny smile. "Maybe the new owner's made a friend!" She sounded entirely too chipper about the prospect. "Now, we're going to go through downtown, and I'll tell you about the ghost who haunts this strip of beach. It's just over near the break in the seawall, near the ice cream shop. Which is different than the ice cream shop by the café that we passed before."

"How many ice cream shops does this town have?" one of the tourists asked as the group began to move along down the sidewalk.

"Only one open now, but three in total. Well, four if you count the T-shirt shop that has a big cooler in the back. Oh, and the place on the dock where you rent kayaks, they sell ice cream there too . . ."

Sophie's voice faded as the group made their way down the main drag. Now that it was safe to move, Cassie leaned over the railing, watching the group disappear into the night before heading into her bedroom. She flipped on the light, looking around with new eyes. Had this been C.S. and Sarah Hawkins's bedroom? Was Sarah's spirit really still here? And would this house be big enough for the both of them?

Of course, the room looked exactly as it had this morning. The ceiling fan whirred above her, stirring stray pieces of hair around her cheek. Her matching bedroom set—purchased from Rooms To Go not long after college—in all its dated glory, the walls still aggressively beige. The scariest thing in this room was the number of boxes she still had to unpack.

"This would all be very mysterious," she told her reflection later that night as she applied her bedtime moisturizer, "if ghosts were an actual thing. Which they're not."

At two thirty in the morning, Cassie was sound asleep. At two thirty-seven in the morning, three of the magnetic words on her fridge moved an inch and a half to the left.

Four

Nick should never have opened his mouth. He'd just wanted a beer on a Friday afternoon.

But it was too late. Vince turned to look over his shoulder, his hands pausing against the tap. "Wait. You said what?"

"You heard me." Nick willed Vince to keep going, but his mental mojo was way off. Vince set the glass down on the bar and turned fully away from the tap, and it was all Nick could do to not groan out loud.

"I need to hear it again." Suppressed laughter made Vince's voice tremble. "Tell me again how you met the cute new girl who's moved to town and called her a tourist. To her face."

"Aren't you a bartender?" Nick waved a hand toward the sadly neglected beer taps behind the counter. "Bartend, will you?"

"I don't know . . ." Despite the doubt in his voice, Vince turned back to the taps, picking up the glass and filling it with lager. "This may become my new bedtime story. You're gonna need to tell it to me again and again."

Nick grumbled under his breath. Why had he bothered coming to The Cold Spot after work? He had beer at home. "Fine," he said. "But in my defense, she's from Orlando. She's not used to places like this."

But Vince was merciless, even as he passed Nick his beer. "Doesn't matter. You fucked up, kid." His wide grin took the sting out of his words, making him look like that cool uncle at the family reunion.

The cool uncle that was into hair metal, that is. The man's look hadn't changed since the early nineties: long curly mullet that had gone more and more gray over the years, a faded Metallica T-shirt with jeans and battered motorcycle boots. His face was lined by years of bad decisions, and his eyes even bore phantom traces of eyeliner.

"She is cute, though, right?" Vince raised one arched eyebrow.

Nick sipped his beer and pretended to consider. Pretended that Cassie's face wasn't already burned into his memory. Pretended that, while he was usually annoyed as hell when someone planted their ass in his café and mooched his outlets and Wi-Fi, he hadn't minded so much when it was Cassie. She could plant her ass in his café anytime she liked.

"Yeah," he finally said. "She's cute." He tried to sound as blasé as possible, even throwing in a one-shouldered shrug to emphasize just how much he wasn't still thinking about that girl he'd just met.

But Vince wasn't falling for it. That was the problem with this town. Everyone knew you too well. Especially Vince, who'd been running The Cold Spot—a nondescript gray brick building on the road leading out of town—since before Nick was old enough to (legally) drink. Vince knew what kind of beer Nick liked: cold and crisp lager, not those floral-scented IPAs, not thick dark beers that were practically chewable. The upside was that Nick could walk in and say "Gimme a beer" like he was a guy in a movie, and Vince would know exactly what he meant.

But the downside was that Vince could tell, just from the tone of

Nick's voice, that Cassie had made an impression. And Vince was just warming up.

"She could be good for you, you know." Vince leaned his elbows on the bar, settling in for conversation. Nick took another sip of his lager, wishing that someone—anyone—would come in. Anything to make Vince go away. "You need to get out more."

"What?" Nick blinked. "In what free time? I'm running a business. You know as well as I do how much time that takes." But Vince had a point. Sure, both of them ran similar businesses, but Vince had time for a side gig at The Haunt, performing stripped-down versions of his old hits alongside Jimmy Buffett covers that resulted in some deeply weird acoustic sets. And besides that, he still had time to hang out at Jo's consignment shop, helping her appraise any musical instruments that came through.

Speaking of which . . . "Oh, did Jo talk to you? She got some new guitars in that she wants you to take a look at." There. Subject change away from his love life. Perfect.

And it worked. Vince all but rubbed his hands together with glee. "Music to my ears," he said. "No pun intended. I'll give her a call tomorrow. You want to come check them out with me?"

"Sure." Nick was known to hang out at the consignment shop after hours, noodling on whatever instruments were for sale. He was a terrible guitar player and even worse on the bass, but those couple of months when Jo had had a drum kit in the shop had been fun. Nick had gotten a lot of aggression out. "Just text me and let me know when."

Vince shook his head. "This is my point, though. You're a young kid—"

"I'm almost thirty." It kind of hurt to say out loud, but seriously. A kid?

Vince kept going like Nick hadn't spoken. "—in the prime of your life. You should be spending time with a special someone, not spending your Friday nights hanging out with a washed-up old guy like me."

"You're not washed up . . ."

"You need a relationship," he shot back.

"I have relationships," Nick said defensively.

The front door to the bar opened, and the two men looked over instinctively as late-afternoon sunlight streamed into the darkened room. He didn't exactly recoil like a vampire, but Nick could feel his pupils screaming down into little pinpricks before the door closed and plunged the bar back into cool semi-darkness.

"You have situationships." Vince tossed the words over his shoulder as he moved to intercept the new customer.

Nick huffed an involuntary laugh into his beer. "Where the hell did you learn that word?"

The newcomer was a stranger, so a tourist. Vince pushed a stained menu in his direction as he turned back to Nick, picking up the thread of the conversation like they'd never been interrupted. "Online," he said. "Haven't you heard? Nineties nostalgia is a thing. The old videos have been getting a lot of views lately."

"Reliving your glory days?" It was Nick's turn to raise an eyebrow. Back in the day, Vince had been the bassist of a moderately successful rock band. But then the grunge era had come along, and flannel didn't look good on a guy like Vince, so he—and his band— had fallen into obscurity. Boneyard Key was as good a place as any to be obscure.

"Always," Vince said lightly. He left the conversation just long enough to take the newcomer's drink order. Long enough for Nick to hope they could change the topic to something else. Because as much as he couldn't stop thinking about Cassie, he didn't want to talk about her. Not yet. She was too new.

But Vince wasn't done. Once the other customer was settled in with a longneck Bud and a bowl of dubious-looking peanuts, he was back at Nick's corner of the bar. "Situationships," he said again, in the confident tone of a Gen Z kid, and not the older Gen X-er he actually was. "You and whatever flavor of the weekend you pick up at The Haunt."

"Hey." Nick was starting to feel offended. "There's nothing wrong with that. I don't lie to them. No one's getting led on here."

"I'm just saying . . ." Vince shrugged. "What if you met a girl who stuck around? Like, a cute girl who's definitely not a tourist?"

"I don't know." Nick took another sip from his beer. "That would certainly change things." Would it, though? Nick hadn't been a relationship guy for quite some time. He had been, back in the dark ages. But he'd learned a long time ago that relationships weren't for him. If he met a cute girl at The Haunt, and she was only in town for a few days, looking for a good time . . . well, Nick was more than happy to help out with that. No strings, both parties knowing from the outset what they were getting into. Knowing that there was an end date from the start, so he couldn't be blindsided when she left.

"Yeah, it would." Vince sounded encouraging. "You should give it a shot. Ask her out. Might as well jump, as Van Halen says."

"There are bands from this century you could quote, you know." But he had to admit that Vince—and Van Halen—had a point. Unbidden, his mind was filled with an image of Cassie's face. Those big dark eyes. A smile he wanted to lose himself in. A wit that gave back as good as she got. Okay, yeah. Maybe there was something better out there for him after all. And maybe . . . well, maybe it could be Cassie.

Seemed like a lot of pressure to put on a woman he barely knew, though.

Regulars began to filter in, just like clockwork, and Nick tilted his head back, finishing his beer and waving to Vince as he headed out. A late-afternoon post-work beer was one thing, but he was way too young to be one of Vince's nightly barflies.

It was dark as he stepped outside, though; that late-afternoon beer had rolled over into an evening beer. The streetlights had popped on, and unseen waves lapped against the shore as he picked up his step, passing the bait shack and the fishing pier. He still had baking to do before tomorrow, and he'd forgotten to eat dinner. Good thing he owned a café; he could just raid his own stash. He was a shit cook, but even he could slap together a sandwich.

There was a crowd about a half block in front of him, huddled together in front of a house. It took Nick a moment to realize they were in front of the Hawkins House—no, Cassie's house. He really should start calling it that. It took a moment longer to recognize Sophie's voice. Of course. It was Friday night. Ghost tour time.

The group moved on before he could catch up to them, Sophie saying something about ice cream shops as they disappeared down the sidewalk and toward downtown. Nick's steps slowed in front of Cassie's house, something he'd never done before. For as long as he could remember, this house was to be walked past as quickly as possible, lest you encounter the spirit of Mean Mrs. Hawkins. But this time he fought his instincts and made himself be still so he could study the place.

It looked . . . well, it looked like a house. Not like the creepy house of his childhood that everyone avoided. Warm and inviting, lights glowed from front windows that used to be cracked and broken. When he was a kid the yard had been overgrown, weeds taking over the wooden picket fence. Those weeds were gone now, and the whole front yard was laid with fresh sod. It looked by all accounts like a charming beach cottage, for probably the first time in close to a century.

It was weird.

While he stood there a light blinked on upstairs, and he forced his feet to move along. The last thing he needed was for Cassie to look out the window and see him standing in front of her house like a creeper.

But Nick gave one last wary glance over his shoulder before he hurried down the street, in case Mean Mrs. Hawkins thought he'd lingered too long. New owner or not, it was still the Hawkins House. She'd been guarding that place for decades; a silly thing like a warranty deed wasn't going to chase her off.

He hoped Cassie was ready for it.

Five

Whoa! Busy morning.

Nick closed his eyes in a slow blink before answering the text. Nothing like running a business while being constantly supervised. It's the chocolate chips I put in the banana bread. Makes the people come running!

There was a long pause before Elmer replied. Heathen.

Hey, I'm just giving the people what they want.

What the people want is for you to stop fucking with the banana bread.

How many times could Nick roll his eyes in one morning?

Elmer was able to read into his silence, even via text. I'm not trying to be a dick, he responded, even though he was totally being a dick. My recipe notebook is still in the back somewhere. There's a lemon pound cake I used to do that I bet would go over great. Maybe try that.

Sure. Nick left the reply vague. He knew what notebook Elmer meant; a battered green spiral-bound notebook—he'd found it the first month he'd taken over the café. Most of the recipes taped onto its pages had clearly been clipped from magazines and the backs of boxes. No culinary secrets there. Nick had flipped through it just in case, but the only thing of note was a photo of Elmer and his wife, Dolores, stuck between the pages in the back. It had been taken in front of the café sometime in the 1970s, judging by the cars parked on the street and the quality of the color of the photo. Funny how the place hadn't changed much since then. He had carefully p... the photo back before leaving the notebook on the upper shelf where he'd found it.

Nick glanced down at his phone, but Elmer had clearly finished giving advice. For now, anyway. He stowed his phone away and got back to cleaning up after the morning rush. It had been a relatively busy morning, especially for this time of year. It was too early for the summer season, but this was a Friday in Florida. There were always tourists, and some three-day weekenders had started to trickle in. The pastry cabinet was almost empty.

The bell over the door chimed, and Nick gritted his teeth. He loved tourists, but he hated tourists. Especially when he'd just finished wiping everything down and it was almost time to set up for lunch. But tourists paid the bills, so he plastered a smile onto his face as best he could. It probably looked more like a wince, but what the hell. Then he looked up and, like his wildest hopes had conjured her, there she was. Messy bun and T-shirt, bag over her shoulder. "Oh. It's you."

"Thanks a lot. It's that stellar customer service that keeps me coming back." But she frowned as she looked around the café. Nick followed her gaze, then he frowned too. Coming out from behind the counter, he stalked to the back table. The one near the outlet. The one that was currently occupied. Theo had been there for almost an hour, nursing that same cup of coffee and reading.

"Don't you have a bookstore to run?"

Theo turned a page, unconcerned, as he shook his head. "I open at noon on Fridays."

"It's close enough to noon. And that's her table." Nick snatched the mostly empty coffee mug. "Let me warm this up for you. In a to-go cup." Behind him, he heard the thud of Theo snapping his book closed before he followed Nick to the counter.

"What the hell?"

"Don't want you to be late." Nick filled a to-go cup with fresh coffee and pushed it across the counter.

Theo took the coffee with a quizzical expression. "Thanks?"

"Just looking out for you, man." He waved off Theo's card. "On me. Don't worry about it." It was the least he could do for kicking the guy out.

Cassie stayed frozen by the door, watching as Theo left, then turned her head to watch Nick clear away Theo's used plate and give the table a quick wipe down.

"What was that you were saying about customer service?" That came out a little more gruff than he'd intended, and Cassie jumped as though startled.

"I said it was stellar." She moved quickly to her table. "Keeps me coming back."

"Ah, bullshit," he said through the smile blooming across his face. "It's the Wi-Fi and I know it."

"And your outlet, of course." She lifted the power cord in illustration before plugging it into said outlet. "Laptop's dead again."

"Hazelnut latte, right?" He moved toward the espresso machine. "What did Buster have to say?"

"You read my mind. Iced, please." She followed him, leaning her elbows on the counter, and Nick tried not to notice her watching him make her drink. "Buster said everything was fine, and the laptop worked when he plugged it in. But I took it to the back porch yesterday since it was so nice outside. And this morning it was dead. Again." She examined the remaining baked goods in the pastry case. "Any cinnamon today?"

He shook his head. "Chocolate chip." He raised his eyes in a question and she nodded. They were already at nonverbal communication. That had to be a good sign, right? Nick pushed that thought down and forced himself back on topic. "That's weird about your outlet."

"It really is. I'm trying to tell myself it's a charming quirk of owning an old house, but when it keeps me from getting work done it's not so charming." The look in her eyes was practically lascivious as he plated the banana bread and handed it to her. She broke off a corner, popping it in her mouth. "Oh, damn. I renounce cinnamon."

"You can like both, you know." He set the coffee down in front of her. "I take it you're staying for a bit?"

She nodded, taking a long pull off her iced latte. The resulting moan made things within him tighten. Things that were inappropriate for a work setting at ten thirty-five in the morning. "I've got a project due by the end of the day. I promise I'll stay out of your way."

"Okay . . ." He tried to sound doubtful, but let's be real. If she kept moaning at him like that, he'd let her do anything she wanted. "Lunch starts in about an hour. It might get a little crowded."

"If it does, I'll give up my table." She held up her hand, prepared to swear on a stack of Bibles.

"Or you could just . . . you know . . . get some lunch. Branch out from banana bread a little."

"I dunno." She broke off another corner of said banana bread. "What's your lunch menu like?"

"It's all right there." He gestured to the chalkboard above his head, hanging on the back wall.

"So extensive." She leaned on the counter, studying it, and Nick caught himself starting to lean toward her in response. "Pretty sandwich forward, I see."

It didn't sound like a criticism, but Nick wanted to apologize anyway. "I'm not much of a cook," he admitted, "but Ramon makes a mean chicken salad."

"Don't sell yourself short. Your baking is phenomenal." She lifted the banana bread plate in illustration as she headed back to her table. "You won't know I'm here, honest."

Yeah, good luck with that. His phone buzzed in his pocket, because of course it did. Elmer had been quiet for far too long. Hey, that cute girl is back! You should ask her out.

Nick's heart was clearly on Elmer's side, leaping at the thought, but he shut that shit down quick. Not gonna happen.

> Why the hell not? You like tourists. You like to DO tourists.

Nick choked, turning it into a cough when Cassie looked his way. Elmer wasn't wrong, but damn. He didn't have to put it like that.

He needed to correct Elmer about one thing, though. Not a tourist. She lives here. Not gonna go there. Even though he wanted to go there. Very much.

> Oh come ON. Live a little, will you? For my sake.

Funny. It was tempting. More than tempting: it made things inside of him light up that had been dormant for some time. But it made him nervous too, like he was about to skydive without a parachute.

Over at Cassie's table, she was frowning at her laptop, and the iced latte at her elbow was almost gone. Well, that was a problem he could fix. It didn't take long for him to make another one, and her frown cleared almost instantly when he approached. "You're a lifesaver," she said as he set down the drink and picked up her empty glass.

"No problem," he said. He nodded toward the laptop. "Everything okay there?"

"Oh. Yeah. Just . . ." Her sigh said the exact opposite. "Three deadlines got moved up without anyone telling me. Everything's due on Monday now, when I was supposed to have another week." She made a disgusted noise and reached for her fresh iced latte. "I was going to unpack some more this weekend, but I guess that's off the table." She took a long pull of her drink, as though mainlining caffeine would help her get through her work stress.

Nick knew when he was dismissed. "I'll let you get back to it, then. Didn't mean to distract you." He didn't know what he was thinking; she wasn't into him. She was here for the caffeine and the Wi-Fi. Not for him.

But her eyes flicked up to his, and her abashed expression made him think that maybe he was wrong. "Please. You're not distracting at all." She closed her laptop with a definitive snap. "Or if you are, I'm not complaining."

"Ah." Well. If that wasn't an invitation . . . It only took a second for Nick to set her empty glass on the counter before returning to her table and dropping into the opposite chair. And then he remembered: he was the worst at small talk. He gestured toward her laptop on the table between them. "So . . . uh. What is it that you do, anyway?" Perfect. Great job. She's annoyed at her work, so the first thing you should do is ask her about it.

"Oh." She looked at her laptop as though she'd never seen it before. "I'm a copywriter. I work on ad campaigns for different brands.

Sometimes it's fun. Sometimes it's a giant clusterfuck." She rolled her eyes with what looked like forced cheer. "You ever have a boss practically hanging over your shoulder, micromanaging everything you do?"

Nick thought about the phone in his back pocket, and Elmer's weird obsession with what Nick put in the pastry case. "Yeah. I know a little something about that."

"It's all so stupid." She huffed out a sigh as she traced a line of condensation down her glass with a fingertip, and something about the movement made Nick catch his breath. "We spent, what, a year or so locked down, working from home? You'd think they would have gotten used to us working independently. But now that almost everyone's back in the office, it's like I have to fight twice as hard to prove I can keep up."

"What brought you all the way out here, then?" Seemed like she was asking for trouble, moving so far away from work. But again, what the hell did he know?

"Lots of things." She looked thoughtful. "Mostly that the house I was renting went on the market. It made me wonder what it would take to buy a place of my own. But everything in Orlando's crazy expensive, of course. So I kept looking farther and farther out until . . ."

"Until you were at the coast?" He snorted. "That's pretty far out."

"Yeah, no kidding." Her lips quirked up. "Y'all don't even have a Publix way out here."

She had a point, but Nick wasn't going to admit it. He liked being *way out here*, in a town too small for a stoplight, not to mention a chain grocery store. "We get by."

"But how do you live without Publix subs?" Cassie shook her head with mock regret. "I really didn't think this through."

"Okay, I admit it's been a long time since I've had a Publix sub—"

"Are you serious?" Cassie's eyes flew wide open. "How can you call yourself a Floridian? There is nothing better in this world than a chicken tender Pub Sub. Toss the tenders in buffalo sauce, add some lettuce, peppers, tomato, and onion, a little squeeze of ranch dressing on top. Maybe grab a side of potato salad . . . the yellow kind that has the egg in it . . ." She was practically in a trance, drooling at the memory, and damn. What would he have to do to get her to look at him like that? Because he wasn't above doing some questionable things with buffalo sauce . . .

He cleared his throat and tried to get back on topic. "It's not all bad. Sure, we don't have chicken tender subs, but Poltergeist Pizza, around the corner, delivers till ten most nights, and—"

"Most nights?" Her eyebrows shot up, but amusement danced in her eyes.

"Yep. Most nights, unless the delivery guy doesn't feel like working late. Or his scooter's busted. Sometimes they'll close up early if it's not busy." He trailed off as he realized that maybe Cassie had a point. Small-town life was definitely its own thing. He just needed to show her the good parts of it. "If it's chicken you want, though, you should check out The Haunt."

"The what?"

"The Haunt." Nick nodded toward the door. "Down on that corner. Technically it's an oyster bar, but it's the place that's open late year-round. You live close; you probably hear them at night."

"Ohhhh. The place that looks like it wants to be a biker bar, but just without the bikes?" She made a nod of understanding. "I've been meaning to go sometime."

"That's the one. Doesn't look like much. I think they do that on purpose to keep the tourist traffic down. But they do a fried chicken on Tuesdays that will change your life."

She smiled, and it was like the sun coming out. He wanted to bend toward that smile like a sunflower. It was that smile that made him bold. Made him want to take Elmer's advice after all. What the hell.

He leaned forward, elbows resting casually on the table. "You know, if you're not doing anything next week, maybe on Tuesday we could—"

The chime of the bell over the door drowned out the end of his sentence, and he wanted to scream. Cassie raised her eyebrows, her eyes alight, and he could almost see the answer to his unasked question sparking in their depths. But duty called, and he stood, managing to conceal his groan of frustration. "Hold that thought."

"Holding." She opened her laptop, but there was a trace of that smile in her voice as he went to the counter. "Hey, Sophie," he said easily. From the corner of his eye, he could see Cassie's head jerk up in reaction. "You need a coffee?"

Six

He was about to ask her out. Cassie was sure of it.

Nick had this look on his face. It had been there ever since she'd vocalized her fantasy about chicken tender subs—seriously the biggest thing she missed about Orlando—and sure, maybe she'd gotten a little carried away. But he hadn't run away screaming. In fact, he'd leaned in closer while they'd been talking, his knees practically touching hers under this tiny table, so close she could have reached his hand. Or he could have touched hers. While they'd talked about fried chicken of all things, his eyes had lingered on her face, and had she imagined it or had his gaze dropped to her mouth, just for a second?

Then he'd cleared his throat, the tip of his tongue touching his bottom lip, and Cassie's heart fluttered in her chest. He'd leaned in closer. *You know, if you're not doing anything next week, maybe on Tuesday we could—*

Then the chime of the bell over the door ruined everything. She'd done her best to be cool about it, but she pressed her lips together to hold in a sigh of aggravation as Nick got up to greet the customer who had just walked in. It was fine. She should let him get back to work.

And she should get back to work herself. Three deadlines on Monday. Ugh.

Cassie opened her laptop reluctantly, preparing to slide back into work mode instead of flirt-with-the-cute-coffee-shop-guy mode, when the name "Sophie" made her jerk her head up, Pavlov style. Sure enough, Nick was talking to a woman across the counter who Cassie was sure she'd seen before. It had been dark and she'd only been lit by the streetlamp in front of Cassie's house, but the glasses and dark curls were definitely familiar. The newcomer was the ghost tour guide from last week.

Now Cassie's heart hammered in her chest for another reason. One that had nothing to do with the cute coffee shop guy. She stared at her laptop screen, her eyes slowly losing focus as she paid attention to the conversation instead.

"You here for the sign-ups?"

Sophie nodded, her dark curls bouncing. "May as well get an iced coffee too. How's it looking for tonight?"

"Let's see." After Nick handed Sophie her coffee and her change, he opened a drawer under the register and slid a notepad across the counter. "Looks like you've got three for tonight. Not too bad."

"Are you kidding?" Sophie sighed as she consulted the list. "It's barely worth doing. Three people?"

"Memorial Day's right around the corner." Nick's voice was consoling. "Just hold out a little while longer."

Sophie nodded with another sigh, but then brightened almost immediately. "Oh hey. You heard that someone bought the Hawkins House, right?"

Cassie's scalp prickled, the tingling sensation traveling across her shoulders and down her spine. She took a pull off her iced latte and tried to refocus her attention to her work, while also not making any unnecessary movements. Time to be inconspicuous.

"Yep," Nick said easily. "She's right over there if you want to say hi." Out of the corner of her eye, Cassie could see him gesturing in her direction and Sophie whirling around.

Welp. So much for inconspicuous. She looked up, trying to act like she hadn't been eavesdropping. "Guilty. You're the one with the ghost tour, right?"

"Guilty," Sophie said right back, her eyes bright and her smile wide. She moved to Cassie's table, pulling out a chair and sitting down. "I'm Sophie, by the way. Or maybe you knew that already."

"Cassie." Her laptop dimmed, then went dark as it put itself to sleep. It felt like a commentary on Cassie's work ethic, and it was irritating, like an itch in her brain. But making a potential new friend in this town felt more important than work right now.

Sophie leaned in, as though she were about to impart a secret. "So, is there really a ghost? You have to tell me."

Cassie hadn't expected that question. Sophie had seemed so authoritative during the tour she'd overheard. Wouldn't she know? "I was hoping you could tell me. I heard your tour last week—"

"You did?" Sophie's eyes lit up as she remembered. "That was you up on the balcony, wasn't it? You scared the crap out of like half the tour!"

Oh, no. Cassie drew in a breath to apologize, but Sophie's voice trembled with suppressed laughter, and Cassie let out her breath again. "You're welcome?"

Now Sophie let her laugh out in a giggle and she nodded. "Anytime you want to do that, feel free. It was great!"

Cassie pictured herself lurking in the shadows of her upstairs balcony, waiting to jump out and say *boo* to the ghost tour every week. She'd certainly done worse things on a Friday night. "The story you told, out in front of the house. Is it true?"

Sophie nodded emphatically. "Oh, yeah. Mean Mrs. Hawkins

has her own chapter and everything." She pulled a book out of her satchel and handed it across the table.

"Her own chapter?" Cassie turned the book over in her hands. *Boneyard Key: A Haunted History.* It was published by one of those small presses that did histories of towns, books that showed up in every "local history" section of a bookstore. This copy was obviously well loved; the cover was bent, with one corner torn away, and the pages inside were studded with colored Post-it notes. She paged through it, pausing at blurry black-and-white photos of Beachside Drive, a street that was already starting to feel familiar. The silhouette of the buildings was the same, but instead of gift shops and restaurants, the streets were lined with a hardware store and a grocery. Another photo showed that the gray squat building on the road out of town used to be a service station.

"The book's pretty comprehensive," Sophie said while Cassie continued to flip pages. "When I started putting this tour together, I found there was more than enough information in here, both about the history of the town and the ghosts. It was written by a local historian about, what, fifty years ago?" She looked over her shoulder to Nick, who leaned against the counter, one leg crossed over the other at the ankle. Cassie hadn't realized he'd been listening in, but he'd obviously been there the whole time. Watching them. A pleased flush crept up the back of her neck, flooding her cheeks.

He snorted in confirmation. "I think calling Mr. Lindsay a 'local historian' might be pushing it. He was our history teacher in high school," he said to Cassie.

"You two went to high school together?" She looked from Nick to Sophie. Sophie looked young, but maybe that was just the way she looked. Cassie wasn't going to judge.

But Sophie laughed. "Oh, no. Nick's an old man . . ."

"Thanks a lot."

Sophie continued like Nick hadn't interrupted. "He was a senior when I was a freshman. We only overlapped by a year."

"If you went to Boneyard Key High in the last forty years or so, you had Mr. Lindsay for history," Nick said, obviously letting the comment about his age slide. "Our parents all had to buy us a copy of that damn book. We were like a captive supplementary income to that guy."

Cassie shrugged. "Not a bad gig if you can get it, right?"

Nick huffed out a laugh. "But yeah. The book was old even back then. Fifty years sounds about right."

Cassie flipped to the copyright page and there it was: the publication date, and confirmation that this book was almost the same age as her parents.

"He was a huge stickler for facts when we were in school," Sophie said. "He must have researched the heck out of everything while he wrote the book. But as far as the Hawkins House goes, it's common knowledge around here that it's haunted. I've never seen any actual activity, though. What about you?" She propped her chin on her hands. "Anything weird going on there since you moved in?"

Sophie looked so eager that Cassie hated to disappoint her. But she shook her head slowly as she handed the book back. "Nothing's gone bump in the night as far as I can tell. Unless ghosts like to mess with the electricity."

Cassie had been joking, but Sophie's eyes flew wide. "Oooh, really? Ghosts have been known to affect electricity. That could be something."

How was Sophie able to talk about ghosts like they were real? Putting on a ghost tour was one thing—that was entertainment. Fiction. This was real life, which didn't have things like ghosts in it. It had deadlines. Three of them on Monday, in fact. "Then old Mrs. H doesn't want me to get any work done," she said. "My laptop won't charge at home."

"Hmmm." Sophie's brows drew together, wheels obviously turning in her brain. "That doesn't match up with anything we know about Sarah Hawkins. I wonder why she'd want to disrupt your electricity?"

"Did you mess with her garden?" Nick was behind the counter again, bustling around but obviously still listening in. "Wasn't that her thing back in the day? Kids picking the roses or something? Wait." He stopped, turning from the batch of sweet tea he was making. "There isn't a garden there anymore, is there?"

"No," Cassie said. "No garden. The sellers put down sod. It's all lawn now." Lawn that looked stupid and was a waste of water, by the way. Now she pictured roses growing along the garden gate, and that mental picture was so much nicer.

"Still." Sophie was determined to stay on topic. "Why would she mess with your electricity? That's got nothing to do with the garden."

"No idea. But I have to come here if I want to get any work done." Cassie gestured to the outlet where her laptop was still plugged in and charging.

"I knew it." Nick shook his head as he added ice and sugar to the tea he'd just brewed. "You really do only love me for my Wi-Fi."

"And the banana bread," Cassie shot back with a smile. "I'm a sucker for cinnamon."

Sophie looked from Cassie to Nick. "You two are a match made in heaven." She slipped the book back into her bag as she stood. "You should come on the tour tonight. On the house. There's plenty of room. I cap it at twenty, but I'm sure you heard, I've only got three people tonight." She waved the notepad in emphasis. "Call it a housewarming present. You can get a little history of your new hometown."

Nick cleared his throat. "Maybe I'll tag along." He picked at an invisible spot on the countertop with a thumbnail, his voice elaborately casual.

Sophie raised her eyebrows. "I've done this tour for five years and you've never gone on it. Since when are you interested in local history?"

"Hey, I love this town. You know that. I've always meant to go on your tour, just haven't gotten around to it." He shot Cassie a look. "Like, how many times did you go to Disney when you lived in Orlando?"

"Not enough to justify the annual pass." Okay, that was a lie. She made her money back on her trips to the Food & Wine Festival alone. And then she spent it all again on the food and wine. Cassie got what he meant, though. When you had a tourist attraction in your backyard, it was easy to forget it was there.

But Sophie wasn't fooled. Her smirk was subtle but it was there. "Sure." She tore the top page off before handing the notepad back to Nick. "See you tonight."

The sound of the bell chiming followed her out the door, and Cassie turned her attention to Nick. "All this ghost stuff. It's really a thing?" It was getting to be a lot. She was okay with cutesy names of various shops, and the iconography almost everywhere she looked. That was touristy, and it was fun. But serious questions about ghosts in her house, and a haunted history textbook as part of the local school's curriculum? That . . . that was a lot of ghosts.

She desperately wanted Nick to make a joke. He was good at those, and she could really use some snark right now to counteract the shiver that was building at the top of her spine. But his nod, while friendly, was serious. Not a stitch of snark in sight. "It's really a thing." He straightened up then, moving to clear away her empty dishes that he'd left on the counter. "I know it all seems gimmicky, something to bring in tourists. And in some ways, it is. But . . ." He paused, staring hard at the rag in his hand before tossing it in the sink behind him. "It's a thing," he said again. "I'm sure Sophie'll explain it tonight better than I can."

Cassie didn't want to end the conversation there, but Nick seemed done. Which was probably for the best. She had a lot of work to do. Especially if she was spending tonight on a walking tour of Boneyard Key instead of catching up on work. She turned back to her laptop, waking it up.

The bell above the door chimed again, and a dark-haired man walked in, raising a hand in greeting to Nick as he headed straight back to the kitchen. "What the hell, man! Nothing's been set up back here!"

"Sorry!" Nick called. "Been a busy morning." He rolled his eyes at Cassie, and she stifled a giggle. "I gotta get back there." He pointed to the kitchen.

She nodded. "See you tonight, then?"

"It's a date."

Cassie's eyes flew to his, taking in the hesitant smile that flashed across his face before he turned to go. She couldn't keep an answering smile from her face as she pulled up an email to respond to. Maybe she'd stay for lunch after all.

Seven

"A *date*, huh?" Ramon was a cheerful guy in general, but the glee on his face right now was next level.

"Keep your voice down!" Nick threw a panicked glance over his shoulder, but the door to the kitchen had swung shut behind him. Cassie couldn't hear them back here unless there was yelling. And neither of them was the yelling type.

"I'm just saying!" Ramon opened the walk-in fridge, checking the stock of everything he'd need for the lunch menu. But he kept talking while he did so; the man was a multitasker. "It's nice to see you so . . ." He trailed off as he stepped all the way inside, and Nick was tempted to close the door on him. Just for a couple minutes, until he stopped talking about Nick's love life.

Instead Nick crossed his arms and leaned a hip against the prep counter. "See me what?" He knew what Ramon was going to say; he just needed to hear him say it.

"You know . . ." Ramon emerged with a block of cheese and a slab of roast beef, carrying them over to the slicer. "Interested. It's been a while, you know? Since Madison—" This time he abruptly stopped talking instead of trailing off. Mentioning Nick's ex's name around him tended to have that effect.

Nick concentrated on taking a slow, deep breath. Hearing her name wasn't the arrow to the heart the way it used to be. She'd left him years ago, and she'd been checked out of the relationship for long before that. But nothing hurt like your first love. Especially when you never had the chance to fall out of love. She'd made that decision for them both. Every so often Nick would wake up in the middle of the night and ask himself: Why hadn't he been enough?

He wasn't still carrying a torch or anything; Madison had doused it long ago. But it was why he didn't date anyone he expected to stick around. He was never going to set himself up for that kind of hurt again. He had his café. He had his town, his friends. Most of the time that was enough.

But now . . .

It's a date.

A date.

The words haunted Nick all through lunch service (Cassie had stayed, gotten a chicken Caesar wrap, and proclaimed her undying love for Ramon. It was a goddamn sandwich; you'd think he'd made her a five-course meal) and into the afternoon. When he flipped the CLOSED sign on the door, locked up the place, and went around to the back stairs, the words echoed in his head to the rhythm of his steps. *It's a DATE. It's a DATE.*

What had he been thinking? He hadn't been, obviously. He'd been a desperate dude who just asked out a girl he barely knew. A girl who mooched off his Wi-Fi and his electricity, and whose only redeeming quality was her love of cinnamon.

And her big brown eyes.

And her dark hair, especially that one lock that fell out of her bun to curl along her cheekbone and down to her chin, following a path he wanted to trace with his fingertips.

And that smile of hers, like the sun. Not on a miserably humid day like today, but on one of those rare days in January, when the air was crisp and a hoodie didn't feel like heatstroke. He wanted to bask in her warmth. He wanted to . . .

Ugh. Fine. It was worth seeing where this date could lead.

As he unlocked the front door to his apartment over the café, his heart raced with equal parts panic and anticipation. Because it really had been a long time since he'd asked someone out, and maybe he shouldn't have waited this long. He was really out of practice at playing it cool when it mattered.

He wasn't sure if his roommate would be there—he kind of came and went as he pleased—and when Nick first opened the door he thought he was alone. Which was good. He wasn't in the mood to talk about any of it: his love life, his lack of one, and the possibility that he may have just accidentally jump-started something in his personal life.

His phone buzzed with a text. Of course. Time for Elmer to make fun of him. For having a date. For not doing an impressive enough job of asking Cassie out.

But the text was from Vince: Guitar night at Jo's! Meet there at 7?

Can't. I have plans. He knew as soon as he hit Send that there would be follow-up questions.

And there were. Plans? You? Since when?

Nick took a slow, deep breath in through his nose as he typed. I have a date. He stared at the words, glowing on the screen. Hitting Send felt like a declaration.

Vince didn't respond for a long moment, and Nick almost put his phone away when typing bubbles appeared. About damn time! Catch you later.

Huh. Nick had been expecting more questions, but Vince must have decided to go easy on him. Nice.

There was another text waiting for him when he got out of the shower. The one he'd been expecting.

Ghost tour, huh? You don't get enough of that at home?

Nick huffed out a laugh. Elmer had a point. He looked up from his phone and spoke out loud, addressing the room in general. "I'm home, you know. Don't need to text."

It took a couple of minutes. Long enough that Nick wondered if maybe he was alone in his place after all. But then he saw it: the ripple in the air, the way an almost-shadow settled in the battered brown leather recliner in the corner near the window. The recliner that had been here since before Nick's time. The recliner that Hallowed Grounds's previous owner had told Nick, under no uncertain terms, to never throw out.

"Yeah," Nick said to the recliner. "I've never been on Sophie's ghost tour, you know. I figure I should probably know what it's all about if I'm going to keep shilling it at customers." It was a poor excuse. Nick knew it. And Elmer sure as hell knew it.

Sure, okay. Nothing to do with the pretty girl who likes your banana bread, even though you make it wrong. This time the response didn't come as a text on his phone, but more like a voice inside his head: words forming as complete thoughts as opposed to a literal voice. It had freaked him out the first time it had happened, not long after he'd moved into this apartment above the café. In fact, it had almost been a deal-breaker. It had certainly been a deal-breaker for the café's last four owners.

But Nick remembered Elmer when he'd been alive: the grouchy old man who'd run this place when Nick was a kid. Hallowed Grounds had been a convenient stop on the way to school, and Elmer always had blueberry muffins and banana bread freshly made in the mornings. There had been something about hearing Elmer's voice again, the nostalgia of it. The memory of when life was simpler, and his biggest problem was math class. The moment that Nick realized Elmer had still stuck around this place was the moment that Nick realized he didn't want to leave, either.

"Of course not," he said, a smile in his voice. "Nothing to do with her at all." He wasn't sure why he bothered to lie; Elmer knew him too well.

Then the cold kicked in. It always did when Elmer was around, and Nick reached for the flannel he kept slung over the back of one of his dining chairs. Having a ghost for a roommate meant he didn't have to run the air-conditioning, even in the height of summer. When you lived in Florida, that was a pretty good upside.

This is good. Elmer's voice bloomed in his head again. *You need to get out more. Life is for the living, you know?*

"So you keep saying." Nick moved to the kitchenette side of the studio apartment. He needed to get back downstairs, get tomorrow morning's prep done before meeting up with Cassie, but he still had some time. "Want some coffee?"

Please.

Nick reached for the can in the cabinet and scooped some grounds into the coffee maker. A half pot was plenty; he didn't need much more caffeine than that, and Elmer couldn't actually drink coffee anymore. But Elmer still loved the smell, and if that pleased his ghost roommate, Nick was happy to oblige.

Besides, Nick was in a good mood. He had a date.

Eight

I t wasn't a date.

Not really.

Yet Cassie had wasted the entire afternoon, first being too distracted to get any work done, and then feeling too guilty about not getting any work done to do anything else. Then it was suddenly six fifteen, and she had to throw a frozen pizza in the oven and figure out what she was going to wear. (She should eat first, right? Nick hadn't said anything about dinner afterward. See? Another reason this wasn't a date and Cassie needed to stop overthinking.)

Her hair was a lost cause; she could straighten it, but she didn't really have time. And the humidity would turn it into a frizzy mess in the few minutes it would take her to walk to the café. So back up in a clip it went, and she threw on a sundress that was hopefully cute enough to make up for it. Then she slicked on some lip gloss and laced up her comfiest walking shoes. It was a walking tour after all, right?

The walk from her house to Hallowed Grounds was all but routine by now, from the cracks in the sidewalk to the shop displays and the white cartoon ghosts fluttering from the flagpoles. The sun had just started to dip low over the ocean, turning everything molten gold, and her sunglasses did little against the glare. Useless. But then she spotted Nick outside waiting for her, and she appreciated the camouflage the sunglasses provided.

He leaned against the lamppost outside Hallowed Grounds, his head turned away from her. His jeans were well-worn without being obnoxiously tight, and the sleeves of his blue dress shirt were pushed up his forearms. The evening sun threw russet-colored rays into his brown hair, which was pushed off his forehead and curled down to the back of his neck. Damn, golden hour looked good on this guy. Then again, she'd seen him in crappy fluorescent light earlier today, and he'd looked pretty nibbleable then.

Nick pushed off the lamppost when she approached. "Hey, you." His voice was warm but not quite flirtatious. Yeah, definitely not a date. Cassie swallowed hard against sudden disappointment.

"Hi." She gave him an unfortunately dorky wave. She'd been so busy ogling him as she walked up that she hadn't even noticed the other tourists, but there were three other people—a white middle-aged married couple and a twentysomething guy with dark skin and a camera bag—milling around in front of the shop. They gave each other friendly, closed-lipped smiles; they were obviously here for the same reason, but not yet ready to engage in actual conversation with each other.

Thankfully Sophie chose that moment to round the corner, greeting everyone with a bright smile. Cassie's return smile was involuntary. The phrase "cute as a button" was invented for Sophie. She couldn't have been more than a little over five feet, her dark hair a riot of curls tamed by a red headband, and her big brown eyes framed by gold wire-rimmed glasses. Her face was round, her nose was small; she could have been a high school senior doing this for extra credit.

But when she addressed the crowd—was five people enough to be considered a crowd?—she was all authority. "Welcome, welcome! I'm so glad you all took the time to join me tonight! First I'm going to collect the fee: fifteen dollars each, please. Then we'll get started! The tour runs about an hour, give or take, and we'll be walking about a mile and a half in total. There are plenty of benches along the way if anyone needs to take a break, and I'm happy to tell more stories to pass the time if need be."

While Sophie moved to the trio of tourists on the other side of the sidewalk, Nick leaned in toward Cassie. She caught a whiff of cinnamon; he must have been baking. Beneath that she smelled clean soap, a scent that reminded her of the ocean off her back balcony.

"You ready for this?" His voice was a low murmur that sent a shiver down her spine. She looked up into those illegally blue eyes, remembering way too late that she should probably answer his question.

"I think so." She smoothed her hands nervously—they were already sweaty, thanks, Florida!—down the skirt of her sundress. Thank God for thin cotton; the night wasn't overly hot, but humidity was eternal. "This isn't going to be scary, is it?" She was very much not one for horror movies.

"Nah." He stuck his hands in the front pockets of his jeans, looking up and down the street as though he were assessing the area. "Most of the ghosts around here are benign. Harmless, you know? The more dangerous ones are usually encouraged to move along."

"Go to the light, or whatever?"

He nodded. "Or whatever."

"Ri-ii-ii-ght." Cassie drew the word out into at least four syllables. Looked like they were keeping up the facade that all of this wasn't bullshit. But that made sense. The other folks here were tourists, paying customers. If he ever broke down and told her the truth—what had to be the truth—it certainly wouldn't be in front of a bunch of tourists who were waiting to hear ghost stories.

"Let's get started!" Sophie situated herself by the door to Hallowed Grounds and clapped her hands together once. Instantly, the disparate group of people milling around fell into place in front of her, resolving into her audience. Cassie was impressed.

"One of the reasons I have us meet here is because it's the best place to start the tour. Which seems weird, right? It's not even open. Hallowed Grounds is one of the longest-running businesses in Boneyard Key. It was founded in the 1930s and was originally a diner, but these days it's more of a coffee shop and lunchtime spot. I usually like to start this tour by telling you the story of the former owner and how he still has a hand in his old business. But we have a special guest tonight. Nick, would you like to do the honors?"

Cassie turned to Nick, a grin spreading over her face. She had no idea he was part of this whole thing!

Nick looked just as surprised. "Uh." He shifted from one foot to the other, looking uneasy. He shot Sophie a glare from under his eyebrows but she was unmoved, meeting his gaze with an easy smile. Finally he gusted out a sigh.

"Fine." He gestured awkwardly to the darkened windows of the coffee shop. "Elmer Buchanan ran this place for years. Decades, even. His dad was actually the one who started the business. It was a diner in the thirties, like Sophie said. When Elmer came back from serving in World War Two, he got married, settled here, and ended up taking over the diner. I don't know when dinner service stopped. Probably when he got older and was sick of staying up late. It was always a breakfast and lunch place when I was a kid." This was not a rehearsed speech. Nick started and stopped, stammered at some points—a stark contrast to Sophie's obviously well-rehearsed patter. Cassie wanted to squeeze his hand, take some of his obvious nervousness into herself to help him out. But that might be too much too soon, so she settled for sending a mental *you've got this* his way.

Sophie nodded. "Elmer took over the place, like Nick said, and it became his life. Especially after his wife died, sometime in the eighties, right, Nick?" She continued after Nick's nod of agreement. "He was a gregarious guy, loved being in the center of town, knowing everything that was going on."

"Not to mention everybody's business." Nick's smile was less stiff now as he fell into conversation with Sophie. Cassie was impressed; Sophie was good at this. "Still does. I've been the fifth owner after Elmer. The other ones didn't want to deal with his . . . uh . . . input."

One of the other tourists—the middle-aged husband—snorted. "I know what you mean. My boss retired three years ago, but he still drops by the firm. Pretty sure he fully expects the place to have burned down without him around." He shook his head. "Some people don't know how to let go."

"That's it exactly." The rest of Nick's obvious nervousness fell away as he seized on the other guy's words. While public speaking wasn't his thing, conversation obviously was. "He texts me all the time. Gets testy with me if I so much as tinker with a recipe. It used to bug me at first. Like, leave me alone, man!" He grinned as the group chuckled. "But I get it. Hard to let go, like you said. So I let him complain, and just nod and smile. It's my place now, and when it comes down to it, I do what I want."

"Nick." Sophie sounded amused. "You forgot to mention . . ."

"Oh. Yeah." Nick glanced at the darkened windows again, let his gaze travel up to encompass the whole building. "Elmer died around Y2K. So, uh. Yeah. He's been gone a while."

A startled laugh exploded from Cassie's throat before she could stop herself, which prompted answering chuckles from the trio of tourists. Nick and Sophie responded with tolerant smiles that made

Cassie's laughter fade as fast as it had come on. She had the unsettling feeling that neither of them was kidding.

Sophie took back the conversation. "I like to start with Elmer's story because he's a perfect example of the kind of spirit that hangs out here." She started down the wide sidewalk, and the group fell in line behind her like obedient ducklings. "Ghosts aren't always scary. Here in Boneyard Key, they're a way of life. Part of the scenery." She led them up the street, past a T-shirt shop. The sun had lowered farther in the sky, sending shadows across the street.

Cassie pushed her sunglasses on top of her head and fell into step with Nick, bringing up the rear of the small procession. "I didn't realize you were part of the show," she said sotto voce, out of earshot of the rest of the tour. "That was pretty cool."

Nick snorted, shaking his head. "I can't believe Sophie put me on the spot like that. We're gonna have words later." But a smile played around his lips—very full, kissable lips, Cassie found herself noticing—that belied his stern tone.

"You sure? You had that story all worked up and ready to go." *Come on*, she wanted to say. *I'm not one of the tourists here.* She wanted him to be real with her, to treat her like a local. But she didn't know how to break through. What was the password to unlock the real story?

"It's not a story." Nick's brow furrowed as he cast her a sideways glance. His voice had dropped, giving them more privacy. "You still think this is all bullshit, huh?"

She opened her mouth to reply but closed it immediately, feeling herself floundering. "I mean . . . you're talking about *ghost stories* here. I get all this—" She waved a hand around, encompassing the shops they passed, all closed up tight for the evening. "But it's a touristy thing, isn't it? Something that sells T-shirts and ghost tours and whatever. I mean, if I go to Weeki Wachee to see the mermaids, I can get caught up in the fantasy they're selling. I can say, 'Oooh look at the mermaids!' I can let myself ignore the hoses they're holding so they can breathe. I know deep down that the tails they're wearing are costumes. I'm not expecting the mermaids to be real."

"This isn't Weeki Wachee, though." He thrust his hands into the front pockets of his jeans again and lengthened his stride to catch up to the group. Their one-on-one conversation was over as quickly as it had started. Cassie picked up the pace, practically trotting to match his steps. *Great job, Cass,* she scolded herself. *If there was any notion of this being a date, you just killed it in record time.*

By the time they were back in earshot of Sophie and her spiel, the group was in front of I Scream Ice Cream, where Sophie was winding down her story.

"So the good news is that if the freezers go down, the ice cream still stays cold!" She grinned while the rest of the group chuckled at her joke. Cassie hazarded a glance at Nick, who was mid–eye roll. He froze for a second as his gaze caught hers, then his expression softened.

"Okay, that one's bullshit." His voice was little more than a breath in her ear, his tone amused. He shot her a shy grin when she looked over at him.

"Yeah?" Her heart surged with hope. He was bringing her in on the joke, like a peace offering. Maybe she hadn't ruined things after all.

The tour group moved on, and he bumped her shoulder with his as they fell into step with the rest. "Sometimes an ice cream shop is just an ice cream shop."

"Okay then, Freud." They continued down the sidewalk that led them around a bend toward the fishing pier. Cassie glanced across the street at her house as they passed it, but quickly turned her attention back to Sophie and her account of the town's history. There would be time for her own personal (hopefully not really) haunted house later in the tour.

"There are lots of theories about what makes Boneyard Key so special. If you're familiar with Cassadaga, which is in Central Florida on the way to Daytona, it was founded largely because of its psychic energy. Something to do with ley lines that I don't even pretend to understand." She pulled a face and the group laughed in response. "Some people think Boneyard Key is the same way. Something to do with the *thinning of the veil . . .*" She made spooky jazz hands to emphasize these last words. "But the general consensus comes from the town's ominous past. We've had our share of tragedies here. Tragedy begets death, which of course begets ghosts."

"Tragedy?" The middle-aged wife glanced around, and Cassie could see her point. The streetlights—wrought iron and made to look like old-fashioned gas lanterns—had begun to pop on as the sky darkened around them. Their warm, cozy light bounced off the closed-up kayak rental and bait shop, painted in cheerful shades of blue and green and orange. It looked like a postcard, or an art print titled *Florida at Night*, not like the kind of setting that tragedy could touch.

"Well, not recently," Sophie clarified. "Boneyard Key was founded in the 1840s, but not here." She led the group across the street and onto the darkened fishing pier, their footsteps clomping hollowly across the wooden slats. "We don't have a great moon tonight"—Sophie peered up as though the crescent in the sky had disappointed her personally—"but if you come back during the day, you can look across the water and see the site of the original settlement. It's called Cemetery Island now, because that's all that's left over there."

Cassie stared as hard as she could, but all she could see in the darkness was a lump of slightly deeper darkness. She'd take Sophie's word for it.

"It's a small barrier island," Sophie continued. "And when people lived there it wasn't much, mostly a fishing and clamming community, but it was settled and thriving. Until the Great Storm of 1897."

"Well, that doesn't sound good." Cassie had mostly been talking to herself, but beside her Nick made a grunt of agreement.

"Hurricanes usually aren't," he said, and she winced in sympathy. Floridians typically took hurricanes with a grain of salt and more than one margarita, but when they were bad, they were devastating.

"They weren't measuring hurricanes yet," Sophie continued, "but they say now that it was probably a Category Four storm, with winds at something close to 145 miles an hour." She nodded as the group gave various gasps and low whistles. "Yeah, it was a big one. Wiped out the town, and most of the island itself. Many of the survivors of the Great Storm took off for points north after that, but a core group of families stayed—we call them the Founding Fifteen. They moved inland and established a new settlement here. They're the ones that made Boneyard Key what it is today."

Cassie leaned into Nick, her voice low. "A tourist town with the most souvenir shops per capita?"

Nick's snort of laughter caught them both by surprise, and Sophie narrowed her eyes at them in mock censure. "As I was *saying*, it was about that time that . . . well, that's when the hauntings started, for lack of a better term."

She sounded so matter-of-fact about it that Cassie could almost forget that Sophie was talking about ghosts. "What was I saying about tragedy and trauma? Suddenly the Founding Fifteen—those families who stayed behind—found themselves able to communicate with those who'd been killed in the Great Storm. Most of those spirits didn't stick around for long; they seemed to want the closure of being able to say goodbye, or seeing that their families were going to be okay. But then, as years went by, some ghosts just started . . . staying."

"That had to have been creepy." The younger tourist in the group aimed his camera toward the water; Cassie couldn't imagine what he'd be able to capture.

"Maybe." Sophie's voice was carefully neutral. "And maybe a little comforting too. Sometimes when we lose someone, it's like we'd give everything to have one final talk with them, you know? The dead aren't always scary."

"The original settlement was called Fisherton," she continued, "but when . . . well, when the weird things started happening, outsiders started calling it Boneyard Key. As a joke. Eventually it stuck, as people who lived here decided that sharing space with the dead wasn't such a bad thing to do." Sophie took a beat to let her words land; she really was a good storyteller. "There's not much left of the original settlement on Cemetery Island—we've had a few more hurricanes over the years that've taken care of any remains of structures, things like that. But during the day you can rent a kayak and go over there. It's an easy trip. There are a couple of foundations of houses, and tucked in the back is the original cemetery." She paused. "It was oddly spared by all of the storms."

Sophie let those final words sink in before she led them off the pier and back onto the sidewalk. Cassie leaned into Nick as they headed down the street. "Do I want to see Cemetery Island?"

He shrugged; saying *meh* with his whole attitude. "If you're into kayaking. And cemeteries."

"My two favorite things." She grinned as Nick was startled into another laugh, interrupting Sophie. She narrowed her eyes at them but was smiling too much to be mad.

"As I was saying, this is one of our most famous landmarks." She glanced over her shoulder then back at the tour group. "I'm not sure what that says about our town, but there you go. People like to take pictures of it, right?" She gestured to the guy with the camera, and he laughed.

"Guilty," he said. "I was planning to get up early to shoot it tomorrow during sunrise."

It was a stilt house built about thirty feet out into the Gulf. Though *house* was a generous term; the stilts were intact, along with two and a half walls. And some of the floor. A little bit of the roof.

Sophie nodded. "Now I'm going to admit that I have no idea if this place is haunted or not. I don't have a whole lot of information on its history. The structure itself is abandoned, and as you can see, the Gulf is slowly taking the house, a piece at a time. Whoever once owned it is long gone. Unlike Nick's friend Elmer, no one dead stuck around, and any descendants moved away decades ago. It's become part of the scenery here in town. We call it the Starter Home." She smiled as the group chuckled. "Just needs a little work, right?"

"Sure." Cassie had to laugh at that. "It's got good bones." How many times had she heard that phrase when she'd been house hunting? Though saying it out loud while taking a ghost tour in a haunted town felt very different.

But Nick apparently appreciated ghost-related puns. "Good one."

They continued around the bend, but Cassie hung back for a moment, gazing at the Starter Home. There was something about it that made her sad. Someone had built that house once. Someone had dreams of watching sunsets over the Gulf from their (probably) cute stilt house on the water. Who had lived there? What had happened to their dreams? Why had they left? She was suddenly very thankful for that somewhat shady flipper who had rescued her house. She hadn't lived there long, but she hated the thought of it sitting there empty and forgotten for all those years, like the Starter Home here.

When she turned back around, Nick was waiting patiently for her, hanging back while the rest of the group continued around the bend and back to the main street leading into downtown.

He raised his eyebrows. "You okay?" He looked from her to the ruins of the stilt house, and back again, like he had picked up on her train of thought.

"Yeah." She kept her voice light, fighting against the sudden melancholy that had come out of nowhere. "All good."

When they caught up to the group, they were stopped in front of her house. Sophie had just turned around, waiting for Nick and Cassie to catch up. Cassie looked at the little gate of her picket fence. Painting it was on her to-do list, and now that she knew the house was a tourist attraction, she mentally bumped it up higher.

She'd heard this part of the tour already, from her balcony last Friday night when Sophie had brought another group by. She'd laughed it off then, but now her heart hammered in her chest. All this walking around in the dark, hearing the history of the town in the places where it happened, was getting to her, and Cassie was starting to see all this ghost stuff in a very different light. What if it was all true? Wasn't a real estate agent supposed to disclose if a house was haunted?

Cassie tried to focus on Sophie's words, but she couldn't hear them over the blood pounding in her ears, so instead she focused on her house. She'd left the downstairs windows open and the porch lights on, which glowed now against the clapboard siding that was painted a soft yellow. Sure, the picket fence needed some paint, and the sod lawn the seller had put in really did look like crap, but there wasn't anything about the place that looked particularly ominous.

". . . She died sometime in the forties." Sophie was wrapping up the story. "The house sat vacant for decades. But . . ." Her voice suddenly switched from spooky back to her bright sunny attitude. "A couple years ago it was purchased. It's been renovated, and now it has a brand-new owner." She threw Cassie a subtle glance and a smile as she started off down the sidewalk, motioning for the group to follow.

The lot next to Cassie's house was vacant and surrounded by an old wooden fence, its whitewash nearly worn away. The faux gas lamp here didn't work, so once they'd left the glow of Cassie's front porch, they were swallowed up by darkness just in front of that vacant lot. But the darkness was short-lived; there was barely enough time to be creeped out before they hit the warm glow of the next streetlight. They were almost back to the downtown area where the tour had started.

"Now there's a little path here, between the dunes, that takes you straight to the beach." Sophie gestured off to the right, and while Cassie tried to follow the movement, the path toward the beach was too dark to make out. "You don't want to head down there now, though."

"Why, is the beach haunted too?" One of the patrons made a *woooo*-style ghost noise, and the group gave a collective chuckle. But Sophie nodded in all seriousness.

"Sometimes. Usually around . . ." She consulted her smartwatch, which briefly illuminated her face. "Oh, yeah, he might be out by now. Let's just say if you take a shortcut through the beach walking home from, say, The Haunt? After a drink or two too many? You may have company." She shrugged. "There's a ghost out there in the dunes that really wants to hang out with drunk friends. If you're sober you may be okay."

"Bring him a beer and he won't bother you." Nick had been quiet for a bit, so when he spoke up now, Cassie jumped, her heart in her throat. He tossed her a crooked smile when she looked at him. "That's what my friends and I always did when we'd go down to the beach to drink. He liked being part of the group."

Cassie's laugh felt forced, as she was still trying to get her heart rate to go down. "There're a lot of rules to these ghosts." She meant it as a joke, the way the guy a minute ago had made that *woooo* noise, but Nick nodded thoughtfully and Sophie, who had heard her, pointed at Cassie in recognition.

"There are! It's weird, right? But you have to remember that ghosts were once people. And just like we all have different personalities in life, those personalities carry on into the afterlife. Now, I don't know the full story of the beach bum—that's what I call him. My theory is that he's someone who was wandering home after a night out and went the wrong direction. Like into-the-ocean wrong direction."

"That . . . he'd have to be pretty drunk to do that." One of the tourists sounded somewhere between impressed and shocked.

"He would." Sophie sounded way too cheerful to be talking about someone's possible demise. Cassie stole a glance from Nick to Sophie. Two lifelong residents of this place, they took all this haunting in stride.

But neither of them lived in a house with the ghost of a creepy old lady who'd whacked her husband. At least, she didn't think they did.

The real estate agent *really* should have disclosed that.

A slight breeze kicked up, cooling the sweat on her skin and ruffling stray locks of her hair. Cassie shivered and leaned in to Nick, who looked down at her with concern.

"Everything all right?" He put an arm around her, chafing one hand up and down her upper arm.

She forced a smile. "Yeah." She wasn't sure if it was the truth. Just like she wasn't sure if this had really been a date. But if she could keep this guy's arm around her, and maybe make him laugh again, well. It wouldn't be the worst night ever. Not even close.

Nine

Nick fished in his pocket for his keys. It had been a long time since he'd been out with a girl, but even he could tell that it hadn't gone all that well. Sure, he'd enjoyed talking to Cassie; she was smart and really damn clever. He'd wanted her to feel welcome in her new town, and thought that Sophie's ghost tour would be a great way to make her feel like a part of things. Sophie obviously agreed; she had all but shaken pom-poms in their direction all night, cheering the two of them on.

But as he unlocked the door to Hallowed Grounds, he could tell from Cassie's face that she had questions. Lots of them. And he was willing to bet that none of those questions were about when she could see him again. So yeah. He'd knocked that shit out of the park.

The ghost tour had come to an end, the trio of tourists sent on their way with a fistful of drink coupons to The Haunt. But Nick wasn't one for karaoke, and when Cassie's quick headshake confirmed that she wasn't either, he'd suggested a nightcap at his closed-up café. Maybe if he was on familiar ground with her, he could salvage things.

"Want a drink?" After flipping the lock behind them, he moved behind the counter and turned on just enough lights that he could see what he was doing. Didn't want to encourage any late-night customers stopping by. "No liquor license, sadly, but I've got some bourbon back here for emergencies. It goes great in hot chocolate." He looked around the kitchen, mind whirling. What else? "Or I could get some coffee going. What do you think?"

"Hot chocolate sounds great." She leaned her elbows on the counter. "Since I hit thirty, I can't do coffee after three or else I'm up all night."

"You're over thirty?" The words popped out of his mouth before he could call them back. *Christ, Royer. You're really killing it with the ladies here.* He could only hope that Elmer wasn't listening in; he'd never hear the end of it.

But to his surprise, Cassie didn't even react. "Thirty-two." Her eyes were as dark as the cocoa he spooned into two mugs. She turned those big brown eyes to him now. "You?"

Well, that was only fair. "Twenty-nine a couple weeks ago." He reached for the metal pitcher by the espresso machine, filling it with milk.

"Oooh, a younger man. I like it." She batted her eyes in light-hearted flirtation that Nick couldn't begin to parse. "Not even thirty, and you own your own business. Nice."

"Oh, yeah." He shot her a glance while the milk steamed, but she didn't seem to be kidding. "I'm the king of everything you can see."

Cassie gave a low laugh, acknowledging his sarcasm. "Seems great to me. It was good enough for Elmer, right?" Her lips quirked up in a smile while he poured the hot milk.

"Whipped cream?" he offered. "It's just the stuff in a can, but it's not bad."

"Yes, please. Let's live a little."

Live a little. Hadn't Elmer just said that to him recently? Maybe he was right.

As if she were reading his mind—and Nick was used to that kind of thing, considering his roommate—Cassie leaned her elbows on the counter. "Tell me more about Elmer."

"What would you like to know?" He passed her one of the mugs before offering up the bottle of bourbon. She accepted both, adding a healthy dollop to her mug before passing the bottle back.

"You really . . . talk to him? Like, for real? This isn't some touristy bullshit. You actually believe in ghosts?"

Nick glugged some bourbon into his own mug. "It's not a matter of belief. It's a matter of fact."

"Fact?" Cassie raised her eyebrows. "You're talking about ghosts here. I'm sorry, it's just hard for me to get my head around it."

"Here." He reached under the counter, where he kept the extra copies of *Boneyard Key: A Haunted History.* During the season he kept those copies up by the register and they sold at a decent clip— here and at every other souvenir shop in town. Mr. Lindsay must have made a deal with the devil back in the day; the book was one of the top-selling souvenirs. Nick himself hadn't read it in years. Not since he'd been forced to, back in school. He handed the book to her. "A housewarming present."

"Ahh," she said. "The textbook." She flipped through it while taking a careful sip of cocoa.

"I know it's a lot to get used to. Especially if you're coming at it from a tourist mindset. Like mermaids at Weeki Wachee . . ." He raised an eyebrow pointedly, even as he regretted bringing it up. The comparison had triggered something in him, and he'd reacted badly. Defensively. He wasn't proud of that.

She looked up from the book, shamefaced. "You know I was kidding about that . . ."

"I know," he rushed to reassure her. "And you weren't far off. It's just that around here, the mermaids are real." He kept his voice casual, like they were talking about something totally normal. Which of course they were . . . to him. If you'd spent your life in this town, lingering spirits were just part of the scenery. Like palm trees and the salty air. But to Cassie, they were still stories, like the fake mermaids or costumed characters at the theme parks. Something to believe in when you're caught up in the moment, but recognize as fiction when you're back home in the real world.

She didn't understand that this *was* the real world. Nothing she'd heard tonight had been fiction. Well, except for that bullshit about the ice cream shop. He didn't know where the hell Sophie had come up with that one.

He suddenly felt exhausted. Couldn't they just skip to the end of this conversation, where Cassie left and he went upstairs to his ghost roommate, and they could both write off this whole damn night? But that wasn't how life worked. No skipping the hard stuff.

May as well try a different tactic. Plunge headfirst into the hard things. Maybe he could get her to believe. "Look . . ." He came around the counter, reaching into his back pocket for his phone as he did so. "Check my texts."

"Your . . . ?" But she put down her cocoa to take his phone and started scrolling through, pausing when she got to what he knew she'd see: text after text labeled Unknown Number. "Damn. You get a lot of spam texts."

"They're not spam. They're all from Elmer."

"Elmer? The guy who used to own this place?" Now those big brown eyes were filled with skepticism. "You're really telling me a ghost can text? How? What kind of phone plan does he have?"

When she put it that way, he had to admit it did sound ridiculous. "I'm not pretending to know how it works. But hand to God, the week after I bought this place, I started getting these texts. Elmer sees everything that happens around here, and texts me to tell me what I could be doing better. Believe me, he has a lot of opinions about banana bread."

"I can see that." She slowly scrolled through, sometimes tapping before scrolling some more. "He's wrong, by the way. Your cinnamon banana bread is great. These are really all from Elmer?" Technically the question was directed at him, but she seemed to be musing out loud. "They do all seem to be from the same person. Can I call him a person?" She glanced up at Nick and he could only respond with a smile and a half shrug. She scrolled a little more, then her eyebrows flew up. "He thinks I'm cute, huh?"

"Oh." Shit. In the veritable ocean of exchanges, of course she'd found those specific texts. The back of his neck burned, and he placed his palm there, soothing the heat. "Yeah. He, ah . . . He's pretty old school. You know. Says what he thinks. Doesn't have much of a filter."

She gave a hum of agreement, a soft sound that went straight down to the base of his spine. He had to sneak in a deep breath before he could look at her again, and when he did, she was a lot closer than she'd been before. She leaned an elbow on the counter, her body canted in his direction, holding his phone toward him so they could both see it. She took another sip of hot chocolate, the pink tip of her tongue peeking out to catch a stray bit of whipped cream from the corner of her mouth.

It was suddenly warm in here, pleasantly warm. Maddeningly warm. Nick felt a little dizzy, like he was about to jump off a high dive.

Oh the hell with it. Might as well jump. Isn't that what those Van Halen boys said? He took a step closer to Cassie, closer to that heat.

"I have to say . . ." He leaned closer, and Cassie licked her lips again, even though there wasn't any hot chocolate left on them. Nick wondered what her lips tasted like. He wondered if she was going to let him find out.

"You have to say . . . ?" Her voice was little more than breath, but it was enough to remind Nick that he'd started a sentence back there. Ages ago, before he got lost in the shine of her lips.

"He's not the only one." He traced the curve of her jaw with the backs of his fingers the way he'd been wanting to, following the line of her errant lock of hair, and Cassie sucked in a breath at his touch. He could relate; all of the oxygen seemed to have left the room. He was feeling a little lightheaded himself.

He asked a question with his eyes, and she gave the tiniest of nods in response before he bent those last few inches. Her mouth tasted like chocolate and bourbon. Nick wanted nothing more than to sink into her, claim her, but he settled for cradling her face in his hands. She sighed into his mouth, the rush of breath doing things to his bloodstream.

But he didn't want to push it. So instead of deepening the kiss, instead of pushing everything off the café counter and hoisting her up onto its smooth surface, he pulled back slowly. Lingeringly. Let his forehead drop to hers and breathed her in for just a couple more moments before he let her go. When he opened his eyes, all he could see was her smile.

"Is this . . ." Nick's voice had stopped working, the words coming out all gravelly. He cleared his throat and tried again. "Is this too soon? I feel like maybe this was too soon."

But Cassie's smile was almost as bright as her eyes. "Feels just in time to me."

So he bent to her again, her smile dissolving under his mouth, and when her hand came up to touch his face, all doubt flew out the window and into the night.

This had been the best date of his life.

Ten

You sure you're okay to walk home by yourself?" Nick glanced over his shoulder as he locked the door to Hallowed Grounds.

Cassie wanted to say no. Even though she could see the glow of her front porch light from where she stood on the sidewalk, she should say that it was a long way to walk all alone after dark. She should ask Nick to walk her home. Anything to make this night last a little longer. Anything to stay near him.

But if he walked her home, she'd invite him inside. And if he'd thought kissing her was too soon, what she'd want to do with him in her house would absolutely scandalize the man. Maybe it was good to have some decorum. Save something for the second date.

So she said, "There's lights most of the way. As long as that ghost on the beach stays where he is, I'll be okay."

She'd been shooting for a joke, but Nick's nod was serious. "He doesn't leave the beach; that's his domain. Just stick to the sidewalk and you'll be fine."

"Will do." Cassie's heart leapt as he stepped forward, his palm curling around the side of her neck. She tilted her head up, her mouth opening under his, and their good-night kiss was as gentle as the breeze coming off the ocean.

What a night.

Cassie walked home under the glow of the streetlights in a bit of a daze brought on by one part bourbon and more than two parts kisses. There was a lot to process about tonight, but two major themes swam to the forefront.

Ghosts were real.

Nick was a damn good kisser.

She wasn't sure which one was scarier. Or more exciting.

Her steps slowed as she approached her house, and she stopped on the sidewalk almost exactly where she'd been during the ghost tour, staring up at it. When she'd bought the place, she hadn't been looking for just a house. She wanted a home. A place—a community—that valued her and made her feel less alone.

Even now, the porch light bathed everything in a warm, cheerful glow. The wicker porch furniture with its plump purple cushions conjured up visions of lazy afternoons and pitchers of lemonade. Out here in the evening quiet, the waves crashed behind the seawall in a hypnotic rhythm, evoking endless summer vacations. This should be the perfect house. The perfect place to make a home.

But . . . She looked down at the book tucked under one arm. Either everyone here was delusional, or the entire damn town was haunted. She didn't like the implication of either one of those things. Could she really make a home here?

The alternative, of course, was returning to Orlando, tail between her legs. Finding a new place with astronomical rent, admitting that her fresh start had been a bust. She could just hear the smug tones from everyone at that next all-hands meeting. The expressions of faux sympathy that she'd failed.

Or worse, they wouldn't say anything at all. She'd continue to be invisible in the group text like she was now. All her contributions lately had been conversation killers; she'd say something about her day, or post a shot of the ocean from her back balcony, and no one would respond. On a good day she'd get a thumbs-up. Cassie felt like she was fading away, like she'd become a ghost herself.

At least Nick answered Elmer's texts.

Nick. Focusing on Nick and the memory of his mouth on hers chased away her gloom, buoying her spirits as she went up the front steps and unlocked her door.

She'd forgotten how warm the night was until she walked into the wall of cold inside her house. Thank God for central air. She sucked in a grateful breath at the shock of cold air and reached for the lamp on the side table, bypassing the wonky light switch by the front door. It didn't take long for her to shiver a little as the lingering sweat on her body cooled. She toed off her shoes and left them by the door before padding into the kitchen to get a drink. The cocoa had been nice, but not exactly hydrating. She rummaged inside the fridge for a diet soda—caffeine be damned—and bumped the door closed with her hip.

When she'd first walked into the kitchen the fridge had looked normal, magnetic poetry words in their usual jumble covering the whole surface of the door in a haphazard fashion. But when she closed the door the words looked like a starburst, lining the edge of the door five lines deep in a big circle.

Except for one word in the middle.

wrong

The soda slipped from Cassie's nerveless fingers, the plastic bottle bouncing off the linoleum. For several moments all she could do was stare at the word in the center of the fridge. But the dropped bottle rolled her way, nudging her foot, and she tore her eyes away, looking down at the floor.

"At least I hadn't opened it yet," she muttered as she picked it up, bringing it to the sink. She'd let the fizz settle and drink that one tomorrow. She closed her eyes, willing the past few moments to be some kind of weird cocoa-bourbon-induced hallucination. But when she turned back to the fridge for another soda, there wasn't a single word in the middle of the fridge anymore.

Now there were two.

my house

And then she remembered. Her front windows were open. She hadn't left the air on. The house was cold for an entirely different reason.

On second thought, Cassie didn't need anything out of the fridge tonight. In fact, she probably didn't need to sleep, either.

Eleven

Nick was in the best damn mood the next morning.

Sure, Cassie was still struggling with the whole "ghosts are real" thing, but she seemed to be getting past her initial skepticism. And then, of course, there was the way they'd said good night . . .

Damn, but that woman could kiss. The memory of her mouth was the reason Nick had woken up with a goofy smile on his face. It was the reason that smile had stayed intact through his shower, his first cup of coffee, and getting ready for the day. Maybe Vince was right. Maybe Nick did need someone special in his life. Maybe this was the beginning of something real. The end of situationships.

It wasn't until he clattered down the stairs that he realized he hadn't gotten her number. So much for a "good morning" text or similar. But that was okay. He knew where she lived. Maybe she wouldn't mind if he dropped by sometime. Like later today, after the café closed. He could bring her an iced hazelnut latte. He could . . .

Nick rounded the corner and there she was, like a remnant of his dreams the night before. She was still in the sundress she wore last night, with a camel-colored oversize cardigan thrown over it. It was way too hot for a sweater, even this early in the day, but Cassie had her arms wrapped around herself, and her eyes were huge in her face. Even bigger than usual. She looked scared. She looked . . .

"You look terrible." He drew in a deep breath through his nose as he tried to keep a neutral expression, when all he wanted to do was pinch the bridge of his nose. He was really the worst at talking to people sometimes.

If Cassie was offended, she didn't let it show. "I need your help."

"You look like you need coffee." He took his keys out of his pocket. "I can help with that. Let me just open up and we can . . ."

"No." Her brittle voice stopped him in his tracks. "I mean, yes," she continued, "coffee sounds amazing. But . . ." She hooked a hand around his elbow, and her touch sent a chill down his spine, and not in a good way. Her hand against his skin was ice cold.

He turned his head slowly and stared hard into her face. Hauntings manifested in all kinds of ways; he was well aware of that. It was a fact he lived with on a daily basis. One of those ways was with extreme cold. Was she . . . ? Could she possibly be . . . ?

But no. She was too real, her eyes were too wild, too alive in her face.

"I need help." Her voice faltered as she repeated the words. "Please." She tugged at his arm weakly, like a child who'd had a nightmare, and Nick's senses went on high alert. This wasn't like last night, when she'd been mildly creeped out by the idea of ghosts in this town. Something was *wrong*.

"Okay," he said. "Okay." He put his keys back in his pocket as he let her lead him up the street. He could open a little late; who was going to reprimand him?

It felt weird, walking through the white picket gate to the Hawkins House. For years—decades, even—it had been the place to avoid. Even long after Mean Mrs. Hawkins had died, it had never been a house anyone wanted to linger near. But the night before, he'd stood in front of the house on the ghost tour and he'd been . . . charmed. It didn't look like a creepy old house anymore. There was a wicker love seat and matching chair on the front porch, with purple cushions and a plethora of throw pillows, and the falling-down porch swing from decades past had been replaced with a brand-new solid wood one that was painted white. It had been a cozy scene, lit up by her porch light.

This morning the cushions were rumpled, some of the throw pillows were scattered on the porch swing, and a crocheted afghan was half tumbled to the floor.

"Did . . ." He paused on the porch. "Did you sleep out here?"

"Yeah." Her keys rattled in her hand, and Nick realized she was shaking. This was serious.

"Hey." He covered her hands with his, took her keys. "Cassie, what happened? Did someone break in? Did you call the cops?"

She shook her head. "I think . . . I think someone was already here. Like . . . before I got here."

"Before you got home last night?" Nick couldn't believe this. Boneyard Key wasn't known for its crime sprees. Sure, sometimes tourists got rowdy during the height of the season and fights broke out, stuff like that. But breaking and entering? Theft? The citizens of Boneyard Key mostly kept to themselves and respected each other's space.

"Before I moved in." Cassie's voice was full of meaning.

"Oh. *Oh.*" It took a second for Nick to catch up. "Did you get a visit from Mrs. Hawkins?" This was big news; no wonder she was freaked. "What did you see? Did she say anything?"

But Cassie took his eager questions as mockery. "Don't you dare make fun of this." Her eyes were pleading.

"I'm not, I swear!" He held up defensive hands. "She's never made contact with anyone before. And usually it's, you know, members of the Founding Fifteen that have the strongest ties to the ghosts around here."

"Then maybe I should do a 23andMe, because she came through loud and clear!" Emotion blazed in Cassie's eyes, which seemed to burn away her fear and steady her hands. She snatched her keys back, unlocking the door and pushing it open. "There." She pointed inside, but her feet stayed firmly on this side of the threshold.

Cassie may have been rattled, but this wasn't Nick's first rodeo. He knew to take stock of the temperature of the room as he stepped inside. Nothing out of the ordinary; no ice-cold breeze brushed his skin as he took tentative steps into the living room.

"The kitchen," Cassie called from behind him. He glanced over his shoulder to see that she hadn't followed him inside; she stayed on the front porch, hopping from one foot to the other while she watched his progress.

"It's okay," he said. "There's nothing here." Of course, he wasn't a hundred percent sure of that. Despite having a ghost roommate of his very own, he wasn't a true expert in this stuff. But he did a slow circle of the kitchen, taking in the unopened Diet Coke bottle in the sink, the neat and wiped-down counters . . . and the magnetic poetry on the fridge. **my house**.

Ah. Okay. To be fair, he probably would have spent the night on the porch too.

Cassie picked her way into the house, her big cardigan wrapped around herself like knitted armor. "I got home last night, and everything was cold. And that was just . . . *there*. Like a message."

"The words?" Nick studied the fridge again. That would be an awful lot for a ghost to manifest. "There's like hundreds of them."

"Not the magnetic poetry; that's mine. They help me think, you know? Something to mess with. But . . ." She swallowed hard and clutched more tightly to her sweater.

Now he was starting to follow. "But you didn't arrange the words like this?"

She shook her head. "First it was just the word 'wrong.' Then I looked away for a second and . . ." She let out a shaking breath. "And then I decided that I'd go sit out on the porch for a little while. And then it was morning. I didn't sleep a whole lot."

"Hmmm. I bet." He looked back at the fridge. It was an older model, and it seemed awfully loud, humming away here in the kitchen. "Do you hear that?"

"No." Cassie looked alarmed. "Hear what?"

"You said Buster looked over the electricity, right?" He took a step closer to the fridge, his head tilted, listening intently. Could a kitchen appliance be haunted on its own?

"Yeah, he said it was fine. Which . . ." She gestured angrily at her laptop, on the table next to where she'd tossed her sweater. It was hooked up to the charging cord, but the other end lay next to the outlet. He bent for it, plugging it in on instinct. He didn't expect anything to happen; it was like that idle light switch flicking you did when the power was out right after a hurricane.

But the laptop gave a chirp, and Cassie gasped.

"What did you do?" They both looked, dumbfounded, at the green light on her laptop, indicating that it was charging just fine.

"I plugged it in. Just . . ." He gestured, miming what he'd just done.

"And it's working?" Cassie stared at her laptop and the outlet as though they'd both betrayed her. There was a low-level buzzing coming from the laptop as it charged. It sounded a lot like the fridge, come to think of it. Maybe there really was something wrong with the electricity in this house. Nick made a mental note to give Buster a call, ask him to come back and make sure he hadn't missed something.

"Maybe it just needed a man's touch." He tipped an imaginary hat. "You're welcome, ma'am." It was a stupid joke, but Cassie gave a thin laugh. This was good; if she was laughing at bad jokes that meant she was coming off the ledge.

She looked a lot better, in fact. Nick had been worried when he first saw her this morning, but now the color had come back into her cheeks, and as she sat in one of her kitchen chairs, her cardigan clutched in her lap, she already looked steadier.

"Okay." Nick took the chair opposite her. "Let's look on the bright side here."

"Really? There's a bright side?" Despite her sarcastic tone, her eyes were pleading.

"You're inside your house again," he said. "That was something you couldn't do last night."

"Huh." She looked around the kitchen, as though just realizing she wasn't still on her front porch. "Good point."

"Are you still afraid of the place?"

"No . . ." She sounded surprised. "Everything looks so normal in the daylight." She leaned an elbow on the table, resting her forehead on her hand. "God, you must think I'm a lunatic. Freaking out like that."

"Not at all." He dared to reach out, run a hand up and down her forearm. Her skin was reassuringly warm now. "You've had a lot of ghosts thrown at you in the last twelve hours or so. It can be intense."

"You think?" She heaved a sigh, but her voice was stronger. A far cry from the terrified woman he'd been confronted with this morning. "I don't know if I'm cut out to live in a haunted house."

"Not many people are," he said lightly, but an uncomfortable feeling began to swirl in his gut. He could almost hear what she was going to say next. This town wasn't going to do it for her. *He* wasn't going to do it for her. Whatever was between them would be over before it even had a chance to start.

But this wasn't about him, he reminded himself firmly. This was about Cassie and the fright she'd had last night. She was running on probably an hour of sleep and had a ghost in her house. It wasn't the best time to grill her on her future plans.

Meanwhile, the time was at the forefront of his mind. He still had to open the café, and he needed to get going. While his heart wanted to stay with Cassie and do anything to make her feel better, everything else inside him needed to leave. He wasn't a "take a personal day" kind of guy.

"Why don't you come back to the café with me? Maybe get a cup of coffee? A latte?" Anything. Anything she wanted. He'd learn to shake an espresso—whatever the hell that was—if that's what she needed right now.

But she waved him off with a weak smile. "I have coffee here. Maybe I should stay home, stop being so scared of the place. Exposure therapy and all that."

"Could work." He hated leaving her alone, but he was already rising from his chair. He really was running late. "You sure you'll be okay?"

"Yeah." Cassie sighed as she spoke, but her nod was firm. "I should probably take a nap or something."

"Might be a good idea," he said. "Your porch looks cozy and all, but probably not for sleeping."

"Definitely not. I don't want to think about all the places I have wicker marks." She rose from her chair and walked him to the front door. "Thanks," she said, grasping his hand. "For everything."

He squeezed her hand. "It's what I'm here for." It wasn't until he said the words out loud that Nick realized it was the truest thing he'd ever said. She'd needed his help, and he hadn't hesitated. He wouldn't hesitate to do the same thing again. "Here." He held out his other hand. "I can give you my number. Text or call if you need any-thing else." He'd hoped for a smoother, more romantic way to get his number into her phone, but this would have to do.

She handed her phone over immediately. "You don't mind?"

"You kidding?" He pulled up a new contact entry and tapped in his info. "Unless you want to loiter outside the café all night." He handed her phone back. "Seriously. I'm here. For whatever you need." His cheeks flamed at the insinuation. He didn't mean it like that, but at the same time he *did* mean it like that.

"Thanks," she said again. Her voice was lower, and maybe she meant it like that too. If Nick were a bolder man he would have kissed her, but there was still something in her eyes that looked shaken. He didn't want to push.

Instead he leaned down, brushing his lips across her forehead. "Sweet dreams." When he pulled back, her eyes were closed, as though savoring the touch of his lips, and she gave a small hum in response. *Work*, Nick reminded himself. *You have to go to work. The people in this town depend on you for caffeine.* It was the only thing propelling him out the door and down the street to Hallowed Grounds. He was five minutes late unlocking the door and flipping over the OPEN sign, but there was no one there to care.

Except Elmer, of course. Where the hell have you been? It doesn't take that long to walk down the stairs.

Emergency, he texted back. Cassie's not used to this town being so . . . He hesitated before finishing the sentence. Would Elmer be of-fended? Ah, the hell with it . . . haunted.

There was a pause before Elmer replied, and Nick spent the time rushing through his opening duties right before the first customer showed up. In fact, it was a good few minutes before Nick's phone rumbled in his pocket. It can be a lot if you're not ready for it.

Wow. That unexpected insight from his ghostly friend made Nick pause, setting down his phone while he steamed some milk. He passed the latte across the counter before ringing it up and wiping his hands on a clean kitchen towel. Are you speaking as one of the haunted or the hauntee?

No comment.

Nick snorted. Elmer certainly had experience being both, and was probably the one person that Nick knew who had that kind of perspective. He'd never thought about what it must be like in Elmer's metaphorical shoes. Had becoming a ghost taken a lot of getting used to? He suddenly had so many questions.

But before he could formulate any of them into a text, Elmer sent another message. The trick is to ease her into it. Show her it's not all scary. Because you and I both know it's not. But she doesn't.

He had a point.

Nick was used to his mornings being punctuated by texts. Elmer knew that Nick was a captive audience and usually took full advantage. But today his phone stayed quiet until halfway through lunch, when it buzzed again in his pocket. He pulled it out, surprised to see that the message was from a 407 area code. Orlando.

It's Cassie, the message read. Thanks again.

You feeling better?

She didn't answer right away, and Nick wasn't sure what to read into that. But he could be patient. Give her time, he told himself. Maybe she was figuring out the nicest way to say that she'd spent the day packing her shit and was halfway back to Orlando.

Nick was always fantastic at hyperbole.

Her response, when it finally came, wasn't nearly as drastic. I'm not scared of my kitchen anymore, so that's progress.

Baby steps, he replied before clicking his phone off. He had an idea. Elmer was right. Cassie needed to see more of Boneyard Key. Beyond the gimmicky ghost tour, and away from what went bump in the night in her house. Nick knew exactly what Cassie needed to see.

He allowed himself a quiet smile as his plan took solid shape in his head, then he turned back to the kitchen. "Still waiting on that chicken Caesar salad, Ramon!" He raised a hand in acknowledgment to the guy in the baseball cap by the window who looked more like a cheeseburger guy than a chicken Caesar salad guy, but what did Nick know? Tourists were weird.

Twelve

While things did indeed look brighter after sleeping in her own bed and not on the porch, Cassie felt antsy all weekend. The magnetic poetry had stayed put since Friday night, but she still considered the fridge off-limits. Thankfully Poltergeist Pizza offered icy sodas along with their pies, and since she'd called them on a night when they actually delivered, she decided to treat herself. There was nothing wrong with eating on the front porch of her home, as far from the kitchen as she could get. Nothing at all.

But being afraid of your own house was, frankly, boring. So, even though the house didn't seem to want her there, Cassie was determined to broker a peace. If there was one thing Cassie was, it was persuasive. She'd never met an unpleasant client she couldn't win over; the same had to be true of haunted houses.

Because, house aside, there was a lot to like about this town. Someone had dropped by from the chamber of commerce down the street with a welcome basket—a sampling of goods from the downtown shops, like a loaf of sourdough from the bakery and a pound of coffee from a place called Spooky Brew. She was on waving-to-each-other terms with the lady who lived in the house across the street, and the produce guy at the market already knew she liked her bananas on the green side. Small-town living had its own charm, as long as she didn't think too hard about the whole haunted part of things.

On Monday morning, she opened her charged-up laptop—how had Nick done that? That remained a mystery—and worked from her dining table, in full view of the fridge. Exposure therapy, as she'd said. And it sort of worked; by Tuesday afternoon she had almost convinced herself that she'd put those words in the middle of the fridge. Not Mean Mrs. Hawkins. **my house**. Cassie's house, those words said.

She almost believed it.

By Wednesday morning she'd developed a backache, because as cute as her dining table was, those chairs were the furthest thing from ergonomic. So she took a risk: she unplugged her laptop and took it with her to the couch. The pillows felt great against her over-thirty back, but the risk didn't pay off: by early afternoon her laptop was at less than five percent battery, fading to black right before she could hit Save. And plugging it in? Did nothing. Of course.

Cassie was pissed. But as she packed the computer in her laptop bag and grabbed her keys, she couldn't be too upset. It was an excuse to go down to Hallowed Grounds, and she'd been looking for one of those all week. Sure, Nick had texted once or twice this week to check on her, and she'd texted back, but she wasn't sure where she really stood with him. Not since her all-nighter on the porch.

It had been awkward, breaking down in front of Nick like that on Saturday morning. Especially after how close she'd felt to him the night before, how comfortable he made her feel. There was a part of her that yearned for him; she'd replay their first kiss, their subsequent kisses, and she'd feel her body moving toward him as though he were right there in front of her. But another part of her wanted to lean back, away from this town and its haunted houses and haunted beaches and haunted whatever-the-hell else. All week, that combination of swaying forward and leaning back had kept her right here, in this house that may or may not hate her, and away from her favorite bearded barista.

But not anymore. Sure, the mystery of her constantly dying laptop was annoying, but it gave her the excuse to see Nick again. Maybe when she was right in front of him, she could figure out once and for all which direction she needed to sway.

She hadn't paid attention to the time, only dimly remembering that she'd worked through lunch, feverishly trying to finish a press release with one eye on her laptop's rapidly draining battery level. She walked through the door of Hallowed Grounds a little after one thirty, and her heart sank. The place closed in less than half an hour; her laptop would never charge in that amount of time. And Nick would be wanting to close up soon. Dammit.

The place was all but deserted. The last lunchtime customer had just left, and Nick was clearing off the table by the window, his arms loaded down with plates and glasses. His face darkened as the bell above the door rang, not looking up from his task. He didn't look angry per se, but he had the expression of someone whose day was ending soon, and he couldn't wait. Cassie felt a full-body cringe coming on; her timing was terrible.

But his face lit up when he saw her, chasing away all of her fears. What had she been thinking, staying away all this time? "Hey, it's you!" He dumped the plates on the counter behind him.

"Live and in person."

"I have to say . . ." Nick put his hands on his hips and cocked his head, taking her in. "You look much better than you did over the weekend."

Cassie snorted a laugh. "That's not really saying much, is it?"

"Things going better with Mrs. H then?" He moved back to the table he'd just cleared, wiping it down with a damp rag.

"I don't know if I'd go that far." She got out her computer cord. "Laptop's dead again."

"Are you kidding?" He tossed the rag onto the table and glared up at her. Well, not *at* her. Hopefully. "Wasn't it charging when I was there?"

"Yep." She popped the *p* as she hooked things up. "But then I unplugged it and poof. Dead."

"That's messed up."

"Yeah. Maybe Mrs. Hawkins is trying to get me fired. Unemployed people get foreclosed on, you know. This could be her way of getting me to leave."

"Hmmm. Seems like a long con."

"She's a ghost, right? She's got nothing but time."

Nick chuckled. "Maybe she thinks you work too much."

"Or she's against women in the workforce," Cassie shot back. Who knew bantering about ghosts could be so much fun?

Nick nodded solemnly, though humor danced in his bright blue eyes. "It was a different time, you know." He shook his head. "Seriously, though. You want me to call Buster again for you? He must have missed something."

Cassie didn't want to bother him. Either of them. But Nick already had his phone out so what could she do but nod?

"Hey, Buster? Nick. Yeah, things are good. You should come by sometime, get some coffee. Elmer misses you." He listened, phone wedged between his ear and shoulder while he gathered the stack of plates from the counter. "Yeah. I know. I'll tell him. Anyway, I was calling about Cassie's house. You know, the Hawkins place? I know you checked it out but there's still . . ." His voice faded as he disappeared into the kitchen, but he was back soon, shoving his phone in his pocket.

"He'll be by tomorrow. That okay?"

"That's great. Thanks."

He waved a hand. "All good. So. Lunch?"

"Are you sure? You're about to close, right?" But her stomach growled in response. God, she was starving.

"Eh." He seemed unconcerned. "Technically. But you need to power up, and I have lots of stuff to do around here after I close anyway. I can hang."

"In that case . . ." She tore her eyes away from Nick long enough to scan the menu board overhead. "I hear the chicken salad is pretty great. I'll try that."

Turned out, eating a chicken salad sandwich at the back table at Hallowed Grounds was the exact amount of time it took for her laptop to charge up.

"I guess it's official," she said with a sigh as she brought her empty plate up to the counter. "I have to hang out here if I'm going to get any work done."

"Damn. That's too bad." Nick didn't put a lot of effort into trying to look sorrowful, which Cassie appreciated. He took her plate and passed her an iced latte. She knew before the first sip that it would have the perfect amount of hazelnut flavoring in it.

She gave a happy sigh. There was nothing like midafternoon caffeine. It was like flirting with the devil: perfect right now, but there would be hell to pay later tonight, when she was trying to fall asleep. But that was Future Cassie's problem. Other things that were Future Cassie's problem: (1) her laptop, which would only have a few hours of battery when she took it home, thanks to (2) the ghost in her house. Probably.

"I don't suppose there's anything on your bulletin board that'll help me with the whole . . ." She waved a hand back in the direction of her house. "With all that?"

The question hadn't been particularly serious, but Nick's eyes lit up. "Actually, I do. Libby."

Cassie blinked. "Who's Libby?"

Nick dried his hands on a nearby towel, then strode with a purpose to the corkboard by the front door; this was a man who knew exactly what he was looking for. On the little table in front of the corkboard, among the tourist maps and brochures, was a stack of business cards, and he plucked one from the pile. "Here you go."

"Simpson Investigations?" She tilted her head as she examined the card. Simple, like Buster's had been, but this one had a little ghost motif on it. "Like a private eye?"

"Like a ghost hunter." He tapped the card. "Nan's about a hundred and fifty, but she's the best."

"I thought you said her name was Libby?" She squinted down at the card. There wasn't a first name on it.

"Libby's her granddaughter. She helps out, but it's really Nan's thing. Remember what Sophie said about the Founding Fifteen? All of us descendants have the whole . . ." It was his turn to wave his hand vaguely. *"Ability* to communicate with the dead. But it's in varying degrees, like a recessive gene or something."

"Like red hair?"

"Exactly. In this case, I'm the redhead in the family. My parents didn't inherit any kind of ability, and neither did my sister. I was honestly surprised when Elmer got in touch." He thought about that. "I was surprised for more than one reason, anyway."

"I can't even imagine." But she could, couldn't she? Was getting a text message out of the blue from a ghost much different than the magnetic poetry message that had happened to her?

"Anyway," Nick said, "Nan has that gene in spades. If it's still hanging around, she can talk to it."

"This town has a ghost hunter." This was the kind of thing she was still having a hard time getting accepting.

"This town has a ghost everything." One corner of his mouth kicked up, and why not. There *was* humor in this, of course there was. Cassie just wasn't there yet.

"Thanks. I'll give her a call. Maybe she can tell Mrs. Hawkins to pound sand."

"Their office is down the street. Past The Haunt, make a left, then a couple blocks inland. I gotta warn you, though."

"What now?" Cassie braced herself for the next shock. "Is Nan really a ghost? Is Libby?"

Nick's laugh diffused her tension. "Nothing like that. More like . . . spirits don't move on from here, typically. They like to hang out."

Crap. She was afraid of that. People in this town didn't seem eager to expel their ghosts. It was all very kumbaya around here. "Well, maybe Nan can help Mean Mrs. Hawkins and me come to an agreement. Like I acknowledge that she exists, and she understands that she needs to leave me the hell alone." She stuck the card in her pocket and took another pull of her coffee.

"That's the spirit . . . I mean . . . You know what I mean." Nick stopped short, realizing what he said.

"Ha." It was a good thing this man made great coffee. The puns were terrible.

"I just mean, maybe Nan can help the two of you coexist. Make living in a haunted house not so bad."

"And then what? We can have sleepovers at our shared house? I can spend my nights gossiping with a lady from the 1940s?" She set down her glass. "I wish I could be as matter-of-fact as you are about all this. You don't find it *weird*?"

Nick shrugged. "I grew up here. It's part of who I am. I've had twenty-nine years to get used to ghosts. You've had, what, a couple weeks? Have you even finished unpacking yet?"

"Nope." He had a point. There was still a stack of boxes in the unused second bedroom that she had yet to tackle. But at this rate, was she going to? Maybe she could consider them a head start if she couldn't handle this whole "haunted town" business and went back to Orlando.

The thought depressed her, made her feel like she was giving up on this fresh start she'd given herself. She picked up her glass and sucked moodily on the straw until there was nothing left but ice. Starbucks had nothing on Nick's skills. The man knew his way around an espresso machine. And she was pretty sure the baristas at Starbucks didn't kiss as well as he did, either . . . Cassie shut down that train of thought. It was going in a weird direction.

Something of her mood must have shown on her face. "I have an idea." Nick leaned his elbows on the counter. "Have you watched the sun set over the beach yet?"

"I've seen the sunset from my back balcony, does that count?" She lived right on the beach, that had to be close enough.

But Nick shook his head. "Nope. I mean on the beach, toes in the sand, sun setting over the water."

"Ah. Then, no."

His smile kicked up. "Wanna?"

She should say no. Was it a good idea to let herself get even more entangled with this guy? Even though everything in her wanted to say yes, sway toward him, she knew she should probably lean back.

She had serious second thoughts about staying here for the long term. How could she live in a town where hauntings were the norm?

But before she could make the right decision—the smart, pragmatic decision—she was already nodding. "Sure. I'm in."

"Great." He straightened up, rapping his knuckles on the counter in front of him. "Meet me at the pier around seven, okay? There's nothing more relaxing than a sunset over the beach, and something tells me you could use a little more of that in your life."

She gave a small laugh. "You're not wrong about that."

"Good. I'd like to show you some things that I love about this place. Maybe I can change your mind about ghosts being scary."

"Maybe." She had her doubts about that, but screw it. She wanted to sway.

Thirteen

Nick got to the pier a little before seven to find Cassie waiting for him, just like they'd arranged. She was turned away, leaning on the railing, her eyes on Cemetery Island in the distance. Nick's steps slowed as he approached. He adjusted the backpack on his shoulder as he let himself watch her while her attention was elsewhere. She'd changed for their date, her linen shorts and blue tank top practically formal wear on this warm evening. Her hair was caught up in a clip like always, but slight tendrils escaped, sticking to the back of her neck in the evening's heat. He wanted to take her hair down. He wanted to spear his fingers through it, separating the strands, and spread it over her shoulders. How long was it? If he pulled her over him, would it fall around them both, hiding them from the world?

He was really getting ahead of himself. He couldn't help it; she had that effect on him.

Nick cleared his throat hard and took a deliberate, heavy step onto the solid wooden boards of the pier, announcing his presence so he didn't startle her. She turned at his approach, and he could only hope that his fantasies about her hair didn't show on his face. But she just smiled, pushing her sunglasses up on top of her head.

"I'll admit, that island's pretty cool," she said. "Is there really a cemetery out there, or was that another bullshit story from the ghost tour?"

"It's really there." He thought about the big headstone, not far from the center of the cemetery. The one that marked where his great-great-grandparents were buried. The one that reminded him that this town was his family's legacy. A legacy he didn't take lightly, despite—or maybe because of—the rest of his family's indifference.

But he didn't want to go into all of that now. Tonight wasn't about that. It was about showing Cassie his favorite spots in town. It was about enjoying a sunset with a pretty girl. "So, you ready?" He nodded back toward the street.

"Sure." Cassie tucked her hands into the front pockets of her shorts, falling in step with him as they headed up the street, away from her house and the downtown area. He wasn't taking her on the ghost tour route; she knew those parts already. "Isn't the beach back that way?"

Nick nodded. "We're not going there yet. Got a little time before the sun sets."

"So where are we going first then?" she asked as they passed Jimmy's bait shack and kayak rental, the ramshackle building locked up for the night. Not a lot of people fishing or kayaking at night, especially this time of year.

"Oh, here and there." He kept the answer vague, hoping to add an air of mystery to the evening. But as they continued up the footpath on the side of the road, which was all but deserted on this Wednesday evening, he also realized that it was possible he'd added an air of serial killer as well. "Like I said before, I wanted to show you some stuff."

Okay, that wasn't much better.

"Stuff?" she repeated with a little laugh, bumping his shoulder with hers. "So specific, thank you."

He huffed a laugh of his own in response. "Stuff that's great about this town. That the tourists don't know about. And the thing is, we kind of like it that way."

"Like a dive bar that you don't want the tourists to find, because they'd ruin the vibe?"

He blinked. That was . . . well, that was very close. "Pretty much," he allowed. "I guess what I'm trying to say is that ghosts . . . hauntings, whatever you want to call them . . . they're everywhere around here. To the point that they're just not a big deal. Don't get me wrong," he rushed to add as a shadow crossed over Cassie's face. "Living with a ghost is a lot. Believe me, I know."

Cassie tilted her head to the side. "You do?"

"You think Elmer just lives in my phone?" He shook his head. "After his wife died, he moved into the apartment upstairs from the café. The one I live in now. And when he died . . . well, he didn't move out."

"So y'all are, what, roommates?" Her voice pitched a note higher, her eyebrows arched, eyes wide.

Nick nodded. "Elmer came with the place, and the previous owners didn't want to deal with him. So I got the business for a song. Your house was a bargain too, right?"

It didn't take long for Cassie to catch his meaning. "I'm just not sure if I can get used to it." Her tone was quiet, voicing something she didn't want to admit, and Nick's heart pitched southward toward the pit of his stomach.

But he kept his voice neutral, when all he wanted to do was plead. "Maybe not." He wanted to connect their minds, so she could automatically see his perspective. But that was not only creepy but a scooch misogynistic, so instead he stuck with his original plan.

"I get it," he said. "Being ambushed in your own house is the opposite of a good time. But that's not what living in a town with ghosts is all about. I wanted to show you some of the cool things about it." No pun intended, but she didn't know that yet. "Okay, yeah, we're a haunted town. But that doesn't necessarily mean scary. For example . . ." They were almost at the stoplight now, where the main road opened up into four lanes going out of town. He gestured in front of them at the nondescript gray building by the street. "This is The Cold Spot."

"Okay . . ." Cassie examined the building, and he tried to see it through her eyes. It didn't look like much from the outside. Hell, it didn't look like much on the inside, either, but that wasn't where they were headed. "Wasn't this in the book? I remember a picture of it. It used to be a gas station?"

Nick nodded. "These days it's a bar. Tourists don't come here much since it's kind of far from the downtown area. It's more of a locals-only place."

"So we're here for a drink?"

Nick shook his head. "We can, if you're in the mood for a beer. Or the worst nachos you've ever had. But that's not why we're here." He led her around the back of the building, where an old Studebaker rusted gently by a service bay door that had been welded shut decades ago.

Cassie laughed nervously. "Well, this doesn't look sketchy at all. Is this where the serial killer is gonna . . ."

Nick knew the moment that she hit it. Her voice faded as he knew it would, and confused wonder suffused her face.

"Right?" he said.

"What the hell?" Her voice was little more than a whisper. She turned in a circle, her hands outstretched, trying to touch the air around her. "Where is this coming from?" She looked toward the bar, and he knew exactly what she was looking for: a stray air-conditioning vent, or a fan. Something, anything, that would explain why the spot she was standing in was a good twenty degrees colder than where Nick stood. Countless people over the years had done the same thing, and no one had ever found an explanation that made sense.

He stepped forward too, joining her in that space. It was like stepping into a blast chiller. The sudden chill raised goose pimples as the ever-present slick of perspiration that lived on his skin in the Florida summer instantly evaporated. He sighed happily, eyes falling closed in a slow blink like a contented cat, an involuntary reaction to the blissful cold.

But she'd asked him a question. "We don't know where it comes from. Mr. Lindsay didn't cover it in the book, and no one's come across any accounts of anything weird happening around here."

A little of the wonder slipped from Cassie's face. "What does that mean? Like . . . someone was forgotten?"

He hadn't thought about it that way, and now the thought made him frown. "I don't know. Maybe. Must have been something from a long time ago, though. Maybe even from before the town was founded. It's been checked out, more than once. One of those cable shows even came out, did a whole investigation with infrared cameras and all kinds of fancy equipment."

Cassie smirked; she knew enough about the town by now to know how that had gone down. "I bet that went great."

"About as well as you'd expect." That crew had been a shitshow. A bunch of social media stars with their bells and whistles, telling Nick, and anyone else in Boneyard Key who would listen, how to look out for spirits and what to do if they saw one. Ghost-splaining, that was what it was. Elmer had a lot to say about those guys; Nick's phone had blown up for days afterward.

He stepped out of the cold spot, where the heat and humidity of the evening was like a wet slap to the face, and extended a hand to

Cassie. "This place gets really popular in the summer. Especially if we get a hurricane and lose power." It was an odd but familiar sight during those times: people lined up to cool off in the town's cold spot after a day of chainsawing trees and clearing away hurricane debris.

"I can imagine." She took the hint—but not his hand, unfortunately—and followed him back around to the front of the bar. "So this place isn't mentioned in the book at all?"

He shook his head as they started back down the street. "My theory is that Mr. Lindsay wanted this to remain a locals-only legend. We don't want tourists hogging up all our cold." He grinned in response to her laugh.

"Then I appreciate you showing it to me."

"Well, sure," he said easily. "You're a local now, right?"

Cassie didn't answer the question, and Nick tried not to notice. Instead she looked over her shoulder, back toward the bar. "We're not going inside?"

"Nah." *No way in hell*, he almost said. He could just picture it if he brought Cassie in there. It was fifty-fifty if Vince would behave himself, and even if he did, he'd give Nick an endless amount of shit the next time he saw him. "Not a very romantic spot," he said instead.

"Where to next, then?" She looked up at him with trusting eyes, a look Nick could get used to.

"Beach sunset time." The timing was perfect; the evening sun had started slanting across the sky, sending burnished orange rays through the Spanish moss draped over the trees lining the sidewalk on the edge of downtown.

The walk through downtown and to the beach bordered on awkward. More than once Nick almost reached for Cassie's hand, but drew back before he did. More than once she swayed into him, bumping their arms together and then apart. Finally, sidewalk gave way to sand, and once they got to the shoreline the clutch of picnic tables came into view, tucked into a small cove. The site of countless family picnics and teenage debauchery over the decades, tonight it was deserted, just as Nick had hoped it would be.

Cassie picked up an empty beer bottle that lay in the sand near one of the picnic tables, pitching it into a nearby trash can as Nick set his backpack down. The backpack was probably overkill considering what was inside, but at least it looked cooler than carrying a shopping bag. He unzipped it, pulling out the single bottle of beer inside. After placing the bottle on the far edge of the table, he sat on one of the picnic bench seats, and Cassie joined him. She toed off her shoes, wiggling her toes into the sand, and he followed suit. The sand was warm on the soles of his feet.

"We splitting that?" She glanced over at the bottle, and Nick wanted to slap himself on the forehead. He was terrible at explaining things sometimes.

"That's not for us. Remember the beach bum? From Sophie's tour?"

It took a second for Cassie to remember, but Nick saw the moment that it clicked. "The drunk guy who hangs out on the beach?" She looked around as though she could see him in the lengthening shadows. Her gaze landed on the bottle again. "Bring him a beer. That was what you said, right? What's his deal? Sophie didn't say much."

Nick shrugged. "My mom remembers him when she was in high school, back when she was hanging out at the beach with her friends. Not a lot for kids to do here on the weekends, you know? Anyway, when I was old enough to hang at the beach, one of my buddies brought beer he'd gotten on a fake ID over in Gainesville. He was going to pour one out for the beach bum and I thought, why not leave it in the bottle so he can drink it if he wants?"

"Like leaving cookies and milk for Santa?"

"Something like that." Nick chuckled as Cassie turned back to the water, where the real show was just starting.

"Look at that." Her voice was hushed. The sun was hanging heavy in the sky now, glowing bright orange, the clouds around it streaked with pinks and purples. The water of the Gulf was blue, reflecting the sky above, highlighted with bright deep gold from the setting sun.

"This was one of my favorite things to do growing up," he said. "When I was confused or pissed off, or just felt like I didn't have my head on straight, I'd come out here and watch the sun go down over the water. It would just . . . I don't know. Clear things up inside my brain. Like a reset."

"Sounds like something out of a Jimmy Buffett song." A smile played around the corners of her mouth, and there was something about it that drew him in. He wanted to lean over. He wanted to kiss the corner of that mouth. She wasn't giving off any *get away from me* vibes. But she also wasn't giving off any *get over here* vibes, and he didn't want to push it.

"I like it, though," she said, her voice soft. "A reminder to slow down." Her eyes scanned the horizon, and he watched her take it all in.

"I haven't done it in a while, though." He hadn't realized it until he said it; when was the last time he'd walked down here and just spent a half hour watching the sunset? So many evenings lately he felt like staying home was the thing to do. Elmer didn't get much company these days; Nick was basically his only option. It was like owning a dog that couldn't leave the house; Nick couldn't exactly take Elmer on a walk. But Nick was all the company Elmer had, so he stayed home. Probably more than he should.

"It's a quiet thing to do," Cassie said, her voice soft beside him.

"And most tourists don't like quiet. They're at the bars, right? Watching this from the outdoor seating at a restaurant, or from their hotel rooms. They're not just gonna come sit at the beach with no other stimulation."

Nick gave a soft laugh. She knew her tourists. But of course she did; she was a Floridian, just not from here. "They need dinner and a show."

"At least."

The sky was lit up in orange and purple and gold, giving way to pinks and dark, dark indigo. The sun was really showing off now, throwing one last brilliant blaze of orange light across the sky. Nick and Cassie sat in comfortable silence, and as the sun disappeared for the night, Cassie leaned in, her head resting on his shoulder. She fit so well against him it was like she'd always been there. He could really get used to this.

Finally the sun slipped behind the water, and the single streetlamp clicked on for the night, triggered by the darkness. The show was over. The sky was dark, yet the heat of the day lingered as the humidity in the air hung on.

Instead of heading back the way they came, toward the sidewalk and downtown, Nick gestured to the water and the long expanse of beach. From here, they could barely see the lights of Cassie's house, twinkling in the distance like stars sent to guide them home.

"I like this," Cassie said. She carried her shoes in one hand, their bare feet sinking lightly into the sand as they walked. The waves hissed against the shore as they rolled in, dissipating close by but never close enough to risk getting wet. "It's like a back road home. I should come this way more often when I'm—"

"Shhh." Nick slipped his hand into hers, squeezing to get her attention. The warmth of her skin against his made everything in his brain skid to a halt, and he had to fight to remember what he was going to say. "You hear that?" He leaned down, breathing the words into her ear. He was trying to be quiet, he told himself. That was why he had to lean in so close. That was why his lips nearly brushed her ear.

She gave a minuscule shake of her head. "Hear what?" Her voice was little more than breath, and he wanted more. God, he wanted more. But he flicked his eyes back, indicating behind them, and he could tell the moment she heard it. Soft footsteps in the sand, five or six feet behind them. She turned to look over her shoulder. Nick turned too, and they could see them—the wet footprints of a strange pair of shoes appearing for a moment or two before disappearing into the sand.

Cassie stopped walking, and the footsteps stopped too, the last prints in the sand slowly fading away. With a glance up at Nick she started to walk again, and he followed. There was a pause, and then the footsteps behind them started up again too. Not fast, not slow. Just a steady stroll, keeping time with them.

Cassie's eyes flew up to Nick's. "Did we pick up a friend?"

"Thought we might," Nick said carefully.

He expected her to react with alarm at the idea of being followed home by a ghost. But instead she smiled. "So he liked the beer, huh?"

"Looks like it." Inside he was cheering. This had been a good idea after all. She had just met a ghost—two really, if you counted the cold spot—and she wasn't freaking out. Maybe she was acclimating. She'd just needed a little time to get used to the quirks of Bone-yard Key.

Her hand tightened in his, and she leaned her head against his arm as they continued up the beach. Yeah. He hoped that she could get used to this. Because he really, really could.

Fourteen

C assie couldn't figure Nick out.

That first night, at the ghost tour—she kept thinking of it as their first date, but maybe she was reading too much into it—he'd kissed her afterward. More than once. And it had been . . . well . . . The feel of his lips on hers, the slow stroke of his tongue against hers, the way his hands had slid up her back—all those sense memories now had starring roles in her dreams. Dreams that she awoke from panting, desperately trying to draw in enough oxygen while the rest of her body calmed and cooled.

But he hadn't so much as kissed her since that night.

Cassie would think he wasn't interested, but all the other signs indicated he was. He was always happy to see her when she dropped by the café with her powered-down laptop. He knew she liked the cinnamon banana bread, and the way she liked her coffee. He wouldn't have taken her on a romantic moonlit walk on the beach after a dazzling sunset last night if he wasn't interested, right? Right?

She was just getting her workday started—i.e., packing up her dead laptop and bringing it to Hallowed Grounds for power, coffee, and a nice ogle—when there was a knock at the door. She blinked for a long moment at Buster, standing there on her front porch.

"Nick said I had to come by," he said, with the air of an old man who didn't like his work being questioned by whippersnappers.

"Oh." She remembered now. "It's just that my laptop still won't charge. I don't know what—" She trailed off because Buster had walked right past her into the house, to where her laptop sat by her bag on the dining table. He took the cord out and plugged it in, and the damn thing betrayed her once again as it beeped to life.

"What is the *deal*?" She put her hands on her hips, disgusted. Was her outlet a misogynist or something?

"No charge." He waved a hand as he walked back out the door. "But Nick's got a point. I must have missed something. Let me get my tools."

"But I . . ." Her protest died as he thumped down the front stairs toward his truck. "I have work to do . . ." she said, mostly to herself.

It was a noisy morning. While Cassie answered emails, and even took a Zoom call on her phone out on the front porch, Buster tested her outlets and then tested them again. He joined her on the front porch, leaning on the doorjamb as she clicked Leave Meeting.

"I found one loose wire. *One*. And I am almost positive that it has nothing to do with your problem."

Cassie had to agree. She couldn't continue like this, having Buster come over every day to plug in her laptop like she was doing it wrong. So once he was gone she found that business card from Nick's bulletin board. Simpson Investigations. She set an away message on her laptop and headed downtown.

Simpson Investigations was a small clapboard building on the main drag, past The Haunt and around the corner, tucked between a smaller T-shirt shop and a place that sold discount crystals and wind chimes. There was nothing about it that looked particularly uncanny, just a plain black sign with the name in stark white letters.

It was so nondescript that it could have been a law firm or an accounting agency. Cassie checked the card in her hand against the building. Address was the same, name was obviously the same. She was in the right place to talk to someone about getting rid of the ghost in her house. So why did it feel like she should have a shoebox full of receipts under her arm?

Then again, what was a ghost-hunting business supposed to look like from the outside? A Halloween haunted house? Should it be festooned in plastic skeletons? Plastic-bag ghosts? Dry ice machine fog?

Inside, a woman not much younger than Cassie who sat behind the receptionist's desk gave her a brisk, professional smile, which only heightened the whole shoebox-of-receipts feeling. "Good morning. How can I help you?"

"Hi." Cassie held up the card. "I got this from the coffee shop. Hallowed Grounds? And I—"

"You have questions." The receptionist's smile remained bright and professional, but dipped a fraction. She ticked the sentences off on her fingers one at a time. "No, it's not a joke. Yes, it's real. Yes, my grandmother can communicate with the dead. No, you can't make an appointment to watch her do it. She can't, as she likes to say, pull a ghost out of her ass."

Cassie blinked. "If she could, I hope she'd charge extra for it."

That got a laugh out of the receptionist, and a little of that professional attitude sloughed away. "Okay, I like you. What can I do for you?"

"Well," Cassie said, "I do have a question, but nothing like those. Nick said I should come by and talk to you . . . or talk to your grandmother? . . . about a ghost in my house."

"A ghost in your house? Now, that's the kind of thing we're here for." The receptionist's blond ponytail swung over her shoulder as she turned to her computer screen. "So where's home?"

Cassie pointed down the street, but the receptionist's gaze was locked on her computer, waiting for the actual address. "1334 North Beachside Drive."

She typed it in. "City and state?"

"Right here and . . . right here."

She looked up from her computer. "You live here? You're a local?" She covered her eyes with her hand. "Oh my god, I'm so sorry. I just assumed you were a tourist."

"I get that a lot." What was she doing wrong around here to make people think she was from out of state? This whole conversation could use a do-over. "I'm Cassie."

"Libby." Her professional smile had melted away by now, replaced by one that was a hundred times more genuine. "You said Nick sent you over?"

Cassie nodded. "He said that Nan . . . er, Mrs. Simpson . . . ? Your grandmother? That she might be able to help me hammer out some peace with Mrs. Hawkins."

"Hawkins?" The name was a squeak coming out of Libby's mouth. "You live in the *Hawkins House*? Oh my god, I can't believe I didn't clock the address when you said it!" Computer forgotten, she put her elbows on her desk, cradling her chin in her hands. "This is *great*. Tell me everything." Libby's entire demeanor had changed from the professional receptionist Cassie had first met. Now she was less "filling out an intake form for a new client" and more "fishing for some great gossip." But Cassie could roll with casual, and there was something so friendly about Libby's big blue eyes, like she was the kindest cheerleader on the squad. The one who'd do your hair for you in the bathroom between classes and always had gum. It didn't take long to tell her everything that had been happening since she moved in.

Partway through the story Libby had turned back to her computer, typing things in. "And nothing's happened since then?" She didn't sound judgmental, or like she didn't believe Cassie. They could have been discussing symptoms of a cold.

"No. Things have been pretty quiet." Sure, Cassie held her breath every time she went anywhere near the fridge, but nothing had changed since last Friday night. None of the magnetic poetry words had moved; **my house** remained in the middle of the refrigerator door. Cassie sure as hell wasn't going to touch them. And at this point, they were, what, evidence? "Do you think she left already? Like made her point and then got the hell out?"

The thought gave her hope, but those hopes disintegrated when Libby shook her head. "I wouldn't think so. If she went to all the trouble to let you know it's her house, she's not planning on leaving anytime soon. But don't worry," she hastened to assure Cassie. "If she was going to hurt you, she would have done it by now."

Cassie wasn't sure how to feel about that. She hadn't even considered that being hurt was on the table. So she settled for a feeble "Yay?"

"That's the spirit. No pun intended." Libby grinned as she picked up the phone on her desk—an old-fashioned push-button landline that looked like a movie prop—and started punching in a number. She held up a finger to Cassie as the call connected. "Hey, Nan? I've got someone here with a job. I think you're really going to want to—"

"Have the boy do it." The voice on the other end was cantankerous, and loud enough that Cassie could hear it through the receiver.

"No, I think you're going to want to—"

But the woman on the other end wasn't letting Libby finish a sentence. "You know I'm getting too old to travel, Liberty. Like I said, let the boy do it. He should be able to handle—"

"*The boy* is doing that job up in Savannah, remember?" Libby was finally able to cut in by speaking a little louder, a little firmer. "You sent him up there last week."

There was silence on the other end before Nan spoke again. "Shit. I forgot." Her voice was contrite, and there was a little wobble in it.

"It's okay, Nan," Libby said smoothly. "I have the calendar right here in front of me. That's why I remembered. And you pay me to remember, right?"

Another silence, broken by a sigh. "Right. So where is it?"

"It's right here in town. The Hawkins House."

There was no silence this time. "What?" Nan barked. "Are you shitting me?"

"I am indeed not shitting you." Libby glanced up at Cassie with a grin, and Cassie couldn't help but grin back. She tried to picture having this kind of relationship with either of her grandmothers. One had died when she was too young to remember her, and the other had called Cassie a slut in the seventh grade when her bra strap showed under her sundress. "The new owner's here, and we think she may have met Sarah Hawkins. Had a couple run-ins, and she'd like us to come check it out."

"Damn right I'm going to check it out. Tell her I can be there on Monday. Noon or so." Libby raised her eyebrows in Cassie's direction, and she nodded in confirmation. Once they hung up, Libby bounced in her seat, clapping her hands together like a child on her way to Disney World. "I knew she'd be excited. She's been dying to get into that house for years. No pun intended."

"People do that a lot around here." Cassie had never realized until now how many ghostly idioms existed in the English language. If she stuck around she was probably going to hear them all.

First things first. Before she decided if she was sticking around, she needed to get these ghostly distractions out of her life. And out of her house. Enough was enough. It was time to confront Sarah Hawkins.

Fifteen

Monday at eleven forty-five there was a knock on the door. Well, not so much a knock as a pound. Nan Simpson was early.

Cassie closed her laptop with a snap; she hadn't been all that focused anyway. In fact, she'd been scattered all morning. The appointment on the calendar—with an actual ghost hunter!—had activated waiting mode in her brain, so she couldn't concentrate on this project brief she was supposed to be reviewing (and removing Oxford commas from, which hurt every time she did it because the Oxford comma was the only good comma, but all these briefs had to follow AP style for some reason . . . but she digressed). So even though Mrs. Simpson was early, the knock on the door was a welcome relief. Maybe she could be more productive after this was over.

Cassie wasn't sure what she expected a ghost hunter to look like. Certainly not like the kindly looking grandmother on her front stoop. She had gray-white curls and wore a purple velour tracksuit in the Florida heat; a large bag made of crocheted granny squares was slung over her shoulder.

"You Cassie?" The question was a bark out of the older woman's mouth. So much for kindly looking.

"That's me. Mrs. Simpson?"

"Call me Nan." Cassie barely had time to nod and step back from the doorway before Nan stepped inside.

"Can I get you anything? Coffee? I think I have some iced tea in the fridge, or a Diet Coke?" Cassie was halfway to the kitchen before realizing that Nan hadn't followed. She turned to find the old woman in the center of the living room, eyes closed, breathing deeply. It was a little disturbing, but maybe this was part of the process? Cassie didn't know anything about ghost hunting.

After a few moments of silence Nan opened her eyes again.

"Coffee would be great. Black." She hitched her bag higher on her shoulder and took a slow turn around the living room, examining everything. "This the original floor?" She tapped on the floor with the toe of one running shoe. Nan didn't look like the kind of person who did a lot of running.

"Sure is." There was still a half pot of coffee she'd left on from this morning, so Cassie got a mug from the kitchen and filled it. "The built-in bookcases are original too, according to the seller, but all the rooms were freshly painted before I bought it. The furniture's mine." She tried to hand the coffee off, but Nan was still looking at everything like she was going to write a report on the condition of the house. Cassie was stuck standing there holding a cup of coffee like a butler until Nan was ready to take it from her.

"Hmm." Nan took a long sip of coffee, then looked at the mug with a grimace. "This is old. If I'd known that, I would have just taken a Diet Coke."

"I'm sorry." Why was Cassie apologizing? She'd been drinking the coffee all morning; it was fine. But apologizing to grandmas when you disappointed them was what you did. "I'll make a fresh pot next time you come over." She'd meant for the words to be sarcastic; when was Nan going to be coming back? Wasn't this a one-time visit? Or was Nan going to be coming by on a regular basis, making sure her home remained ghost-free? Maybe there was a contract for Cassie to sign for an annual ghost inspection.

"Mmm." Nan took another sip, so the coffee couldn't have been that bad. "She misses the cabbage roses."

Cassie looked at her blankly. "Who? The what?"

"Cabbage roses." Nan gestured toward the walls with the coffee cup. "The wallpaper that was here before."

"You were here before they renovated the house?"

Nan shook her head. "Sarah Hawkins died in 1942. Two years before I was born. I've never seen anyone live in this house. Never been inside." She said those last words softly, almost to herself. Then she picked back up the thread of what she was saying. "The wallpaper. Pink cabbage roses on a soft green background. She'd picked it out, put it up herself. It matched the roses she grew outside. She was proud of it. The work she'd done to make this house hers. A home. She doesn't hate the paint, but she keeps saying over and over that she misses the cabbage roses."

Cassie's breath left her body in a whoosh, and she stepped back, groping for the chair she knew was right behind her. It was a race to sit down before her legs gave out. "She?" It was a question she knew the answer to, but it seemed right to ask it.

But as critical as Nan had been about the coffee, she didn't scoff at the seemingly unnecessary question. "Sarah Hawkins." Her voice was gentler than Cassie expected.

"She really is here, then." It was a rhetorical question, but Nan nodded anyway.

"Oh, she's here. No doubt about it. I clocked a feminine spirit the second I walked in the door. The floors felt like a hug—yes, I know how stupid that sounds. But there's nothing but love in that old wood, at least as far as she's concerned. I figured it was original to the house. But when I asked for a message, she kept showing me pink cabbage roses. On the walls. And outside."

"Wow." Cassie let her gaze travel over the living room walls, which were painted an inoffensive but boring shade of beige. When she first saw the house, even before putting in an offer, she'd imagined painting it a livelier color. Pink, she realized now with a start. She'd thought of painting the living room either a soft pink or a muted green. The color of the cabbage rose wallpaper that Nan was talking about now.

Damn.

Nan nodded. "She misses those roses something fierce." She headed now for the kitchen, and Cassie got up to follow. She was about to direct Nan's attention to the fridge, and the message that lingered there, but Nan saw it immediately.

"Clever. You do that?" She turned to Cassie with raised eyebrows, and Cassie shook her head.

"No. That was what I told Libby about. When I got home Friday night, first it said 'wrong.' Then it changed to that."

"Not the message. That's obviously from Sarah. I mean the magnets. The words." She stepped closer to examine the hundreds of little words on the refrigerator.

"Oh. Yeah. Those are mine. Magnetic poetry. I've had it for ages. It's just a thing I have. It's not like I got it to communicate with . . ." Cassie couldn't let herself say the word out loud. It made all of this too real.

But Nan looked impressed. "It's a great idea, though. Not all spirits can use them, of course. The afterlife is weird, and spirits come through in different ways. But the ones that can make things move . . . I like it. I'm gonna tell Libby to get some of these." She thrust her coffee mug back into Cassie's hands before rummaging in her bag and drawing out a notepad and pen, scribbling down a note. "Magnetic poetry, you called it?"

"Yeah. Glad I could help." Cassie desperately wanted to bring the conversation back on topic. "So about the, uh, spirit that's in my house. Sarah Hawkins? How do we get rid of her?"

"Oh." Nan put the notepad and pen away before turning back to Libby. Her expression was almost sympathetic. "Oh, no, honey. Sarah's not going anywhere."

"What?" The word exploded out of Cassie's throat, much louder than she'd intended. But disappointment was a loud emotion.

Nan didn't react to her outburst. "Not all spirits need to be gotten rid of."

"But . . ." Cassie sputtered. "I thought she was Mean Mrs. Hawkins? Chasing people with sticks and whatnot?"

"I thought so too." Nan looked around the kitchen with a puzzled expression.

"Then, don't we want to get rid of that?"

"Typically, yes." Nan was silent for a moment, concentrating. "But I'm not getting that from her. She's not mean. I don't think she ever was. She loves her home. Maybe there's nothing wrong with letting her stay."

There's a lot wrong with it, Cassie wanted to say. *It's my house now. Not hers.* But arguing with a ghost through a third party felt petty somehow. Childish. Cassie took a deep breath through the annoyance. After all, hadn't Nick mentioned this could be a possibility? He seemed to be just fine with a ghost roommate.

This was all getting a little too weird. Ghost stories were one thing, but living in one?

First things first. "Then can she stop scaring the shit out of me?" She gestured toward the fridge.

That got a chuckle out of Nan. "I don't think she meant to scare you. Think of it from her perspective."

"From the ghost's perspective," Cassie repeated dully. "Think of it from the perspective of the ghost who's haunting my house." Was she the only one who realized how ridiculous that sounded?

"Sure." Nan took her mug back, draining it before putting it down on the counter. "She's been here, by herself, for . . . well, for longer than I've been alive." She gestured at herself in emphasis, and Cassie had to admit the visual drove the point home. "She's been watching this house she loves deteriorate, nothing she can do about it. Then some asshole comes in, tears out her cabbage rose wallpaper that had probably all but disintegrated anyway, and paints her living room this shitty vanilla color. Then you show up, move your things in, make this place a real home again. And don't get me wrong; I'm sure she loves that. But then—then!—you put those little words up on your fridge, and she can move them. She can get a message across to you. Imagine how that would feel."

"Oh." Cassie swallowed around a sudden lump in her throat. When had that happened? When had she gone from angry to sad? She blinked away tears that blurred her vision. When Nan put it that way, her heart ached for Sarah. But . . . "She said 'wrong.' What's wrong? Is she really that pissed about the wallpaper?"

"Hmm. I don't think that's it." Nan brushed wizened fingers over the words on the fridge, closing her eyes. She didn't move for several minutes, and Cassie got a little concerned. It was almost like the old woman had gone somewhere else, leaving her body behind like a car in a parking lot to come back and pick up later. Silence stretched out in the kitchen, gradually becoming awkward. Just as Cassie began to wonder if she should intervene in some way—was it possible for someone to fall asleep standing up?—Nan dropped her hand, stepping back and opening her eyes.

"She doesn't have a problem with you." For the first time since walking into the house, Nan sounded tired. She sounded old. She didn't protest when Cassie took her arm and guided her to a seat at her kitchen table. "She doesn't have a problem with you," she said again as Cassie pushed a glass of water in front of her. "No, she thinks you're just fine." Nan took a deep breath and a sip of water, both of which seemed to energize her. "It's Sophie she has a problem with."

"Sophie?" Cassie sat back in her seat opposite Nan. "The girl who does the ghost tour?"

Nan nodded. "She says Sophie's getting it wrong. That's the most I could get out of her." She passed a hand over her eyes. "It's hard to listen that deep."

"But how would she know?" Cassie asked the question to the room at large. "Sophie's never been here. I mean, sure, she's outside, and the ghost tour goes by here every Friday night. But she . . ." Cassie's voice trailed off as she remembered. She liked to open the windows in the evenings sometimes, to get the breeze off the ocean. She'd left them open that night when she'd gone to meet Nick for the ghost tour. Had that let Sarah hear Sophie's spiel? Or had she always heard the spiel, and just now decided to try and set the record straight with Cassie's magnetic poetry?

Whatever it was, it was time to believe. No more explaining it away. Ghosts were real and she lived with one. "What about my laptop, though? Most of the time when I plug it in, I can't get it to hold a charge. Is that Sarah too?"

Nan looked at the laptop, which sat now on the table between them, still plugged in from when Buster had been there the other day. It was all charged up now, because Cassie was scared to unplug it and upset the status quo. Nan prodded at it with her forefinger, but nothing happened. "Hard to say," she finally said. "I mean, spirits messing with electronics is nothing new, so it's possible. But I'm not getting anything from Sarah off of it." She shrugged. "We've got a lot of ghosts here in town, but that doesn't mean they're behind everything that happens. Sometimes it's just as simple as shitty wiring." She opened her bag again, peering inside. "There's a great handyman, Buster Bradshaw. I've got his card here somewhere. He could . . ."

"He's been." At least it was good to know that Buster came highly recommended around here.

"Tell him to look again. I bet he missed something."

Great. That was absolutely what Buster wanted to hear from her.

Nan levered to her feet, and Cassie was relieved to see that she seemed steadier now. "That goes for me too," she said as Cassie walked her to the door. "Anything else weird happens, you give Libby a call. She'll get me over here." She paused at the door. "In the meantime, see if you can get Sarah to talk a little more."

"How?"

"Use your words." Nan nodded back toward the kitchen. "She's been alone a long time. She might like to talk."

Cassie closed the door behind Nan, then looked over her shoulder at the magnetic words on the fridge. She could relate, couldn't she? To being lonely. To wanting someone to talk to.

Maybe she and Sarah weren't so different after all.

After dinner, Cassie settled in on her sofa. It had been a while since her last reality television binge, and she was ready to turn her brain off for a little while. No ghosts, no cute guys who ran cafés, no poor financial decisions with janky plumbing and a stuck kitchen window. She reached for the remote on the side table, and promptly knocked it to the floor instead. She swore softly as it slid across the wood floor like a hockey puck to rest under the sofa, thudding against the back wall.

"Of course." With a long sigh she hauled herself off the sofa and lay on her stomach. But no matter how far she stretched, her finger-tips just barely brushed the remote. Resigned, she got to her feet and tugged the sofa away from the wall.

"All this to watch gorgeous people in tiny bathing suits try to find love." She slipped behind the sofa to pick up the remote when something near the baseboard caught her eye. When she'd moved in, one of the first things she'd done was direct the movers to nestle the sofa next to the built-in bookshelf; the blues and creams of the sofa matched the bookcase perfectly and it looked made for this room.

But now . . . she bumped the sofa with her hip, nudging it a little farther from the wall so she could kneel on the floor. At the side of the bookcase, just above the baseboard, there was a small place where the texture of the wall changed. It wasn't large, maybe three inches or so, but this close Cassie could see it clearly. Wallpaper. A piece that had been missed when the flippers stripped the wallpaper and repainted the room, it was wedged between the baseboard and the built-in bookcase. Cassie picked at it with her fingernails, but it was stubborn. Obviously the painters had given up on it and just given it the landlord special: paint over it and pretend it doesn't exist.

Her manicure kit was on the coffee table, and it only took a few seconds and a pair of nail scissors to extract the piece of wallpaper. The colors were obscured by the cream-colored paint, of course, but when Cassie tilted it toward the light she could make out the texture. It was a floral print in the shape of a round, unfurled rose.

A cabbage rose.

"Okay." She sighed at the ancient wallpaper. "Okay." Hotties in bathing suits could wait. She studied the scrap of wallpaper as she walked back into the kitchen. Then she studied the words on her fridge before selecting the two that would work best for this.

"All right, Sarah." She raised her voice like she was calling to someone in the other room, but maybe Sarah was right here, looking over her shoulder? How did ghosts work, anyway? "I get it. These guys did a shitty job on your house, and you're pissed about it, right? If this is the wallpaper that Nan was talking about, it was green and pink with cabbage roses on it. I'm not gonna lie, wallpaper is kind of a pain in the ass, and given the choice, I'd rather paint the room a different color. But it's not my choice; it's yours. So I need you to tell me. What do you miss?" She held the wallpaper scrap to the fridge with one hand. "I have two words here. If you are dead set on the cabbage roses, choose the word 'flower.'" Cassie lay the magnet over the wallpaper. "If you just want it repainted in those colors, choose the word 'color.' Leave the word you want in the middle." That magnet went over the wallpaper next, and between the two of them they held the wallpaper scrap securely against the fridge.

She held her breath as she took a step back. She wasn't sure what she expected, but nothing happened. She let out a sigh as the adrenaline that came from talking to a ghost faded into a slight hum in her blood.

"Maybe you need a minute to think." God, it was weird, talking out loud to thin air like this. But she was committed now. "Take your time. I can't do anything about it tonight anyway, and I really want to watch some TV. You can join me if you want."

She scooped up the opened bottle of merlot on her counter and brought it and a glass back into the living room with her. "I bet you've never even *seen* reality television. Or any television at all, huh?" Now that she'd started talking to invisible people who might be listening, it was hard to stop. "Mrs. H, you've got a lot to catch up on. This show is called *Romance Resort*, and it's the worst. All these hot people are living together in this island paradise. They say they're looking for true love, but we all know better. It's all about hookups and drama." She pointed the remote at the television. "You're gonna love it."

The opening credits rolled, the bikini-clad people were impossibly gorgeous, and Cassie felt her brain click off. She needed this. She had no idea what the future held, but she could stick around for now. To help Sarah out. Nothing wrong with that.

Three episodes later, in the darkened kitchen, where there were no windows open and therefore no breeze, the wallpaper scrap twitched against its magnetic captors.

Sixteen

"Oh, I meant to say . . ." Libby handed Nick her debit card to pay for her lunch order. "Thanks for the referral."

"You mean Cassie?" Nick kept his eyes on the card reader machine and tried his damnedest to sound casual, but the smile that played around his lips probably gave him away. He couldn't help but smile when Cassie's name came up.

Libby noticed. She clucked her tongue at him. "Of course I mean Cassie. You've been sending a lot of referrals our way that I don't know about?"

"Nope, just the one." He chanced meeting her eyes as he handed her card back, but the amusement in her expression only made his smile widen.

"Well, thanks again. Nan loved getting into the Hawkins House." Libby tucked her card away. "She said the activity there was off the chain."

"Your grandmother did *not* say 'off the chain.'"

A laugh bubbled out of her. "Okay, you got me there. In any case, she couldn't stop talking about it last night."

"So Cassie's got ghosts?"

"Oh, she's definitely got ghosts," she said in the matter-of-fact tone that someone who didn't live in Boneyard Key might use to say a house had termites. Though around here the ghosts were definitely more welcome. "But get this." She leaned her elbows on the counter, and even though Nick had at least three tables of customers waiting for their lunch orders, they could wait. Ghost gossip was the best gossip.

"Mean Mrs. Hawkins isn't mean." Libby raised her eyebrows. "Can you believe that?"

"Huh." Nick wasn't expecting that. "You sure it was her, then?"

"Nan was pretty sure. There were a lot of details about the house—the way it used to look inside, stuff like that. Who else could it be?" Libby straightened up again. "But Nan said the presence was gentle. Kind, even. She apparently talked about her roses, and that she misses them. That was like the main theme. Weird, huh?"

"Really weird." Nick was taken aback. All his life he'd heard about Mean Mrs. Hawkins. How could all those stories be wrong?

Libby shook her head. "Sounded more like she was lonely. Happy to finally be able to communicate with someone. Kind of sad, you know?"

"Yeah." The word *lonely* echoed in Nick's head. A relatable notion. He thought about Mrs. Hawkins rattling around in that house, abandoned for however many years. About someone finally hearing her after all this time. He suddenly had a little more sympathy for Elmer and his incessant texting.

From behind Nick came Ramon's voice calling "Order up!" along with the clatter of plates being deposited into the window. He really did need to get back to work.

"How did Cassie take the news?" He tossed the question over his shoulder on his way to delivering the roast beef sandwich to the guy in the far corner and a Cobb salad to the woman at the table by the window. More and more tourists every day, and it wasn't even Memorial Day yet. It was shaping up to be a busy summer.

"She was kinda mad at first, Nan said." Libby waited till he was back by the counter to pick up the conversation string. He grabbed the last plate—roast beef sandwiches sure were popular today—and practically threw it at the customer at the other end of the counter. All these lunch orders were interrupting this very important conversation. "She was more focused on getting Mrs. H out of her house as opposed to understanding why she's there. Which . . . I guess that makes sense. I try and remember that not everyone grows up with this stuff. It's a lot to take in when you haven't been tapped into it all your life."

"No, I get that." He thought that Cassie had been making progress. Sure, he still remembered her stricken face when Sarah Hawkins had first made herself known, when Cassie had said she wasn't cut out for this. But he also remembered her face as they watched the sunset together and talked about ghostly roommates. He thought she'd been coming around to the idea. Maybe he'd been mistaken. "I'm glad she's okay, at least," he finally said. "She was pretty freaked out when it first happened."

Libby narrowed her eyes, studying him. "You *like* her!" She practically crowed the words.

Nick narrowed his eyes back, mocking her. "I like her fine."

"Yeah, he does." Ramon walked through the swinging door to the kitchen, take-out box in hand. He usually just threw them up on the ledge with the regular orders, but Libby ordered a BLT with extra crispy fries every time, and Ramon had a crush on Libby. Hence the personal delivery.

"I knew it!" Libby sounded triumphant as she took the box from Ramon, but she made no move to leave. Nick wished she would; he didn't need his love life dissected in public like this. "This is great! Cassie seems really nice. I'm thrilled for you—"

"Don't start." He didn't mean to interrupt her, but it was time to quash that line of thinking. "We don't even know if she's sticking around."

"Well, of course she is." Libby popped open the take-out box and selected a fry. "She just bought a house." She said the words slowly, as though explaining a complex concept. "People who buy houses generally stick around."

"Right," Nick said. "But she didn't know she was buying a *haunted* house. That changes things."

"He's just being a chickenshit," Ramon said. "You know how he is. Scared to let people in."

Nick whipped his head around and glared at his cook. When the hell had Ramon become his therapist? "I let people in."

But Libby nodded sagely. "He's right," she said while Ramon glowed at the praise. Traitor.

"Just let her in, Nick." Libby continued munching on her fries.

"You know, if you were gonna eat it here you could have just said." Nick passed her a plate, but Libby kept eating out of the take-out box.

"Not every girl is gonna be like Madison, you know."

"Libby . . ." He tried to put as much warning into his voice as possible, but once again, Libby was immune.

"Nick." Libby leveled a look at him. "Your best friend is a guy who died a couple decades ago."

Nick leveled a look right back. "I don't exactly have a choice. It's not like Elmer's gonna go away." He sent a quick glance up toward the ceiling. *Sorry, man. You know what I mean.*

But Libby wasn't done. "Have you had a real relationship since Madison left? It's been *years* since you two broke up."

He threw up his hands. Libby meant well, but even though he had moved on from his ex, hearing her name still felt like needles on his skin. "Who the hell am I gonna date around here?"

Libby's smile was slow and sly. *Checkmate*, it said. "There's Cassie. You could date her."

Nick opened his mouth to argue, but Libby had him there. While his ex's name was needles, Cassie's was like a drink of water on a hot day.

Libby took advantage of his silence. "You know what I think?" She picked up one half of the BLT, inspecting the quality of the bacon. "You should go check on her. Maybe see if she's feeling better about Mrs. H today."

"Sure," Nick said slowly. "I could do that. Maybe after closing, I'll . . ."

Libby waved a hand, the one not holding the sandwich she was still theoretically not eating here, as she took a bite. "Or you could go now."

"Now?" he repeated. "We're in the middle of lunch."

"Technically it's the end of lunch," Ramon said, and he wasn't wrong. The three orders Nick had just delivered were working on their food, and no one new had come in. The lunch rush was indeed over.

That didn't mean he didn't have work to do. Once the café closed he still had to clean up. Start on the next day's batch of banana bread. There was also this chocolate chip cookie recipe he wanted to try that had the tiniest sprinkling of sea salt over the top . . .

But he was already untying his apron. "There are a couple pieces of cinnamon banana bread left over. She might like them."

Ramon nodded sagely while Libby polished off the first half of her sandwich. "Don't want 'em to go stale," he said.

It didn't take long to bag them up. "You sure you're okay handling things for a little bit?" But Nick was already halfway to the door.

Ramon made a shooing motion. "I know how to work a cash register. Go say hi to your girl. Just don't fuck it up."

"Wasn't planning on it." He glanced over his shoulder one more time to see Libby starting on the second half of her sandwich.

"Do you think I could get a Diet Coke here?"

Nick scoffed as Ramon all but dashed for the soda fountain. Ramon had been nursing that low-key crush on Libby since eighth grade. But hell, who wasn't. Just about everyone had a crush on Libby back in those days. Except Nick. He'd chosen her cousin, which had turned out to be a terrible idea.

But Madison was the past. The future was just up the street.

Cassie didn't answer the door at first. Nick rang the bell a second time and stood there just long enough to feel desperate. He glanced around the porch, then back down the street. Maybe she wasn't home? Maybe—

The door swung inward with a speed and ferocity that had Nick falling back a step.

"Sorry!" Cassie said. "Sorry. Were you there long?" She gestured at the massive pair of black headphones hanging around her neck. "I thought I heard the doorbell, but I couldn't tell if it was part of the music or not."

"You listen to doorbell music?"

She smirked and rolled her eyes, gesturing him inside. "I listen to lo-fi mood music. You know, while I'm working. Helps me get in the zone. They just put me on this new ad campaign, some hippie granola company, and they want us to completely redo their social media. I have permission to make as many Grateful Dead puns as I want."

"Groovy." Warmth bloomed in his chest in response to her smile. Ugh, Libby was right. He liked her. Like, *liked* her. Nick closed the door behind him and held out the bag. "There was some leftover—"

"Oh my god, is that banana bread?" Cassie snatched the bag and peered inside. "You are a lifesaver. I'm just now realizing that I forgot to eat lunch." She cocked her head. "Actually, I'm not sure I had breakfast. Does coffee count?" she asked as she led him toward the kitchen.

"No." So much for freaked-out Cassie. She was either taking this whole ghost thing much easier than anyone suspected, or she was pushing it down in favor of her job. "I think maybe you work too much." That wasn't something he usually said, at least not out loud. He started work at the crack of dawn, after all. Who was he to criticize anyone's work habits? Then again, he usually remembered to eat.

"Probably," she agreed easily. "But it's either that or obsess about my haunted house, right? Speaking of which, check this out!" She dug among the papers on the table for a moment, emerging with a scrap of paper that she pushed into his hand.

At first he thought it was a torn receipt, but it felt thicker. "Wallpaper?" He ran a thumb over the surface before holding it up to the light. He could almost make out the pattern, but it had been painted over with white paint.

"Wallpaper," Cassie confirmed with a nod. "But she doesn't want new wallpaper. It's the color she misses. Which, thank God, because repainting a room is so much easier."

Nick shook his head, as though that would jar a thought loose. He knew the words she was saying, but not the context. "What . . . ?"

"The *wallpaper*," she repeated, as though that would make it clearer. She opened the fridge and took out two bottles of soda, offering him one. "Nan Simpson came by yesterday, right?" She bumped the fridge closed with her hip. "And she kept talking about cabbage roses and wallpaper. But I didn't find this"—she indicated the scrap of wallpaper in his hand—"till after she left. They missed it when they were remodeling. Looks like they painted over it instead of getting it off the wall."

"Sounds about right." Nick had gotten a few quotes from contractors when he'd first bought the café, and he knew all about ones that cut corners.

"But then. *Then!* I asked her. Does she want the pink and green colors back? Or does she want the cabbage rose print? And she answered me! Look!" She pointed to the mess of words on her fridge, and sure enough the word **color** was in the center. The word **flower** lay on the floor in front of the fridge, obviously rejected.

"Damn." Nick was impressed. "She answered you. That's . . ." He couldn't put into words what he was feeling. And he really wished he could, because the feeling swelled something in his chest. It was like pride, but warmer than that. Deeper than joy. But there was something buzzing in his chest too. Like the aftermath of a swarm of bees. Something that felt tight. Felt like panic. "Cassie, this is huge. There are people that have lived here their whole lives— Founding Fifteen and everything—and haven't been able to communicate like this."

"What?" Her forehead furrowed. "I thought it was normal around here to talk to ghosts. Isn't that this place's whole . . . thing?" Her gesture encompassed not just her kitchen, her house, but the entire town.

Nick shook his head. "It depends. I think of it as more like a talent. Like drawing or being good at tennis. It can be trained, for sure, but natural ability helps a lot. Family members in the Founding Fifteen can have the talent in spades, but it's still going to vary from person to person. And then, of course, not everyone cares or wants to develop it."

"Ah." She looked at the fridge for a long moment. "And your family's part of the Founding Fifteen?"

He nodded. "Neither of my parents have the ability, therefore they think it's a load of crap. They live over in The Villages now. And my sister Courtney left for college when she turned eighteen and never came back."

Cassie gave a low whistle. "So you're the last Royer standing, huh?"

Nick tried to give a casual shrug, but his jaw had suddenly clenched tight. "Something like that." It was a sore subject, and not one he'd meant to bring up. It was weird sometimes, to be the only one in the family who took the legacy seriously. Sure, Boneyard Key had become a cheesy tourist destination, but it was also their ancestral home. As much as anything in Florida settled barely at the end of the nineteenth century could be called "ancestral." People in Europe would probably laugh themselves into hysterics at the notion.

Anyway, he felt possessive of the town. In a way that no one else in his family did.

If Cassie noticed any of this inner turmoil, she didn't let it show. "Nan thought it might have to do with the magnetic poetry. Makes it easy for her to communicate."

"She'd know better than I would, for sure." He followed her gaze to the scattered words on the fridge. "Not all ghosts communicate the same. Elmer's never moved stuff around. He talks to me in my head. Or on my phone."

"In your head?" Cassie's eyes widened. "That sounds creepy."

She had a point. "It's not as bad as it sounds. I guess I got used to it."

"I think I'd prefer the words on the fridge."

He chuckled. "You're in luck then. Looks like she can move things, and you have things that she can move. Who knows, maybe it really is as simple as that."

Cassie considered that while Nick turned his attention back to the wallpaper scrap in his hand. "So she wants you to paint, huh?" He scraped at the white paint with his thumbnail, trying to get to the . . . what did she call them? Cabbage roses? He didn't know the difference between that and a regular rose.

"Yep. Pink and green. I've already called Buster, and he's got a few weeks free. He's going to come by soon, and we're going to put a list together."

"A list of what?"

"Other stuff that needs fixing." She started ticking them off on her fingers. "The shower upstairs has a leak. They never put baseboards in the second bedroom upstairs, and one of the windows is painted shut. This window in the kitchen doesn't close properly; learned that the hard way the first couple days, so I can't even open it now. And of course that electricity thing that never resolved itself; we're gonna need to take another crack at that." She gestured to her laptop. There was something about the sight of it, open on her kitchen table, papers and notes scattered all around, that made Nick feel like he was intruding on her life. Like she was a professional, and he was just some guy who owned a diner. Inferior.

But he pushed down the feeling and focused on Cassie. Because she was right *there*, warm and soft, and it was the easiest thing in the world to slip an arm around her waist and tug her closer. "You're going to make this house beautiful," he murmured into her hair. She made a soft humming sound in response, leaning into him, and his blood stirred. What other rooms in this house needed fixing? Maybe her bedroom? Because he wouldn't mind taking a look right about now.

Cassie sighed, her dark eyes still slowly scanning the room. Probably making to-do lists in her head; she was that type of person. "I do want to make it beautiful," she said, her voice low, talking more to herself than to him. "And maybe I could . . . I don't know . . . recoup some of what I put into the place."

His blood cooled fast. "What do you mean?"

"You know, when it's time to sell. Improvements build equity. Increase the value."

Nick let his arm fall limply to his side as realization dawned. "You're selling?" Of course. She wasn't sticking around, either. *Let her in*, they'd said. What bullshit.

"Not tomorrow or anything, but at some point." Her dark eyes scanned the kitchen. "You have to admit, this house is a lot to take on. More than I thought it would be. The listing should have said 'two bedroom, one and a half bath, renovated in a half-assed manner, free ghost with purchase.'" Her laugh sounded mocking. To Nick, to Sarah Hawkins, to all of Boneyard Key. "I probably would have thought twice before putting in an offer then."

"Right. So you're . . ." Nick couldn't finish the sentence because the buzzing sensation in his chest had gotten stronger and moved upward, like his head was suddenly full of bees.

Cassie must have noticed the change in his tone, because she turned back to him. "I don't know." Her voice was soft, almost gentle. "I don't know what I'm going to do, Nick. I want to just start with painting the living room and see how it goes."

"See how it goes?" His voice was harsh in his ears, and he didn't like how it sounded.

"Yeah. I mean, I still have work to consider." She gestured to her laptop setup, and the sight of it made him even angrier. Cassie's overly patient tone felt condescending. Dismissive. It all made the buzzing in his head louder. "How am I going to keep my job if I have to come down to the café every day just to power up my laptop?"

"You're welcome there anytime. You know that." It was like his electricity wasn't good enough for her or something.

"I know that." Her calm voice just made him angrier. Why was she placating him? "But it's not exactly convenient, is it?"

"So you're saying you don't want to see me?" He was picking a stupid fight. There was a part of his mind that was fully aware of that. But the rest was filled with buzzing, growing even louder now. The buzzing said that she was wrong. That he had to put her in her place.

What? said the sane part of his mind. But that part wasn't in charge anymore.

"No, I get it," he said, even as Cassie opened her mouth to answer him. "Work comes first for you, right? What's going to happen when you get married? Aren't you going to want to give your husband children? Shouldn't that be the priority, not a career?"

"When I *what*?" Cassie looked stricken and she fell back a step, away from him. "Who the hell is talking about having kids?"

"Are you saying you don't want a family? What the hell is wrong with women these days?"

What the hell was wrong with *him*? Why had he just said that? He didn't mean that.

Yes, he did.

No, he *didn't*.

Silence stretched between them. Cassie's eyes were wide and her face had gone white, except for two bright spots of red on her cheeks. Her mouth was open in a little O as she stared at him, stunned. Nick didn't blame her. He sounded like a raging asshole, and that wasn't like him at all. But the buzzing in his head had grown so loud that he couldn't think straight. Red crept into the edges of his vision, the rage making his chest so tight that he couldn't breathe. He wanted to yell. He wanted to cry. He wanted to . . .

He wanted Cassie to stop looking at him like she had no idea who he was. Though she had every right to; Nick had no idea who he was, either.

But Cassie wasn't looking at him. She was looking past him, and when he turned around he realized her attention had been caught by the refrigerator. The words in the middle, where Sarah left her messages, had changed.

get him out

The buzzing faded as he stared at the fridge, the words burning their way into his brain. Even the goddamn ghost wanted him out.

"I think . . ." Cassie's voice behind him was shaky. He looked back at her, taking in her tight expression. Those warm brown eyes had gone cold. "I think maybe you should go."

"Yeah, I can tell I've overstayed my welcome." What had he been thinking, dropping everything to run over here like a lovesick puppy?

He wasted no time getting the hell out of there. He practically leapt down the front porch steps, and the buzzing in his head stopped the moment he crossed through the front gate and his feet hit the sidewalk. The farther he walked, the quieter everything got, and by the time he made it to the café it had faded completely, along with his anger. His heart raced from more than just the walk as he paused at the door. He felt like he was waking up from the worst dream he'd ever had.

What had he said? And why had he said it? He turned to look back at the Hawkins House—Cassie's house. That whole conversation—no, call it what it was, a fight—felt like it had happened to someone else.

But it hadn't. It had happened to him. He'd said some pretty shitty things to the girl he was trying to date.

Inside Hallowed Grounds, Libby lingered at the counter, chatting with Ramon and sipping on her Diet Coke. Her take-out box was long gone. She and Ramon looked up at him with matching gleeful smiles, which faded as they got a good look at him.

"What happened?" Libby asked.

Nick didn't know how to answer that.

"I think I fucked up."

Seventeen

Wow, had he fucked up.

Cassie tried to put the whole thing aside, concentrate on work for the afternoon. But not even her secret love for puns and jam-band music could lighten her mood. All she could see was Nick in her kitchen, his ridiculously handsome face screwed up in a grimace, his gorgeous blue eyes dark like they'd been poisoned, spouting some bullshit about her job, about marriage and kids, like he was doing some 1950s cosplay.

That had hit her hard. She'd had no idea that kids were so high on his list of priorities. But she shouldn't have been surprised. That was the default; women were supposed to be wives and mothers. It was her fault for being different. Defective.

But it was his eyes that had been the most unsettling. Normally they were such a clear flawless blue, but in her kitchen they'd been dark and angry. She added *fix kitchen lighting* to her endless to-do list for the house; it was obviously too dark in here.

She logged off a little after six, tossing her headphones to the table and massaging away the beginnings of a headache in her temples. What a shitty day.

She reached for her phone, pulling up the group chat. It had apparently been hopping while she'd been working: twenty-seven messages, mostly a spirited debate about car seats. Not something she could weigh in on anyway.

Nick was such an asshole today . . . Wait. Had she even filled them in on who Nick was? She backspaced and started over. This guy I've been seeing was such an asshole . . . Maybe she should give more specifics. They didn't know any of the history, so she'd really have to start from the beginning, right?

> So I'm pretty sure my house is haunted, and the ghost likes to communicate by using the magnetic poetry on my fridge. And today the guy I'm seeing here was a real asshole, and . . .

This text was quickly turning into a paragraph. Cassie tried to be as concise as possible, filling everyone in while knowing she was leaving out key details. But good enough. She was just about to hit Send when another text popped up in the chat.

> I totally agree with Monika! That was the car seat we got when our little arrived, and it's been fantastic.

They were still talking about car seats. If Cassie hit Send now to share her own problems, she'd be derailing the convo. She read through the text she'd created, then held her thumb down over the backspace key until it was gone. Then she clicked her phone off and tossed it to her table. Who cared.

Her chest tightened, and tears blurred her vision. Goddammit, she did *not* want to cry. She was fine. She was strong. She didn't need a man who was going to go off on her like that. Not every group text was about her, and she didn't need them to be.

But a small sob came from her throat as she pressed the heels of her hands against her closed eyes. Sure, she was fine and she was strong. But she was so *lonely*.

The ringing of the doorbell cut through her gloom, the unexpected sound bringing her out of her chair. Was Nick back for round two of yelling at her? She was still dizzy from round one.

The last thing she expected to see was Sophie, balancing a pizza box. Libby was just behind her, a tote bag in her hand and sympathy in her eyes.

"Hi . . . ?"

"I was at Hallowed Grounds," Libby said. "Earlier today."

"Oh. Great." Now their arrival made sense. She could only imagine what Nick had said about her when he got back there from her place. He'd been an absolute dick, yet for some reason he'd been mad at her? Utter bullshit.

Sophie nodded solemnly. "We thought you might want this." She held up the pizza in illustration, but what they were really offering was what Cassie had been craving for ages now. Friends. People to talk to, and even better, ones who understood the weird-ass things that went on in this town.

She also saw it for what it was. Sure, it was sympathy pizza. But it was also gossip pizza. Anything Cassie said could and would be held against her when Sophie and Libby reported back.

But Cassie didn't care. She had half a mind to sell the house and get the hell out of here. So fuck it; let them talk. Let Nick tell the town what a bitch she was. He was the least of her concerns.

Besides, that pizza smelled incredible, and she was suddenly starving.

Inside, she cleared off her kitchen table while Sophie set the pizza down on the counter. Libby dug into her tote bag and pulled out a bottle of red wine and a six-pack of lager. "Both go with pizza," she explained, "and I didn't know which you liked better."

Cassie smiled. "I'll get the corkscrew."

A half hour later, they'd destroyed the entire pizza and most of the bottle of wine while Cassie filled them in on what had happened with Nick this afternoon.

"Wait." Sophie's eyes went wide behind her glasses. "He said what?"

"I know." She still couldn't believe it herself. His vitriol had come out of nowhere, and she hadn't been able to get him out of her house fast enough. She picked a pepperoni off her last slice and popped it in her mouth. "Sorry to disappoint," she said while she chewed.

"No, it's just . . ." Sophie shook her head. "That's not Nick. He's a nice guy. Always has been."

Cassie snorted. "Believe me, he wasn't this afternoon." She pointed at the fridge. "Even Mrs. H had had enough of his shit."

"Oh wow. Nan was telling me about this." Libby got up and moved closer to the fridge, examining the magnetic poetry. "She really does move those around, huh?"

Cassie nodded. "It's feeling less and less weird the more it happens."

"I don't know." Libby gave a little shudder. "I know this is Nan's thing, the family business and all, but sometimes it still gives me the ick."

"She really put that phrase up when Nick was here? Like she threw Nick out?" Sophie asked.

"More like she strongly suggested it," Cassie said. "She can move these little words around, but not whole human beings. As far as I know." God, wouldn't that be something. Today, magnetic poetry; tomorrow, people. Would Mrs. H evolve, like a Pokémon?

Libby shook her head, still staring at the fridge. "I'm trying to remember any time Nick got thrown out of somewhere."

"I can't picture it," Sophie said. "I've known Nick since . . ." Her voice trailed off while she thought. "I don't remember a time in my life that I haven't known Nick."

Libby nodded in agreement. "Sure, sometimes he gets mad. Everyone does. And boy, can that man hold a grudge."

"Yeah, but he's such a nice guy," Sophie said. "He's never been . . . I dunno. Misogynistic or angry like that."

"Do you think it's because you talked about selling the house?" Libby polished off the wine at the bottom of her glass.

"I don't know," Cassie said. "Would that really upset him that much?" Sure, they'd had a couple nice evenings out together. And more than a couple very nice kisses. But that didn't make them committed to each other or anything. No hearts were being broken here. Yet.

But Sophie gave a low "*Ohhhhhh*" of recognition. "I bet that's it. If he thinks you're leaving town . . . that's a sore subject with him." She and Libby locked eyes across the kitchen, and the two of them nodded in unspoken agreement. Cassie suddenly felt very tired. It was exhausting sometimes, feeling like you didn't have people.

But maybe these two weren't being exclusionary. After all, they were here, and they'd brought sustenance. They weren't leaving her on read and then sending selfies from happy hours that Cassie wasn't part of anymore. They were trying. Maybe Cassie should too.

"He did tell me," she said tentatively, "something about his parents leaving town? And his sister?"

Libby nodded. "And Madison." She said the name quietly, her eyes dropping to the floor.

"Madison?" Cassie echoed. She looked from Sophie to Libby. "I thought his sister's name was Courtney?"

"Oh, it is." Libby sighed. "Madison's my cousin. She and Nick were high school sweethearts. Prom king and queen, all that."

"Okay . . ." Cassie drew out the word. "And now?"

Sophie sighed. "Now she's more like his childhood trauma."

"The long and short of it is," Libby continued, "he loves this town, and she didn't. She left, and he stayed here."

"Ah." Cassie reached for the wine bottle, but it was empty. She shook the last few drops into her glass before giving up. "And he's still holding a torch for his first love?"

"I wouldn't go that far." Libby toyed with the stem of her wineglass. "I love Mads, but she didn't treat him great. She strung him along for a few years when she really should have let him go. It got kinda messy there at the end."

Sophie nodded. "Really messy. I haven't seen him date anyone since then, and they broke up, what, five years ago?" She looked over to Libby, who nodded in confirmation. "He'll go out with a tourist for the weekend, but that's about it. It's like he doesn't want to commit to someone who's going to leave him behind again."

"I really thought he'd changed. I thought . . ." Libby didn't finish the thought, just gave Cassie a sorrowful shake of the head.

"His family left, his sister left, his girlfriend left," Sophie said. "If you started talking about leaving too . . ." She shrugged. "Maybe it set him off?"

"Maybe." It still seemed like an extreme reaction. Nick had been set off the way you'd set off a Roman candle. Explosive. Chaotic. "Whatever it was, he was a dick. I don't think he and I are going to be friends anymore."

Sophie cocked an eyebrow. "I saw y'all on the ghost tour. There was nothing 'friends' about you two."

"Well, there's no more of that, either." Now there was something to mourn. The way that, no matter the time of day, Nick smelled faintly of coffee and cinnamon. The way his hand felt on the small of her back: solid and sure. The curve of his smile and the rasp of his beard when he kissed her.

There'd been a spark between them, that was for sure. Something that felt real in a way she hadn't felt in a long time. But that spark had been well and truly doused this afternoon. Cassie let herself hold on to that regret for another moment, mentally pouring one out for what could have been between her and Nick.

Then she pushed the regret away completely. These were still new friends, and she couldn't break down in front of them. There hadn't been nearly enough wine for that.

Besides, she had more important things to discuss with Sophie. It was a relief, getting the topic of conversation off her. "Speaking of the ghost tour, I've been meaning to talk to you."

Sophie perked up, seizing on the new topic. "About the ghost tour? You want to tag along again? I don't have very many signed up for Friday, so you're welcome to join. Any warm bodies to help it look like a crowd."

"No. I mean, sure, that sounds like fun. Count me in. But I'm talking about Sarah Hawkins. The story you tell on the tour about her and her husband. You said you got that from that book, right?"

Sophie nodded while Libby gathered up the pizza box and paper plates. *A Haunted History?* That's the one. Do you need a copy? I mean, Nick has them at the café, but the bookstore carries it too."

The café. Ugh. God, she was gonna lose Hallowed Grounds too, wasn't she? She'd already come to think of the place as a second office. Sure, it was out of necessity when her laptop wouldn't charge, but Nick never seemed to mind too much, and the banana bread was a bonus.

"I have a few copies at the office," Libby chimed in, bringing Cassie back on topic. "Honestly, try to avoid getting a copy of it in this town. It's kind of everywhere."

"Oh, I've already got one." She went to the bookshelf in the living room. She'd left it there the night of the ghost tour, after coming home on the heels of her first kiss with Nick.

Cassie brandished the book as they settled onto her living room set. "How sure are you that this book is accurate?"

"Pretty sure." Sophie and Libby exchanged another look, but this time Cassie was less annoyed. They weren't trying to leave her out; they were bringing her in.

"Mr. Lindsay wrote it a million years ago," Libby said.

"And it was part of our high school class, remember?" Sophie's brow furrowed as she took the book from Cassie's hand, flipping through it as though she didn't have a battered, dog-eared copy at home. "Wouldn't he want his book about the history of the town to be accurate?"

"You'd think," Cassie said. "But Sarah thinks otherwise. She says you're getting it wrong."

"I'm . . ." Sophie dropped the book into her lap. "Sarah *told* you that?" Her voice was hushed, and her eyes darted around the room, as though she could spot Sarah lurking in the shadows. Cassie didn't blame her; she'd just started coming around to the idea of communicating with ghosts herself. It helped that Sarah was moving the magnets around more; more exposure therapy for Cassie.

"She did." Cassie gestured back to the fridge. "When I got back from the tour that night, she said 'wrong.' I don't know what part of the story is wrong. Maybe all of it, I don't know. And then she said 'my house.'"

"We know it's her house, though," Libby said. "No one's disputing that, right?"

Sophie shook her head. "The whole story can't be wrong. We know she was married to C.S. We know he died. And we know that Sarah stayed on, and scared the kids as she got old, until she died here too."

"We know all of that for sure?" Cassie didn't want to argue. She was the newcomer. But there had to be something they were missing.

"As sure as I can be." Sophie spoke slowly, as though she'd never had cause to doubt the story she was telling, but now was rethinking everything. "I mean, I didn't fact-check the whole book, because I figured . . ."

"You figured he wouldn't have any reason not to be accurate."

"But what if he was full of shit?" Libby's voice was hushed and a little dramatic after two glasses of wine. "Think about it. What if he just . . ." she waved a hand, "made it all up? Who was going to contradict him?"

"No." Sophie shook her head hard. "He can't have made it up. It's got to be accurate. I base the entire ghost tour around that book!" She pressed her palm to her forehead, looking stressed.

"I'm not saying he made the whole thing up," Cassie rushed to reassure her. Apparently she wasn't the only one whose world was being rocked tonight. "I'll look into it, okay? Maybe I can, I don't know, ask Sarah to elaborate?"

"Oh, good idea." Libby nodded emphatically. "Anything you need, let me know. We're happy to help you out." She gestured to include herself and Sophie, who nodded in agreement.

Cassie threw a glance over her shoulder into the darkened kitchen. She was gonna need a bigger fridge.

Eighteen

When Nick first took over the café, he found something unexpected in the back room that made him smile. Old and weathered, it was a relic from Elmer's day, but still relevant. Especially on days like today: a random Wednesday in early June, during the calm before the metaphorical storm. Tourist season was about to begin in earnest, so today was a great day to take time off and hang that old weathered sign on the door. CLOSED. GONE FISHING.

Nick was a terrible fisherman, but that wasn't the point. The point was to wake up before the sun and amble to the pier in the predawn light. Vince was busy getting his boat in the water, and Nick's job was to get the bait. Thankfully, Jimmy's opened early.

Jimmy's—the bait shack and kayak rental shop by the pier—looked like it was fashioned out of driftwood and held together with duct tape and a prayer. It had looked like that for as long as Nick could remember, and had somehow maintained that same appearance of "about to collapse" through several decades and at least four hurricanes. Jimmy himself didn't look much better: with a cracked and aggressively tanned face that showed every minute of decades spent in the sun, he was usually barefoot in board shorts with a regular rotation of stained and faded Hawaiian shirts. But his eyes were alert, twinkling beneath his battered Vietnam Veteran hat, and he gave Nick a smile when he approached.

"How's that girlie of yours?" Jimmy got down a battered five-gallon bucket and started scooping minnows out of the tank. He hadn't charged Nick a deposit in years; he always remembered to bring the bucket back.

Nick shook his head. "Not my girlie, I'm afraid." He'd never had a chance, had he? Sure, he thought they'd been building toward something. Cassie had been a breath of fresh air in a life that had become stale, and he'd been looking forward to finding out what would develop between them.

Jimmy shook his head in sympathy. "You fuck it up already, boy?"

"In record time," he said wryly. If only this conversation would end in record time.

But Jimmy barked out a laugh that was more like a wheeze and reached for his can of beer, cracking it open with one deft hand while handing Nick his bait bucket with the other. "Been there," he said. "The trick is in how you apologize."

"I dunno." Nick rubbed the back of his neck. "I don't think this is something I can fix with 'sorry.'" It had been almost two weeks now since that day at her house when he'd lost his mind, and they hadn't spoken since. He'd seen her, of course—this town was microscopic. But Cassie was impressive, the way she could avoid him like they had all the space in the world. If they were at the grocery store at the same time, she'd linger in the frozen food aisle until he was done with produce. She'd even managed to keep the entire pier between them during the town's Memorial Day picnic.

"Then don't make it about sorry." Jimmy took a swig from his Miller High Life, the gold can glistening in the morning sun. It was noon somewhere, right? "Sometimes it's gotta be more than that."

He pointed at Nick with his beer. "If she's worth it, you'll figure out what that is."

It was very, very early in the morning, and Nick was getting life advice from a borderline alcoholic who probably didn't own shoes. But thankfully the sound of Vince's boat cut through the early morning quiet, and Nick was able to escape, hauling the bait bucket to the boat slips adjacent to the pier. He took a deep breath of salt air and looked out over the water at the sky, pink with dawn. He needed this.

Not that he ever caught anything. But it was an excuse for Vince to get his boat out: a vintage teak Chris-Craft that he'd bought when one of his old songs was used for a commercial, then licensed for a film. There was a cooler full of sandwiches and beer, kept very separate from the bait bucket after one disastrous afternoon a couple years ago. Sometimes they talked, but not always. More often than not Vince sang under his breath as he cast out his line, a hand tapping out the rhythm of one of his old hits against the hull. These days were about enjoying the sunrise: watching the dark indigo of the barely-still-night sky transform slowly to deep pink and finally the blue sky of morning. It was about relishing the quiet morning, the soft lapping of the water against the boat, before the heat set in and ruined everything.

Nick didn't want to talk, as Vince was well aware. They'd already been through everything, over a couple longneck Buds at The Cold Spot one afternoon. No need to hash it all out again. Instead, they cast out their lines and settled down for a leisurely morning.

"Finally saw those guitars that Jo wanted me to look at. She only rescheduled on me twice." Vince took a sip from his travel mug of coffee—not quite time for that first beer of the day yet.

"Yeah?" Nick didn't have anything to say to that, so he just made the appropriate sound, letting Vince keep going.

"Yeah. They're good. The Strat's in amazing shape—I told her she should sell that one online. She'll get more for it than just letting it collect dust in the back of her shop." He fell silent, squinting as he scanned the water, and there was something about his face in the early morning light that reminded Nick that Vince was a lot older than he was. He sometimes forgot that Vince had lived a whole life before moving to this town.

Finally, Vince let out a long breath. "Anyway. None of them were the right one."

"The right one?" That was a new one on Nick. "I thought you were just helping her appraise them. I didn't know you were looking for one yourself." He didn't know shit about music, but that could make sense. Didn't guitarists have collections of favorite instruments?

"You never know." Vince kept his eyes out on the water. "Good to keep your eyes open for the right one. You never know when it's going to come into your life."

Nick made a noncommittal sound and reached for the cooler. Screw it. If Jimmy could have a beer this early, so could he.

After an hour or so of catching nothing, they reeled their lines in and Vince started up the boat again, steering them toward the causeway. The bridge formed an arc over the water, leading away from Boneyard Key and to the highway. Early morning sunlight reflected off tall buildings in the distance. It was getting close to rush hour, and Nick could picture the highway packed with cars, on their way to offices and chain stores. Life and bustle that Nick knew nothing about. That had never been his life.

But it had been Cassie's. A life that she clearly missed. She'd made that clear when she'd started talking about selling her house. Recouping some of her losses.

"You ever miss it?" Nick jerked his head toward the mainland. "City life, bright lights, all that stuff?"

Vince scoffed. "Nah. I mean, I got some good memories, but I like where I am now. Wouldn't trade it for anything."

"Yeah. Not my thing, either." But his gaze lingered. If she chose to return to the life she'd left behind, he wasn't going to try and stop her. He'd forfeited that right on that Tuesday in her kitchen.

Sometimes when he couldn't sleep at night he'd hear himself lashing out, saying shit he'd never meant to say. Stuff he didn't even really believe. He had no idea where any of it had come from; all he could remember was the anger he felt. The angry bees in his chest, the buzzing in his head.

Maybe it had come from her talking about leaving. He looked out toward the bridge again. Just like his family had left. Just like Madison had left. It must have pushed a particular button inside of him. A button that he didn't even know he had.

The morning grew hotter and neither of them had caught anything worth keeping; eventually Vince pointed the boat toward home. As Nick helped him tie it up, a breeze cut across the back of his neck, cold and startling. He looked up sharply at the dark clouds that had gathered just offshore.

Vince saw them too. "Storm's coming. I thought it might. It was getting too damn hot out there today." In contrast, the temperature was now dropping steadily. Time for an afternoon thunderstorm.

It was a good one. Nick had just enough time to return the empty bucket to Jimmy's and get to his apartment over the café before the deluge. While the rain fell, it looked like Armageddon outside, or at least the back half of a hurricane. But within a half hour it was gone; the sun blazed down, drying the puddles from the sidewalks in a matter of minutes. Soon the only remnants of the storm were the remaining clouds that were more of a dirty gray than a fluffy white.

Summertime in Florida. The rainy season was here.

Something Vince had said that day, about waiting for the right one, stuck with him. It stuck with him as he strolled down to The Haunt for a burger, and as he brought two more beers with him to the beach at sunset.

The afternoon storm had left lingering clouds in the sky, just enough to make the sunset spectacular. Colors blazed across the horizon, but Nick picked at the label on his beer, feeling uneasy.

The right one. There was no reason to think that Cassie could be the right one, but something inside him still wondered if she might be. Cassie had cracked open a door in his heart that he'd kept closed for years. She reminded him how it felt to be with someone else and really open up to them. Not for a weekend. Not for a couple weeks on vacation. But day to day. She reminded him how it felt to want to share himself with someone else.

The sunset didn't even look as peaceful anymore without her. Nick levered himself off the edge of the picnic table, dropping easily to the sand. Time to go. He cracked open the last beer, leaving it behind on the table before heading home in the gloaming.

The sun was all but gone, and as Nick hit the sidewalk on Beachside Drive, the streetlights winked on. He paused in front of his café, his gaze traveling up and up, to the window of his tiny apartment. He'd left a light on, but it didn't look cozy or inviting.

Being alone had been a comfort for a long time. Being alone meant you didn't need to depend on anyone else. You couldn't get hurt.

But tonight, Nick didn't like the way being alone felt. It felt too much like being lonely.

Nineteen

It was annoying, honestly. How much the sunset reminded Cassie of Nick.

It had been a long day. Hot and humid, just another Florida day broken up by a midafternoon thunderstorm. From her place at the kitchen table, Cassie could hear the rumble of thunder outside, like a distant promise. That was followed almost immediately by the patter of the first hard raindrops against her window. It would be a perfect day for snuggling under a blanket with a cup of tea and a good book (and the air-conditioning cranked down to a polar setting to justify said blanket), but sadly, she was a grown-up with a job. Life really wasn't fair.

By the time the rain stopped she'd uploaded the last bits of the ad campaign for the granola company, humming "Scarlet Begonias" under her breath as she closed her laptop for the day. She loved days like this, where things were buttoned up by the end of the day and she could check things off her list. To celebrate, she decided to take a glass of wine down to the beach at sunset.

But it wasn't much of a celebration. Sure, the sunset was gorgeous—that was a no-brainer. Cassie watched the colors blaze across the sky and reflect over the water, and she knew she should be grateful.

She *was* grateful. How amazing was it that she lived here, in this little cottage by the water? She'd never dreamed of this as she'd stumbled home to her downtown apartment after yet another girls' night out. She'd had no idea then how much she would love the quiet of the night, the stars, the soft sound of the ocean against the shore practically in her backyard. A Shakespeare quote popped into her mind: "An honor I dream not of." She was pretty sure he was talking about marriage, but it made sense here. Cassie had never imagined a life like this, and now she was living it.

But as she watched the sky darken and the sun disappear beneath the horizon, all she could think about was Nick. They'd watched the sunset together, not too long ago. It had been a perfect evening, and it had felt like a true beginning of something.

What the hell had happened? She took a healthy sip of wine, and her phone weighed heavy in her pocket. Calling him would be so easy, and yet it was impossible. Every passing day widened the gap that had grown between them, and Cassie didn't know if she wanted to bridge it. His outburst hadn't been her fault. Nick had been the one with the attitude, the one to set a match to what they'd been building. Why should *she* be the one to reach out?

She scowled at the last remaining daylight and turned back toward home. She'd only taken a few steps when she heard the footsteps behind her, walking when she walked and then stopping when she stopped. A cold sliver of fear slid down her back before she remembered. The Beach Bum. Ugh. The last thing she wanted at this pity party she was throwing for herself was a tagalong.

"Get lost, Casper." She threw the words over her shoulder and picked up the pace, speed-walking the rest of the way home. The footsteps stopped before she hit her property line, and she immediately felt bad. It wasn't the Beach Bum's fault, was it? And that was all this guy had, following people around on the beach.

Great, she thought as she washed out her wineglass. Something else to feel like shit about.

Cassie distracted herself by opening her mail. It was a good mail day; she'd found an Etsy seller who made customized magnetic words for her refrigerator. The seller probably wondered why Cassie needed words that pertained to home improvement; there probably weren't a lot of people wanting to stick words like "baseboards" or "linoleum" or "carpet" on their refrigerators. But this was exactly what she needed; if Sarah Hawkins wanted to have input on what the house looked like, Cassie needed to communicate with her.

It didn't take long to swap out some of the more esoteric words in her collection, making room on the fridge for the new words. This wasn't about poetry anymore. This was about conversation. Sarah Hawkins hadn't had a voice for a very long time now, and Cassie was going to do her damnedest to let her use it.

"Okay, Sarah. Let's tackle something easy first. Paint colors." She scooped up a handful of paint chips in shades of green and pink that she'd picked up from the hardware store. They each went up on the fridge under a magnet. "Keep the ones you like and toss the rest." Talking to absolutely no one in the middle of her kitchen was getting less weird by the day, and she didn't know how to feel about that.

Speaking of talking to no one . . . before going upstairs for the night, Cassie picked her way across her backyard and to the seawall. She peered out into the darkness, but didn't see anything other than the moon reflecting off the water. No sign of the Beach Bum who'd followed her home.

But just in case . . . "Here." She plonked a bottle of water onto the low wall dividing her house from the beach. "You may not like this as much as beer, but listen. You need to hydrate." Was that true? Did ghosts get dehydrated? She had no idea.

But the bottle of water was gone the next morning.

So were most of the paint chips. Only two remained under their magnets: a soft, barely-there pink and a dark sage green. The rest were scattered on the kitchen floor. The chosen colors coordinated beautifully, which didn't surprise Cassie in the least.

"That works," she said to nobody as she made a tick mark on her mental to-do list. Buster was coming over later this afternoon to talk about renovations, now that she had the magnetic words to use to consult Sarah.

To Buster's credit, he didn't bat an eye when Cassie told him about the ghostly input. "Makes sense" was all he said. "It was her place first."

They made sure to discuss the renovations at her kitchen table, so all of Sarah's contributions could be clearly seen. Cassie and Buster never saw the words on the fridge move, but they also kept themselves from looking there too often. The idea of watching Sarah form her thoughts felt too voyeuristic, too much like watching someone change their clothes. Instead, Cassie left a teaspoon sitting on the table between her and Buster while they discussed what work needed to be done to fix what the flippers had done so shoddily. If Sarah wanted to weigh in, the spoon between them would spin slowly, and they'd both look over to the fridge to see what her thoughts were. (**linoleum ugly never like. carpet go. wood floor nice.**)

She had no opinions on the master bedroom. Cassie asked, more than once, but Sarah's answers were always short and in the negative. **your room now**. She was letting Cassie decorate it the way she wanted, which she appreciated. But she still wasn't sure if she was staying; she may be doing all this work on the house in order to sell it once Sarah was happy. Even so, she decided to paint this master bedroom her favorite color—soft blue and white accents that made it feel like she was falling asleep in a cloud—even if ultimately it was for someone else to enjoy. Or to paint over. She couldn't decide which was worse.

It didn't take long for Buster to become a fixture in the Hawkins House. During the next week he dropped by to tackle some of the smaller things himself. She could finally open her kitchen window, just in time to keep it tightly closed, because it was too damn hot outside and the air conditioner would be running nonstop until at least November. The larger things went on a separate list for him to tackle with his teenage grandsons when they came home for summer break.

"They're great at painting," he said. "Those kids will be able to knock out the living room, and the kitchen if you want it, before you can even blink. And if you're wanting to change out these cabinets, I'll get the boys to help me with all that lifting too." He placed a weathered hand to the small of his back at the thought.

"That'll be great," Cassie said, already picturing the chaos of trying to attend meetings from her laptop in the kitchen while all that was going on. But she couldn't risk unplugging and moving to another room; she didn't have Hallowed Grounds as a backup anymore. So chaos it was.

One evening, she noticed as she took her dinner out of the microwave that there was a new message on the fridge. One thing about ghosts, they were stealthy when they wanted to be.

television island again

"Television . . ." Cassie swore as she peeled back the film from the plastic tray, giving herself both a steam facial and mild first-degree burns. "Island? Do you mean like a kitchen island? We don't have one of those in here. Or a television." She opened the fridge for some water, and when she closed it again there was a new message.

stupid television people

Now it clicked. "Oh, you mean *Romance Resort*?" Great, her ghost was getting hooked on reality television. "You're right, we're behind, aren't we? I think there's a couple episodes saved up." She carried her meal out to the living room; apparently she was eating in front of the TV tonight. "Only one at a time, though. Binge-watching can rot your brain."

After the mediocre microwave lasagna and even more mediocre television, Cassie curled up on the sofa by the front window with *Boneyard Key: A Haunted History*. Reading it felt just like taking the ghost tour. When Sophie had said she'd used the book to create her tour, she hadn't been kidding. Which wasn't necessarily a bad thing; a story was made that much richer, that much more immediate, when you were standing right there where said thing happened. It was a smart business model, and Sophie obviously had a good thing going here.

When she got to the story of Hawkins House, Cassie took a sip of wine and started reading aloud. Because who knew who might be listening. And who could help get the facts straight.

"The Hawkins House was built in 1899 by William Donnelly . . ." Cassie started reading aloud, but it didn't take long for her voice to trail off. Like the rest of this book, it was Sophie's ghost tour verbatim. There was nothing in here that Cassie hadn't heard before. Therefore, there was nothing that Sarah Hawkins hadn't heard before, either.

"Well, that was pointless." She sighed and tossed the book down on the table. "Sorry, Sarah," she called toward the kitchen. "I thought there might be something I didn't already know in there, but it's the same old shit. House was built by William Donnelly, then acquired by your husband. You two moved in, and then a few years later he died. And then . . ." She didn't want to finish the story that was written in the book. How do you tell someone, *You became the town's scary lady in the old house on the corner*? It felt rude, somehow, to point it out to her non-corporeal face.

Something clattered to the floor in the kitchen, and Cassie jumped to sit up straight on the couch. She leaned forward, peering into the kitchen, but she couldn't see anything from that angle. She wasn't scared, she told herself as she went to investigate. Sure, it had gotten dark a little while ago, and sure, her house was confirmed to be haunted. But she and Sarah were watching reality TV together. They were friends now.

The kitchen was empty, and in the dim light from above the stove it took a minute for Cassie to find the spoon. The telltale spoon that sat on the kitchen table. Now it was in the middle of the floor, its filigree handle pointed toward the fridge.

Oh. Cassie swallowed as guilt rushed through her. Sarah had probably been spinning that spoon on the table like mad, but Cassie hadn't seen because she'd been in the other room. She stepped closer to the fridge, to see Sarah's message.

wrong

my house

Cassie sighed. "You said that before. I remember, because it scared the shit out of me. Can you be more specific? When was it your house?" Her mind whirled with possibilities. Had Sarah built this house? Had she bought it?

She didn't even realize she was musing out loud until the spoon bumped lightly against the side of her foot. She looked over at the fridge again. The words **my house** were still there, but now they were followed with **before**.

Okay. Now we were getting somewhere. Maybe. "Like before you and your husband got married? Did you buy it from that Donnelly guy? Could women buy houses in those days?" Cassie wasn't a property law girlie, but she remembered a factoid she'd read online. Something about how women couldn't even get credit cards in their own names until around the 1970s. Was owning a house the same thing? Had Sarah's name been erased in favor of her husband's? Was that what she was so pissed off about for all this time? Being misrepresented in property records?

She deliberately didn't look at the fridge, and waited till the spoon spun again to check for an answer. There were three separate lines this time; Sarah Hawkins was getting more and more verbose.

man closer friend
build house
then me

Cassie stared at those words like they were one of those old-school Magic Eye puzzles, and if she looked at them long enough, they'd make sense.

"Okay, starting with the easiest first. 'Build house, then me.' So that Donnelly guy built the house, then you . . . bought it or whatever. But . . . 'man closer friend' . . ." She sounded out the trio of words, as though that would help them make more sense. It wasn't Sarah's fault; she was limited by the words on the fridge, and could only say so much as a result. Time to go back online and order more packs of words.

There had to be a better way to go about this. Cassie had never been very good at fact-checking—at work that had always been someone else's job. She just wrote the copy. But maybe she could handle this. Maybe she could fact-check Sarah's life.

She had to. Right now Sarah didn't have anyone else in her corner, and from the sounds of it, she hadn't for a long time.

But Cassie was in her corner now. And she was going to see this through. Help the ghost in her house however she could. Thankfully, this damn town was full of ghost experts. She pulled out her phone and sent Libby a text. Only in Boneyard Key could she make an appointment at the local ghost hunter's office for first thing in the morning.

Cassie had high hopes, but the next morning Libby shook her head with a puzzled expression. "'Man closer friend'? What is that supposed to mean?"

"I wish I knew." Cassie had stayed awake far too late last night, trying to connect those words to something, but she'd come up with nothing.

Nothing except the incredible need for caffeine, and the coffee in her cardboard to-go cup was terrible. She took another sip in an act of optimism. Nope. Still awful. She'd stopped by Spooky Brew—the coffee shop next door to Libby's office—on the way over here, and now she understood why Libby walked the extra couple of blocks to Hallowed Grounds.

Cassie sternly reminded herself that she didn't miss Nick, or his excellent coffee. Or his vivid blue eyes, or his smile. Or his hair, that was just long enough to curl along the nape of his neck . . .

Anyway. Screw Nick. Cassie choked down another sip of coffee and forced her brain back on topic. "I was thinking maybe she meant 'boyfriend'? A man that's closer than a friend? But 'love' and 'lover' are right there on the fridge, so I'd think she would have used one of those instead."

"That would make more sense." Libby tapped a pencil against her bottom lip, thinking. "Maybe she meant family? Family is closer than a friend. A man who's closer than a friend, like a brother or cousin or something."

Cassie hadn't considered that; she'd been so stuck on the boyfriend angle. She tried to visualize the words on the fridge—were there any terms for family? She couldn't think of any. Libby may be onto something. She added that to her mental list of custom words to order.

"Well, besides that . . ." Cassie dug in her bag. "I spent the morning doing some research. Property records were a bust; her name doesn't appear anywhere. But she died in the forties, and online searches don't go back that far. Maybe I could go down to the county courthouse? See if there's anything there?"

"Hmm. Maybe." Libby's voice was doubtful. "I'm not sure how helpful it'll be."

"I looked up census records too." Had Cassie done any actual work this morning? No. No, she had not. She'd already resigned herself to catching up on projects later tonight. But this whole thing with Sarah and the house itched in her brain too hard to let it go.

"Oooh. Gimme." Libby stretched out her hands. "Census records are a good start. We do a little genealogy research sometimes, so I could probably do some more digging if it helps."

"That's the 1910 census." Cassie handed it over. "It's got Charles and Sarah living there. And that pointed me to their marriage record." She handed that over too.

"Oh, good. Because from there you can . . ." Libby looked from one document to the other with a frown. "Crap. Never mind."

"Never mind? Never mind what?"

Libby handed the papers back to Cassie with an apologetic look. "Sarah's maiden name is Blankenship. That's not one of the Founding Fifteen. And neither is Hawkins, but we already knew that; Charles came to town a little after 1900."

"Which means?"

"Which means that Sarah must have moved here after the Great Storm. If you research any further back you're leaving Boneyard Key . . ."

"Which isn't helpful." Cassie looked at the papers with a scowl before shoving them back in her bag. "So a dead end, then." She really noticed how many idioms were morbidly themed now that she lived in a haunted town. "I don't suppose your grandmother can come out to the house again? See if Sarah can give her something a little more useful than her preference of wallpaper?"

Libby shook her head as she reached for her cup of coffee. Hers was in a to-go cup from Hallowed Grounds, and Cassie was insanely jealous. But she forced herself to pay attention. "It doesn't work that way. Nan's never able to get more than one visitation from a spirit. It's like a recording just for her, and that's it."

Cassie took a swig of her own coffee; maybe it would taste better once it had cooled off? Nope: lukewarm dirt. "What about you? Maybe you can give it a shot?"

"Me?" A laugh bubbled out of Libby and she shook her head. "That whole 'talking to the dead' gene that the Founding Fifteen have totally skipped me. Skipped my dad too. We think Nan got the last of it, and now the ability in our family is all used up."

Cassie clucked her tongue in sympathy. "That sucks."

"It's okay. That's why I'm the office manager." There was something slightly brittle about her cheerful expression. "I'm able to make myself plenty useful."

"I'm sure." Cassie turned her to-go coffee cup around and around in her hands. It was still half-full; she didn't want to pitch it in Libby's empty wastebasket. She'd have to carry it home with her and dump it there.

"You know what you need . . ." Libby picked up her pencil again, twirling it in her fingers before tapping the eraser end on her desk. "You need someone that was around when Sarah was alive."

If that were said in any other town, it would be a joke. Hilarious. *Yeah, let me just find the nearest centenarian and see what they can tell me.* Florida was full of old people, but that was pushing it.

But of course, this was Boneyard Key. All she needed to find was a ghost that was easy to communicate with that had been alive back then. Cassie's gaze drifted to Libby's Hallowed Grounds cup as a terrible idea began to form. This was probably a mistake, but what the hell. At least she'd get a decent cup of coffee.

Twenty

Nick's days and nights had started to bleed together in a way they had never done before Cassie moved to town. He could call her. In fact he *should* call her, but then there was that whole "what would he say" thing, which always stumped him. And then a few more days went by, long days at the café becoming long nights alone.

Busy mornings helped. More and more tourists were stopping by in the morning as the summer heated up, and most of the banana bread and muffins had been sold. But like clockwork, he glanced up to the door around ten thirty. Sure, Cassie hadn't come through that door for a while now, but he couldn't help it. This late-morning dead time had become Cassie's time. When she'd breeze in with her perpetually dead laptop and beg for a latte and an outlet.

Ramon had given him shit about it for a couple of days—the record amount of time it had taken for Nick to screw things up with her. But the longer Cassie's absence went on, the less frequent the jokes became when it was apparent that it was no longer funny. Even Elmer had stopped bringing it up, and Elmer liked bothering Nick about *everything*. Nick's life plodded on, and Cassie just became yet another person who didn't stay in it.

But she hadn't left yet. Buster's truck had been in her driveway more often than not, so she was still fixing up her house. He hadn't lost her for good. *The trick is in how you apologize,* wasn't that what Jimmy had said? Nick thought again about those shiny glass buildings on the other side of the causeway, the life Cassie had left behind. An idea dropped fully formed into his head, and he knew. He just *knew* how he could show her that he knew her. That he listened. That he wasn't that guy in her kitchen a couple weeks ago.

He had some errands to run after work. Get what he needed, *then* call her.

The bell above his door chimed, interrupting his gloomy thoughts, and at first all he could do was blink. It took a moment or two to realize that Cassie was really in his doorway. She wasn't a mirage conjured by his lonely heart.

"Hey." She hiked her bag up on her shoulder and glanced around.

"Hey." His voice felt rusty, like he hadn't used it in a while. He cleared his throat hard while Cassie cast cautious glances around the café. What was she looking for? Witnesses, in case he started berating her out of the blue again?

But then she took a sidestep toward the trash can by the door, furtively tossing in a blue take-out cup. Spooky Brew? She'd gotten coffee at Spooky Brew? Damn, she must really hate him; their coffee sucked.

They stared at each other for a few awkward moments until the door behind Cassie crashed open, the bell over it ringing frantically. Cassie jumped and whirled as Ramon came barreling through the door.

"Whoa!" He stopped himself with a hand on Cassie's shoulder, and Nick had never been jealous of someone else's clumsiness before. Ramon looked from Cassie over to where Nick stood behind the counter, then sagged with exaggerated relief.

"Thank God you're here," he said dramatically. "Look, I don't know what my man here did, and I'm sure he deserves you being pissed at him. But please, I'm begging you. Tell him how to fix it. I'm so sick of the moping."

Nick rolled his eyes. "I don't mope." He tried not to notice Cassie suppressing a smile.

"You mope." Ramon grabbed a clean apron from under the counter and started into the kitchen.

"You're fired!" Nick called after him.

"No, I'm not!" The swinging door bumped closed behind him, leaving Cassie and Nick alone again.

The awkward silence persisted. "Hey," Cassie said again.

"Hey." This was going great. But she was still here, so maybe this was an olive branch? Maybe she was here to bury the hatchet? Hopefully not in his face?

"You . . . ah." Cassie's stroll to the counter was overly casual. "You don't have any banana bread left, do you?"

"Sure do. It's just plain, though. I hope that's okay." He hadn't been able to touch the cinnamon recently. "You want a latte to go with it? I know for a fact that Spooky Brew can't pull a shot of espresso to save their life."

A tentative laugh burst from her, and the sound released some of the tension in Nick's shoulders. "Yeah." She glanced over her shoulder to the trash can, and when she looked back at him there was a hint of a smile in her eyes. "Yeah, that would be great."

Nick tried to act casual, but it was hard when just a small smile from her made him feel like he'd won the lottery. "You got it." He glanced back at her while she fiddled with her bag. Silence settled between them again, broken up only by the hiss of the espresso machine.

Cassie didn't look at him. She looked out the front window, down at the counter. She didn't move to that back table. She didn't get out her laptop and plug it in. "I should probably take it to go," she finally said. "I've got a ton of work to catch up on."

"Oh. Sure." Nick told himself not to be disappointed even as his heart plunged down into his shoes. There was no reason for him to expect things to just snap back to how they'd been. Just because she came by for some decent coffee didn't mean she was here to hang out in her satellite office in his café.

"No, I mean, I just . . . I didn't bring my laptop." Cassie shifted from one foot to the other. "I wasn't planning to come by here."

"And then you had the coffee at Spooky Brew and changed your mind?" Nick reached for a cardboard to-go cup and purposely didn't look to see how his joke landed.

She didn't respond at first, but when he turned around she looked rueful. "Their coffee really sucks," she finally confessed, the laugh escaping her sounding more like a sigh as her shoulders relaxed.

"You gotta come here to get the good stuff." He smiled down at the cup as he swirled in the milk. He didn't bother with latte art since he was popping a lid over the top of it.

"Don't I know it." Cassie took the coffee and the slice of banana bread he'd wrapped up for her. She tucked the banana bread into her bag and came out with her wallet.

Nick waved off her gesture to pay. "No charge." He took a deep breath. It was now or never. "Consider it a long overdue apology for the things I said. I was a dick that day. I'm really sorry."

"Yeah." Cassie watched him carefully as she put her wallet away. He wasn't sure if she was agreeing to accept his apology, or simply agreeing that he'd been a dick. Or both; that was certainly an option.

"I don't know what happened. Maybe Sarah was messing with me, I don't know. I can't explain away what I said, but I promise I didn't mean it. I'm so sorry for hurting you, Cassie. I swear I'm not that kind of guy." He paused. "Which is, of course, exactly what someone who *is* that guy would say. But seriously, ask anyone. Ask Ramon back there—" He jerked a thumb over his shoulder. "Ask Sophie. Or Libby."

"I know." Cassie sighed. "They've already stuck up for you. Well, not Ramon. I haven't asked him. But . . ." She seemed to think for a moment before nodding decisively. "I'm actually here to ask a favor."

God, yes, anything. Nick clamped down on his back teeth to keep from sounding too desperate. "Anything you want." Perfect. Great job of not sounding desperate.

Cassie raised an eyebrow. "Anything? What if it's illegal?" A teasing smile played around her lips—the best thing he'd seen all day.

Nick leaned his elbows on the counter, staring right into her eyes. "Anything," he repeated.

She broke the stare first, fiddling with the strap of her bag again. "You said Elmer died in the year 2000, right?" Nick nodded at the non sequitur, but Cassie wasn't done. "Do you know how old he was when he died?"

Nick's phone buzzed in his back pocket almost immediately, and he fought to keep his face impassive. Elmer chiming in already. But Cassie was finally talking to him again. Nick wasn't interrupting this conversation for anything. "I'm not sure exactly, but at least eighty? Maybe eighty-five?"

Cassie appeared to do some quick math in her head, then her eyes lit up. "Okay, that might work."

"Work for what?" His phone buzzed again, and Nick considered throwing it in the trash.

"Well, you know how you and Elmer text?"

"Painfully aware of it," he said as his pocket buzzed again and again.

Another smile. Even a little bit of a laugh this time. "And it happens pretty regularly, right?"

Now he let himself chuckle with the irony. "Most days."

"You can just text him whenever you feel like it?"

"Huh." He'd never thought about that before. "Elmer usually texts me first. Does that matter?"

"Maybe not." But the answer was more of a question. Cassie took a deep breath; Nick could tell that this was her gearing up for the actual favor. "Do you think he might have known Sarah Hawkins?"

Oh, wow. Something else he'd never considered. He knew that the ghosts in town had been real people with real lives, but he'd never thought about their lives before their deaths. Who they'd known. How far back their history went.

And Elmer . . . of course Nick had known him when he was a kid. But Elmer had always been that old man who ran the café. Boneyard Key was a small town, though, and the history didn't span very many generations. So it stood to reason . . .

"If he was in his eighties when he died," Nick spoke while he thought, working out the math in his head, "he would have been born, what, before 1920? So yeah, that sounds like they might have overlapped. When did she die again?"

"Sometime in the 1940s." Enthusiasm lit up her eyes; he'd obviously answered correctly. "So the favor . . . Do you think you could ask Elmer about her? And that maybe he'd answer? I'm trying to piece together more information about her life, but it's hard to come by, and her vocabulary is pretty limited. You know, the words on the fridge."

"I'm aware." His voice was brittle; he remembered the words on her fridge. **get him out**. Yeah, he remembered those words all too well. Nan might think that Sarah Hawkins was a gentle spirit, but she'd manifested as Mean Mrs. Hawkins to Nick; she was obviously not a fan of his. What had he done to offend her? Had his grandpa pissed her off a few decades back or something?

Cassie's expression softened; she remembered the words too. "What I mean is, there's only so much she can tell me. I get it; Sarah isn't your favorite person right now, but do you think . . . ?"

"Sure," Nick answered immediately. He wasn't going to hold a grudge against a ghost. That would just be petty. "Believe me, if there's one thing Elmer likes to do, it's talk. If he knows anything about Mrs. Hawkins, it'll be harder to get him to shut up." The phone buzzed in his pocket again as if to illustrate his point, but Elmer could wait. This conversation was a hell of a lot more important. "I'll ask him about Sarah under one condition."

The enthusiasm drained from Cassie's eyes, replaced by suspicion. Oh, no. That wasn't the look he wanted to put on her face. "What's the condition?"

His heart pounded as he took the leap. "Have dinner with me. Let me prove to you that I'm not that guy." Nick held his breath. This was his chance. If she said no, he wasn't going to ask again. He wasn't *that* guy, either. If a girl said no, she said no.

Cassie took a cautious sip of her latte, considering. "Sophie and Libby really like you. You've got some good friends there."

That wasn't a yes. But it also wasn't a no. "I really do." He cocked an eyebrow. "So . . . ?"

She studied him carefully. Nick wasn't sure what she was looking for in his face, but she must have found it, because her sigh ended with a cautious smile. "Okay."

Relief swept through him. He was going to get a chance to make this right. "Okay. Meet me here at eight."

"We're eating here?" She raised her eyebrows, and her flirty smile was the best thing he'd seen in weeks. "Nick Royer, are you gonna cook for me?"

He shook his head. "I'm a shitty cook, believe me. You don't want that."

"You don't want that!" Ramon called from the back, and Nick hung his head. Of course he'd heard everything. He should be annoyed, but he was in too good a mood now. She'd said yes. The whole café could catch on fire for all he cared.

"See?" Nick gestured behind him.

She held up a placating hand, that smile still lighting up her face. "Okay, I believe you. See you tonight."

The bell over the door chimed as she left, and Ramon came out, leaning in the doorway to the kitchen as they both watched her head up the street. Then he turned back to Nick with a grin. "Niiiiiice."

Nick rolled his eyes. If it wasn't Elmer bothering him about his love life, it was Ramon. "Shut the hell up."

"I'm just saying, that was smooth. Help her out, get her to agree to a date in return." He held out a hand for a fist bump. "Good job, man."

Nick did not fist bump back.

It wasn't until lunch was almost over that he remembered his phone and pulled it out of his pocket. His home screen was entirely covered with texts. What a surprise.

Almost eighty-five. I died the day before my birthday. How's that for a kick in the ass?

Ask her out! I know you fucked it up before, but try try again!

ASK HER OUT YOU DUMBASS

Of course I remember Mrs. Hawkins. Ask me anything. Isn't that what the kids say? Hahahahaha

> ASK HER

> Oh you asked her out. Good job!

> Please don't cook for her

Nick cleared away all the notifications with a chuckle. Thanks, he typed. I'll get back to you about Mrs. H after tonight.

Tonight. The word had never felt so good.

Twenty-One

Cassie should have said no.

Yes, she wanted to help Sarah Hawkins. And sure, going through Nick to talk to (text to?) Elmer may have been the only way to accomplish that, short of putting the *Oxford English Dictionary* on her fridge, one word at a time. But on the face of it, going out with Nick again was a bridge too far. She'd written the guy off in her head a while back, and there was no point in letting him back in.

But there was something about the way his face had lit up when she'd walked through the door of Hallowed Grounds that morning. Like she was a miracle, and all he wanted was the chance to bask in her miracle-ness. He'd missed her.

And fine, she'd missed him too.

Besides, the man made damn good coffee. Whenever Cassie started to reconsider her date that night, she remembered the atrocity that was Spooky Brew's dark roast and did a full-body shudder.

She wasn't going to dress up, though, she told herself as she changed her earrings for the third time. She'd been in Boneyard Key long enough to know that there wasn't much around here worth dressing up for. No five-star restaurants, no jacket or tie required. Cute shorts and sneakers would get her in anywhere in town.

Nick was waiting for her right at eight, leaning against the wall

near the darkened entrance of Hallowed Grounds. He looked so
much like he had the night they'd gone on the ghost tour together
that she thought she'd gone back in time. He wore jeans and work
boots but he'd changed his shirt to a gray button-down. The sleeves
were rolled up, and he had a large bag slung over one shoulder.

"We going on a road trip?" She indicated the bag.

He huffed out a laugh, pushing off the wall and glancing down at
the bag as though he just noticed it was there. "No. No, this is dinner." Now that he was close, she could see it was an insulated bag,
sagging with the weight of its contents. "Don't worry. I didn't cook."

"What is it?" She reached for the bag as though he'd hand it
over. She knew better, and he shook his head.

"It's a surprise." His hand moved as though he wanted to hold it
out for her to take, but then he dropped it. They weren't there yet.
Not by a long shot. But Cassie fell into step next to him on the sidewalk as he led them in the opposite direction from her house, past
The Haunt and down the street. The lights to Poltergeist Pizza flick-
ered; the delivery guy must have felt like working tonight.

She knew where they were going right away, once they hit the
sidewalk that snaked between the buildings and toward the water.
Eventually the concrete of the sidewalk gave way to sand, until her
Keds began to sink gently into the earth with each step. It didn't take
long for them to reach the clutch of picnic tables, where they'd
watched the sunset together before.

Nick set the bag down and Cassie took a seat on the opposite side
from him. After unzipping it, he pulled out a six-pack of beer in
green glass bottles. "I couldn't remember if you were a beer person
or not," he said apologetically. "I've got some sweet tea in here too,
and some waters." He popped the top off one of the beers, setting it
to the side. For the Beach Bum. Of course. Cassie liked that she
knew that. It made her feel like a local.

"I like that you thought ahead. I'll take a tea." He passed her one, a plastic bottle with a blue label. Cassie blinked at it; this was a Publix label.

When she looked up, Nick was holding his own bottle of tea toward her in a mock toast. She tapped the mouth of her plastic bottle to his, and they each took a sip.

As Nick turned his attention back to his bag, Cassie stretched up on her toes, leaning across the table in an attempt to see what else he'd brought. But Nick caught her, narrowing his eyes and tugging the bag a few inches closer to his side of the table.

"No peeking," he chided, but he didn't keep the secret long as he kept unpacking. Food now: potato salad and pasta salad in little plastic containers. More Publix labels: the packaging was as familiar as the back of her hand. But her heart absolutely soared when he drew out two oblong, paper-wrapped packages.

"Are those *Publix subs*?" She couldn't keep the squeal out of her voice or the excitement out of her body as she practically scrambled on top of the table to get to them.

"Wait, wait!" But Nick was laughing as he held the sandwiches over his head, out of reach. "This one's yours." He handed her one of the paper sleeves. "I hope I got the order right."

Cassie plopped to the picnic bench with her prize, sliding the sandwich from its sleeve and unwrapping the familiar logo-ed deli paper. She groaned in ecstasy as the sandwich was unwrapped. "Look at you, beautiful." The chicken tenders had been tossed in the perfect amount of buffalo sauce, the veggies were crisp, the bread was fresh and soft . . . this was a perfect Publix sub. She picked up one of the halves and took a bite. It was sensory overload: the spicy-tangy taste of the buffalo sauce exploding across her tongue, the pillowy bread giving way to the crunch of the fried chicken and veggies.

"Oh my god." She held a hand to her mouth while she chewed. "This is amazing." A Publix sub was something she used to grab once a week or so, usually when she was grocery shopping anyway because the last thing you wanted to do after unloading groceries was cook. But she hadn't had one in a while now, so the nostalgia of it made her eyes mist over.

"Should I leave you two alone?"

Oh, right. For a moment there she'd forgotten that Nick was across the table from her, one eyebrow raised while she shoved a sandwich into her mouth.

"Where did you get this?" She took a swig of iced tea, sweet and cold, the perfect complement to the sandwich. "There isn't a Publix anywhere nearby."

"In town? No, there isn't." He nodded in confirmation. "But there's one on the other side of the causeway, down the highway a ways."

Cassie stopped chewing as his words sank in. She knew where he meant; she'd driven past that shopping center more than once, on her move out here and more recently when she'd had to hit a big-box hardware store. But Nick was downplaying his effort; he'd driven at least an hour to get there. Each way. To pick up her favorite sandwich. He'd gotten her order exactly right and she'd told him about it once, some several weeks ago.

This wasn't just a sandwich. It was an apology. A declaration. Somehow that made it—and Nick—even more delicious.

While she'd been pigging out on her sub, Nick had sat down across from her, his back to the water, unwrapping his own sub and cracking open the potato salad—the yellow kind, with the egg. He'd gotten that right too. Cassie's heart swelled as Nick glanced up at her with an apprehensive smile.

"Thank you." She tried to imbue as much meaning as she could into the words. He'd gone to a lot of trouble to show her how much he meant his apology. She needed him to know that the effort wasn't wasted.

Nick ducked his head, pink flushing the tops of his cheeks. "Of course."

He suddenly seemed very far away, all the way across the table like that. "You know, this sunset's shaping up to be a great one. But you've got your back to it." She patted the seat next to her in invitation, and he raised his eyebrows.

"Yeah?" The flash of hope in his eyes was humbling, and Cassie smiled.

"Yeah."

It took less than a minute for Nick to switch sides, tugging his sandwich across the table by one corner of the waxed paper. Cassie took the opportunity to check out his sandwich—knowing someone's Publix sub order was important. It was a key insight into their character.

But she frowned at what she saw. "You don't like chicken tenders?" His sub looked like a classic Italian combo, made up of cold cuts and veggies, loaded down with an herbal dressing. Which was fine, but . . . it wasn't a chicken tender sub.

"I do." He shrugged. "But we're the opposite here. The fried chicken at The Haunt has spoiled me for all other chicken, while Publix did the same for you. I almost went with the Cuban, but—"

Cassie made a noise of acknowledgment while she chewed and swallowed. "No, you gotta have the right kind of bread for a Cuban."

"Exactly. I didn't want to chance it. I figured I couldn't go wrong with an Italian sub."

Cassie gave a hum of assent around another bite of her sandwich. "I still have to try The Haunt's chicken. Tuesdays, you said, right?" Nick nodded while chewing, his eyes carefully on the sunset in progress over the water and not on her. She understood. He'd made this apology, but he wasn't going to push further. It was her turn. "Maybe we can do that sometime soon?"

He looked at her then, and she held her breath as he swallowed his bite and took a long drink of tea. "Just be prepared to have your life changed."

"I can't think of a way that my life hasn't changed recently. What's one more?"

Nick gave a bark of laughter, the sound so unexpected that she grinned to hear it. "Good point," he said. He handed her a plastic fork from the bag and offered her the carton of potato salad. They passed it back and forth, eating in silence, letting the crash and hiss of the waves against the shore fill the quiet between them, while the sun setting over the water provided a show of its own.

Nick cracked open a beer and cleared his throat. When he finally spoke his voice was soft, hard to hear over the sounds of the ocean. "Growing up, there was this girl. Madison."

Cassie gave a start of recognition. Libby and Sophie had told her this story already. But she should let him tell it too. It was his story, after all.

He didn't look at Cassie while he talked; he sipped at his beer and kept his eyes on the sunset. "We knew each other all our lives— most kids do when you grow up here—but I don't think we really noticed each other till we were in high school. Then she became everything. You know how it is."

Cassie made a murmur of agreement. "First love is powerful." She got that. They imprinted on you, shaped your DNA, made you part of the adult you are today.

"We stayed together through college, at least I thought we did." Bitterness crept into his voice then, and Cassie glanced over, trying to read his face in the growing dark.

"That doesn't sound good."

"It wasn't." Nick sighed. "I thought the plan was college, then back here to Boneyard Key. My family's lived here as long as I can remember. So has hers."

"Founding Fifteen, both of you?"

Nick nodded. "There's a responsibility that comes with that. This whole ghost thing . . . before it was a way to sell T-shirts, it was . . . it's always been something real. And kind of sacred. My roots, you know? This town is special, and that means a lot to me." He paused for so long that Cassie wondered if she was supposed to say something. He studied his hands, ignoring the blazing sunset in front of them.

"Madison didn't think the same way," he finally said. "She felt trapped here. She went off to college and for her it was a way out. She couldn't wait to get out of this town and start her life. Leaving Boneyard Key was when her life began—those were her exact words."

"A life without you," Cassie said quietly. She didn't feel jealous.

"Yep. That's what she wanted. A life without this town. Which meant a life without me. But she didn't want to tell me. She was putting it off. Putting *me* off. First it was both of us going to college. Then she wanted her master's degree. Then a doctorate . . ." A muscle jumped in his cheek as his face clouded over with memory. Suddenly his rant about women and careers, as misogynistic as it was, made a little bit of sense. It was no excuse, but she could see now that his words were coming from a place of deep hurt.

Nick continued. "That was fine, you know. I get wanting an education, and ambition is good. But all this time I thought we were moving forward together. I waited for her, while she was off getting these advanced degrees. But it turned out she'd left me years ago. Left me behind. She just never bothered to actually tell me. It was . . ." His voice trailed off as he stared unseeing at the sunset, his eyes unfocused, lost for the moment in memory. Then he blinked and met Cassie's eyes with a small, sad smile. "Well, it sucked, obviously."

Cassie was startled into a snort. "Obviously."

"So I was back home, living with my parents, still trying to figure out what I was going to do. And then they dropped the bomb—they were moving. Dad's a tax accountant, and they were getting more and more clients in The Villages, so it just made sense for them to move there. They were about that age anyway."

"Sure." But she got where that was going. Nick, as a young man in his twenties, would have no desire to move to a retirement community. To spend his days driving around the place in a golf cart and playing bingo.

"Right before they moved, Elmer's place shut down again . . . It had gone through a bunch of owners since he died, and the place just couldn't stay open. The last guy was some entrepreneur from out of town, selling the business for a song. I thought, making coffee's pretty easy . . ." This time his smile reached his eyes, in response to Cassie's laugh. "Elmer texted me the first day I got the keys, and then it all made sense. Why all these out-of-towners couldn't make the business work. They didn't know how to deal with Elmer. Or the Beach Bum. Or any of it. But I did. It was like . . . confirmation that I belong here. That Boneyard Key is my home, and I did the right thing by staying here."

He gave a long sigh, and all trace of a smile was wiped from his face. "That's the only reason I can think of for why I acted the way I did at your house. Why I lost my shit. It was like you couldn't wait to leave here too. But the things I said, that's not me."

"I know." She laid a hand on his arm. The cotton of his shirt was crisp and his skin was warm underneath. His biceps tensed under her hand, then relaxed.

"I appreciate that." He turned his head to look at her, and even in the almost-dark, his eyes were so easy to get lost in. She didn't know what it was about this guy, but being with him felt like coming home after a long day. How could this Madison chick want to give this up? Give him up?

So she let herself thread her arm through his, hugging him to her side. She let herself lay her head on his shoulder, looking out toward the water and the last remnants of sunset. She let herself forgive him. Because it really seemed like he could use a break.

Nick tilted his head, laying his cheek on top of her head. She felt more than heard his sigh. "The sunsets look so much better with you." The words were little more than breath, stirring her hair.

"I couldn't agree more." Her voice was an answering murmur. She could live the rest of her life in this one moment and be perfectly content.

But Nick's mind was still on that one terrible afternoon. "The worst part," he said, "was your face. I can close my eyes and still see how you looked at me. I never want to put that look on your face again."

Cassie remembered that moment too; it was like all the blood had drained from her face, her chest. She'd been frozen, unable to move but so cold at the same time. He'd been talking about a woman giving her husband children as though it were the only thing they were good for.

As long as they were sharing their core wounds . . . "I can't have kids." The words fell out of her mouth and seemed to hang in the air between them. "It's a whole medical thing that I usually don't bring up on dates."

His brow furrowed and he turned his head away from the sunset and toward her, his expression darkening with concern. "Are you okay? Like . . . healthy?"

"Oh. Yeah, I'm totally fine," she rushed to reassure him. "There's just . . . certain parts that don't work properly." She gestured around her abdomen in a wide arc. "Not accommodating to growing babies." Now she knew why she didn't bring this up on dates. Ovarian cysts and endometriosis weren't sexy under the best of circumstances. But Nick had just told her some hard truths of his own, she may as well share hers.

Cassie took a deep breath. "It was fine in my twenties," she said. "I was working on my career, getting established and all that. The last thing on my mind was starting a family. But the thing about being a woman in your thirties is that being a mom becomes the default to the rest of the world. All your friends are doing it, and before you know it, babies are the main topic of conversation, and you can't relate. More and more you get these targeted ads geared toward 'busy moms'—like you can't be busy if you aren't one." Her sinuses started to tingle, and she blinked fast against threatening tears. "It's one thing to not want kids. But it's another when you don't even get to decide. When everyone around you is starting a family, you're just left there. Feeling defective."

"Hey." Nick's hand covered hers. Squeezing lightly, sending reassurance her way. "There's nothing defective about you. Not a damn thing."

Cassie sniffed once and knuckled the emerging tears from her eyes. Enough. She was not the self-pitying type. She tried for a laugh, but it came out choked. "That's not what you said that day. That's what hit me so hard, and hurt so much."

His hand tensed on her arm. "I swear to God that wasn't me. That day, at your house, I wondered who was saying those things, and why they had my voice." He shook his head as he stared out at the water. "I don't think those things. I'm not the family-and-babies type, either."

"I buy that," she said. "Libby and Sophie . . . they said you don't do relationships. Ever since the thing with Madison. Is that . . . ? Do you . . . ?" She hated to bring it up, but if he was going to bring her Publix subs and say nice things about her and watching sunsets together, they should probably figure out where they wanted to take this once and for all.

Nick got where she was going with her question. He straightened up, and while he didn't exactly pull away from her, she dropped her arm and sat up straight too. "They're right," he said. "It's hard, dating in a town where you've grown up with damn near everyone and they know your entire life story." He studied his hands, picking at his cuticles. "Apparently I'm more of a situationship kind of guy."

"Situationship," Cassie repeated. She could feel her eyebrows crawling up her forehead.

"That's what I've been told. You know. A little more than a one-night stand, a little less than going home to meet the parents. If someone's in town for a week or two, I show her a good time, and . . ."

"And then she goes home. No mess, no commitment."

"It's just easier to not get involved," Nick said. Then his eyes went wide as he turned to her. "I mean, it's nothing personal. Nothing against you. You're great. You're more than great. I just . . ."

"I get it," she said even as her heart fell. But she couldn't expect any promises of a real future with this guy when she couldn't promise the same. She didn't know if she was sticking around herself.

"Here's the thing," she continued, steeling her courage. "I like you, Nick."

His eyes softened, and his quick intake of breath at her words lifted her soul. "I like you too." He dropped a hand to hers, tangling their fingers together. "More than I've liked anyone in a long time."

"Then how about this: we take it day by day. No strings. No pressure." She wanted to cringe at how pragmatic she sounded. She could be running a meeting instead of proposing a relationship. "What do you think?"

"Yeah?" Nick studied her face, and Cassie met his eyes with her own.

"Yeah. Let's see where this goes." Maybe this was the right move for both of them. Neither of them was in the position, physically or emotionally, to promise anything.

Darkness had fallen around them while they talked, and now the sole light blinked on behind them, breaking whatever spell had fallen over them both. Cassie threw away the trash of their picnic while Nick packed away the leftovers.

"Wait." She held out a hand as he started to zip his insulated bag closed. "Did you say you had some waters in there?"

"Oh. Yeah." He reached in, handing her a bottle. "Here you go. This one's still cold."

"It's not for me." She opened it, tossing the cap into the trash. Then she set it on the edge of the table, next to the beer Nick had left out for the Beach Bum when they'd first arrived.

"What . . ." Nick's brow furrowed. "What the hell is that?" he asked, as though he hadn't just handed the bottle to her.

"Water," she said primly.

"For the Beach Bum?" Nick shook his head. "He likes beer. You're doing it wrong."

But Cassie waved him off as they started up the beach. "Nah. He likes it. Trust me."

Twenty-Two

Nick was sure he was dreaming and would wake up soon in his bed. There was no other way to explain it.

He walked down the beach, an arm around Cassie's shoulders. The darkness around them had done nothing to relieve the heat of the day, but she was snuggled against his side as though she needed him to keep warm. Their walk home was illuminated by the moon, bright and nearly full. It shone off the water and on the wet sand they walked on. The world was dark yet bright at the same time, and the glow felt like something warm and alive.

Nick had tried not to hope for much from this evening. Clearing the air between them at best, hearing that she never wanted to speak to him again at the worst. His brain was especially good at the worst-case scenarios. But reality had blown his pessimism out of the water.

She got him. She really did. She understood his reluctance for relationships, and she was okay with it. Relief had loosened something in his chest, and he felt like he was able to take a good deep breath for the first time in a long time.

In fact, it wasn't until they were halfway to Cassie's house, the soft steps of the Beach Bum behind them (apparently he was okay with bottled water, like Cassie had said), that he remembered the other reason for seeing her tonight.

"So. Ah . . . Elmer let me know that he knew Sarah Hawkins."

"Oh! He did?" Cassie stopped walking, pulling him to a halt. Her eyes were wide with surprise. "I . . . I forgot all about that. What is wrong with me?" She gave a rueful laugh. "God, dangle a chicken tender sub in front of my face and my priorities go right to hell."

"I'll keep that in mind." He dodged her good-natured swat, his smile widening. "He said you could ask him anything."

"That would be great. There's so much I don't know." He could see the wheels turning in her head. Checklists and plans being made in real time while he watched. "There's Sarah herself, her house. The way it used to look. I really want to do right by her, but she's not the most forthcoming." She shook her head. "It doesn't help that I think she's getting hooked on reality TV. It's distracting her a little bit."

"Hooked on what?" That was a new one. Or was it? Was Elmer looking over Nick's shoulder when he watched TV alone at night? He probably wasn't as alone as he thought he was.

Cassie didn't answer at first, an embarrassed flush coming over her cheeks that he could see even in the dark. "I'm not going to apologize for watching reality television," she finally said.

"Nor should you." He kept his voice even. Calm. Free of judgment.

"It's excellent brain candy after a long day of work."

"I'm sure it is." It had never been Nick's thing. Something about women fighting each other, and roses? And flipping tables?

"But Sarah is getting a little too into it. I try to ask her if she likes the cabinet handles I picked out, and she's all, *When are we watching* Romance Resort? I told her: all that TV is gonna rot her brain." She paused. "Do ghosts have brains left to rot?"

"I try not to think too hard about stuff like that." He had, once upon a time. But the logistics of ghosts and how they existed gave him a headache.

"Probably wise."

"If I can help at all . . . I dunno, about talking to spirits, how to communicate, how to feel about what they say . . ." He tried to make his shrug as casual as his tone. "You know where to find me."

"You make it sound so easy. Talking to the dead. Getting first-hand accounts of things that happened a century ago."

"Like I said, try not to think about it." A smile tugged at his lips. "Going with the flow is the key to sanity around here."

A laugh spilled from her, and she bumped his arm with her shoulder. "I missed you."

Oh. Nick wasn't prepared for how that simple statement rushed through his blood, made everything inside him feel a little more urgent, a little more . . . *more.* "I missed you too. It had become the best part of my day, seeing you walk through the door."

"I'll have to start coming by the café again, then. But only if you start putting the cinnamon back in the banana bread."

"Done." They started walking again, her arm wrapped around his, and of course the footsteps behind them started up again too. Nick spared a fleeting thought for the Beach Bum, hanging around all this time while they talked.

Cassie did too. "Was he just standing behind us, waiting for us to start walking again?"

"Maybe."

She gave him a sideways glance. "You really don't think about this stuff too hard, do you?"

"I try not to," he said. Was he wrong for thinking that way? Should he be more like Cassie, questioning everything and trying to learn all the *why*s for every spirit that lingered here in town?

She was quiet for a minute. "I want to think about what to ask Elmer," she finally said. "Do you think I could come by in a day or two? Is that okay?"

"Come by anytime you want," Nick said, and he meant it. The morning rush, the lunchtime crowd, three in the morning. He would welcome her anytime. "I can't text him right this second, anyway. He only manifests at the café. Or the apartment over the café. The building itself seems to be his domain. Anywhere else is out of range for him."

"Out of range? So, like, the café is the only place he gets any bars?"

Nick had to chuckle. "Something like that. That place was his life. His afterlife too, I guess."

"And he's okay as a roommate? No bumps in the night?"

"Nah. The only thing I have to do is make coffee for him sometimes."

"Do I want to know how a ghost drinks coffee?"

"He doesn't drink it. He just likes the smell. You know, when you grind beans fresh, and then brew a new pot? He loves that."

"He's not wrong; that's the best smell in the world."

Nick had to agree. "Yeah. So I don't mind too much."

"You must drink a lot of coffee, then."

"I don't always drink it." His stomach churned at the thought. "Usually I'll grind up just a little. Brew up a cup or two, enough to keep him happy."

"You're very good to your ghost," she said primly. Her hand slid down his arm to catch his.

Nick threaded his fingers through hers and held on tight. "I try."

This was so nice. Everything felt easy with Cassie now that they'd cleared the air. Which was why Nick couldn't explain how, once they'd cut through the break in the seawall and made their way back to the sidewalk, his shoulders began to tense up. That tight feeling in his chest, which had been easing all evening, suddenly made itself known again.

"You okay?" Cassie's voice was concerned.

"Yeah." But he was gripping her hand tighter, his whole body practically radiating tension. He didn't get it. They'd cleared the air. They were starting over. No pressure. No strings. That was what he wanted, and she was fine with it. There was absolutely nothing to be nervous about.

His steps slowed as they approached Cassie's house and she opened the latch at her front gate. He couldn't get enough air around the boulder that had set up residence in his chest. Cassie went through the front gate and though he tried to follow, he didn't get far. The static in his head was back, growing with every step until it was an almost unbearable din, filling him with an anxiety-fueled anger. It was just like last time, just like . . .

He stopped walking, watching her start up the front steps. She was halfway up before she turned around.

"Hey." She went back down the steps to where he stood on the front walkway. "You okay?" She'd asked that twice in, what, two minutes? He needed to get it together.

"Yeah," he said, when everything inside him said *no*. There was a hell of a lot of emotion coming from that house, all aimed at him with the delicacy of a firehose. There was no way he could step foot in that house. "I think . . . I think Mrs. Hawkins doesn't like me much." He spoke carefully; the last thing he wanted to do was spook Cassie. Make her think her house was threatening, when she had to go inside and live there. She couldn't see what he could, didn't feel what he did. It was like the house was threatening him personally.

"Still?" Cassie gave an annoyed sigh as she looked over her shoulder at her house. He tried to see it through her eyes. The porch lights were on, as well as the light in the upstairs windows. The house looked inviting, serene. Except for the buzzing in his head. The buzzing told him that there was something under the surface of all this serenity. It was like a malevolent force reaching out, asking for help. It all felt very Anakin Skywalker, asking him to turn to the dark side.

He wasn't going to do that. He took a step backward, then another, till he was back on the sidewalk on the other side of her front gate. Then he reached for the gate, swinging it closed. The buzzing didn't stop, but it quieted down, like the volume had been turned down. The tension in his chest eased, and he could breathe again.

Cassie followed him but stopped just inside the gate, a barrier between them now. "Did she say something to you?"

"No. Not in words." He looked up at the house again, at its inviting glow. He hated that it didn't apply to him. "It's emotion, and it sounds like static. Or a really loud buzzing noise. Or . . ." He trailed off with a frustrated shake of his head. "It was like that the last time I was here too. When I . . ."

"When you went off for no reason?"

"Yeah. She's really angry about something, and she seems to be angry at me."

"I don't get it." Cassie looked over her shoulder at the house too. "Nan didn't say anything about her being angry, or vengeful, or anything like that. Maybe I can try to talk to her. Get her to knock it off."

"No, it's okay." Nick held up a placating hand. "Ghosts are allowed to feel what they feel, and—"

"I don't care." Cassie crossed her arms, looking like a petulant teenager. "I'm doing my best to help her out here, and the least she can do is let my date into my house every once in a while."

"Every once in a while?" Nick's attention snapped back to her. The hell with the angry ghost in her house; this was much more important. "You saying you want to see me again?"

Cassie huffed a stray lock of hair out of her face, and when she met his eyes, Nick felt it in his gut. "Of course I do," she said. A smile teased around her mouth. "You said you'd talk to Elmer for me."

His heart dipped, then soared again. She was teasing him. He liked it. "But what about when Elmer's not involved?" He grasped the slats of the fence with both hands, leaning toward her. "Or Publix subs? What if it's just me?"

Her hands were warm against his, holding on to him while he held on to the gate. Nick caught his breath as Cassie stretched up onto her toes to meet him over the barrier. "I kinda like it when it's just you." Her voice was a murmur just before her mouth brushed across his, and she took his gasp into her mouth. Oh. He'd forgotten how good it felt to kiss her. How much he wanted to sink into her softness. If only there wasn't this damn fence between them. If only there wasn't all this buzzing. If only Sarah Hawkins didn't hate him so much.

Cassie pulled back way too soon, laying a hand on his cheek, rubbing her palm across the scruff of his beard. "I'll talk to Sarah," she said. "Because believe me, I'm going to want to have you inside the house at some point." Her voice was low, urgent, and it did things to Nick's insides. There was innuendo there, and he wanted more.

"And I'd like to be inside . . . your house. At some point." He raised an eyebrow and her cheeks flamed in response. He flipped his hands under hers so he could entwine their fingers. "But for now I'll just say good night."

"Good night." She squeezed lightly on his hands before letting go. She backed away, up the front walk, until her heel bumped against the bottom step. He stayed on the sidewalk, rooted to the spot under a streetlight until Cassie was up the front steps of her porch and inside. The sound of her front door closing echoed down the street to him in the quiet of the night, finally setting him free to find his way home. As he headed down the sidewalk the weird, stat-icky buzzing that had filled his head was gone, but he could still feel it there somewhere—a faint, unsettling whisper tickling the back of his brain, getting quieter as he walked away, a radio station losing its signal. Its absence was a relief, but why was it there at all? Until they figured that out, he wasn't going to be hanging out much at Cassie's place. That was for sure.

It wasn't until the next morning that he remembered they hadn't exactly set a date for the talk (text? chat?) with Elmer. But he barely had time to feel disappointed, because there she was, coming through the door, square in the middle of the lunchtime rush.

"Hey." He threw her a quick smile as she walked through the door. "I'm a little tied up right now, but if you want to give me a min-ute, we can . . ." His voice trailed off as she took her laptop and charg-ing cord out of its bag, a sheepish expression on her face. "Come on. Again?" He tried to sound grumpy, he really did. But he couldn't help it; his heart was soaring. Cassie was back at her table in his café and all was right with the world. Suck it, Spooky Brew.

"Look, it wasn't my fault." But Cassie was already laughing. She was glad to be back too.

"Did you unplug your laptop?" He shook his head at her in mock despair as he wiped down the counter. The counter was perfectly clean, but this made him look busy and he didn't have to go too far away from her.

"Well, yes, but—"

"Sounds like it's your fault then."

"But it was so nice out this morning!" she protested. "The breeze off the ocean was gorgeous up on the balcony. Plus I had a meeting and I . . ." She tried to look contrite but the grin messed it all up. "Okay, maybe I wanted to show off my beach view a little."

"Can't blame you there. You want some lunch?"

She shook her head. "I had a sandwich a little bit ago. I really am only using you for your outlet." But her smile took the sting out of the words as she approached the counter, stretching up on her toes to get closer to him. She looked so much like she had last night, by the garden gate, that he automatically leaned in toward her. To hell with professionalism in the workplace. He placed his hands flat on the counter and met her halfway in a quick, sweet kiss hello. Apparently they were at that stage now, and that was fine with him.

He lingered for just a moment too long, distracted by the way her smile felt against his mouth. Then Ramon yelled "Get a room!" from the kitchen, and the moment was broken.

"Coffee?" he asked.

"Please." The color was high in Cassie's cheeks as she dropped back to her heels. Had he put that color there, or was it Ramon's commentary? She returned to her table in the back. "I promise I'll be out of your hair soon."

He waved her off. "I kind of like you in my hair. May have to add you to the electric bill, though."

"You wouldn't dare." Her dark eyes danced at him, and everything in him lit up like Christmas. He liked the way he felt around her. He was determined to go more than a few days this time without fucking it up.

Nick had never been the best at customer service, but today he was worse. Just a little bit shorter with the customers, just a little more eager for everyone to get the hell out of his place so he could turn his attention back to Cassie. But she was patient, typing away at her laptop, until the lunch rush had slowed to a trickle. She took out her earbuds when he brought a second hazelnut latte to her table. "So . . . do you think there's a good time we could try the whole . . ." She waved a hand in his direction, a gesture that could mean anything from *text your ghost roommate* to *take off your pants*. Nick was pretty sure it was the former, but he sure as hell wouldn't say no to the latter.

"This?" He took his phone out of his pocket and waved it at her as he headed to the register to cash out a customer. "It's not like it's a secret. Just about everyone knows that Elmer exists."

As if on cue, the customer—an elderly guy who Nick was pretty sure knew Elmer when he was alive—took his change, dropping the coins and a single into the tip jar, giving Nick a nod that was more of an upward jerk of the chin. "Tell him hey."

"You got it, Mr. Maddox." He bumped the cash drawer closed then glanced at Cassie. "See?"

She held up a defensive hand, her eyes on her laptop as she tapped a few keys. "Point taken."

"We can bug him after I close up. He's been kind of quiet today, and it's been nice to run the place without his micromanaging." He held his breath, expecting his hip pocket to buzz with some kind of protest. But the phone stayed silent.

Cassie nodded. "I'll drink this fast."

"Take your time." Like Nick was ever going to kick her out. "I can close up around you."

She took another sip of her latte. "I can wait."

But that was a lie, Nick noted with amusement. As two o'clock came and went, what was left of the lunch crowd trickled out one by one, much too slowly as far as Nick was concerned. He looked over at Cassie, practically vibrating as he cashed out the last person, and when the place was finally empty she was out of her seat like a shot, heading over to the counter. "Now?" she asked, as eager as a kid wanting to see what Santa had left.

"Now what?" Nick kept his eyes down, smiling an innocent smile at the salt and pepper shakers he'd suddenly decided it was time to refill. He was teasing her, but he couldn't help it.

Cassie threw a sugar packet at him, and he dodged it neatly. "You know what! Can we text him now?"

"I thought you were here because you had work to do?" That earned him another sugar packet. "Okay! Fine!" He held up his hands, deflecting a third one, before motioning her behind the counter.

"Oooh, everything looks so different from back here." Cassie gazed around, peeking at the spaces under the counter, craning her neck to take everything in as though she'd been ushered into some kind of secret world. "All this power," she continued, sidling over to the espresso machine. "I could make my own coffee and everything."

"You could bake your own banana bread too."

"Wow," she deadpanned. "How do you not let all this go to your head?" There was a sparkle in her eyes. Damn, but he loved her brand of sarcasm.

"Ramon," he replied. "He keeps me humble."

She nodded. "I can see that."

Just then Ramon burst out from the kitchen, as though his name had summoned him. "You need me for something?" He wiped his hands on his apron.

Nick shook his head. "We're good here. You can take off. I can finish up."

"You sure?" He looked out into the empty café. "Looks kinda busy out here." Nick half expected a tumbleweed to make its way through for emphasis.

Nick nodded. "I'm a pro. I got this."

Ramon waved him off with a chuckle, shucking his apron as he left. Nick locked the door behind him then returned to Cassie behind the counter, pulling his phone out of his pocket. But when he pulled up his messages he was at a loss. He'd never initiated a text chain with Elmer before. The texts came in, and he replied. Every new conversation came in marked Unknown Number and started a new thread. How would this work? Should he just reply to the most recent one? Would Elmer receive it, or had he already spiritually moved on to the next burner phone?

Before he could decide what to do, his phone buzzed in his hand, nearly sending him out of his skin.

> You looking for me?

Well. That answered that. Cassie gave a soft gasp next to him as he responded. Sure am. You good to talk?

> What the hell else am I doing? I don't exactly have a full schedule these days.

"Whoa," Cassie breathed. She stared at the screen with wide eyes. "That's . . ." She swallowed. "Words on the fridge are one thing, but this . . ." She shook her head in wonder. "That's really a dead guy."

Well, you don't have to put it like that. The response appeared like magic on the screen. Nick snorted, and after a moment Cassie laughed too, the sound thin.

"Good point. I apologize," she said into the phone, like they were on speaker. "Wait." She looked up at Nick. "Do you need to type that, or can he hear me?"

"Either/or," Nick replied as Elmer's response came through. I can hear you. Nick insists on typing because it's more civilized or something. Seems like more work to me.

"I like to text," Nick said, very pointedly typing the same words as he spoke them. "It makes all this . . ." He circled his hand around his phone. "Seem more normal. That okay with everyone?"

"Yep." Cassie popped the *p* while Elmer responded Sure on Nick's phone. "So do you want me to . . ." She held out a hand for his phone. "I can type questions to him if you want. Or you can. Whatever works for you."

"Ahh, it's fine. We can skip the middleman. Just talk." Normality was overrated at this point.

"You sure?" Cassie leaned away from him, pulling her own phone out of her back pocket. Nick was flummoxed. Did she think Elmer's answers would show up on her own phone? But before he could tell her that it didn't work like that, she pulled up her Notes app to a very full screen. Of course. She'd come prepared for this.

"Okay." She consulted her list while Nick tilted his phone toward her. Which was pointless; Elmer wasn't listening through the phone's microphone, but again. Whatever kept this whole thing semi-normal. "You said you knew Mrs. Hawkins, right?"

Not much, myself, came the response. She was already a widow when I was a kid. My dad talked about old C.S. like he was a god or something around here. And he didn't think much of Mean Mrs. H.

"Is there anything you remember about her? Was she really mean?"

One thing about Elmer's texts: they popped up fast. Faster than anyone could conceivably type out words. That was plain with the lengthy responses that showed up now on Nick's screen. Kids in the neighborhood started calling her Mean Mrs. Hawkins, and Pop thought it was funny. But she never seemed mean to me. I thought she looked sad.

"Sad?" Cassie glanced up at Nick, almost to confirm what they had both read. "Do you think she missed her husband?"

Nick shook his head. "That doesn't make much sense. Everything now implies that she offed her husband. That's a pretty big stretch from grieving widow."

Beats me.

"Yeah." Cassie sighed. "We've got to be missing something."

Sorry I can't be more help. I was just a kid in those days.

"No, no, I get that," Cassie hastened to assure him, but Nick narrowed his eyes.

"You said you knew Mrs. Hawkins," he said. "'Ask me anything,' that's what you said. Why are you bullshitting us now?"

Oh come on, kid. You knew I was bullshitting you. What, you can't do math? She was in her forties when I was born.

Nick tossed his phone to the counter. What a waste of time. He wanted to be mad at Elmer, but could he blame him? Dude was lonely, and for the first time in decades someone had come to him for help, instead of just ignoring his good-intentioned suggestions.

Cassie picked up Nick's phone, studying the words Elmer left. "It's okay." Her voice was soothing. Probably just the kind of thing Elmer wanted to hear. "But you're the only one we know who was around in those days. Any little detail you can remember might be important."

At first there was a pause, and Nick wondered if Elmer was gone. Once again, Nick had always been the one to end the conversation with him; as far as he knew, Elmer would talk forever, given the chance.

But then the typing bubbles appeared, followed far too quickly by a paragraph that took up Nick's entire screen.

> She liked music. The windows in her house were almost always open, and you could hear music playing. Classical pieces on a phonograph, and sometimes she played the piano. You could see her from the street when she played. She always had roses growing by her garden gate. Big, round ones. She loved those roses. Sometimes kids would sneak into her garden and pick them, and she'd chase them out. But she didn't sound angry. She sounded almost scared. Like the roses were poison, and she was trying to keep the kids from getting hurt.

For a long moment neither Nick nor Cassie spoke. "The roses were poison?" Cassie finally said. "That . . . that doesn't make any sense."

> It was LIKE they were poison, not really poison. Damn Nick, you're right. It's hard to get your meaning across like this. Which is weird, since it's nothing but words.

"It's all in the tone of voice," he murmured, something he had said to Elmer more than once. But had Elmer ever listened? Nope. What a surprise.

> Point is, Elmer continued, I always had the feeling she wasn't trying to keep people away to be mean. It was more like she was trying to keep them safe from something.

"Could have fooled me." Nick's mind went to last night, to the bees and the static that kept him from going too close to Cassie's house. Was this Mrs. H's way of chasing him away, since she couldn't get her hands on a stick? He didn't give a fuck about her roses that weren't there anymore anyway.

Cassie obviously remembered too. She slid an arm around his, hugging his arm to her. "I couldn't get any answers out of her last night. She said she didn't want to hurt you. Then she said 'get him out' again, just like . . ." She swallowed hard. "Just like she did that other time."

"Yeah." He blew out a frustrated breath. "So she still doesn't like me, and now she's lying about it." He squinted at the phone. "Can ghosts lie?" He directed the question to Elmer, who responded almost immediately.

> Sure we can. I said I liked the color you painted the café, remember?

"Hey." Nick looked around the pale blue of the café. He'd closed down the place for two weeks during the off-season a couple years back, giving the inside a fresh coat of paint and updating some of the appliances. He was still paying off that small business loan, but it was all worth it. At the time, Elmer had said he liked the color. What an asshole.

But Cassie wasn't buying it. "Why would she lie to me, though? All this time, she's wanted to be heard. And she's never been outright aggressive toward me. I mean, she's weirdly insistent about the house being hers. I'm about to leave my closing papers out in a conspicuous place just to get her off my back on that. But she's never actually been unfriendly."

"Even though she scared the shit out of you?" For as long as he lived, Nick was never going to forget Cassie's face that early morning after Mrs. Hawkins had first made contact. Cassie's haunted expression was the most chilling thing he'd ever seen, and he lived in a town populated by ghosts.

But Cassie's memory was shorter. "That wasn't her fault," she said. "She was trying to get her point across."

"She sure did that."

"No, I mean it. Can you imagine being this . . . this incorporeal spirit, unable to make anyone realize you're there, and suddenly there's all these words on the refrigerator and you can send a message? Like, Elmer . . ." She directed her words toward the ghost inside Nick's phone now. "It had to be amazing when you realized you could text people, right?"

Nick swallowed a chuckle as Elmer responded You have no idea. He still didn't have a firm grasp on how it all worked when it came to Elmer, and he doubted that Elmer did, either. Before he'd died, Elmer had interfered with the running of "his" café the old-fashioned way: by showing up daily, criticizing the coffee, and badgering the new owner with feedback until he gave up and sold the place. Then Elmer started in on that new guy, until Elmer's sudden death from a heart attack. Not long after that, the second new owner made a crucial error: he got a cell phone with texting capability. And then the texts started coming.

Nick had been the first one who could roll with all this. And while he'd patted himself on the back more than once for being so nice to the grumpy old ghost, this was the first time he'd really considered what it must mean to Elmer. To have his voice heard, in a time when you should be silent forever.

Nick could relate, after all. Sure, he was surrounded by friends here in his hometown, but there were times when he'd never felt so alone.

He looked down at his phone with new eyes. If Cassie could put all this effort into helping the ghost in her house, one she wasn't even sure she wanted hanging around, the least he could do was listen to Elmer a little more often. That was what friends did for each other, right?

Twenty-Three

"Good morning, Sarah!" Cassie clattered down the stairs and into the kitchen, sending her thanks, as she always did, to Past Cassie, who had set the timer on the coffee maker the night before. Past Cassie was so good to her sometimes.

She stuck two slices of bread in the toaster and poured herself some coffee, talking all the while. "Now, Buster is coming by in the afternoon to talk about the kitchen floor, so I hope you have some opinions on that for me. I want to—" Her voice trailed off as she opened the fridge for the milk.

man for pink girl is bad

"Oh, for . . ." Cassie poured milk into her coffee and reminded herself to be patient. This was all very new to Sarah. The twenty-first century, communicating with the living. Reality television. "You mean Wanda, right? The one in the pink bikini on *Romance Resort*? You know as well as I do that girl has terrible taste in men. It really shouldn't have been a surprise when she ended up picking Noah."

Cassie slathered butter on her toast. "I'm sure she'll get tired of him soon. Don't worry about her, okay?"

She put the butter and milk back in the fridge, in time for a new message to appear. **bad man**. Sarah seemed really hung up on this. Didn't she know how reality TV worked? No, of course she didn't.

"Listen," she said. "These relationships aren't permanent. They last maybe three days, tops. And those are the committed ones. She doesn't have to stay with him forever." She crunched through a piece of toast. "In fact, I bet by the end of the week Noah will be history. He's kind of a dick, you know? And Wanda may be horny right now, and blinded by a perfect set of abs, but she's not stupid. Now about those flooring choices . . ."

Cassie took a long sip of coffee before looking back at the fridge, letting Sarah take her time. But the words, when they changed, made Cassie's heart drop to the shoes she didn't have on yet.

my man bad

She very carefully swallowed her last bite of toast as a chill that had nothing to do with the AC made the hair on her arms stand on end. No, Sarah Hawkins wasn't a grieving widow. From the looks of things, she was still a frightened one, a century after her husband had died.

"Okay." Her voice was small in her own kitchen. "It's okay, Sarah. He's gone. He can't hurt you anymore." But it wasn't that easy, was it? Trauma can linger, apparently even after death. She made a mental note to reschedule with Buster. The kitchen floor could wait a day or two.

Meanwhile, she had to get to work. She packed up her bag with her notes. Another day, another dead laptop. It was nice having Hallowed Grounds back as her own personal office space. It was even nicer to have Nick back in her life.

From the looks of things, he was just as happy to have her back in his life too. Was there a better sight in the morning than his smile when she walked through the door of his café? "Morning."

He leaned across the counter and she stretched up on her toes to kiss that smile with her own.

But he frowned when she dropped back to her heels. "You taste like coffee." He narrowed his eyes. "Did you drink outside coffee?"

"I had some in my kitchen this morning," she said. "Is that a crime?"

"And now you want more coffee, I bet."

"You know it." Her usual back table was occupied, along with almost every other table in the place, so she made herself at home at the counter, taking the seat at the end near an outlet.

He clucked his tongue at her, turning to the espresso machine. "Too much caffeine. It's bad for you."

"It keeps me going," she replied cheerfully, opening up her laptop. She half expected Nick to argue with her further, but by the time she logged in there was an iced hazelnut latte in front of her. She glanced up at Nick, who dropped her a wink and a half smile before turning to the next customer who'd come through the door.

The downside of sitting at the counter at Hallowed Grounds instead of her usual table in the back was that Nick was too close by. Too distracting. Cassie was getting zero work done. Sure, her document was open. She'd even made a correction or two on the draft of the press release for the granola company. But her mind wasn't on it. Her mind was on Nick. The way he moved behind the counter with masculine grace, pivoting from the espresso machine to the pastry case. The way he greeted the regular customers by name and the tourists with a veneer of politeness.

In fact, that was the upside of watching Nick work. She had a front-row seat to a one-act improv play: Nick Versus the Tourists.

"Excuse me." A dark-haired man called in Nick's direction as though he were hailing a cab in Manhattan in the 1980s. When Nick didn't respond right away (because he was handing a to-go cup across the counter to a woman with dark hair and darker eyeliner), the man said it again. He had the air of someone who didn't like repeating himself, and looked like he'd probably invested too much in crypto.

If Nick was annoyed, he didn't let it show. Too much. "Yeah, what's up?" He wiped his hands on a towel before throwing it over his shoulder. "What can I get you? Something from the pastry case?"

"There's a lot of carbs in here." Mr. Crypto frowned at the pastry case as though it had offended him personally.

Nick nodded. "It's a pastry case."

The man sighed and shook his head, and Cassie noticed that his hair didn't move a millimeter. Incredible. "Do you not have any protein options?"

"It's a pastry case," Nick repeated with exaggerated patience. "Not a lot of protein in pastry."

"You don't have egg bites? Avocado toast with an over-easy egg?"

Cassie pressed her lips together hard, picturing Nick making avocado toast. He probably didn't even know—or care—what an egg bite was.

"Nope," Nick said, a little too cheerfully. "You want protein? Here's what you do." He pointed out the door. "You go out of here, make a right. Walk all the way down and around the bend to the pier. There's a little place there. Jimmy's."

Mr. Crypto's face lit up. "And they have better options there? I mean, they have to, right? Look at this place." He scoffed, as though laughing in the owner's face was the key to getting good customer service.

"I don't know about better," Nick said. A smile started to break across his face, a slow progression. "But ask for Jimmy—he'll be the one with no shoes on—and he'll rent you a fishing pole. You can take it over to the pier, catch all the damn protein you want."

Cassie couldn't help it. A snort escaped her, and she clapped a hand over her mouth. She wasn't the only one. The conversation had attracted a little attention, and one older guy—had to be a local—all but guffawed in Mr. Crypto's face, which had burned bright red as he turned on his heel and stalked out of the place.

"Not a great business model," Cassie said to Nick after he left. "Don't you want tourists coming back?"

Nick shrugged. "Not that guy."

She snorted again and turned back to her work. She really should get this press release finished before lunch.

But life had other plans. No sooner had she woken her laptop back up than Sophie dropped onto the seat next to her at the front counter. "I was hoping I'd find you here."

"She's already taken the tour," Nick admonished from the other side of the counter.

"Three times," Cassie said.

"Three?" Nick raised an eyebrow. "Soph, you can't make the poor woman be your constant warm body when your crowds are thin."

Sophie rolled her eyes. "It's not that." She waited for Nick to wander off before turning back to Cassie. "I was wondering if . . ." She clasped her hands together, released them, then tapped nervously on the counter with a fingernail. "If you've . . . I don't know . . . if you've talked any more with Sarah recently?"

"Well, yeah," Cassie replied. "We talk a lot. As often as you can talk to the incorporeal spirit of the woman living in your house, that is." She was shooting for a joke, but all she could remember was this morning. **my man bad**.

"Were you able to figure out if there's more to her story? Have I been getting it wrong all this time?"

"Sophie." Cassie dropped her voice as though imparting a

secret. "It's for tourists, right? I don't think the ghost tour police are going to come and take you away if your stories aren't accurate."

"They should, though!" Sophie looked miserable. "I worked hard on that tour. On finding the most interesting stories, mapping out a route that shows off our downtown area. Figuring out the right mix of history and ghost stories. I've been proud of it, you know? And to find out I've been lying all this time . . ."

Cassie could see where she was coming from, but . . . "What about the ice cream shop?"

"What about it?" Sophie's brow furrowed. "Which one?"

Cassie gestured down the road, which really did nothing to narrow things down. She could throw a rock from the front door of Hallowed Grounds and hit at least three ice cream places. "I Scream Ice Cream. I missed the beginning of that story, but Nick said that you made it up."

"He did?" Sophie looked over her shoulder toward Nick. He poured a cup of coffee and popped a to-go lid on it, oblivious to their scrutiny. "I didn't make it up," she said, turning back to Cassie. "It's in the book! Why would he say I made it up?"

Oh, no. What the hell had Cassie started? "He didn't use those exact words." Actually, the exact word he'd used was *bullshit* but she wasn't going to tell Sophie that. "He just said that it wasn't true. I figured you sprinkled in some more colorful stories for the tourists."

"I don't do that." Sophie leaned back in her chair with a sigh that was bigger than she was. "That's what I was afraid of." She rummaged in her messenger bag, pulling out her battered copy of *Boneyard Key: A Haunted History*. "I'll admit, I haven't actually reread this book in a while. At least not since I finished putting this tour together, and that was over five years ago. I looked through some parts of it the other night, and now I know he got some stuff wrong.

Simple stuff! He said that Eternal Rest—you know, the motel over that way—is one of the only buildings that isn't haunted, and I know that it is! The Eriksons have been running that place for four generations, and lots of their family members have stuck around."

Cassie cocked her head. "Then why isn't it part of the tour?"

"Too far away." Sophie flipped through the book while she talked. "The tour is an hour long, give or take. Eternal Rest is only a mile down the road, but if we trekked all the way there and back on foot it would take too much time. Plus not all tourists want to walk that much, so you have to take that into account too."

Cassie nodded slowly. There was more involved with putting together a walking tour than she would have suspected. "So what you're saying is . . ."

"I have to rewrite the tour." Sophie tossed the book to the table with a thump and buried her face in her hands.

"Okay. Hey . . ." Cassie grasped Sophie's wrist. "Hey. You can do this."

"I don't know." Sophie's voice was muffled by her hands. "It's so much to research."

"Tell me about it." Her mind drifted back to Sarah. She had a lot of research to do too.

"Why don't you talk to Theo?" Nick came by to clear away their empty glasses, but he'd obviously been eavesdropping. "I bet he can help."

Sophie groaned at his suggestion, letting her forehead thunk to the countertop. But Cassie was stumped. "Who's that?"

"Theo," Nick said, as though repeating the guy's name would clear everything up. It didn't.

"He's an asshole." Sophie was still face down on the counter, her voice muffled.

"He is not." Nick rolled his eyes and turned back to Cassie. "He runs the bookstore. Boneyard Books? Anyway, there's a little history museum in the back of the bookshop. Kind of his pet project."

"Seriously?" Cassie had walked by the bookstore a few times but hadn't made it inside yet, which was frankly a crime. But the building wasn't that big; how did they get a whole-ass museum in there?

"It's not much, believe me. The town's been here, what, less than a hundred and fifty years? Not that much history to document. His focus is mostly on the Founding Fifteen."

"His focus is on being an asshole." Sophie lifted her head up then, adjusting her glasses. "He took my tour once, back when I started. I swear all he did was sigh and shake his head the entire time. I thought his head was going to fall off." Her tone of voice said that she wouldn't have minded if it had.

"He can be a little bit of a stickler for accuracy," Nick said tactfully. "But if accuracy is what you're looking for . . ."

"And it is," Cassie reminded Sophie, her voice firm. "Look, I'll go with you, okay? Strength in numbers and all that." She closed her laptop. The hell with it; that press release wasn't due for a few more days. Sophie needed backup. And maybe Theo knew something about Sarah Hawkins and her bad man.

Twenty-Four

Boneyard Books was one of the only shops in town that had always been a bookstore. Just about every other shop on this street had once been something else: bank, hardware store, grocery. Everything a small town needed to keep itself running. But of course these days Boneyard Key ran on tourism, so everything was geared toward tourists, with most of the shops selling airbrushed T-shirts, shot glasses, and other crappy souvenirs—basically anything you could slap a cartoon ghost on. The formerly utilitarian buildings were now painted in eye-catching pastel colors, perched on the edge of wide sidewalks that invited strolling. *Come spend your money*, the pale blue and pink and yellow paint said. *Then go home.*

When Cassie paused at the doorway to Boneyard Books to study the facade, Sophie didn't argue. She seemed to be stalling anyway; she really didn't like this guy.

"Oh, this is cool." The outer wall near the door was made to look like carvings of various children's book characters, all of them reading books. Depicted across the bottom of the facade, along the sidewalk, was a long line of books on a long bookshelf. The titles were all classics: Dickens and Austen and Hemingway and Fitzgerald. Cassie ran her fingers over *The Great Gatsby*.

"Yeah." Sophie's voice was flat. "It's neat."

"Oh, come on." Cassie straightened up to smile at Sophie. "He can't be that bad."

Sophie didn't respond, she just folded her arms and waited. Cassie shook her head and reached for the door. The old-fashioned bell over it announced their presence, and their feet echoed in the empty shop. Cassie didn't see a single soul among the stacks.

"Huh," Sophie said. "Doesn't look like he's here. We should come back . . ."

"Can I help you?" The voice came from the front counter, behind an enormous stack of books. Cassie ventured farther in, peering around them to find a man who could only be Theo.

He was a little younger than she was, and a little bit taller. His sandy-colored hair could use a cut and, let's face it, a style a little more modern than the 1960s. With his tortoiseshell glasses and button-down shirt with an even more buttoned-down vest over it, he looked like a time traveler come to visit modern-day Florida.

Despite his buttoned-down look—not to mention Sophie's prejudice—his smile was open and friendly.

"Anything I can help you find?" He closed the book he was reading—something leather bound and old—and unfolded himself from the stool behind the counter. Oh. Never mind. He was more than a little bit taller than Cassie.

"Yes, actually," Cassie said. "Are you Theo?"

"I am."

"Yes" came a voice behind her. Sophie had finally followed her into the shop, and as she and Theo stared at each other, Cassie could have sworn the temperature dropped about twenty degrees. Not from a ghostly presence this time, but from pure animosity.

"Sophie." So much for open and friendly, but the nod Theo gave her at least bordered on polite.

Which was more than could be said for Sophie. "Hey." Well, this was going great.

Cassie forged ahead. "I . . . well, we . . . okay, I . . . was hoping to find some more information on the town's history. Something that's maybe . . . ah, a little more in-depth than *Boneyard Key: A Haunted History*?"

His eyebrow went up in a perfect arch. "More historically accurate, you mean?" From behind her, Sophie sucked on her teeth. Loudly.

"So you know for a fact that it's not?"

He waved a hand. "Oh, it's fine for tourists. The rudimentary history of the town is correct—Cemetery Island, the Great Storm, the founding of the town—that's all basic stuff and covered pretty well. Have you been on the ghost tour yet?"

"Yes, she's been on the ghost tour." Wow. Cassie had never heard Sophie so snippy before.

"I sure have!" Cassie said cheerfully, as though she could talk over Sophie's ire. "That's why I'm here, actually. There's . . ." What should she say? *I'm here to fact-check the ghost tour*? She couldn't say that in front of Sophie. "The ghost in my house would like her story to be told correctly."

Theo said nothing for a long moment. He opened his mouth, closed it. "Are you . . ." He cocked his head. "You're not Cassie Rutherford, are you? You own the Hawkins House now?"

"That's me," she said. "Word's gotten around town, hasn't it?"

"It has," he agreed. "Not that it takes long. If you're wanting local history, *real* local history, I have a couple things you might like." He moved out from behind the counter, his walk brisk, and he didn't look back; he seemed to just assume Cassie could keep up. "Along this wall is our local interest section." He gestured toward a shelf as he walked, but he didn't slow down. "University press stuff, local authors, books about the Indigenous history of the town, its role over the years as a colony before Florida became a state. If you're wanting to delve into the town's past, that would be a great place to start. It's mostly accurate."

"Mostly?" Cassie tried to speed-read the titles on the local history shelf while Theo zoomed past them. Dude was tall and he could walk *fast*. "You mean as accurate as *A Haunted History*?"

Theo threw a smirk over his shoulder. "Something like that."

"You could have told me, you know." Sophie's voice was breathless; she was a good foot shorter than Theo and was struggling to keep up with them. "That *A Haunted History* wasn't accurate. That the tour wasn't accurate. Instead of just letting me run around all this time, telling everybody fake stories."

That stopped him in his tracks, so suddenly that the two women nearly crashed into his back. He turned to them with a puzzled expression. "I thought you knew," he said to Sophie.

"How was I going to know?" She put her hands on her hips and glared up at him, like a mouse staring down a giraffe. "I was going off of the book, which I was told was a good source!"

"I certainly didn't tell you that," he retorted. "And your tour is fine. I never said it wasn't—"

"No, except when you scoffed your way through it!"

Theo continued as though she hadn't interrupted. "And it's fine for tourists. I figured you were selling them on a fun time, getting them to buy the book at the end. I didn't think you cared."

"Of course I care." Her voice was small, hurt. A staring contest ensued between the two of them, and Theo was the one to blink first, a sheepish expression coming over his face.

"I'm sorry," he finally said gently. "And I'm sorry that I scoffed at your tour. It's just that . . . That damn book's been a thorn in my side for years. Historical inaccuracy bothers me like nothing else."

"Me too," said Sophie. "Believe it or not."

Theo considered that, then nodded decisively. "I believe it. Come on." He led them to the back of the shop, to a curtained-off doorway leading to what looked like a storeroom. A small sign to the right of the doorway read BONEYARD KEY CULTURAL CENTER AND MUSEUM. It seemed like a lot of pressure for one storeroom to handle.

Theo pushed the deep burgundy curtain to the side and ushered them inside. "I usually ask for donations, a couple dollars, something like that. But you're both residents, so . . ."

"Thanks," Cassie murmured as she stepped through the curtain. The place looked . . . well, it looked like a museum that was set up in a storeroom. It was larger than she'd expected; each of the four walls had groupings of what could generously be called museum displays: framed photographs of varying ages and degrees of disintegration. A glass cabinet in the center of the room held antique fishing implements, along with pieces of brick that must be important for some reason, while a shadowy corner in the back had two tall filing cabinets with a card table set up next to them.

While Theo headed directly for the filing cabinets, Cassie found herself wandering to the far wall, which focused on the early history of the town and its settlement. Her attention was caught by black-and-white photos of a cemetery. Some of the tombstones had toppled over or were broken in half, and most of them were overgrown with vegetation. *Cemetery Island, 1954*, read the small placard next to the photos.

"Oh, wow." Her fingertips hovered over one of the photos, tracing the curve of a tombstone. She could just barely make out the name on it. ROYER. A shiver prickled the back of her neck. That was Nick's family, right there in front of her in literal black and white. His attachment to Boneyard Key made a lot more sense to her now.

His link to this town wasn't just sentimental. It was tangible. His roots were right there, where he could visit them. She wouldn't want to move away either if she had something like that.

"This cemetery really still exists?" She aimed the question at Sophie, Theo, anyone who cared to answer.

"Yep," Sophie answered from right behind her, while Theo's assent came from the other side of the room. Cassie glanced over her shoulder to see Theo's back to them, a drawer to a file cabinet open as he rummaged through it. "You have to take a kayak out there," he said, "and make sure you hose yourself down with bug repellent first. The mosquitoes are merciless."

"I'll keep that in mind," she said. "But these photos are from the fifties. And the tombstones look in pretty rough shape back then. You sure they're still there now?"

"They absolutely are." He sounded certain, and a little pissed off—who was Cassie to doubt him? "The historical preservation committee goes out twice a year to clean up the graves." He had come up behind her while she was studying the black-and-white photos and stood next to her now, two file folders under his arm. He tapped a fingernail against the glass of a framed picture she hadn't noticed, off to the right and in color. "That's from the early 2000s." The broken tombstones were still broken, but one of the toppled-over ones had been set to rights. The sun streamed down on the little cemetery through the Spanish moss that hung from the live oak trees around it. Where the black-and-white photos looked more . . . well, *haunted*, the color photo showed the cemetery in a serene setting.

"Historical preservation committee?" Cassie asked. "Is it really a whole committee, or is it just you?"

Theo pretended to look offended. "Sometimes I can rope a couple people into helping me." He gave her an assessing look. "How good are you at kayaking?"

His smile said that he was kidding, but now that he mentioned it, Cassie could think of worse ways to spend an afternoon. "I could be taught." She indicated the folders under his arm. "What are those?"

Theo looked down at them, as though just remembering they were there. "Ah. Yes. This one is for you—" He handed one folder, so thick it was practically overflowing, to Sophie. "This is all documentation that focuses on Beachside Drive and the downtown area. If you really wanted to start looking for ways to improve your tour . . ."

Sophie took the folder with a firm nod. "This is great. Thanks." She started to open it but it was so full that documents began to spill out. She slammed it closed again with a sheepish look.

"There's a table right over there." Theo indicated a small table near the entrance, under a huge framed painting of a blond woman. Then he turned to Cassie, handing her the other, much thinner folder. "Hawkins House," he said. She followed him to the card table by the filing cabinets, setting the folder down. While there wasn't a lot of documentation, the folder was filled with photographs taken of the house over the years. Cassie spread them out gently, taking her time to study each one.

The first black-and-white photo she picked up was badly faded with age. But Cassie recognized the lines of the house, the rooftop and the gingerbread trim around the balcony. Even the picket fence looked the same, and right behind it . . . Cassie knew the general shape of cabbage roses by now. Mrs. Hawkins's roses.

"I don't know if the photos themselves are helpful at all . . ." Theo's voice sounded apologetic. "While I have plenty on the Hawkins House, I don't have all that much on Mr. and Mrs. Hawkins themselves." He shook his head. "They're not in the Founding Fifteen. That's really what my focus is here."

"Right." Cassie let her gaze wander over the room, at the photos and displays, as though an answer might jump out at her. "But where did Sarah come from? She's not in the Founding Fifteen, so she must have moved here, right? But where were her people? Were there other Blankenships in town?"

"Blankenships?" Theo blinked. "Who are the Blankenships?"

"Sarah Hawkins. Her maiden name was Blankenship." Had she really stumped the history guy?

He looked thoughtful. "Are you sure that's right? I don't think I've seen that name anywhere. In any of my research." He gave a pointed look toward the filing cabinets. "And I've done a lot of re-search."

"I can see that." But Cassie had her own research, and she dug in her bag for it now. She handed Theo the marriage license she'd printed out, and he studied it thoughtfully.

"Obviously you're right," he said, handing her back the paper. "But I don't know of any other Blankenships. None are buried at Cemetery Island, and none appear in Boneyard Key. So where did Sarah come from?"

"That's what I'm asking." They both turned back to the documents on the table, and Theo pulled out photocopies of records and handed them to Cassie.

"Original deed, in the name of William Donnelly."

"No way! I'd been looking for that!" She seized it as though it would hold all the answers. But of course, it held zero answers. It was a land deed, in very fancy and almost illegible handwriting, granting Donnelly the land on which he later built the house. Which was great, but it didn't tell her anything she couldn't get out of *A Haunted History*.

"Warranty deed." Theo handed her another piece of paper. "William Donnelly to Charles S. Hawkins in 1904."

"1904. That's when Charles and Sarah got married. But . . ." The chain of title was clear, even to Cassie, who didn't know squat about real estate. Donnelly owned it, then C.S. Hawkins. Why did Sarah insist it was her house, if it was never really hers? There must be something she was missing.

She put the papers aside and turned her attention back to the photographs. Theo narrated as she worked her way through them.

"These came from all over. Some were from the newspaper, which was started in 1899, once Boneyard Key—well, Fisherton, as it was called then—was established. Like this one"—he plucked one from the pile—"I'm pretty sure that's William Donnelly there. He was an architect, originally from Cincinnati, and he had a hand in designing most of the downtown area, as well as a few of the more prominent houses."

"So why wasn't it called the Donnelly House?"

"Alliteration?" Theo's lips quirked up in a smile but Cassie couldn't tell if he was serious, so she made a noncommittal hum. The photo in her hand was likely the oldest one in the folder, since the home looked newly built. A man—Donnelly, she presumed—stood at the garden gate, wearing pants and a long coat in the noonday sun. Cassie couldn't imagine dealing with all those layers in the Florida heat. And before central air-conditioning? People must have been built differently back then. The wide brim of his hat obscured most of his face, but what wasn't obscured were the roses. More cabbage roses, by the garden gate.

Cabbage roses. In 1899. Years before C.S. Hawkins bought the house and lived there with his wife, Sarah.

Something in the background caught her attention too. "What's that?" She pointed at an out-of-focus smudge. She could barely see a peaked roof, but it was out on the water. Who would build a house on the . . . She let out a soft gasp as it clicked into place. "Is that the Starter Home?"

"Good eye." He took the photo back. "Donnelly designed and built that too."

"Wait, he did?" Sophie's voice came from the other side of the room. "I've been telling everyone . . . Mr. Lindsay said in his book that nobody knew who built it."

"Mr. Lindsay never asked me," Theo replied dryly. "Maybe that's the first part of the tour you can revise."

"You bet your ass I'm going to revise it," Sophie grumbled as she turned back to her reading.

"Anyway," Theo continued. "The sand the Starter Home was built on proved to be unstable, so it wasn't lived in for very long. The pier leading out to it fell apart years back, and of course there's not much left now."

They continued sorting through the photos, but this time Cassie took care to notice the Starter Home in the background. For many of the photos it looked the same, but eventually she could see the house begin to deteriorate. It seemed the damage occurred when a hurricane swept through; every time the Starter Home lost part of its roof or another stilt or two, the Hawkins House would lose some of the Spanish moss on the trees or entire branches. One photo even showed roof damage partially repaired; Cassie made a mental note to have her roof checked. Just to make sure.

Eventually, Cassie and Theo put the photos of the house itself in chronological order, lining them up side by side along the edge of the card table. There were a few non-house photos left in the folder. One was a posed studio portrait of a young woman with dark hair piled in curls on top of her head. Even though the photo was in black and white, her eyes were startlingly light—blue or possibly green. Cassie reached a hand up to touch her own messy bun. She didn't look a thing like the woman in the photo, but there was something in the way she wore her hair. The shape was the same. And there was something in her expression that made Cassie feel like she was seeing an old friend for the first time.

"Sarah," she said softly, and Theo nodded.

"Correct. That's Sarah Hawkins's wedding portrait."

Cassie couldn't take her eyes off it. All this time she'd been picturing Mean Mrs. Hawkins, a grumpy old lady who chased children with sticks. But before she was any of that, she was young Mrs. Hawkins. Young Sarah Blankenship, even. Her whole life ahead of her, with no idea that she would end up dying old and alone, haunting the house she had lived in for so many decades.

She put the photo down and picked up the matching photo: a wedding portrait of Sarah and a man who had to be C.S. Hawkins. But her mind rejected it at first. "Oh God," she said. "He's so old!" Mr. Hawkins had a white beard, dark brown eyes, and an expression that could only be described as hard. He didn't look particularly happy in his wedding picture, but then again, neither did Sarah.

"Mr. Hawkins was definitely an older gentleman." Theo sounded like he was doing his best to be diplomatic. "They were only married about a decade or so before he died. Heart attack, they say." He shrugged. "Of course, they blamed it on Sarah. Gossip about him not being able to keep up with such a young and lovely bride."

"Ew." Cassie clucked her tongue. Based on these two in their picture, there was no way that this was any kind of a love match. She studied Sarah's expression again. Resigned, sure. But there was something in the set of her eyes, almost pinched. Her hands were clenched tightly together in her lap, not holding on to her husband's arm. His arm was around her, though; his fingers dug into her waist so tightly that Cassie could see wrinkles in the fabric, even in this old a photo.

She remembered the words on the fridge this morning: **my man bad**. He sure as hell looked it.

She put the photo down; she didn't like the vibe it was giving off, and if there was one thing she'd learned about this town, it was that vibes were to be listened to. She cast her gaze across all the photos: the house, the wedding portraits, the cabbage roses. There was something, just in the corners of her brain, but she couldn't catch the thought. It was like she was looking at a jigsaw puzzle; she knew she had all the pieces but she couldn't see how they fit together.

God. Living in this town was becoming a bad scavenger hunt. What the hell was the prize at the end going to be?

She looked up at Theo. "I don't suppose I could borrow these photos? Just for a little bit? Or make copies?" Maybe if she could spend a little more time with them, figure out what questions she could ask Sarah with her limited ability to answer, Cassie could discover what she was missing.

Theo was silent for a long moment. "Well," he said finally, "that depends. How well do you think you'd be able to kayak in oh, say, three or four months from now? Follow-up question: How do the both of you feel about grave preservation?"

A groan came from the other side of the room, but a slow smile spread across Cassie's face. "I think we can work something out."

Twenty-Five

"S o they didn't come to blows?" Nick poured coffee into two mugs, but spared a glance over his shoulder to Cassie, sitting on the sofa in his apartment.

She shook her head. "By the time we left they were getting along. I think Sophie may even ask Theo to help her rewrite some of her tour."

"Wow." He splashed milk into her coffee before bringing both mugs over, setting them on the battered coffee table in front of the couch. "Miracles do happen."

Another miracle was currently happening right now, here in his apartment. Nick had always thought of his place as just a place to crash, not big enough to be called a home. Hell, it was barely big enough to be two rooms. But with the sky outside growing dark, the lamp on the side table on, and a pretty girl on his couch, the whole scene looked pretty damn cozy.

He could absolutely get used to this.

The thought was less of a jolt to his system than he expected it to be. He filed it away for now and forced his mind back on topic. "And he just let you walk out of there with the file on your house?"

Cassie nodded, patting her trusty laptop bag at her feet. "I basically had to swear a blood oath not to lose or damage anything. Plus,

I think I just signed up for the historical preservation committee. Is that really a thing?"

"Oh, it is. And you're not kidding about the blood oath. Did he tell you about the mosquitoes out on Cemetery Island?"

She pulled a face. "He did. Guess I'm stocking up on bug spray." She blew across the surface of her coffee before taking a sip, then sent him a sideways glance. "So when you asked if I liked kayaking and cemeteries, you were speaking from experience."

Nick's laugh was a short bark. He thought he remembered every detail of the ghost tour, that first evening spent with Cassie. But he'd forgotten about that. He'd acted nonchalant, because Cassie was new in town. She was definitely not on board with ghosts yet, and scaring her off was the last thing he'd wanted to do. "Yeah, I go out there with him as much as I can. It's actually kind of pretty." That was putting it mildly. Nick always felt a sense of peace when he went out to Cemetery Island. A sense of connection. Especially when he was weeding around the graves of his ancestors. Being there reinforced the idea that he belonged here. There was something about knowing you shared DNA with the bones beneath the ground.

Cassie nodded thoughtfully. "I saw pictures. Your family's out there, huh?"

"The big headstone? Yeah, that's my great-great-granddad. He died not long before the Great Storm, so he was one of the last burials out there. I think they rowed someone out there in 1898, after the storm, to bury them there, but after that they started a new cemetery on the mainland." Nick took a long pull of his too-hot coffee, punishing himself for this ridiculous small talk. He had the girl he liked in his place, and he was talking about cemeteries, rowing corpses across the bay? Because cemetery talk got all the girls hot? What the hell was wrong with him?

But Cassie was long past scaring off now. She took the conversation in stride, like any other longtime resident of Boneyard Key. She took another sip of coffee before setting the mug down, curling her feet under her, clearly getting comfortable. That was fine with Nick; she could stay forever as far as he was concerned. "He's got some great photos," she said, her mind clearly back on Theo and his little museum. "Not just of the cemetery, but of downtown. The pier. The Starter Home. And my house." She finished the list with a sigh. "There were even some pictures of Sarah and C.S. Hawkins. She was really pretty. He looked like a dick."

Nick had seen photos of C.S. Hawkins here and there, but he couldn't remember ever seeing what old Mrs. H looked like. There was something to that, of the husband being remembered as a great man while the wife was lost to history, that maybe deserved thinking about further, but Cassie was right there, snuggling into his side. He left his mug on the coffee table in front of them and slid his arm around her shoulders, tugging her closer. She laid her head on his shoulder with a contented sigh. Nick almost let out a happy sigh of his own. This was nice.

Her hair smelled clean, like no-nonsense shampoo, and somehow that seemed exactly right for Cassie. She turned under his arm, tilting her face up to his, and it also seemed exactly right to lower his head, brushing his mouth against hers. The sound of her breath catching in her throat sent a thrill through his blood, and that was all it took for him to settle his mouth over hers, prolonging the kiss. Deepening it. Her hand was flat on his chest, warm through his T-shirt, and he wanted to cover her hand with his and press it closer. But his hands were busy, taking out the clip in her bun, letting her hair tumble down over her shoulders. Nick caught some of the long strands, twirling them between his fingers.

Cassie's hand slid up his chest, curling around the back of his neck, and the light scratch of her nails sent a hard shiver to the base of his spine. It was too much; it wasn't nearly enough. He tugged, she moved, and before long she was in his lap, her thighs straddling his, their bodies rocking gently through their clothes like a couple of teenagers in the back seat of a car.

He pulled at her hips, tugging her impossibly closer, then his hands drifted upward, settling in the dip of her waist, flirting with the hem of her T-shirt. Her shirt was soft. Her skin underneath was softer. She gasped as he slid exploratory fingers under her shirt, tracing her skin there.

"Is this okay?" Speaking was hard; speaking involved forming words with his mouth, and his mouth was much happier exploring the smooth skin of her neck. He found the spot where her neck met her shoulder and he bit at it softly. She sucked in a breath and rocked against him, her fingernails digging into the back of his neck.

"More than okay." Her words vibrated against his mouth as he worked his way up her throat. "If you stop what you're doing I may kill you."

Like he had any intention of stopping. "Yes, ma'am." While his mouth claimed hers again, his hands ventured higher until he reached the band of her bra. She whimpered as his fingertips found the undersides of her breasts, tracing them through the thin cotton. Her thighs tightened around him when he cupped her breasts in his hands, thumbs running across the hard peaks of her nipples through the fabric of her bra. Too much fabric. They were wearing too many clothes. He had his hands on Cassie, but he wanted Cassie's hands on him. He wanted . . .

Through the almost-deafening sound of blood rushing through his temples on their way to parts south, Nick heard the unmistakable sound of leather creaking. The recliner by the window. Elmer's chair.

No. He didn't want that. That was the last thing he wanted.

Cassie stilled in his lap. "Did you hear something?" She was breathless, practically hanging from the back of his neck.

No, he wanted to say. He didn't hear a goddamn thing. But she'd already stopped kissing him. Dammit.

The blood had stopped rushing anyway. He stilled his hands and sighed. "Looks like we're not alone."

Damn right, you're not alone! Since he was home, the words appeared in his head and not on his phone. Nick wanted to laugh. He wanted to cry. He wanted to throw that goddamn leather recliner out the window.

"Oh, God. He's here, isn't he?" Cassie was still on Nick's lap, but it was now more of a sit than a grind. "And he can . . . see us. Right? He can see us."

Nick let his head fall forward to rest on Cassie's shoulder while his hands settled on her waist. "I swear he wasn't here when we started," he said. "I'm not into kinky shit like that."

"Me neither." She still sounded breathless, but she'd stopped clutching the back of his neck. Now her touch was more comforting, sliding up into his hair, rubbing his scalp in soothing motions. Nick didn't want soothing. He didn't want to be comforted. But his body calmed, almost against his will, and he finally took a long breath that only shuddered a little. He raised his head, finding Cassie's lips with his own, but his kiss was now to bank the fire between them instead of stoke it.

"Give me a minute," he said through a soft laugh. "And I'll walk you home."

Awww. Don't stop on my account.

Nick gritted his teeth. "We are absolutely stopping on your account."

"Oh my god!" Cassie turned wide eyes to the leather recliner.

But her laugh gave her away; she was more amused than shocked. "Elmer, you pervert!" she chided.

A laugh burst from Nick's chest. God, this woman was perfect.

"So does that happen a lot?"

"Say again?" Nick leaned across the high-top table they currently shared in the back corner of The Haunt. After their spiritual douse of cold water, they fled Nick's apartment, electing to satisfy a different kind of hunger instead. Unfortunately, their sense of terrible timing continued; there was a Jimmy Buffett cover band playing tonight, and the place was packed. But Nick had gone to high school with the barback, and he'd managed to score them this table near the bathrooms. Probably because it was tiny and nobody else wanted it. But it worked for them.

Cassie finished chewing her bite of cheeseburger. "Does it happen a lot?" She leaned in. "Getting cockblocked by a ghost?" She practically yelled the words into his ear so he could hear her over the steel drums and guitar coming from the other side of the bar.

Nick choked on his swig of beer and concentrated hard on swallowing it instead of spewing it across the bar. "No," he finally said through a cough. "That does not happen often. Ever, actually."

"Never?" She raised her eyebrows. "Haven't you lived with Elmer for a while now?"

His cheeks heated as he nodded. "I'm . . . uh . . . not in the habit of bringing girls home." He wasn't lying; when he hooked up with a tourist he always went back to her place. Hotel rooms and vacation rentals were a lot sexier than "haunted studio apartment over the café I own" any day. "I didn't know he was going to show up, I swear." He frowned down at the remnants of his fries. "I don't know why I thought he'd have a little sense of propriety. Why start now?"

"Aww, he was happy for you!" Cassie leaned across the table and gave him a friendly punch on the shoulder.

"You're really not upset?" It almost seemed like too much to wish for.

Cassie shook her head, popping the last bite of her burger into her mouth. "I mean, okay, it's a little weird. But he's cool with me, right?"

Nick considered that. Elmer hadn't said one way or the other, but Nick had a feeling he'd be hearing about it if Elmer didn't approve. "Pretty sure he is."

"Well, then." She grinned. "It's like getting Dad's approval. Or maybe your weird uncle. What's not to like about that?"

She had a point.

Nick snagged an extra longneck on the way out—open container laws were loosey-goosey around here, and besides, the bartender knew Nick wasn't going to drink it. They deposited the beer at its usual spot on one of the picnic tables, and if Nick backed Cassie up against one of those tables, hoisting her up to finish the thorough kiss he had started at his place, well, the Beach Bum didn't say a word about it.

They took the beach route back to her place, Nick's arm slung over her shoulders, Cassie snuggled into his side. The sounds of the steel drums grew fainter and fainter as they left that side of the beach, and the gentle sounds of the waves took over. An ocean-scented breeze kicked up, teasing long strands of Cassie's hair out of its bun to snag themselves in Nick's beard. He smoothed her errant hair behind her ear, planting a kiss on her temple as he did so.

Being with Cassie felt so right, so normal, that it was easy for Nick to ignore the static as they approached her house. It was nothing but a faint buzzing as they paused outside her picket fence.

Cassie turned to him, her back to the gate. "Are you sure you can't come inside?" She twined her arms around his neck, fitting her body close to his, and holy hell Nick was ready to agree to anything. Everything.

"I don't know." He dipped his head down, stealing first a quick kiss, then a second longer kiss. "Do you think Mrs. H can put up with me for a few minutes?"

Cassie raised one arched eyebrow. "Are you saying it's only gonna take a few minutes?"

A growl emanated from Nick's chest, a sound he didn't even know he could make. "Absolutely not." His hands were on her hips now, pulling her flush against him. He could barely hear the buzzing at all now over his mind roaring at the thought of having much, much more than a few minutes alone with Cassie.

He slanted his mouth over hers, drinking her in like she was water on a hot day. Cassie fisted one hand in the front of his T-shirt, pulling, while she fumbled behind her for the gate latch. It probably would have been easier if they'd stopped kissing, but Nick wasn't about to let that happen and apparently neither was Cassie.

Finally the gate gave way, the two of them stumbling through it and up her front walkway, kissing and pulling, clutching and sighing. If they didn't get into the house soon, there was going to be an extremely public display of affection going on, and Nick wasn't sure if Cassie was that kind of girl. He definitely wasn't that kind of guy.

Cassie stumbled as she hit the front step, and Nick broke the kiss long enough to catch her under the elbows.

"You okay?"

"Yeah." Cassie panted as though she'd been running, her hands still clutching the front of his shirt. She looked up at him, her eyes glassy and her lips kiss-swollen. "You?"

He knew what she was asking. And truth be told he wasn't great; the static was back, threatening to drown out everything. But he focused on the woman in front of him. She was important. She was worth a little dizziness.

So he smiled as best he could. "Never better." She reached for him and he went gladly, making their way up the steps and to her front door. Nick pressed her against the solid wood, claiming her mouth, her neck.

Yes, this was what he wanted.

What he was meant for.

What *she* was meant for.

That was what women were for. To possess. To own.

And Cassie was his.

She belonged to *him*.

The thoughts rang through his head, getting more and more wrong, to the rhythm of the buzzing that got louder and louder and just.

Wouldn't.

Stop.

It took every bit of strength he had, but Nick wrenched his mouth from Cassie's. He dropped his hands from her body, stepping back one step, then another. The buzzing howled in an angry crescendo, but he ignored it.

"I can't," he gasped. He grabbed blindly for the banister, holding on to it for dear life as he took one step down, then another.

Cassie sagged against the front door, letting it hold her up. "What is it?" She sounded confused, taken aback, and not a little bit horny. "Is it . . ." She followed him down the steps. The farther he went, the quieter the static became until he was on the sidewalk again, the garden gate firmly shut between them.

"Well." His voice was shaky in his own ears. "Here we are again."

Cassie's sigh seemed to come from the bottom of her toes. "This is *bullshit*," she said. She looked over her shoulder, directing her fury toward the house. "You hear me, Mrs. H? This has got to stop!"

"I don't understand." He clutched the pickets of the garden gate, his nails digging into the wood in frustration. "What the fuck does she have against me? I haven't done anything to her."

"I think I know," she said darkly. "But I'm not sure . . . I need to figure out how to make it right. Give me a little time, okay?" Her hand on his cheek felt cool, calming. Everything he didn't want to be with her.

Now that Nick was away from the house, the buzzing in his head faded and he felt exhausted. Wrung out, like he'd just run a long distance. "Okay." The word was a long sigh. It wasn't okay. Not even a little bit. But then he couldn't help but find the humor in it. "I guess I'm not the only one being cockblocked by a ghost."

Cassie huffed out a laugh. "Fantastic. We both live alone, you know. You wouldn't think it would be this hard to be . . . uh . . . alone together."

"In a town full of ghosts? I'm not surprised, to be honest."

"Great," she grumbled. But she reached for his hand, threading their fingers together, and he held on tight. "I don't suppose there's an unhaunted seedy motel around here or anything?"

"Well, there's the Eternal Rest, out by the highway. It's not too bad, actually, and . . . oh. You said unhaunted?" Nick shook his head. "Never mind."

"Terrific."

Nick tugged at her hand, stepping closer to the closed gate while Cassie did the same on the other side. The gate was short enough that it only separated them from the chest down. Which still sucked, but Nick could work with it for the moment. He was a patient man, and Cassie had a plan. Or she was working on a plan. Something.

He reached over the fence, cupping her cheek with one hand.

"Figure things out with Mrs. H soon," he said. "Because I want you, Cassie Rutherford. And I want to find a way to make this work."

Cassie's dark eyes shone in the porch light as she looked up at him. She caught her lower lip between her teeth and Nick thought that was a great idea. He leaned forward and captured her mouth with his, pouring an entire night's worth of sexual frustration into that good-night kiss.

"We'll make this work," she said against his mouth when he finally let up. "I promise."

Nick was going to hold her to that. As he walked home alone (again), his mind felt surprisingly clear, and he cast his thoughts back to Cassie's front porch. The smell of her skin, the feel of her hair. But those weird, intrusive thoughts ruined the memory of kissing her on the front porch. Where had they come from? It reminded Nick of those college days when he'd made poor life choices and gotten blackout drunk at one party or another. The next day would be filled with snatches of memory, and mild horror at things he'd apparently done. *I said what? I threw whose phone into the lake?* It was like those things had happened to someone else, someone who coincidentally wore his face.

But those thoughts had been in his own head. They'd been *his thoughts*. Right?

The Beach Bum saw Nick safely to The Haunt, where the steel drum band was still going strong. But he didn't stop for a nightcap. He wasn't in the mood for company. He headed toward Hallowed Grounds, then up the back stairs to his apartment. Alone. Again.

But this was Boneyard Key, after all. "Alone" was a relative term.

Twenty-Six

It had happened again.

It hadn't been a trick of the light. Cassie was sure this time.

When Nick had pulled himself away from her and fled down her front steps, for the space of a couple of racing heartbeats his eyes had bored into hers.

Those eyes had been dark brown. As dark as her own.

He'd been harder to see down by the gate as they said good night, but the streetlight had caught enough of his face for her to see that his eyes were their regular blue again.

A bad feeling had settled in her gut, like a punch to the stomach. She had a pretty good idea of what was going on. She had questions to ask, but with Sarah's limited vocabulary, she had to ask them just right if she wanted to get the answers she needed.

Cassie woke up the next morning to an unexpected text from Nick. Check your mailbox. Not even bothering to get dressed, she shoved her feet in some flip-flops by the door and flip-flopped her way to the mailbox by the street in her pajamas. The rich smell of cinnamon and bananas greeted her when she opened it, and inside was a foil-wrapped loaf, still warm.

Tampering with mail is a federal offense you know, she texted back after her first slice.

> They'll never take me alive.

Cassie laughed out loud in her empty kitchen, her hand clapped over her mouth to stifle the sound and catch any stray banana bread crumbs. God, she really liked this guy. The warm glow in her chest from cinnamon banana bread and the memory of Nick's body against hers dimmed quickly, though, when she remembered how everything had ended the night before.

She called off work; it was time to get to the bottom of this.

Another cup of coffee, and then she got to it, unpacking the photos and documents from the folder she'd borrowed from Theo. She lined them up the way they had been the day before, the time progressing in chronological order across her coffee table. Then she opened her latest Etsy package of custom magnetic poetry pieces, placing them on the fridge in random places.

Once she was done, she stepped back and cleared her throat, which had suddenly become very dry. "Sarah? I hope you're here today. I really want to talk to you."

It took only a few seconds before the spoon that Cassie had used to stir her coffee rattled from its place on the saucer that still held banana bread crumbs. She exhaled a long sigh. "Okay. Good. So, there are some new words up here. Family words, like 'husband' and 'brother' and 'father,' stuff like that. You were trying to tell me about how the house was yours, do you remember? You said 'man closer friend,' which I took to mean he was closer than a friend to you. And I spent money on these custom words so I really hope I'm right.

"Were you talking about William Donnelly? The man who built this house? Was there a connection between you two? Can you tell me?"

Cassie stared hard at the fridge, waiting for a response, but nothing happened. Then she remembered that she never watched Sarah move the words; maybe she was waiting for privacy. Cassie busied herself by wrapping up the leftovers from her breakfast and putting her dishes in the dishwasher. Then she turned around. There was one word in the middle of the fridge; a word that was worth every penny she'd spent on it.

uncle

"Uncle?" Cassie repeated. "William Donnelly was your uncle?" Her mind spun with this new information.

But Sarah wasn't done. When Cassie looked up again the words had changed.

mother father dies

child goes uncle

big rain wind

"Big rain wind . . ." She made a disgusted noise in the back of her throat. "Cassie, you dumbass. You live in Florida and don't have 'hurricane' on your fridge?" But self-flagellation could wait. She turned her attention back to the fridge, translating each line of the message one at a time. "So your parents died. You were sent to live with your uncle, before the Great Storm. You were here for the Great Storm?"

And with a mental click, puzzle pieces began to fall into place. There wasn't a record of any other Blankenships in Boneyard Key because Sarah was the only one. But she wasn't an outsider; she was actually part of the Donnelly family, whose history here wasn't documented because he didn't stick around. Sarah Blankenship had been absorbed from one man's family to another, with no trace of her own name.

Man, fuck the patriarchy sometimes.

That would be an easy enough thing to verify. Cassie turned to her laptop; she'd splurged on a membership to a genealogy website a while back when she'd first started digging into Sarah's past. She flipped it open and . . . dead. Of course. It wouldn't charge at all now when she was at home. She'd chalk it up to it being old and just give in and buy a new one, but it would work just fine when she plugged it in at Hallowed Grounds. Or when Buster would plug it in. Or that time Nick had done so . . . Basically anytime a man plugged it in, it worked.

Man, fuck the patriarchy again. Even her electricity was involved.

There was something to that. Another puzzle piece. But Cassie could only handle one of those at a time, and right now she was working on Sarah's past. With a sigh she reached for her laptop bag. Buster would be here any minute to fix the showerhead in the upstairs bathroom, but he had a key. She left a note on the table asking him to check the electricity one more time. Couldn't hurt, right?

"I'll be back in a bit!" she called out to the empty house. "If there's anything else you want to let me know about, feel free! I'll check the fridge when I get home."

Her heart pounded a little faster the closer she got to the café. Nick's gift this morning had been unexpected and all the more perfect because of that, but was it also a message? They were all about no pressure, no strings. Was this saying he wanted more? Was this saying he wanted less? Like *I like you, but please quit coming by the café every damn day*? She glanced idly in the window of I Scream Ice Cream as she walked past, remembering what Nick had said about it on the ghost tour. *Sometimes an ice cream shop is just an ice cream shop.* Maybe banana bread was just banana bread.

Nick glanced up from behind the counter, and his smile looked like the sunshine after a summer rainstorm. So she'd probably been overthinking it. As usual.

"You done already?" He tossed a towel over his shoulder in the style of every clichéd diner owner in every movie or television show. "You're not supposed to eat an entire loaf of banana bread in one sitting, you know."

"You didn't leave me a latte to go with it," she shot back. "How was I supposed to enjoy it like that?"

"I had to keep you coming back here somehow."

"You know I love you for more than your banana bread." Her breath caught in her throat as the words left her mouth. She meant it in a teasing way; she'd said that kind of thing more than once to him. But Nick's eyes widened, just long enough for Cassie to see that this time, those words had had an impact.

She really shouldn't have said that. *No pressure, no strings*, she repeated to herself. Get a grip.

But Nick put his elbows on the counter, leaning toward her, an easy smile on his face. "I'll take what I can get."

Okay. They were okay. She relaxed into a smile as she stretched onto her toes, leaning over the counter for a kiss. "You can't leave one of those in the mailbox, either."

"Good point." God, his smile felt good against her mouth. She opened her eyes to watch Nick press his lips together for an instant as though to savor the kiss. "Iced hazelnut?" His gaze lingered on her mouth in an extremely distracting way, and Cassie forced her brain back on task.

"Yes, please," she said. "And power." She headed to her table in the back corner; Nick was just too damn distracting. "I think I'm going to just have to bite the bullet and rewire the whole damn house at this rate."

"That sounds nice and low stress."

"Oh, yeah. Won't dip into my nonexistent savings at all." Her laptop gave a pleasant chirp as it started charging, and Cassie tsked at it. Her logical brain reminded her that it wasn't her laptop's fault and her electricity worked fine; she had working lamps and appliances and hair dryers and all kinds of things. There was just something about her laptop and her house that didn't get along. Sarah Hawkins seemed to have something against Cassie working from home. It was the twenty-first century; Sarah Hawkins needed to get with the program.

That thought flashed in her mind like the neon ghosts in the coffee cup outside of Hallowed Grounds, and she knew she needed to pursue it further. But then Nick dropped off her iced hazelnut latte, along with a kiss on top of her head, and safe to say that put her mind on other, more pleasant things.

"Whatcha working on today?" He glanced down at her laptop, his hand flat on her back between her shoulder blades. Something about his touch was so grounding; it was like being connected to him was the most comforting thing in her life. It felt right. So right that it was almost unremarkable.

"Research," she said. "On Sarah Hawkins. Enough is enough."

"I couldn't agree more," Nick said. "Getting a little sick of that bitch."

"Hey." Cassie looked up with a frown. "Don't call her that."

He held up defensive hands. "Look, she's not my biggest fan. I don't want to take it personally, but she's making it hard."

"I get that. But she's my roommate. There's got to be a reason for all this. And I'm going to figure out what."

"If you say so." There was still an edge to his voice, but he kissed her hair again before leaving her to it. Cassie took a long sip of her latte—heaven—then brought up the genealogy website. Last time, she'd only gone as far as to confirm that C.S. and Sarah Hawkins lived in Boneyard Key in 1910, but now she brought up the 1900 census and searched for William Donnelly.

The result came back almost immediately. Donnelly, William.

Age fifty-seven, occupation: Architect. The next line however, was where she struck gold. Other members of the household: Blankenship, Sarah. Age nineteen. Relationship: Niece. No occupation listed.

"Gotcha," Cassie whispered at the screen. If she ever needed any confirmation that Sarah's spirit was really in her house, here it was. The fridge had said earlier this morning that Donnelly was her uncle, and now here was the proof in a PDF. But this new knowledge sent a chill down her spine and her brain down a rabbit hole. Why did William Donnelly leave town? How did C.S. Hawkins enter the picture? She wasn't sure what search terms she needed to enter to get the answers she sought.

But maybe her answers weren't online. Cassie all but chugged her latte as she repacked her computer bag.

"You charged up already?" Nick waved off Cassie's debit card when she tried to hand it to him.

"Not quite. But I need to talk to Theo."

Nick's brow furrowed. "I thought you already talked to him."

"What, are you jealous?" She stretched up for another over-the-counter kiss. "I found something that I want him to see."

"Hmm." Nick looked skeptical, his gaze sweeping her up and down. Cassie's cheeks heated up, and this time when she reached across the counter it was to swat him.

"Not like that! Pervert."

"I'm just saying . . . you and him, alone in that museum of his . . . try and behave yourself."

Cassie snorted. "I'll see what I can do."

But when she arrived at Boneyard Books, picking her way back to the museum side of the shop, she pushed aside the curtain and found that she wasn't alone at all.

"Hey." Sophie waved from one of the seats at the card table.

"Please tell me you haven't been here all night."

Sophie's mouth twitched in a smile as Cassie dropped into the seat opposite. "Of course not. But there's so much here . . . so much I never knew about. I took the morning off to do some more reading."

"Took the morning off? You have a day job?"

Sophie raised an eyebrow. "Ghost tours don't exactly pay the bills, you know. I work from home. Medical transcriptions, stuff like that."

"Oh. Nice." Cassie could relate to working from home, and how easy it was sometimes to sneak off when something more tempting was itching in your brain.

"What about you?" Sophie folded her arms on the table, over the papers scattered from their file folder. "What are you doing around here?"

"I found something." She pulled out her laptop and powered it up.

"What did you find?" Theo's voice came from the doorway, and Cassie jumped and spun in her seat.

"Where the hell did you come from?" The front counter had been deserted when she'd walked in, so she'd expected him to be back here in the museum.

"The classics section." Theo tugged on his brown tweed vest and straightened his tie, looking exactly like someone who would hang out in the classics section. It was probably the sexiest part of the store to him. "Some new books came in I had to shelve. This place is occasionally a bookstore, you know." His voice was chiding, but his eyes sparked with humor.

"I'll try and remember that," Cassie said with a smile of her own. "Anyway . . ." She turned back to her laptop, pulling up the documents she'd hastily downloaded at Hallowed Grounds. "Take a look."

Theo adjusted his glasses as he leaned over Cassie's shoulder. "Sarah Hawkins was Donnelly's niece?"

"Before she was Sarah Hawkins. When she was Sarah Blankenship." Cassie nodded. "That explains why you didn't know the name; she was the only one. Plus, she told me this morning that she was his niece, so it all tracks."

"Wait." He straightened up. "She told you?"

"Oh, yeah," Sophie chimed in. "Cassie has these words on her fridge, and Sarah moves them around when she has something to say."

"Really?" Theo looked at Cassie with new interest. "That's . . . that's genius, actually."

"Thanks. It's been touch and go, but it seems to be working." Cassie felt like a little bit of an asshole, taking credit for this innovative plan to communicate with the dead, when it was really a happy accident.

"I'll say." Theo looked at Cassie's screen with unfocused eyes, and Cassie could all but see the wheels turning behind his light green eyes. "So Donnelly built the house and lived in it with Sarah. Then Sarah married Hawkins and he got the house . . ."

"That means Sarah lived there the whole time," Sophie chimed in. "The house was always hers."

"But not hers at the same time," Theo said. "Her name was never on it. It was more like her dowry or something."

"And then Donnelly left, Hawkins died, and it was just Sarah and the house again. For all those years." Cassie sat back in her seat. "And all those years, it's been called the Hawkins House, like she didn't matter."

Theo shrugged. "History's written by the living, after all. Mr. Lindsay wasn't exactly a protofeminist. *A Haunted History* is going to show his bias."

"Yeah." Cassie sighed. Fuck the patriarchy one more time. "But it's not like this has been buried all that deep. Why didn't anyone put this together before?"

"Nobody cared enough to." Theo's eyes flicked over to Sophie in apology, and her gaze went to the table and the papers she was studying.

That made the breath whoosh out of Cassie's body. That, more than anything else she'd seen and heard these past few months, drove home the point that Sarah Hawkins had died alone. No friends, no family. No one to miss her. All she'd left behind were her beloved cabbage roses, and those were long gone.

"I'm going to get this right." Sophie's usually small voice was strong, backed with steel. "I know this ghost tour's just a stupid thing for tourists, but I owe it to these people I'm talking about. If I'm going to tell those stories, I need to tell them right."

"I know you will." Theo's voice was kind. "Anything I can do to help, let me know."

"Same here," Cassie said. "I still have the Hawkins House stuff at home. Come over anytime if you want to take a look."

Sophie's smile was thin, but genuine, and Cassie could relate. Her mind was in a jumble, turning over these moments of Sarah's life that she'd just figured out. But the puzzle pieces were clicking into place now.

Twenty-Seven

Cassie knew that Sophie was determined to get things right when it came to the ghost tour, but she hadn't expected her to show up that next Monday afternoon with a bag of Chinese takeout.

Cassie blinked dumbly at the food. "We have a Chinese place here?"

"They keep it quiet," Sophie said with a smile. "They're over behind Eternal Rest, and are only open three days a week right now. Even less during the offseason."

"That's . . . that's pretty quiet," Cassie agreed.

Sophie hoisted the bag. "I was hoping to bribe you with chicken lo mein to see that research on your house."

Cassie opened the door wide. "Come on in."

They made short work of the lo mein as Cassie took Sophie on a little tour of her own, narrating the photos that were still lined up on her coffee table. "Maybe you can help me," she said. "There's something here, and I'm just not seeing it. I think I've been looking at these pictures too long."

"Is this them?" Sophie picked up the wedding photo, studying Mr. and Mrs. Hawkins. "He looks kinda mean, doesn't he?"

"He does . . ." Cassie trailed off as another mental puzzle piece clicked into place. *Mean. My man bad.* Good Lord. She'd been so excited about the family tree discovery that she'd forgotten the other, very important thing that Sarah had told her.

"Sarah." Cassie kept her eyes on the wedding photo as she raised her voice, directing it toward the kitchen. "Did your husband ever hurt you? Is that how he was bad?" She knew the answer to this question already, but damn did she want to be wrong. She steeled herself before going into the kitchen to look at the fridge.

yes

"Wow." Sophie's eyes were huge behind her glasses. "That still gives me the shivers, her moving the words around like that. Do you ever get used to it?"

"Trying to," Cassie said absently, more focused on Sarah's answer and what it meant. She glanced down at the photo in her hand, then back up at the fridge, and the message had already changed.

husband want baby

no

man bad

"He . . . he wanted kids, and when they didn't come he got angry?" Cassie blinked hard against sudden tears. Go back a hundred years or so and that could have been her. With a husband who thought she was useless because she couldn't have children. But it wasn't her fault, any more than it was Sarah's.

little pain

more control

Cassie nodded. "So it wasn't so much that he hit you as he was a controlling douchebag. Got it."

"You really should have that as one of the words she can use." Sophie stepped closer to examine the words on the fridge.

But Cassie had more questions to ask. "Did you ever hurt him?" That was the big question, and both she and Sophie held their breath. They couldn't see the words move, but suddenly just one word was in the middle of the fridge.

no

Cassie exhaled a huge sigh. She wasn't roommates with a murderer. She could work with that. "But people thought you did."

people wrong

"Yeah, I get that now." Sophie looked around the kitchen, as though she could spot Sarah by the table and address her face-to-face. "I'm sorry. I didn't know. We're going to get it right now, I promise."

"We are." Cassie wasn't sure if she was reassuring Sophie or Sarah. "We're trying to get to the bottom of everything. I want to get your side of the story. I know it's hard, since you only have so many words to work with."

The words on the fridge may have provided a limited vocabulary, but Sarah had a lot to say.

husband control

after death free

but not

"Okay, so I was right about your husband being controlling. After he died you felt . . . free?"

Sophie nodded. "I mean, that's a little dark, but fair."

"Yeah, but . . . 'but not'? What does that part mean? Free but not free?" Cassie turned to Sophie, who shrugged.

"Plenty of reasons, I'd think. It's not like women had tons of autonomy back then. She was a product of the nineteenth century, right? It's not like she could go out and get a job. If she was an independent woman back then . . . Maybe that's what she was being judged for?"

"Maybe?" But that didn't seem right. Cassie paced the downstairs, from the kitchen to the living room and back again, while she thought. Sure, it had taken some time to get used to all this ghost stuff, but now that she had, Sarah wasn't threatening. She wasn't mean. She was kind. She was lonely. She liked watching garbage television.

Cassie was having a hard time reconciling all that with the story of Mean Mrs. Hawkins chasing kids away from her house. Why would you want to keep innocent—or not-so-innocent—kids away? Why not put up a NO TRESPASSING sign if you wanted people out?

Thoughts of signs were still in her head when she slowed in front of the coffee table, lingering in front of the photos of the house that were lined up in chronological order. She sat down on the couch in front of them, imagining where she'd hang a NO TRESPASSING sign. Maybe on the gate itself? No, there were too many roses; the sign would get lost.

Except there weren't too many roses. Not always. Cassie picked up the first photo, the earliest one, taken when the house was newly constructed. Roses bloomed along the fence line, and now that she looked at the photo more closely, there was a white out-of-focus smudge in the background that was vaguely woman shaped. Was that Sarah, working in her garden?

Cassie followed the progression of the cabbage roses as she examined the photos in order. Lush rosebushes in full bloom suddenly disappeared. Three of the photos had no roses at all. What those photos did have was C.S. Hawkins. Standing in front of this little seaside cottage like he was lord of some great manor.

"Not a fan of roses, this guy," she murmured.

"Cassie!" Sophie called from the kitchen. "She's doing it again! The words changed. It says 'roses useless.' Does that mean anything?"

"Yeah." Cassie returned to the kitchen, photos in hand. "See, look at these pictures. She had roses in her garden before, but while she was married—while C.S. was around—they were gone."

"Because he said they were useless?" Sophie frowned, looking at the photos. "Flowers are there to be pretty. They're not supposed to have a function."

But more puzzle pieces started to rotate in Cassie's head. So close now, just out of reach. "Sarah's attention was on her garden, on the things that made her happy. And not on her husband. Not on giving him a family."

Sophie sucked in a breath, and Cassie looked at her, then to the fridge. The words had changed again.

get him out

Those words again. The first time Sarah had used that phrase had been that day that Nick was there. He'd stood in her kitchen, his eyes flashing dark and almost frightening, saying the most awful things before she'd kicked him out. How her own interests should be irrelevant compared to a husband and family. Outdated, misogynistic thinking; it had all been so unlike Nick. But it was right in line with the opinion of a man from the early nineteen hundreds.

A man who wanted to control his wife.

A man who thought a woman's main purpose was providing children.

A man with dark brown eyes.

get him out

Sarah had never been talking about Nick.

She was talking about C.S. Hawkins.

When he'd died, Sarah said she was free, but not.

Because he'd stuck around too. His spirit was bullying her, and anyone else who might come around her home.

So she'd kept everyone away. Even the neighborhood children, who might get too close. For decades she'd borne the brunt of his temper. Alone.

Well, not anymore. Not if Cassie could help it.

"You're right," she said to her refrigerator. "We need to get him out. But we're gonna need some help first."

"Get who out?" Sophie asked, but Cassie had already scooped up her phone. She punched up Libby's number and waited impatiently for her to answer.

"Libby? Can a house have more than one ghost in it?"

"Sure it can." Libby had obviously been doing this for too long to let a question like this faze her. "Whole families can linger behind together."

Cassie turned back toward the kitchen, where Sophie watched her with wide, slightly confused eyes.

get him out was still displayed on the fridge. *Working on it, Sarah.* "Do you think Nan could come over? I think she missed a spot."

Nan's tracksuit was pink this time, practically glowing in the late-afternoon sun when she and Libby arrived on Cassie's front porch. The first thing the elderly woman did when she walked inside was look around Cassie's freshly painted living room with an appraising eye.

"Nice colors," she said. She looked around again. "Don't see any cabbage roses, though. Didn't she say she missed the roses?"

"She did," Cassie confirmed. "But given the choice she said she'd rather have the color of the wallpaper than the actual wallpaper itself."

"She said . . ." Nan's voice trailed off, mystified, but then she caught sight of the refrigerator and that seemed to jog her memory. "Right," she said. "You and Sarah have been using your words, huh? Very good." She headed toward the kitchen, with Cassie, Sophie, and Libby trailing after her like ducklings.

Nan examined the fridge, which still said **get him out**. "Not exactly subtle, is it?"

"Nope." Cassie took a deep breath. "I'm pretty sure there's a second ghost in this house. C.S. Hawkins? I think he stuck around too." She watched Nan's face carefully. Cassie sure wasn't the ghost expert in the room—hell, she wasn't even the second-best expert in the room. Or the third. Was she ghost-splaining here?

"Really?" If Nan was offended by the implication that she'd missed something the first time around, she didn't show it. Instead she walked slowly back out to the living room, turning in a circle. It was the same thing she'd done the first time, when she was getting a feel of the place. Was she seeing something different this time around?

Apparently she was. She stopped short in the center of the living room and took a sharp breath. "Oh, there you are. Where the hell have you been?" She fell silent then, her eyes closed, concentrating. "Hiding behind your wife, I bet. Typical." Her voice was little more than a murmur, and she seemed to shrink into herself the longer she stood. Cassie wanted to take her arm, wanted to offer her a chair, but she was pretty sure that touching a medium at this point in the proceedings was a no-no. She hazarded a glance over at Libby, who was worrying her bottom lip with her teeth, her eyes fixed on her grandmother. She looked concerned, but no more than anyone would over the well-being of your average octogenarian. That made Cassie feel better, the way that bored-looking flight attendants made her feel calm when the plane hit turbulence. Libby knew what was going on, and she wasn't alarmed.

"Damn." Nan's voice was stronger now, rougher. "He really doesn't like you." Her eyes opened, focused on Cassie.

Cassie blinked. Was that something she should be concerned about? "Uh. Sorry?"

"Work." Nan practically spit the word as she shook off the remainder of whatever trance she'd been under. "He doesn't like that you work. Not just you. Women in general. Says he tried to stop you, stop your machine."

"My machine . . ." Cassie repeated, then the light bulb came on in her head as another puzzle piece slid into place. "He keeps my laptop from charging." Then she sucked in a breath as the mental light bulb surged suddenly brighter. "Only when *I* plug it in. Because I'm a woman."

Sophie made a *tsk* sound with her tongue. "What a misogynist."

"No shit." Libby folded her arms on her chest. "Fuck that guy."

"Language, Liberty." Nan cut her eyes to her granddaughter. Libby looked chastened, though she rolled her eyes in Cassie's direction when Nan wasn't looking.

"Yeah," Nan said dismissively, walking back to the kitchen with a purpose this time, plunking her shoulder bag on the kitchen table. "He's gotta go."

"He does?" A surge of relief swept through Cassie. Imagine being able to plug in her laptop and having it work. Imagine being able to kiss Nick in her kitchen anytime she wanted. Cassie could imagine a lot of other things she'd like to do with Nick in her kitchen. But she forced her brain back on topic as one thing bothered her. "I thought you said you don't like to banish spirits. That it was okay for them to stick around."

"Not if they're assholes." Nan said the words slowly, as though explaining to a toddler. "And this one's an asshole. Therefore, he's gotta go." She started rummaging through her impossibly large bag, pulling out a few things: a Costco-size container of salt, a water pistol for some reason, a child's plastic bucket capped with a lid, a fistful of white taper candles still wrapped in plastic. "Libby, get the poker out of the car."

Now Libby was all business; not an eyeroll to be seen. "Yes, ma'am."

"So what . . . what is all this stuff?"

Nan laid a hand on the water pistol. "Holy water. Salt, obviously. Sand. The candles are for protective energy. The poker is made of iron; some spirits react to iron, so it's always good to have it around."

"Right." Cassie nodded dumbly. "So this is . . ."

"An exorcism," Nan answered, as though it were the kind of thing she did every day of the week. Which, considering her line of work, she probably did. "We're getting rid of Mr. Hawkins."

Nan paused in her preparations and cocked her head, as though she were listening to something. Or someone. "He wants to know where your man is," she said. "He says your man should put you in your place." She sounded disgusted. "This guy. Real piece of work." She pulled a pocketknife out of her bag and started peeling the plastic off the candles.

"My man?" But Cassie knew right away. Nick. The relief that swept through her made her sway on her feet, chasing away any lingering doubts about him. He'd been right after all. The way he acted, those things he said . . . he'd said it wasn't him, and he was right. It was all C.S. Hawkins.

"He tried to tell you," Nan said. "He came close once, when . . ." Her voice trailed off, lost in thought. "When the boy was here. The boy is weak. He needed to get you under control."

Sophie let out a nervous giggle. "Mr. Hawkins doesn't know Nick that well, then. That's not like him at all."

"Nick, huh?" Nan looked up. "The coffee shop boy?" The front door opened, and Libby brought a fireplace poker inside, laying it on the table next to the rest of Nan's supplies.

"What about Nick?" Libby asked.

"Go get him too." Nan made a shooing motion toward the door.

"No!" Cassie called out, but the front door was already banging shut behind Libby again. She turned to Nan. "You don't need him for this." Her voice shook; all she could remember was when Nick's eyes changed. Those dark brown, angry eyes that didn't belong in his face. She didn't like seeing him that way. Mr. Hawkins's problem was with her, not Nick. There was no need to put him through this.

But Nan shook her head. "He keeps saying he wants to talk to your man. Again. That means he's talked to him before. If we're going to get rid of him, we need to bring him to the surface. I think your boy there might be the key." She ripped the plastic off the last candle, then started taking out small candleholders. She handed them all to Cassie. "Your living room is the biggest room in the house, we'll set up in there. Start with the candles—one at each compass point. Then you girls can move the furniture out of the center of the room. We need space to work."

Cassie decided not to argue. This was her very first exorcism, after all. At this point, all she could do was watch and follow directions. And trust that Nan would keep them safe.

Keep them all safe.

Twenty-Eight

It had been a busy day, especially for a Monday. Nick could tell that summer was here, from the uptick in tourists as much as from the rising temperatures that kept people inside and as close to the air conditioner as possible. Folks up north were trapped in their houses by snowstorms in the wintertime, but in Florida it was the opposite. Summer brought the most oppressive weather, though it inexplicably brought the tourists as well.

Well, they could have the outdoors this time of year. Let them rent the kayaks and stand-up paddleboards and slowly broil in the hot Florida sun. Nick wished them well and hoped they had enough sunscreen. (And enough bug spray, if they were heading to Cemetery Island.) The only outdoor activity on his docket was another day of fishing with Vince on Wednesday. But the plan was to head out well before sunrise and be back by midmorning, when the humidity really settled in like a wet blanket over your face.

Nick followed the last customer to the door, flipping the latch with satisfaction. It had been a long, busy breakfast rush followed by a slightly tamer but still hectic lunch crowd. It didn't take long to set the seating area to rights, stacking chairs on tables so he could mop the whole floor later. But for now, he had banana bread to make for tomorrow.

The kitchen was sparkling clean; Ramon always left the place spotless after the lunch rush. Nick took a moment to enjoy the silence of the empty café and the tranquility of a perfectly clean kitchen, knowing he was about to mess it all up. Then of course he'd clean it. Again. There was something so comfortable about a routine that never changed; it was something he could rely on.

And in the back of his mind, there was Cassie. She wasn't supposed to be part of his routine. No pressure, no strings, remember? Yet his favorite thing in the morning was her smile when she walked through his door. And his favorite thing in the evening was the way the sunset threw golden light in her hair, and the way she nestled into the hollow of his shoulder, fitting like a piece of him he hadn't realized was missing.

Maybe once he was done here he could give her a call. See if she wanted to watch the sunset.

Of course, that was about all they could do, he remembered with not a little bit of irritation. He couldn't go into her house, and with Elmer hanging out like a Peeping Tom, she couldn't spend much time at his. Too bad he couldn't hang a sock on the door, let Elmer know to fuck off for an evening . . .

But that gave Nick an idea. With the first batch of banana bread in the oven, he reached for the green spiral notebook on that upper shelf. He flipped through it till he found the photo of Elmer and his wife. The facade of the café looked mostly the same except for the neon ghosts Nick had added a couple years ago.

"Okay, Elmer. Let's make a deal." He tossed his phone to the counter before flipping over the first few pages. "I bake whatever you tell me to, and you give me a night alone with Cassie. Sound good?"

The answering buzz came immediately, sending his phone dancing across the counter. *Pound cake. Lemon, if you have the stuff for it.*

Nick's smile lifted the right corner of his mouth. "Oh, I've got the stuff for it. You're on." It didn't take long to find the recipe—it was pretty basic, like everything else in that notebook. But there was nothing wrong with sticking to the basics. He threw himself into baking, trying to take his mind off the fact that he hadn't heard from Cassie since she left the café that morning, right before lunch. No pressure, no strings. They were both adults, with careers and habits formed long before they came into each other's lives. He was cool with that.

But he also missed her. He'd meant to catch her before she left, ask when he could see her again. But she'd left right as things started to pick up at lunchtime. She was there when he took a customer's order, but by the time he'd turned the order in to Ramon she was gone. It was fine, he told himself as he poured the cake batter into a set of loaf pans. It was her routine these days, since her laptop still wouldn't hold a charge at home. Spend the morning at the café, charging up, then work at home in the afternoon. As he mixed up a batch of lemon icing to drizzle over the top of the pound cake, he reminded himself that he and Cassie were fine.

But no pressure and no strings also meant no progress. And while Nick had been fine with those kinds of relationships for as long as he could remember, he suddenly felt stifled. Not by Cassie, but by the lack of her. Things between them felt like they were stuck in first gear, and Nick suddenly wanted to put the hammer down. See how fast they could go.

Maybe they wouldn't go far. She wasn't committing to him the same way he wasn't committing to her, and for all he knew she was still planning to sell the house and go back to Orlando.

But so what? Her leaving town didn't mean they had to end. Orlando wasn't *that* far away, and people did long-distance relationships all the time. All he knew now was that he liked his life with

Cassie in it and didn't want to think of a life without her. They could make it work. They would find a way. Maybe he wouldn't mind a few strings after all.

Yeah, he was definitely calling Cassie tonight. They had things to discuss. And things to do that didn't involve talking.

There was a knock at the outer door to the café right as the timer went off for the cakes. Nick ignored it, letting the knocking continue while he took the loaf pans out of the oven. There were always going to be Those People who thought that because they were on vacation, rules didn't apply to them. Rules like closing times: they wanted a coffee and it didn't matter that the coffee shop had closed hours ago. Couldn't he just open the doors and serve them anyway? People seemed to pack extra audacity when they went on vacation.

The kitchen was filled with the aroma of buttery sugar and lemon, making Nick's mouth water. He hoped Elmer could smell it. It was a little more effort than the banana bread he could make in his sleep at this point, but he had to admit Elmer was right. Totally worth it. He set the loaves to cool next to the finished banana bread. He'd ice them tonight and then pack it all up later, ready for tomorrow.

He fired off a text: hope I did it justice, before glancing around, gearing himself up to clean the kitchen. He'd just started stacking dishes in the sink when his phone buzzed with a response; he dried his hands on a kitchen towel before throwing it over his shoulder and picking up his phone.

> Perfect. Smells just like I remember. You're not bad at this!

Wow. Rare praise from Elmer. Nick smiled, a warm feeling blooming in his chest.

Meanwhile, someone was still knocking on the fucking door.

Nick threw the kitchen towel to the counter in a private display of temper, then he sucked in a deep breath through his nose as he barreled through the swinging kitchen door and into the café proper. He knew how to deal with folks like this—snarky and just this side of rude—but his annoyed stride halted when he saw a familiar blond ponytail through the front window. Libby.

Why the hell was Libby knocking at the café like she didn't know he was closed? But the look on her face made Nick's heart stall in his chest; something was wrong. Now he couldn't get the door open fast enough, unlocking the latch and throwing back the bolt with nerveless fingers.

"What is it?" The words tumbled out of his mouth as he pulled open the door. "Is it your grandma? What's wrong?"

Libby shook her head, ponytail swinging frantically to keep up. "It's Cassie."

"Cassie?" His heart gave a great thump, nearly stalling in his chest. "Is she okay?"

Libby shook her head. "We need you. Come on. Nan's at her house right now." She looked over her shoulder, toward the Hawkins House, and ice pooled in Nick's stomach.

"Okay." He darted out the door, closing it behind him before he realized—keys. He needed his keys to lock the door. And he should probably take his phone too. "Hold on." It only took a moment to dash inside, back to the kitchen, to scoop up his phone from the counter and his keys from their hook. His hip caught against the corner of the counter on his way back out, more than one stool crashing to the ground, but he didn't notice the pain.

As he stepped onto the sidewalk, pulling the door closed behind him and fumbling with his keys to lock it, he glanced back into the café; had he turned the oven off? He didn't give a shit; the whole place could burn down for all he cared. Cassie needed him, and nothing was going to get in his way.

But he had the presence of mind to fire off a text (Is the oven off?) while he was still under the awning before he locked the door. He could only hope that Elmer's range reached to the sidewalk, and he practically sagged with relief when he got an immediate reply (All good in here; go help your girl!). He was already heading up the sidewalk, his long strides forcing Libby to trot to keep up with him, as he stowed his phone away along with his keys.

"What's happened?" he asked. "Did Mrs. H turn on her?" Just the thought of it had him seeing red. Cassie had bent over backward to try to understand her ghostly roommate, and now this? Mrs. H could fuck with him all she wanted; he was used to it by now. But if she'd done something to hurt Cassie . . .

But Libby shook her head. "It's not Mrs. H," she said. "It's *Mister* H."

"Mister?" Nick stopped short, facing Libby. "Where the hell did he come from?" But something clicked in his brain. The bees, the buzzing . . . the aggressive static. The masculine, outdated thinking.

Holy shit, it *was* Mr. H after all.

Libby filled Nick in on everything on the rest of the walk to Cassie's house.

"From what we've been able to figure out, Mrs. H has been keeping him at bay all this time. First while she was alive, and then . . . afterward."

"Strong woman." Nick conveniently forgot that he'd hated Sarah Hawkins all of five minutes ago. "Bet he hates that."

"Yep. And then Cassie came along, and then *you* came along. Mr. H wants to control Cassie, and he's trying to get you to do that for him."

Nick had to scoff at the notion. "Fuck that."

"Exactly."

They reached the Hawkins House, and the sight of Cassie sitting on the top step filled Nick with relief. Whatever was going on hadn't touched her yet. She looked fine. She looked . . .

Pissed.

She came storming down the steps of her front porch, her face like thunder. "Absolutely not," she barked as she met Nick at her front gate. She put her hands on the gate, as though that would keep him out. She glared past him to Libby. "I told you not to get him."

Libby tsked. "Nan said to get him, so I got him. That's how it works."

The front door opened, and as though summoned, Nan Simpson stood on the front porch in all her pink-track-suited glory. She looked out into the yard, taking stock, then nodded. "Good," she said. "The boy's here. Let's get this started."

Nick looked up at Nan, then to Libby and finally to Cassie. "What exactly are we getting started?"

"An exorcism," Libby replied cheerfully. "Haven't been part of one of these in a while. Should be fun."

"They're not *fun*." Nan shook her head at her granddaughter as Libby pushed open the gate to head into the house. "Go inside, double-check everything. Tell me if I missed something." She looked back at Nick and Cassie, who were still rooted to the spot, the gate firmly shut between them again. "Come inside when you're ready. It's time C. S. Hawkins crossed over for good."

As the front door closed behind Nan, Cassie heaved a sigh. Then she turned her attention back to Nick, worry etched in her expression. He reached out, smoothing a thumb across her forehead. She closed her eyes at his touch. "I really don't want to involve you in this," she said, her voice soft.

Nick shook his head. "Don't care. I'm in." He took her hands in his—her fingers were freezing, despite the heat of the late afternoon—threading their fingers together.

Her face softened, and that only strengthened his resolve. "I don't like what he does to you," she said. "I don't want to put you through that."

"I don't love it, either." Even now, on the other side of the gate but this close to the house, Nick could hear the static, a faint buzz in the back of his brain. It dared him to cross into the yard, even as everything inside him urged him to turn and flee. But he was stronger than that. And it was time to tell her. Everything. "Cassie. I want to be with you."

She blinked up at him in surprise. "What happened to 'no pressure, no strings'?"

"You happened." He reached for that lock of hair that always fell out of her messy bun, catching it to twirl it between his fingers. "Give me all the pressure. All the strings. Lay it on me."

He bent toward her, over the gate. She caught her breath, and then he caught it, brushing his mouth over hers. Her kiss lay waste to the thick wall he'd built around his heart, around his soul. He didn't need it anymore. When they came up for air, he pressed his forehead to hers, breathing her in. "I want to be with you, Cassie," he said again. "I know that there's a lot going on right now, about to banish a ghost from your house and all, so my timing is absolute shit. But you have no idea how good it feels to say that to someone. How good it feels to feel that way. I know you still might be leaving town, so I don't want to pressure you. But . . ." He was babbling now, his thoughts spilling through his brain and out of his mouth faster than he could keep track of them. But these feelings were so new, so strong, that he couldn't hold them back.

Cassie pulled back, her brown eyes studying his, and Nick

wanted to lose himself in those eyes. Hell, he already had lost himself. He just needed Cassie to find him.

"I want to be with you too." Her words sent his heart soaring, but her face was still worried. She threw a glance over her shoulder, to the house where everyone was waiting for them. "But I don't want you involved in this. There's got to be another way."

Nick would like that too, honestly. But . . . "Apparently Mr. Hawkins only really appears for me. So if I can help get him out of here, then that's what I'm going to do." He took a breath and, very deliberately, unlatched the garden gate. Then he stepped through, into Cassie's front garden.

The static took up residence in his head almost immediately. Buzzing that was almost painfully loud. But Nick wasn't afraid of it anymore. Now he knew what it was: C.S. Hawkins dialing in, trying to find the right frequency to get Nick to do his bidding.

Wasn't gonna happen.

"Nick." Cassie's voice broke through the static and calmed his heart. She squeezed his hand. "Are you sure about this?"

He squeezed back. "It's for you. I'm in. I'm all in."

Twenty-Nine

Cassie didn't want to go inside. She didn't give a damn about ghosts anymore. At that moment, all she wanted was to pull Nick away from prying eyes, down the street if necessary, and ask him what he meant by "I'm all in." It wasn't exactly an *I love you*, but it wasn't *not* one, either. That moment, where it was just her and him there at her front gate, felt like one of those moments you needed to pause, to remember every detail, because it was a moment you were going to remember for the rest of your life. The way Nick's hands felt, cupping her face. The way his eyelashes were a little spiky as they framed those clear blue eyes of his. The way he smelled faintly of lemon sugar, carried on the light breeze that surrounded them. His voice, his words, the way he talked so fast it was like his mouth was trying to keep up with his brain. Cassie wanted to hold him close and live in this moment for the rest of her life.

But she couldn't. Because there was a malevolent spirit in her house, bullying everyone he was able to reach, and that asshole needed to be evicted. And this gorgeous, perfect man in front of her was apparently the key to making that happen.

So instead of dragging him out of there to a place where none of this could touch them so she could ask, *What exactly do you mean by "I'm all in"?*, she gripped his hand tightly and led him up the stairs and onto her front porch. There was something about the way he walked, with slow, deliberate steps, that made Cassie's heart hurt. It was obvious that this was hard for him; every time he'd been to her house recently he hadn't even made it inside the front door. She didn't understand what C.S. Hawkins was doing when he affected Nick like this, but it was obviously uncomfortable at best and painful at worst. This whole exorcism thing had better be quick.

Cassie stepped carefully over the threshold of her front door. Nick hesitated for a long moment before following. Once on the other side of the threshold, he exhaled a long, slow breath.

"Okay." He smiled at Cassie. "See? It's not so bad."

He was lying. Cassie could tell by the set of his jaw, a slight squint in his eyes, that it was indeed bad. Really bad. What kind of torture had he just signed himself up for, for her sake? Cassie hated this, but all she could do now was support him to the end.

She gave his hand a reassuring squeeze. His eyes were still that bright, impossible blue, but she knew that wasn't going to last. It was about to get much, much worse.

Nan was waiting in the living room, with Libby and Sophie behind her in the kitchen like acolytes in casual summer wear flanking their track-suited high priestess. Sophie chewed on a fingernail, her eyes darting around, while Libby kept her eyes on her grandmother. But Nan only had eyes for Nick and Cassie.

Cassie, meanwhile, only had eyes for her living room. While she'd been outside, the room had been completely transformed. The curtains were drawn, turning the room into an intimate scene. Those tall, white taper candles glowed from where she'd placed them earlier. All the furniture had been pushed up against the walls, like they were going to throw a dance party in the living room. Even the circular area rug had been rolled up and moved aside. In the middle of the empty space was a large, almost-completed circle laid down with what looked like sand. Cassie pointed to it. "That better vacuum up afterward."

Nan rolled her eyes, while a smile played around Libby's mouth. "It'll be fine," Libby murmured, as Nan gestured to the circle.

"Right. In there, you two."

"Both of us?" This surprised Cassie, but she wasn't upset about it. She wasn't about to let go of Nick's hand anyway.

But Nick lingered, eyeing the circle. "What is that?"

"Salt," Nan said. "Mixed with sand from Cemetery Island. Powerful stuff. Grounding. It's good when you're trying to get a spirit's attention."

"All I usually need to do is change up the banana bread recipe." Nick's lips turned up at his attempt at a joke, but his voice was thin, his smile tight. He cleared his throat. "What happens when we step in there?"

"Libby's going to close the circle behind you," Nan said. "C.S. Hawkins seems to like you, so we're going to see if you can attract him to you. Once he's here and attached to you, he'll be trapped in the circle, and we can concentrate on getting him out."

"Can't say that I've ever been bait before." Nick rolled his head around his neck, then shrugged his shoulders, like he was warming up for something.

Cassie tugged gently on his hand. "Are you sure about this?"

He turned his gaze to her; his eyes had darkened, but they were still blue. Cassie's heart skipped a beat. It was starting already. But his smile was gentle, sincere, and just for her. "Don't worry," he said. "It'll be fine."

She wasn't sure about that, but before she could say anything else, Nick stepped through the opening and into the salt-and-sand circle, and what could she do but follow? As soon as they were inside, Libby was there, pouring more of the sand and salt mixture in the gap they'd just stepped through, closing the circle behind them. Cassie caught her breath, waiting for something to happen. Nothing did. No energy shift, no dramatic explosions.

"You all right?" She looked up at Nick.

"There's nothing wrong with me." It wasn't Nick's voice anymore. Not completely. It was harder, meaner. Cassie dropped his hand in alarm, and if she could have taken a step back without disturbing the circle she would have. It had happened in an instant, and so much more intensely than it ever had before. Nick put his hands on his hips and rotated in a tight circle, taking in the living room in its entirety. "What are you all doing in my house?"

"The house is mine." Cassie's chest felt tight as she spoke. She meant those words, more emphatically than she'd ever meant anything in her life. It was almost like she was saying them more loudly, saying them twice. At the same time. "Not yours. It was never yours, Charles." *Nick,* she thought. *His name is Nick, not Charles.* But Nick's eyes had gone dark, dark brown, and there was something about his face, something about the way he held himself, that made Cassie want to shrink back, flinch away from him. Which was ridiculous. She wasn't afraid of Nick. He'd never hurt her.

But Charles would. Charles had. The knowledge was immediate and certain, and Cassie understood what had happened. C.S. Hawkins had taken over Nick, that much was obvious. But Cassie had been taken over too; Sarah was right there with her. Inside her head. Ghostly reinforcements had arrived.

It was confusing inside her brain, like watching two movies at the same time on a split screen. She tried to relax, share the space inside her head, while her instincts struggled against it. *C'mon, Sarah. Let's get him.*

Meanwhile, Nick looked coldly smug, an expression that Cassie wanted to slap off his face. "We're married, *love*." He spit out the term of endearment, making a mockery of it. "This house became my property on our wedding day. *You* became my property." He stepped forward then, gripping her arm with one strong hand. The Sarah inside Cassie's head flinched, pulled against his grip, but Cassie just got angry. Nick wasn't like this; this asshole inside his head was making Nick behave in a way that wasn't normal, wasn't natural.

Suddenly, Nick's head jerked back and he gave a grunt of surprise. He dropped Cassie's arm and fell behind a step, his hand going to his face, which was suddenly . . . wet? Cassie whirled to look over her shoulder. Nan stood a few feet away on the other side of the circle, the water pistol trained on Nick.

"Woman!" Nick's voice was a bark as he wiped water from his eyes. "What do you think you're doing?" That earned him another squirt to the face, as though he were a cat on the kitchen counter.

"What are you doing?" Cassie echoed the question, but in a harsh whisper.

"Holy water," Nan said matter-of-factly. "Spirits don't like it much. At the very least, it got his attention."

"Because you shot him in the face with a water gun." This exorcism was getting out of hand. But as she turned to face Nick, his face screwed up in a scowl, she had to admit he looked ridiculous. Water dripped from the end of his nose, and his hair was wet, curling on his forehead. Even the part of Cassie's head that had been taken over by Sarah felt lighter, less threatened.

It was easy now for Cassie to take control and do the talking for Sarah. "It doesn't work like that anymore, *Chuck*." She mocked his tone of voice, spitting his name, turning it into an expletive. "You've been dead for a while, so you've missed out on a lot."

Nick scoffed, his dark eyes flashing. "What are you talking about?" It was creepy to see Nick acting like Not-Nick, but Cassie shook that off. She had more important things to focus on.

"I'm talking about jobs. Women have them now, you know. I can tell that you're really against it—believe me, I know. This whole stunt with my laptop. What were you trying to prove?"

Nick looked at her like she was an idiot. "I don't know what that thing is. But you talk to it, you tap on it. You sound like a businessman when you talk to it, you know." He scoffed again; that seemed to be C.S. Hawkins's signature move. "You look ridiculous."

Cassie glanced over her shoulder at Nan. "You can shoot him again." She leaned away from Nick as Nan took aim, landing three good shots to his forehead. Nan was a sharpshooter with that thing.

Nick looked furious as he raked back his now soaked hair. "Ridiculous," he said again. "Like a cat wearing a costume."

"We do that too now, you know." God, Nan was right; this guy was a dick. "Cats in costumes. I don't have a cat, though. Maybe I should get one. Get a nice little necktie for it; he'd look great." From outside the circle, Nan clucked her tongue and Cassie got the message; they were getting off topic. "You really thought if you made my machine not work that I wouldn't be able to either?"

Not-Nick's laugh was without mirth. "Why not? It seemed to do the trick."

"Well, it ends now, old man." Inside Cassie's head, Sarah sucked in a frightened breath. *It's okay*, she reassured the ghost. *Trust me.*

"Of course, it doesn't," Sarah's husband said, using Cassie's boyfriend's body. "As I've said, you are property. This house too, property. Mine. What can you possibly do without your man's say-so?"

"So many things." Cassie crossed her arms. "You think I need a man to live my life? Let me tell you what I need a man for: nothing. Not a goddamn thing. I bought this house all on my own."

There was that damn scoff again. "Impossible." But there was something happening. A struggle in Nick's face. Tension in his body. His fists clenched, then slowly relaxed again.

"Keep going." Nan's voice was a calm and steady lifeline for Cassie to grab on to. "He hates an independent woman. Piss him off some more. That's the key."

Cassie could do that. It was actually kind of fun. "Not impossible." Her smile was bright and so very fake. "Women can get mortgages these days. I own this place outright." Well, she would after thirty years of payments, but he didn't need to know that.

She took a step closer to him, while internally Sarah rebelled. Sarah didn't want to be any closer to Charles's spirit than she had to, and Cassie didn't blame her. But C.S. didn't want Cassie to come any closer, and what he didn't want he was going to get.

Sure enough, Not-Nick fell back a step. He held up a hand. "Get away from me, you . . ."

Cassie raised her eyebrows. "What? What could you possibly call me that would bother me in the least? Do you have any idea how irrelevant you are? Forgotten? After tonight, this house won't even have your name on it, and your existence will be erased. Just like that." She snapped her fingers, and Not-Nick flinched. He actually flinched. This was good. She could do this.

"Nobody will talk about you," she continued. "No one's going to visit your grave. Hell, no one has in years. No one's even going to remember your name when this independent woman is finished with you." She took another step toward him, then another. He backed up as far as he could, but when his foot reached the edge of the circle he stopped, as though his back were against a brick wall.

His dark eyes stayed fixed on her, wide, as she stepped up to him, very much in his personal space.

"But you know what I'm going do?" She put her hands up, cupping his face in her palms, her voice a low murmur. "I think I'm going to take out another credit card. Maybe even . . ." She wet her lips with the tip of her tongue, leaned in, and whispered in Not-Nick's ear, as seductively as she could. "Vote."

His face went red, mottled with rage, then he sucked in a huge breath. Before Cassie could react, Nick dropped to the floor, boneless.

"Shit!" She dropped down beside him, pulling his head into her lap. Outside of the circle, Sophie and Libby let out identical cries of alarm. For a stunned heartbeat she couldn't comprehend what had happened. Had she killed him? But Nick's chest rose and fell under her hand, his heart thumping strongly against her palm. Cassie closed her eyes and let relief flood through her body. C.S. Hawkins was gone. At last.

But then Cassie realized that Sarah was gone too, from inside her head. Outside of the circle, Libby gasped.

"The circle!"

Cassie followed her gaze to where Nick's booted foot had scuffed the salt and sand circle, breaking it. Alarmed, she turned toward Nan, but she was the only one in the room who was both conscious and unconcerned.

The elderly woman closed her eyes and breathed deep. "He's gone," she said finally. "His anger burned him up from the inside out until he couldn't withstand it."

"But what about Sarah? She was right here." Cassie tapped a finger against her temple, and her eyes filled with tears. When she first got here, all she'd wanted was a ghost-free house. But Sarah had become a friend. Had they repaid her by banishing her too? Was she still stuck with her husband? Had Charles managed to keep his hold over Sarah, drag her with him to wherever he'd gone?

But Nan seemed unfazed. "When Nick broke the circle she was free of your head. Simple as that. She's still here. It's her house, after all." Her lips twitched in a smile.

Cassie's laugh was like a sob, an involuntary heave of her chest. As her barely conscious boyfriend stirred and her friends peered at her inside the remains of a summoning circle, supervised by an octogenarian, Cassie realized that she finally felt at home. The house may be Sarah's, but it was hers too.

She was home.

Thirty

It was surprisingly easy to clean up after an exorcism.

Granted, Nick wasn't fully conscious for a few minutes, so it was possible he missed a lot. But before he knew it, he was sitting next to Cassie on the couch, one hand clasped between both of hers, while Sophie and Libby pitched in to set her living room to rights. He wanted to help, but his legs didn't seem to be working well. Plus, he didn't want to let go of Cassie's hand. She felt like the only thing keeping him upright and awake.

He ran a hand through his hair, pushing it off his forehead. His hair was wet. Why was it wet? His face was wet too, and the front of his shirt. Like he'd been bobbing for apples but with no fruit to show for it. What the hell had happened while he was out?

A riot of pink obscured his vision, and he blinked blearily up at Nan, hovering over him. She shoved a tall glass of water into his free hand. Then she stood over him, arms crossed, until he got the hint and drank, though it seemed like the last thing he needed right now was water.

"You okay?" Her voice was brusque, but kind. Pale blue eyes in a wrinkled face studied him with interest.

He nodded, but not too hard because there was a very real

chance that his head would fall off his neck. It had been that kind of
day. Everything felt muffled, like he was ensconced in plastic wrap,
removed from the world in front of him.

Then it hit him—why everything felt just a little off-kilter. "The
noise is gone." His voice was thick, raspy, as though he hadn't used
it in months. "The static . . . the buzzing. It's all gone. It's so quiet
now." The absence of the noise was so loud in his head. This plastic-
wrapped feeling could fuck off any time now.

But Nan just nodded sagely. "Being possessed can take it out of
you," she said. "Make sure you rest tonight." She looked a little
drained herself. Nick wasn't clear on how Nan's abilities worked,
but it had obviously taken it out of her too.

A full-on conversation was too much for Nick to handle just
now, so instead he gave a heavy nod as he set the glass down on the
newly reset coffee table. Huh. That hadn't been there a minute ago.
He looked bewilderedly around the room. The salt-and-sand circle
had been completely swept away, and the area rug was back in its
place. It was as though the past couple hours had never happened,
and Nick wondered if he'd dreamed all of it. Or was he dreaming now?

Libby helped Nan out the front door, her focus clearly on her
grandmother, but Sophie lingered. "Are you sure you're okay?"

Nick had no idea who she was addressing, but just in case, he
started another tired nod that would hopefully cover his ass.

Thankfully Cassie spoke up. "Yeah. We're okay." She looked at
him, as though confirming, and he nodded again. Nan wasn't kidding; he was exhausted.

Case in point: he looked up again and Sophie was gone. The sun
had set completely, and with the front curtains drawn the living
room had grown dark, lit only by the soft glow of the lamp on the
table in the front window. For an extended moment neither of them

moved or spoke, but then Cassie sprang to her feet. The sudden movement made Nick jump, woke him up even more.

"I'm sorry," she said. "I know it doesn't matter much in the scheme of things, but I have to know." She padded to the kitchen, and once Nick was sure that his legs worked, he followed. Her laptop was sitting on her kitchen table, the unplugged cord dangling to the floor. They both held their breath as she plugged it in. There was a beat of silence, and then the chirp of her charging laptop rang out like a chime.

"I'll be damned." Nick's tired smile felt good, like he'd accomplished something today.

Cassie stared at her laptop, hands on her hips. "It really was him, all that time." She shook her head slowly. "I'm gonna have to call Buster and apologize. I kept making him come out here and check, and there was never anything wrong with the wiring. There was just an asshole of a ghost living in my house."

"And now he's gone." Nick punctuated the words with a sigh of relief. After all these years C.S. Hawkins was gone, taking his misogynistic bullshit with him. Now it was just the two of them, alone in her seaside cottage that they now had all to themselves.

"Are you sure you're all right?" Cassie asked. "You've had kind of a busy night."

A laugh burst from him. "That's putting it mildly."

"I'm half tempted to call in sick again tomorrow. Do you think my boss will accept exorcism as an excuse—"

Her voice cut off, and Nick turned to see her facing the fridge, her mouth sagging open. Then she cleared her throat hard. "You know what, let me get you some more water. Nan seemed to really insist on you being hydrated . . ."

When she bustled out of the kitchen to get his glass from the living room, Nick got a clear view of the fridge, and he'd been wrong.

Of course, it wasn't just the two of them here in the house. Sarah was here too. And her message was for him.

kiss her

Good thing Nick had lived with Elmer all this time; he was used to having a ghost as a wingman. *Good idea, Mrs. H.*

He followed Cassie into the living room, plucking the glass from her hand and setting it back on the coffee table. "Remember all those times?" His voice was as casual as he could make it, with his heart hammering in his chest and his blood simmering in his veins. "Those nights I walked you home but couldn't get past your front gate?"

She nodded dumbly, her eyes huge in her face. He loved those eyes. He loved that face. "It's okay," she said, waving a hand toward the kitchen. "I know Mrs. H is being a bit of a matchmaker there, but that doesn't mean you have to . . ."

"You think I don't want to kiss you?" The hell with that. Stepping close to her was as easy as breathing. "Oh, I want to kiss you." Sliding his hands into her hair and slanting his mouth over hers was even easier. She was warm under his hands, soft and pliant, and when she snaked her arms around his neck he wanted to shout with joy. But he would have had to stop kissing her to do that, and he wasn't about to.

"You sure about this?" Cassie's voice was breathless when they finally came up for air. He'd done that to her. He was about to do a lot more to her.

"Are you kidding?" He had never been so sure about anything in his life. How did she not know that by now?

But she pulled back, her dark eyes dancing with humor. "Nan said you should take it easy tonight. I don't want to overtax you or anything." She patted his chest, as though he were a child who needed to calm down.

Nick nodded with mock sincerity. "We'll take it slow." Her smile against his mouth was delicious, but it didn't take long to kiss that smile away. Her mouth opened under his, eagerly letting him in, and the stroke of her tongue against his set his blood on fire. Now that he was in Cassie's house—and the only ghostly spirit present was on his side—he wasn't sure how he was going to let her go.

Thirty-One

This wasn't the first time Nick had kissed her. Far from it. But being in his arms in this moment felt brand new. She fisted her hands in his T-shirt, anchoring herself to him and to his kiss. He held her like she was something to be treasured. He kissed her like he was offering her his entire soul.

Before tonight, there had always been something awkward, something about being here in this house with him that just felt *wrong*. But that tension was gone now, and her home felt warmer. More welcoming. And Cassie wanted to show him just how welcome he was. To her home, and everything in it. Herself included.

"You know what this is?" Nick murmured the words against her skin as he kissed his way down her throat.

"What?" Cassie couldn't begin to guess. She knew what a kiss was, so that couldn't be it. She also knew what that hard line in his jeans was, pressing against her lower belly. Besides, brain power was quickly leaving the building, especially once he started tracing her collarbone with the tip of his tongue.

He didn't stop kissing her to answer. "It's the first time we've been alone. We don't have Mr. H to mess with my head. No Elmer being a creep."

Cassie hated to contradict him. She really did. But . . . "What about Sarah? She's still here, right?"

Nick froze. "Shit." He slowly let her go, taking one deliberate step back from her, while Cassie's body practically swayed toward his. Oh, she was definitely swaying. There was no more leaning back where Nick was concerned.

"Sarah?" She raised her voice, casting a desperate look around the house. "Any way you can give us some privacy? Please?" She had no idea how this would work, if this even would work, but it was worth a try.

The house was silent, and the words didn't move on the fridge. How were they going to know if she heard them? But then a door closed upstairs, making them both jump.

"Did she just close herself in your bedroom?" Nick looked mournfully toward the stairs. "I had plans for that room."

Cassie shook her head, her eyes scanning the ceiling as though she could see through to the upstairs. "That was from the back of the house. The second bedroom. I can't imagine that ghosts use doors like we do. Maybe she was just making the point. Giving us privacy."

"Hmm." He looked back at her then, and the fire in his eyes made Cassie forget how to breathe. She knew exactly what was going to happen next, and it was about goddamn time. She yearned for him, the way he obviously yearned for her. But now that the moment was here, it was hard to believe.

"You hungry?" Suddenly nervous, Cassie took a step, then two, toward the kitchen as a saving grace. "I think there's some frozen pizza in the . . ." Her throat went dry as Nick shook his head slowly. He advanced on her, step by slow step, eyes fixed on her like a lion looking at a rabbit. Her heart was certainly beating at a rabbit-like speed.

"Later." His voice was a low growl, something she'd never heard from him. He ran his hands up her arms, to her shoulders, finally gripping the back of her neck with one strong hand.

"Later," she echoed, her head feeling loose on her neck as she nodded. "So what about now?"

"Now?" His other arm slid around her, hand flat on the small of her back, bringing her hips flush against his. This close, there was no mistaking what he was in the mood for. Cassie had to hold herself back from squirming against him, like a teenage girl facing her first erection. "Now, I plan on fucking you on every surface in this house."

"Oh." She wasn't used to that kind of language from Nick, but she could sure as hell work with that. A tiny, maniacal giggle escaped from her mouth just before he bent down to claim it. Every atom in her body celebrated. *God, yes, finally!* Her laughter died quickly as more serious, more passionate emotions took over. Her whole world shrank down to her and Nick and his mouth, his tongue, his hands.

Her hands went back to his T-shirt, this time with purpose, tugging at the fabric and pushing upward, until he got the hint and reached a hand behind his head to pull it off. She caught her breath at the sight of him, toned and well muscled without being showy, lightly tanned from a life at the beach, his chest furred with soft brown hair. He closed his eyes as she laid her hand flat on his stomach, his breath sighing out of him while she stroked up his chest, between his pecs, to his shoulder. His skin was warm, as though he'd absorbed the Florida sunshine into himself, and even though it was mid-June she craved that heat. She stepped back in, stretching up onto her toes to kiss him again.

He groaned against her mouth, his hands tightening on her hips before moving upward, ruching the fabric of her T-shirt as they went. "My turn." Letting go of him was the hardest thing she'd ever had to do, but she reluctantly raised her arms so he could tug off her shirt. Impatient, she reached behind her back to unclasp her bra, sliding the straps down her arms and letting it join the growing pile of clothing on her living room floor.

Nick caught his breath, his eyes darkening in a way that had nothing at all to do with ghostly possession. "Oh," he breathed. "Shit."

Cassie's laugh was throaty. "Just what every girl wants to hear when she takes her bra off."

"Get the hell over here." Nick slid an arm around her waist, and this time when he started kissing her he was on a mission. Her body crashed against his, warm bare skin against warm bare skin. His mouth traveled across her cheekbone and to her neck, immediately finding that place behind her ear that made her knees sag. While he lingered on her throat his hands were busy, skating up her sides, tracing the dip of her waist to the swell of her breast. Callused fingertips skimmed the sensitive skin on the undersides of her breasts, thumbs gliding across her nipples before stopping to circle the hardened peaks. All Cassie could do was cling to him, her nails digging into his shoulders while he wreaked havoc on her body.

But he wasn't done. He stooped down, his mouth traveling lower. His beard rasped against the insides of her breasts as his mouth followed her sternum down the center of her body, sinking lower and lower until he looked up at her, on his knees in front of her like a supplicant. The emotion overflowing from his clear blue eyes made Cassie catch her breath.

"Cassie, I . . ." He closed his eyes as she slid a hand through his hair, her fingers smoothing through the russet waves. He was so far away down there, but when she moved to kneel, he stopped her with gentle but firm hands on her hips. She trembled as he moved soothing fingers across the soft skin of her belly, following the waistline of her denim cutoffs. She didn't notice when he popped the button, but the sound of her zipper was loud in the quiet room. She had to hold on to his shoulders for support as he hooked the shorts and her underwear together and pulled gently, her last garments whispering down her legs to the floor.

She should feel self-conscious, she thought, standing here in her own living room completely naked, while Nick was on his knees in front of her, still wearing his jeans. But her blood was running too hot to care. Her body practically ached for him, and the longer he knelt in front of her, the wetter she became under his gaze.

"God, you're perfect." He leaned in, placing a kiss just below her belly button, and a whimper escaped Cassie's mouth at the contrast of his soft lips and rough beard. "Is this okay?" He looked up at her as he kissed an inch lower, then another. One hand skimmed up her leg, her inner thigh, urging her legs to part slightly for him.

Cassie was beyond language. Every muscle in her body was wound tight, and God help her, Nick was going to give her the release she needed. She bobbed a nod, her eyes captured by his. "If you don't touch me soon I think I'm gonna scream."

"Oh, you're gonna scream no matter what." He smirked—he actually smirked!—at her, but before she could give him any shit for it, his mouth drifted lower. Lower. She only had a moment's warning, his hot breath against her most sensitive skin, before his tongue was there, licking gently, so very, very gently, at her clit. At the same time, his hand cupped her, so hot, but she wanted more. She only had time to drag in one frantic breath before he slid a finger inside her. A second one joined the first, his hand pumping her gently while his mouth increased the suction.

Cassie didn't scream, but she did moan an awful lot, her body swaying against him as he held her up. She braced shaking arms against his shoulders when he added a third finger and his tongue licked harder. Her trembling legs barely held her up as everything inside her wound tighter and tighter. And then she was there, over the edge, coming apart and being remade under his hands and his mouth. When the waves finally subsided and Cassie was back in her body, Nick sat on his heels and slowly, slowly pulled his hand from her. His eyes stayed trained on hers as he licked his fingers clean, and that was it. She dropped to her knees.

"Holy shi—" She didn't let herself finish the sentence; she was too busy pulling his face toward hers, kissing him hard, taking her taste back onto her own tongue. A good orgasm like that usually left her boneless, but in his arms she was energized. She wanted more and wasn't going to wait one minute longer.

It was a group effort to get Nick undressed, but soon enough the rest of his clothes joined the pile of discards. As they stretched out together on the area rug, Cassie had never been more thankful that the living room curtains were closed. But then Nick rolled to his back, pulling Cassie with him, and his body was warm and hard and soft all at once, and as she sank into his kiss Cassie stopped thinking about living room curtains. She stopped thinking about anything at all. Her senses were full of warm skin, legs twining together, the hardness of his cock nudging against her, and her hips rocking softly in response. It was easy, so easy, to hitch a leg over his hip, slide herself along the length of him, teasing them both. If she moved up just a little more, he could slide . . .

"Wait." His hands were iron bands on her shoulders, pushing her away. He looked wild, his dark pupils almost eclipsing his blue eyes. His hair was tousled, his breath coming fast and hard in his chest. "Protection. I don't have . . ." He sighed in frustration as he let his head fall back to thud against the floor. "I didn't know I'd need to bring condoms to an exorcism."

"It's okay. No kids coming from me, and I've been on the pill since I was a teenager." Cassie knew this was an important conversation to have, because pregnancy wasn't the only worry. But let's face it, the last thing she wanted to do right now was have an important conversation. "How about you? Do you always use condoms?"

Nick nodded. "Yeah, always. I had a physical over the winter, everything was good then. And I haven't . . . well. There hasn't been anyone since then."

"I'm clean too." Goose bumps broke out over her skin at the implication. She'd always used condoms with her long-term partners, but could they . . . ? Were they going to . . . ? "Do you think we could . . ."

"Go without?" Nick's breath gusted out of him, and his fingers flexed against her skin, digging in. "God, Cassie. That would be . . ."

"Yeah." She gave a single, decisive nod before reaching for him. Or maybe he reached for her. Didn't matter. A heartbeat later she was in his arms, rolling under his body, on the area rug in the middle of her living room. Something in the back of her mind reminded her that they were about to have sex for the first time in the same spot where they'd exorcised the ghost of C.S. Hawkins, but she left that thought in the back of her mind where it belonged, and she got back to more important things. Like kissing Nick like her life depended on it. He kissed her hungrily, his weight settling over her, pressing her down into the floor, and Cassie opened her legs beneath him, cradling him, welcoming him in. They both caught their breath as his cock nudged her entrance, hard skin meeting wet skin, and he started the slow slide inside. Nothing in the world felt like this. So naked, so open. Cassie felt like she was sharing her body for the first time.

Nick groaned as his hips met hers, seated fully inside. "Christ." The word was a harsh exhalation in her ear. He thrust once, twice, a quick sharp rock into her body and back out again, never fully withdrawing from her. He laughed then, a guttural, desperate sound. "I swear I usually last longer than this, Cass, but right now I gotta . . ."

"Please." She tilted her pelvis, bringing her thighs up on either side of his hips, holding on tight. "You can impress me with your stamina next time." Because there was going to be a next time. A lifetime full of next times, if she had anything to say about it.

With one hand planted next to Cassie's head for leverage, Nick grasped Cassie's thigh, pulling up farther. The change in angle was like flipping a switch, sending Nick into a frenzy. He thrust hard, harder, and Cassie gripped his shoulders, then the back of his neck, holding on for the ride. His fingers dug almost painfully into the soft skin of her thigh, and the room was filled with the sounds of their sighs and their bodies coming together.

After a few moments his movements began to stutter, his rhythm faltering. He rocked against her deeper, as though trying to reach every part of her. Cassie felt a release starting to build again—so soon after her last one!—and she dropped one hand, sliding it down her stomach, down to where they were joined. It wouldn't take much, just a few strokes . . .

"God. Yes." Nick's head dropped as he looked down, watching her. Watching them. "Touch yourself. Bring yourself there. I know you can. Come on . . ."

His words spurred her on, and before she knew it she was coming again, harder than before, her muscles tightening around him inside her, her legs tightening around his body, her hand tightening in his hair. The sounds of her orgasm were swallowed up by his kiss as his mouth plundered hers, as he finally lost all control. His hips drove into hers one more time, his body shuddering, his hands clutching.

They spent an eternity there together, on the living room floor, while their hearts slowed to a normal rhythm and their breaths calmed. Finally, Nick raised one weak arm.

"One surface down." He made a lazy check mark in the air, as though knocking an item off a to-do list. "What else you got?"

Cassie didn't have the energy to laugh. The most she could do was a delighted exhale. "Give me a minute," she said. "Once I can walk again, I'd be happy to give you a thorough tour of the Hawkins House."

Thirty-Two

C assie was so beautiful that it hurt.

She looked purely blissed out, which Nick hoped was from the several orgasms but could very well have been from the frozen pizza they'd finally heated up when they ran out of energy. She sat across from him at the kitchen table, wrapped in a black-and-yellow floral bathrobe, her dark hair loose, flowing down past her shoulders, and when she gave him a tired smile it felt like a dart to the chest.

Because he knew the truth. The painful, unfortunate truth.

He loved her. He loved her with everything he was. And he still might have to let her go.

"So." Oblivious to his turmoil, Cassie popped the last bite of pizza crust into her mouth and brushed her hands off. "That's the downstairs."

Nick nodded solemnly, trying to play it cool. His heart really shouldn't be beating this fast, despite all the cardio they'd just been doing. "Nice place you've got here," he said. "This tour has been exceptionally thorough so far."

"I'm known for being detail oriented. My poor kitchen counters, though." Cassie glanced over her shoulder, and he followed her gaze, his blood simmering at the memory of the things they'd just done over there. "They'll never be the same." When she turned her gaze back to him, though, her eyes were more serious.

"Hey." He started to reach for her, but something in her eyes made him lean back in his chair. "What's the matter?" Up until now, he'd loved every look he'd put on her face this evening. But he didn't like the way she looked now.

She stared at her hands, folded on the table in front of her, picking at a thumbnail. "What happens now?" The question practically fell out of her mouth, and her eyes widened as though she hadn't meant to say it out loud. But she didn't meet his eyes; her gaze remained fixed on the table.

"Now?" Nick was confused by the question. "Well, we've covered the downstairs, so if you're not too tired maybe we can continue the tour? We can skip the stairs themselves, though. I'm almost thirty; I don't think my knees can take that."

That made her look up, brought some humor back into her eyes. "Same." Her lips twitched in a smile. "The rug burn from the living room is bad enough." Her cheeks pinked, obviously remembering the cause of that rug burn, and Nick wanted to crawl across the table and kiss her again. It was so nice, being able to do this. To be here with her. Alone here with her.

But she wasn't done. "I mean now. Tomorrow." The pink in her cheeks drained away. "Next week, next month. What you said before, about being all in? Is that . . . Did you mean that?"

"Yes." His answer was as abrupt and immediate as her question had been. "I meant it then, I mean it now." His brow furrowed. "You believe me, right?"

"Sure." But her eyes slid away from his, back down to her hands folded in front of her on the table. "But it's been an emotional night. There was a lot going on. That's over now, and once you're thinking clearly, you'll remember that you don't do relationships, and . . ."

"Listen. I told you. None of that matters anymore. Give me all the strings. All the pressure. I want it all with you, Cassie." Sitting here with her, Nick couldn't remember why he'd ever thought otherwise. Situationship Nick didn't exist anymore; he'd been banished from this earth, just like C.S. Hawkins had. All he wanted was Cassie, and wasn't that a kick in the head. Because he couldn't have her. Not long term.

He took a deep breath, which did nothing to help the ache in his chest. But fuck it. She needed to know, and he needed to be brave enough to say the words. "I know you're not staying. Just my luck, right? Always falling in love with the woman who doesn't wanna stay." He couldn't look at her. Instead he stared hard at the center of the table, boring the pattern of the woodgrain into his retinas. "But I can't help it. I love you, Cassie. I'll love you as long as you're here in Boneyard Key, and you'll take my heart with you when you go. I don't know if there's room for me in your life when you're back in Orlando, but if there's any way we can—"

"I'm staying." The words were a nuclear bomb in the middle of the small kitchen, stopping Nick's words and almost stealing his breath.

"You . . ." He chanced a look up at her, and there she was again. All huge brown eyes, shining in the low light of the kitchen, and long dark hair against pale skin. Painfully gorgeous.

"Yeah." Her smile dawned across her face. "Say it again."

Nick's heart soared so high that he'd need to retrieve it from the ceiling later. "I love you." He cocked an eyebrow. "Now you say it again."

Her smile widened, and when she blinked a tear hit her cheek. "I love you too."

His breath caught; how long had it been since he'd heard those words? But those weren't the words he was looking for. Not now. "And?"

"And . . ." She caught her bottom lip between her teeth. "And I'm staying."

"There it is." He stood up, tugging her to her feet, because it had been minutes now since he'd kissed her, and this would be their first kiss as a couple in love. He couldn't wait one more second for that.

"To answer your question," he said many, many moments later, "I think what happens now is we take this party upstairs. I've only gotten half of the tour."

Cassie gave a hum of assent as he stood up, tugging her to her feet as he did so. "I think I know the perfect place to end it."

The tour ended sometime around midnight, with both of them wrapped up in each other and in Cassie's duvet. Slow kisses eventually transitioned into sleep, and an hour or so later the door to the second bedroom swung slowly open on its hinges. After that, the house was completely silent.

Nick had never been so happy to get so little sleep.

His commute was also longer than normal: a quick walk down the block instead of down the stairs as the sun just barely crested the horizon. The streetlights were still on outside as he left Cassie's house, and they blinked slowly out around him as he lightly jogged down the street, trying to get the blood moving in his veins. He was tired. He was sore, having used muscles last night that he hadn't used in quite some time. He wanted a long, hot shower and to get back in bed with Cassie. Instead he got a lukewarm, thirty-second shower in his place above the café, his hair still wet and curling ridiculously on his forehead when he opened Hallowed Grounds at five minutes after seven.

Thank goodness for all the prep he'd gotten done yesterday, right before he'd gone over to Cassie's house, gotten possessed, and his entire life had changed. He sliced the lemon pound cake and banana bread, filling up the pastry case before starting on the daily batch of blueberry muffins. Same old morning routine, but his life was no longer the same old life. This morning felt like the beginning of a new era, and he couldn't wait to see what happened next.

"Someone looks happy this morning." He'd been so absorbed in his thoughts that he hadn't even heard the chime over the door. Libby had her elbows on the counter and a smug expression on her face. "I was dropping by to see how you were feeling—"

"And to get coffee." He moved to the espresso machine to start her morning latte without being asked.

"And to get coffee," she confirmed, "but mostly worried about you and Cassie. Y'all do okay last night?"

Nick almost dropped the milk jug. He glanced over his shoulder and Libby arched a brow. "That obvious, huh?"

"Oh, pretty obvious." Her smile widened. "Glad you two managed to work everything out. Sophie and I have been getting sick of y'all dancing around each other the way you have been."

"Look . . ." Acting stern would probably work out a lot better if he wasn't fighting a grin. "Things have been complicated between Cassie and me."

"And now?"

"Now they're much simpler. Thanks to your grandma." He popped a lid on her latte and handed it across the counter. "Coffee for Nan today or no?"

"No." Libby's smile dipped as she straightened up and accepted her latte. "She's at home today. Resting. Last night really took it out of her, though you know she won't admit it."

"That sounds like her." But that punctured a small hole in Nick's shiny balloon of a morning. His brow furrowed. "She gonna be okay?"

"I think so." But Libby's eyes were serious as she took a sip. "She doesn't do a lot of those, you know. Banishings. Even when she was younger. She's very much a live and let live . . . well, afterlife and let afterlife?" She shrugged. "Anyway, it takes more energy to fight a spirit than it does to just understand one. She should be okay after a couple days of rest."

"Let me know if we can help at all." He was part of a *we* now. Incredible. He waved off Libby's offer of payment as his heart swelled, tightening in his chest in the most delightful way. "No charge. Exorcism special."

Libby snorted. "Say hey to Cassie for me. Tell her I'll talk to her later."

The rest of the morning was the same familiar routine, yet everything was different, and his day had a new shine to it. Theo chose a slice of the lemon cake instead of a blueberry muffin, making a short noise of pleasure around the mouthful.

"This is good." He washed it down with a sip of his usual coffee. "You should make this more often."

"I think I might." Nick glanced up toward the ceiling, surprised Elmer hadn't weighed in on Theo's reaction. It wasn't like him not to seize every opportunity he could to point out when he was right.

Theo didn't notice, breaking off another corner of the cake while he paid for his breakfast. "Oh, by the way. Any idea how Cassie's doing with the Hawkins House research? I keep meaning to check in on her."

Nick didn't even know where to begin. "You should ask today. I bet she'll have an update." Understatement.

Breakfast rush ended with Jo and her damn herbal tea, along with a gloating text from Elmer about the lemon cake.

> Told you. That lemon cake has always been a winner.

Nick was impressed at Elmer's restraint. He started to respond when the door chimed again. Nick looked up to see Cassie stroll in like she owned the place. Which, hell. She could ask him and he'd turn over the keys in a second. Along with anything else that would keep that smile on her face.

"Iced hazelnut?" She hoisted her laptop bag in illustration, and Nick's heart fell.

"You're kidding me. What happened?" Her laptop woes had been solved last night, hadn't they? Was C.S back? Had they gone through all of that for nothing?

But Cassie's eyes danced. "Nothing. I guess I got used to working here. Something about the ambience." She strolled up to the counter, dragging a finger across the surface between them. "Plus, between you and me, there's this guy who works here. He spends a lot of time texting on his phone?"

Nick nodded, not quite trusting his voice.

"Anyway . . ." Cassie came around to his side of the counter. This close, she dropped her voice to a low murmur. "Don't tell him, but I think he's kinda hot."

"Oh yeah?" Her T-shirt was thin cotton, and he could feel the heat of her skin under his palm as he smoothed his hand around the curve of her waist. Now that he knew what that skin looked like, tasted like, keeping his hands to himself was a special kind of torture. He dipped his head, brushing his lips against her temple, her cheek, before whispering in her ear. "If it helps, I have it on good authority that he has a thing for you too."

Cassie gave a happy sigh of relief. "That's good news."

"So you don't just love me for my Wi-Fi?" He was teasing, but his voice came out low, thick. His hand slid around to the small of her back, and God he loved the way she fit against him.

She shook her head, and a lock of hair fell out of her messy bun to brush against her cheek. When she spoke, her voice was low and intimate. The exact opposite of teasing. "I love you for so many reasons."

He groaned, letting his forehead rest against hers. "Cassie," he whispered in the heartbeat before his lips touched hers, "I love you too."

"Ugh. Get a room, you two." Nick had been so absorbed in Cassie that he hadn't heard the door chime, but when he reluctantly pulled away from Cassie there was Ramon, standing just inside the door with his arms crossed. He tried to look stern, but his crooked grin gave him away.

Cassie had the grace to blush, but Nick wasn't going to apologize. "Don't you have lunch prep to get started?"

"Sure do." Ramon shook his head as he came behind the counter, slipping past the two of them. "It's about damn time, by the way."

Cassie slid her arms around Nick, cuddling herself close and laying her cheek on his chest. "I couldn't agree more."

"Just keep it out of my kitchen," he said as he pushed on the swinging door. "That shit's unsanitary."

Cassie was the last to leave Hallowed Grounds, packing up her laptop a little before two, just as Nick was counting down the register and saying goodbye to Ramon.

"Any plans tonight?" He kept his voice casual as he finished up the closing paperwork.

Cassie shrugged as she slung her bag over her shoulder and met him at the register. "A couple things to finish up this afternoon, then I'm free as a bird." She gave a satisfied hum as she lifted her head to kiss him. "You wanna come by tonight?"

"Thought you'd never ask." One more kiss, on her mouth and then on her forehead.

"Feel free to pack a bag. I think Sarah likes having you around."

Cassie's grin fueled his own. "I think your roommate's as much a pervert as Elmer is."

Nick was still grinning when he locked up the place and jogged up the back steps to his apartment. His afternoon shower was more leisurely, and he took the time to throw a change of clothes into a duffel bag. He stopped short in the kitchen, dropping the bag on his kitchen table.

"Ah, shit, Elmer." He moved to the coffee maker, which had sat neglected now for over twenty-four hours. "I haven't made you any coffee, man. I'm sorry." He spooned in a half pot's worth. He was undercaffeinated today; he could certainly use it.

Within minutes the coffee was burbling and Elmer's familiar cold chill had seeped into the room. Likewise, Elmer's voice seeped into Nick's brain. *Been a while since you've been out all night. Good for you! You and your girl finally make it happen?*

"Gross." Nick poured himself a cup of coffee and sat down on his couch. The battered leather recliner shifted in the afternoon sunlight that leaked through the half-closed blinds. "But it turned out Sarah Hawkins wasn't a mean old lady. You were right."

I'm always right.

Nick kept talking, like he hadn't been interrupted by a ghostly voice in his head. "Her husband was there too, and he was the mean one." He took a sip from his mug. "He's gone now, and Cassie's house is hers again. Well, hers and Sarah's. I think Mrs. H is sticking around. They seem to be friends."

In his head there was silence, and at first Nick thought Elmer was done communicating. He rarely gave notice before ending conversations. But half a cup of coffee later he was back. *Speaking of sticking around, it's time I was off too.*

Nick sat up straighter. "Off? What do you mean?" Panic fluttered in his chest.

I was never supposed to stay here for good, you know. I just wanted to know that someone would take care of my café after I was gone. No one else ever listened, or took my advice.

"Oh yeah. And I've been so open to feedback." *Don't go,* Nick wanted to say. But he forced himself to stay calm and listen. This was the most Elmer had ever volunteered before about why he'd lingered in Boneyard Key. Nick owed it to him to listen.

Yeah, but you've been kind. You make coffee for me. You answer me. And then you made my lemon cake.

"The lemon cake? Was that all you wanted me to do before you moved on? Why didn't you say so?"

Use your brain. You think I stuck around pouting because you didn't make my lemon cake? God, you're a dumbass.

Nick choked on his next sip of coffee. Setting the mug down, he coughed until his lungs were clear. "Thanks, man. Always there to make me feel good about myself."

That's the point. You don't need me to do that anymore. You've got your girl.

"I think you're right." Despite this blow he was being dealt—he had gotten really used to having Elmer as a roommate—Nick couldn't help but smile at the thought of Cassie being his girl.

You've got this town, you've got friends, if you'll let yourself lean on them for a change. And now you've got Cassie. Even though there's still a chance you'll fuck it up—

"Thanks a lot."

But the voice in Nick's head continued like he hadn't interrupted. *I feel better leaving you behind now that I know you're not alone.*

"You stuck around for me?" It was suddenly hard to swallow, and Nick had to blink hard to clear his vision.

Of course I stuck around for you. You think I really give that much of a shit about banana bread?

Nick choked out a laugh around the tears that threatened to fall. "I hope that where you're going is a better place for you."

Dolores is waiting for me. At least she'd better be—we were married forty-seven years, and when she went first, she promised she'd wait. She's a hell of a lot better company than you are.

Nick pinched the bridge of his nose, conveniently swiping at his eyes with his index finger and thumb. "Then you really should get going. You've kept her waiting a long time."

Damn right, I have. And Nick?

"Yeah?"

Get rid of this godawful recliner. It's a piece of shit.

Another involuntary laugh, and this time Nick didn't even bother trying to hide his tears. "You got it." But he was lying; he was going to hang on to that chair until it finally fell apart.

It took a few minutes for the cold to truly dissipate. Even the leather recliner looked different somehow. Duller. Emptier.

Nick picked up his phone. All the texts from Elmer, from every single unknown number, were gone. Wiped, as though they'd never happened.

Elmer was truly gone. Wasn't that a kick in the ass.

As much as he told himself that this was what Elmer wanted, and

he was happy for the old guy, Nick was going to miss him. Elmer had
been a voice in his head and a thorn in his side for a long time now,
and he wasn't sure what he was going to do without him.

But Elmer wouldn't want to hear that. Life was for the living, as
he liked to say. So Nick scrolled through his contacts and punched
up a number.

Cassie answered right away. "Miss me already?"

"You know it." He tried to sound casual, but his voice was too
strangled, and Cassie noticed immediately.

"Hey. What is it?"

"Elmer," he finally choked out. "He's gone."

"Oh, Nick, no. I'm sorry." She didn't ask what had happened, or
how it had gone down. She honed in on the important question.
"Are you okay?"

"Yeah. I think I am." It was only a little bit of a lie. Elmer was
right. It was time to look forward. "So hey, I was thinking," he said,
desperate to change the subject.

"About what?"

"It's Tuesday. Fried chicken night at The Haunt."

"Ooooh." He could hear the smile in Cassie's voice. "I hear it's
life-changing."

"Meet you there tonight?"

"Or . . ." Her voice faltered, then returned stronger. "Any way
you could get it to go? Bring it over here?"

"Dinner at your place?" The thought was so warming. "I like the
sound of that." Dinner with her, sunsets over the water with her,
endless nights in bed with her. He liked the sound of all of that.

"Dinner at my place where neither of us has to cook." Now the
smile in her voice was a laugh.

"I like the sound of that even better." He leaned back on the sofa,
crossing his legs on the coffee table. "Remember, you don't want me

cooking." He grinned as her warm chuckle came through the phone. "Let me do the prep for tomorrow and I'll pick up dinner on the way over, okay?"

"Sure. But I have to say, I don't know if I need life-changing chicken. My life's pretty great the way it is right now."

"Yeah." This time the tight feeling in his chest had nothing to do with grief, and everything to do with the woman on the phone. She'd changed his life for the better, and he couldn't imagine living it any other way. "Mine too."

Thirty-Three

Nick was later than he wanted to be. He'd hoped to catch the sunset with Cassie, as the start of a new nightly tradition. But duty called and took longer than he'd expected. The new kid he'd hired for the summer was opening up tomorrow for the first time. So Nick took the opportunity after breakfast prep to revise the opening checklists—all the boring but necessary things so that he didn't get a frantic phone call while he was out on the boat with Vince. By the time he'd locked up for the night and picked up dinner, the sun was low on the horizon and the streetlights were winking on.

It was heady feeling, walking right through Cassie's front gate and up the steps like he had every right to be there. For most of Nick's life, this house had been falling down and forlorn. That front window used to be a broken half pane of glass, and a good portion of the boards on this very front porch had been missing. Now the lights on the porch glowed in welcome, and it no longer looked like a place you'd dare your little sister to run up to and knock on the front door. Now it looked like a home. Cassie's home. And he was finally welcome.

Inside looked like home too. The kitchen table was set with two place settings, and in the middle was a salad in a wooden bowl. But the most important thing was Cassie, barefoot in her denim cutoffs and oversize tee—her work-from-home uniform. Her smile was the warmest, most welcome glow of all.

"Now, I told them it was your first time with their fried chicken, so they made a fresh batch just for you." He set the box of chicken next to the salad, and a Styrofoam container of fries next to that.

"I feel so special." Her smile twinkled at him as she opened the box and pulled out a drumstick. The noises she made as she took her first bite bordered on obscene and made Nick forget all about food.

"I told you. Life-changing, right?"

"I maintain my allegiance to Publix, but this isn't bad at all."

Nick rolled his eyes good-naturedly and dug in himself. He had to remember that despite everything, she was still new in town. Plenty of time to bring her over to the right side of things.

He had very specific plans for after dinner, mostly including him and Cassie and her bedroom upstairs, but they had just started clearing their plates when a spoon perched on the edge of the table fell to the floor with a clatter. Nick bent to retrieve it, and when he straightened up the words **television island** were displayed in the middle of the refrigerator.

"What's television island?" He dropped the spoon into the open dishwasher. "Does she mean kitchen island? You don't have a television in here." He was going to have to learn Sarah's language if he stuck around, wasn't he?

"She means *Romance Resort*." Cassie loaded their plates into the dishwasher. "It's her favorite show." She looked sheepish. "I'm sorry. I forgot. I promised her we would watch it tonight. She went through a pretty bad ordeal, what with her husband and all."

"That's okay." Nick could think of worse ways to spend an evening than next to Cassie on her couch. Besides, he'd been through an ordeal with Sarah Hawkins's husband too. He understood.

After dinner, Cassie snuggled into him on the couch, her head nestled against his chest—oh yeah, he could think of *way* worse ways to spend an evening—and pulled up her library of recorded shows. "So it's kind of like *Survivor*, but horny." She flashed him a grin. "You're gonna hate it."

Nick wouldn't say he hated *Romance Resort*. He was mostly astounded at the teeny-tiny swimsuits they all wore. Could they really show that many butts on network television?

"This is really what Sarah wants to do with her afterlife? Watch this crap?"

"Hey." Cassie giggled as she lightly swatted at his chest. "Love me, love my ghost."

Well, that was an easy decision. He caught her hand and pressed it to his heart. "Oh, I definitely love you." He bent his head, laying a kiss on her forehead, her cheek, the tip of her nose. She closed her eyes, giving a happy hum in response.

On the television, a girl in a barely-there pink bikini pushed an overly muscled guy into the pool, declaring she was over his bullshit. But Nick wasn't paying attention, because Cassie was warm in his arms, and the scent of her shampoo made him dizzy. He leaned down to catch her mouth with his, sinking into a kiss that didn't need to be hurried. There were no barriers between them now; they had all the time in the world.

"I was thinking . . ." Her mouth moved against his, punctuating each word with another kiss. "That recliner of Elmer's."

"What about it?" How was Cassie thinking at a time like this? Nick wasn't doing his job right. He kissed his way up her throat and behind her ear.

"I was thinking it might look nice over there . . ." Nick reluctantly raised his head to follow where she was pointing, over by the front window. "In that nook. Cozy, you know?"

Nick caught his breath while his heart continued to pound. Was she asking what he thought she was asking?

He swallowed hard. "You're right. It would."

"And I have a lot of space in my closet upstairs. I'm only using, say, half of it."

"Really?" He hadn't thought of himself as a domestic guy in a long time, but damn if what she was offering didn't sound perfect. "I hardly have any closet space in my apartment."

"Just something to think about," Cassie said. Her hand lingered on his cheek, her fingertips tracing his cheekbone. She looked at him with wonder, as though she couldn't believe he was there. Nick knew the feeling. Her mouth was right there, kiss-swollen and inviting, and he couldn't resist another second.

It didn't take long for Cassie to straddle him on the couch, their kisses becoming deeper, their hands wandering over and under clothes, rivaling the making out that was happening on the long-forgotten television screen.

"It doesn't have to be tomorrow or anything . . ." Cassie gasped as he tugged gently on one earlobe with his teeth. Nick liked that sound. Would she do it if he bit the other earlobe? A worthy experiment. He grasped her chin, turning her head to the side and kissing a path to her other ear. Damn, she made the same sound there too. Incredible. "Just something to keep in mind, in case your place ever feels too small." Her voice was breathless, her chest heaving against his, her fingers twining in his hair.

"My place is always too small," he murmured into her hair. He skimmed his hands up her sides, pushing that soft T-shirt up to reveal even softer skin.

She pulled away and looked at him, her expression suddenly unsure. "Probably too soon for that kind of thing, huh?"

But the astonishing thing was, it wasn't. It was just like the night Nick had kissed her for the first time. On paper, it was probably way too soon. Nick should probably be scared of this kind of commitment, but this was different. This was Cassie. And everything with her felt just right.

He shook his head and pulled her close. "Feels just in time to me."

Much later that night, while they were sound asleep in Cassie's bed, magnetic words moved to the center of Cassie's fridge. A special message for Nick to find in the morning.

welcome home

Epilogue

S unsets came much earlier in January.

At five on the dot, Cassie logged out of her laptop, firmly closing it for the day. For the weekend. It was Friday night in Boneyard Key, and she had someplace to be. After filling a plastic tumbler with white wine and getting a bottle of water out of the fridge, she headed down to the beach. Nick was already there, straddling the seawall.

"There you are." He took the bottle of water from her hand, twisting off the cap and setting it on the seawall next to an open bottle of beer. Cassie scooted onto the wall, swinging her legs over to sit next to him.

"Just in time." She gestured with her wine toward the horizon, where the sun hung low in the sky.

Nick nodded, dropping a kiss on her temple as she leaned against his shoulder. "Show's just about to start."

This was their favorite time of day, and they always tried to spend it together. Some days were easier than others; with Florida currently full of snowbirds, Nick's two o'clock closing time often stretched to three or four. But he was always home before sunset, waiting for her on the seawall with an open beer for the Beach Bum.

Home. Not just her home, or Sarah's home. But Nick's home too. They'd spent that dead season in August—when it was too hot even for tourists—moving his things into her house, and the space over the café was back to being storage for the first time in years. After a good cleaning, Elmer's leather recliner was a cozy addition to her front window—the perfect place to read in the evening tucked under Cassie's crocheted afghan.

Combining their lives had been just as easy. Especially at the holidays: half the time with Cassie's parents in Orlando, then up the Turnpike an hour and a half to The Villages where Nick's family gathered. Sure, Cassie's mom's eyebrows had crawled up her forehead when Cassie announced at the Thanksgiving dinner table that she and Nick lived together, but she'd sent them home with extra pie, which was the surest sign that he was now a member of the family. Likewise, Nick's family had welcomed Cassie at Christmas with open arms; his sister Courtney had even drafted Cassie to her team for the annual (strictly unauthorized) neighborhood golf cart relay race. They'd won.

During those first few months they kept checking in with each other—is this too soon? Are we rushing things? But Nick fit into Cassie's life as easily as she fit into his, and by the time the new year ticked over, it was as though they'd always been together. Like two puzzle pieces that had found each other, just in time.

A breeze kicked up as the world darkened around them, and Cassie gave a shiver and pulled the sleeves of her hoodie down to cover her hands.

"Cold?" Nick wrapped an arm around Cassie, tugging her close, sharing his heat.

"Mmmm, a little." But she wasn't going to complain. She loved being cold enough to snuggle into Nick. Hoodie weather only lasted so long in Florida, and she was going to cherish every moment of it.

"Come on, let's get inside. I'll finish making dinner." He swung around and hopped off the seawall, holding a hand to help her down.

"Oh, no." She jumped down without his help. "I've got it."

"Oh, come on," he said as they headed back toward the house. "It's just grilled cheese sandwiches. It's not like I can screw up grilled cheese sandwiches."

He screwed up the grilled cheese sandwiches.

"It's only on one side this time." Nick set the plate in the middle of the kitchen table with an apologetic grimace. All the sandwiches looked perfect: golden brown and cut on the diagonal, oozing with melty cheese. Then Cassie picked one up and turned it over; the other side looked like a charcoal briquette.

"I don't understand." She dropped her half sandwich to her plate. "You run a café. How are you so bad at this?"

"See, I don't think of it as being bad at cooking." Nick put a couple sandwich triangles onto his plate before starting the surgical process of peeling off the burned half of the sandwich. "I think of it as job security for Ramon."

"And I'm sure he's grateful." Cassie dipped her spoon into her bowl of tomato soup—thank God she'd been in charge of that—and gave it a taste. At least that had turned out well. Then she followed his lead, picking off the burned pieces of bread from her sandwich. "Who knows, maybe you can make open-faced grilled cheese sandwiches a thing."

Nick snorted. "Not if I'm trying to do it on purpose. I'd probably set the kitchen on fire." His eyes, bright with amusement, met hers across the table, and Cassie had to laugh.

"Yeah. Maybe you should stick to coffee."

"True. Elmer always said that was what I did best."

Cassie studied him from across the table. His voice had softened, the way it always did when he talked about Elmer. "You miss him, huh?"

He nodded around a bite of mutilated cheese on bread. "I'd never admit it to his face, but I do. My phone's so much quieter these days."

Cassie's soup spoon vibrated next to her bowl, striking it with a faint clink. Automatically her gaze went to her fridge.

window

"Oh!" Cassie stood up, dropping her napkin next to her plate before hurrying to open the kitchen window. "It's time already." They'd meant to finish dinner beforehand, but time had gotten away from them. It took a while to ruin a perfectly good plate of grilled cheese sandwiches.

Nick looked at the fridge, then at the clock on the microwave. "Damn. I'm late." He stood up too, following Cassie to the living room, where they opened the windows wide. Then he bent to give Cassie a kiss. "See you after."

It was meant to be a quick peck—an *I'll be right back* kiss. But Cassie couldn't help it; she reached up and slid her hand around the back of his neck, holding him there so she could linger. She still wasn't used to this: his mouth on hers, the way his touch warmed her to the core. She lived for these little moments, for his slow, lazy smile against her lips as he took his time kissing her. He was thorough, his arms sliding around her waist and pulling her hips into his, making a promise he would keep later that night.

"Damn," he said again as he finally, reluctantly pulled away. "Now I'm really late."

"Oh no. I'm sorry." Cassie wasn't sorry. Not in the least. She leaned against the doorjamb, watching with a hazy smile as he trotted down the front steps and through the garden gate, hurrying down the street toward Hallowed Grounds. Then she poured a second glass of wine and made her way to the upstairs balcony off of their bedroom. It was her favorite spot to watch the ghost tour come by. She left the door to the balcony open in case it was Sarah's too. With all the downstairs windows open to the night air, Sarah was guaranteed a good vantage point no matter where she was in the house.

It was mid-January, so the Christmas lights that were strung around the downtown area would be coming down soon. She'd loved the way they'd lit the town in a bright glow, with her house just on the edge of it all. She and Nick had taken their lights down from the house last weekend, so tonight she sat in relative darkness. The night was cool by Florida standards—just cool enough for a tomato soup and grilled cheese dinner and leaving the windows open in the evenings. The salt air teased locks of Cassie's hair free to dance in the breeze, and she pushed them behind one ear.

Cassie settled into her bistro chair just in time. Low murmurs of conversation came from the sidewalk below, broken up by a cheerful, authoritative voice as they approached her house.

"And here we have the Sarah Hawkins House." Sophie's voice rang out loud and clear. She always spoke a little louder when she gave this part of the tour, since she knew who was listening. "It was built in 1899 by William Donnelly, shortly after Boneyard Key was established here after the Great Storm of 1897. Not long after that, Donnelly left for points north, deciding he'd had enough of Florida. And after that storm, who could blame him?" She paused as a couple of the tourists chuckled, the way they always did at that little joke.

"He planned to leave the house in the care of his niece, Sarah Blankenship. We think her intention was to rent out rooms to the visitors who had started to congregate here in Boneyard Key. There hadn't been a hotel established here yet, and the income would help when women didn't have a lot of opportunity to earn a living.

"Sarah had helped Mr. Donnelly design the house, especially the gardens, and she loved this house tremendously. She was looking forward to living here—just her and her cabbage roses—but then William Donnelly met C.S. Hawkins. *Mean Mr. Hawkins*, we like to call him." Sophie pitched her voice low, in the spooky storytelling voice she was so good at.

Cassie nodded along as Sophie continued to tell the story. It had taken months, and several sets of custom magnetic poetry, for Cassie and Sophie to get the entire story out of Sarah. She didn't seem to harbor any ill will toward her uncle who had married her off. She understood, in a way that Cassie and Sophie didn't, that William Donnelly thought he was doing right by his niece—seeing her married to a wealthy pillar of the community. And while the wealthy part certainly came in handy for Sarah once she was a widow, there was no way any of them could have known that Mr. Hawkins would linger for so many years after his death, trying to control Sarah from the great beyond.

"Sarah lived in this house alone, taking the brunt of her jerk of a husband's behavior, not letting anyone else come inside the house for fear that he might harm them too."

"Now, wait a second," one of the tourists piped up from the back of the crowd. "I bought a copy of *Boneyard Key: A Haunted History* yesterday, and it doesn't have any of that in there. It says that Mrs. Hawkins was the mean one. So what's the truth?"

Some confused mutterings punctuated this statement, but Sophie didn't sound fazed. "That's an excellent question. The *Haunted History* book has been the authoritative text on the history of the town for decades now. But when the Sarah Hawkins House was purchased by its current owner last year, new information came to light. I'm actually working on a more accurate history of Boneyard Key and its inhabitants—living or otherwise—with the help of a local historian. We're hoping to publish it sometime next year. I have business cards back at Hallowed Grounds with our website information, if you want to stay updated."

Sophie tossed a look up toward Cassie's balcony, and Cassie waved, even though it was too dark to be seen. "Okay! Now, as we go back toward downtown, I want to remind you that Hallowed Grounds will be open when we get back to where we started. Feel free to grab a coffee or snack for the road. The lemon pound cake is really to die for. No pun intended, of course."

Cassie grinned at the joke as the tour group filed away, then took her empty glass inside, closing the door to the balcony behind her. "Okay, Sarah," she said as she headed down the stairs. "Story time's over. Hope you enjoyed it."

It was getting a little chilly downstairs, and as a Floridian, Cassie was far too stubborn to turn on the heat if she didn't have to. She closed the living room windows, looking out into the yard. The cabbage roses practically glowed under the front porch light. It was the wrong time of year for them to be blooming, of course, but that wasn't a surprise.

The roses had taken very little effort on Cassie and Nick's part—a couple trips to the local garden center, and a weekend of digging and planting. After that, they grew perfectly and bloomed lush and full, filling the front yard with color and a sweet scent. Cassie barely even had to water them. Sarah apparently took care of the rest.

Cassie glanced at the clock on her way to the kitchen to do the dishes. Nick should be home in about an hour or so, once the tour group came through and filed out. He was almost out of copies of *A Haunted History*; Sophie and Theo's book couldn't get finished quickly enough. Cassie couldn't wait to get a signed copy of her own.

Her mind drifted as she did the dishes, the way it often did. Sudden memories of her old life in Orlando. Happy hours that had become less and less happy, feeling more and more lonely and unfulfilled. Leaving the group chat had been one of the hardest things she'd ever done, but sometimes it was good to leave behind things that no longer fit. It left room for new friendships to grow, and for the ones that really mattered to bubble up to the surface. Two work friends had already come to visit her, declaring her home a delightfully child-free haven when they needed a break.

Things were so different now. Tomorrow she would kayak to Cemetery Island with Theo and Sophie while Nick worked at the café. Once Nick was off work they'd grab a beer together at The Cold Spot, and then probably wander down to The Haunt to see Vince debut a new acoustic set he'd been working on. Then they'd come home, where Sarah Hawkins kept a careful, ethereal eye on them. She was a perfect roommate, and since Nick could roll with having a ghost for a roommate, he was the perfect boyfriend.

Okay, he was the perfect boyfriend for other reasons too. Many, many other reasons.

Dishes done, Cassie hung her kitchen towel on its hook by the fridge. The last thing she saw as she turned off the light was a new message on the fridge.

thank you

"No," she said to Sarah. "Thank *you*."

Acknowledgments

Every time I sit down to write one of these, I become overwhelmed with gratitude. Writing a novel can be frustrating, lonely work, but when I get to reflect on the journey that brought me to this finished book, I remember all the help I got along the way, and I feel so, so grateful that I get to do this.

I remember telling my long-suffering agent, Taylor Haggerty, about what I wanted to write next, spitballing lots of ideas at her like "beach houses" and "ghosts." Before long that became "beach ghosts," and she got excited. Thank you for believing in me, even when you come back with questions like "How can a ghost text?" Our jobs are weird sometimes! And extra thanks to Jasmine Brown for keeping me on track and occasionally in blurb jail when I need it.

I was thrilled when my rock-star editor, Kerry Donovan, was up for taking this fictional trip to Florida with me. It's rare to have someone who really gets what you're trying to say, and the way she speaks my characters' language is, well, spooky sometimes. The team at Berkley remains unmatched: Mary Baker, Genni Eccles, Jessica Mangicaro, Kristin Cipolla, and Kaila Mundell-Hill. Thank you, thank you, for all that you do.

I'm so in love with the cover Sarah Maxwell created for this book! She brought Nick and Cassie, and the Hawkins House, to such perfect life.

The music of Jimmy Buffett was essential while writing this book, and his passing has left such a hole in the world. Give the album *Banana Wind* a listen sometime; it's underrated. Thanks for all the music, Jimmy. Bubbles up.

Before I send in a book I do a lot of angsting and second-guessing. Luckily, I have the best critique partners in the world, who read (and re-read) chapters and tell me what I need to hear when I need to hear it. Gwynne Jackson, Vivien Jackson, Lindsay Landgraf Hess, and Annette Christie, I couldn't possibly do this without you.

One of my favorite things to do when I write is procrastinate. But thankfully, Eva Leigh is right there in my phone, texting me that it's time to sprint and lifting me up when I'm feeling low. Denise Williams invited me on a weekend writing retreat and not only did we write tons of words together and laugh a lot, I also saved her from a moth. My own local writing buddy, Sarah T. Dubb, was always willing to meet me for writing mornings over sourdough toast and cold brew coffee.

Morgan Lee has been my husband, my best friend, and my partner in adventure for coming up on three decades now. Thank you for always believing in me, having my back, and supporting me in all my creative endeavors. (And for letting me get a dog at the worst possible time.) I can't wait to see where life takes us next!

Special shout-out to two very important things I miss about Florida: the chicken flautas from Tijuana Flats (with a side of Smack My Sweet Ass and Call Me Sally from the hot sauce bar) and the Publix chicken tender sub (with provolone cheese, onions, lettuce, and ranch: you are the perfect sandwich and I miss you so much). Honorable mention to the cheese rolls at Napasorn in Orlando.

Finally, I want to thank all the readers who have followed me from the world of the Renaissance Faire to the Gulf Coast of Florida. BookTok and Bookstagram remain a mystery to me, but the love you've shown my books over the years is absolutely second to none. I quite literally wouldn't be doing this without you, and I can't thank you enough for believing in me, reading my books, and connecting with my characters.

In the midnineties, my then-fiancé and I moved to Florida, intending to stay only a year or two. We stayed almost exactly twenty-five years. It was hard saying goodbye to our favorite places: the serenity of Cedar Key, the history of St. Augustine, our home in quaint Mount Dora, the unique aura of Cassadaga. It was even harder to believe that I would no longer live where Disney World was in my backyard, every body of water had at least one alligator in it, and I could grab a Publix sub when I was grocery shopping. Getting to return to Florida, if only in my mind, while getting to know these characters in Boneyard Key has been such a joy, and I hope you enjoyed the trip with me.

Don't miss

Well Met

by Jen DeLuca.
Available now!
Continue reading for a preview.

~

I didn't choose the wench life. The wench life chose me.

When I pulled into the parking lot of Willow Creek High School on that late-spring morning, I had very little on my agenda. No doctor's appointments for my big sister, no school obligations to shuttle my niece to. The only thing I needed to do was get my niece to the sign-ups for the Renaissance Faire. We were five minutes late, so it was going great so far.

Caitlin huffed from the back seat as I threw my little white Jeep in park. "Em, we're late!" She managed to stretch both my name and that last word out into at least three syllables. "What if they don't let me sign up? All my friends are doing this, and if I can't, I'll—"

"They'll let you sign up." But of course she was out before I'd even unbuckled my seat belt. I wasn't going to call her back. I didn't have that kind of authority over her. At barely ten years older, I was more a big sister than an aunt. When I'd first come to stay with my older sister and her daughter, April had tried to get Cait to call me "Aunt Emily," but that was only a short hop away from Auntie Em and Kansas jokes so we'd abandoned it quickly. My relationship with the kid had settled into more of a friendship with overtures of Adult In Charge.

This morning, Adult In Charge was kicking in. No way was I leaving a fourteen-year-old by herself in a strange situation, even if it was her high school. I grabbed my coffee mug from the cup holder and started after her. She couldn't have gone far.

My cell phone rang from inside my purse when I was halfway across the parking lot. I fished it out and kept walking.

"Did you find it okay?"

"Yeah, we're good. Hopefully this won't take too long."

"Oh, God, you don't have to *stay*." April sounded slightly horrified by the prospect. "You just need to drop her off and come back home."

I held my breath and tried to analyze her tone through the crappy cell phone connection. The past few days had been rough as she'd started weaning off the pain medication. "Everything okay?" I tried to sound as casual as possible. "Do you need me to come home?"

"No . . ." Her voice trailed off, and I stopped walking and listened harder.

"April?"

"No, no, Emily. I'm fine. I'm right where you left me, on the couch with coffee and the remote. I don't want you to feel like you have to . . ."

"It's fine. Really. Isn't this why I'm here, to help you out?"

Another pause. Another sigh. "Yeah. Okay . . ." I practically heard her shrug. "I feel bad. I should be doing this stuff."

"Well, you can't." I tried to sound as cheerful as I could. "Not for another couple months at least, remember? Doctor's orders. Besides, this 'stuff' is what I'm here for, right?"

"Yeah." A tremble in her voice now, which I blamed on the Percocet. I'd be glad when she was off that shit for good. It made her weepy.

"Drink your coffee, find something awful on television, okay? I'll make lunch for us when we get home."

I hung up, shoved my phone back in my purse, and once again cursed out the driver who had run the red light that night. A vision of April's SUV popped into my head, that twisted lump of silver metal at the junkyard, and I pushed it aside. Caitlin had been asleep in the back seat, and somehow she'd walked away with nothing more than some bruises and a sprained ankle.

My sister hadn't been so lucky. Mom had stayed with her while she was in the ICU, and by the time April was home from the hospital a week later I'd moved in, so Mom could go home to Dad in Indiana. My older sister needed a caregiver for a while, and my niece needed an Adult In Charge who was mobile, so I was here to stay.

As for me . . . I needed a change. A couple weeks before the accident I'd lost not only my boyfriend and my apartment, but all my plans for the future. Willow Creek, Maryland, was as good a place as any to lick my wounds while I took care of April and hers. Smack in the middle of wine country, this area was all rolling green hills dotted with small towns like this one, with its charming downtown storefronts and friendly people. Though I hadn't seen any willows yet and as far as I could tell there weren't any creeks, so the name remained a mystery.

I picked up the pace and pushed through the double doors, finally catching up with Caitlin outside the high school auditorium. She didn't look back at me, running down the aisle instead to join a handful of kids roughly her age clustered in front of the stage, getting forms from a guy with a clipboard. The auditorium was filled with clumps of kids embracing like long-lost relatives who hadn't seen each other in years, even though they'd probably sat next to each other in class the day before. There were adults around too, sprinkled here and there, but I couldn't tell if they were chaperones or participants. Then one of the adults turned around and his black T-shirt said HUZZAH! across the front in huge white letters, and I had my answer.

I took a long sip of coffee and sank into a chair in the back row. My job as taxi service was done. I checked the time on my phone. One hour until I needed to be back to pick her up, which wasn't enough time to go home. Willow Creek was a small town, but April lived on one end of it and the high school was on the outskirts at the other. I pulled up my list-making app. I'd picked up refills of April's meds the previous day, and this Renaissance Faire tryout was the only other thing on my list. Was there anything else I needed to get done while I was on this side of town?

"Are you here to volunteer?"

One of the adults I'd spotted before—cute, blond, shortish, and roundish—had splintered off and now hovered at the end of the row where I was sitting. Before I could answer she took a form off her clipboard and pushed it into my hands.

"Here. You can go ahead and fill this out."

"What? Me?" I stared at the form as though it were printed in Cyrillic. "Oh. No. I'm just here to drop off my niece." I nodded toward the group of kids at the front.

"Which one's your . . ." She looked down the aisle. "Oh, Caitlin, right? You must be Emily."

My eyes widened. "Yeah. Good call. I keep forgetting how small this town is." I'd come here from Boston, and had grown up outside of Indianapolis. Small towns weren't my thing.

She laughed and waved it off. "You'll get used to it, trust me. I'm Stacey, by the way. And I'm afraid you kind of have to volunteer." She indicated the form still in my hand. "It's a requirement if a younger student wants to be part of the Faire cast. Anyone under sixteen needs a parent or guardian in the cast with them. I think April was planning to volunteer with her, but . . ." Her sentence trailed off, and she punctuated it with an awkward shrug.

"Yeah." I looked down at the form. "You can't call it volunteering, then, can you? Sounds more like strong-arming." But I looked over at Cait, already chatting with her friends, holding her own form like it was a golden ticket. I read through the form. Six weeks of Saturday rehearsals starting in June, then six more weekends from mid-July through the end of August. I was already playing chauffeur for Caitlin all spring and summer anyway . . .

Before I could say anything else, the double doors behind me opened with a bang. I whirled in my seat to see a man striding through like he was walking into an Old West saloon. He was . . . delicious. No other way to describe him. Tall, blond, muscled, with a great head of hair and a tight T-shirt. Gaston crossed with Captain America, with a generic yet mesmerizing handsomeness.

"Mitch!" Stacey greeted him like an old friend. Which he undoubtedly was. These people probably all went to this high school together back in the day. "Mitch, come over here and tell Emily that she wants to do Faire."

He scoffed as though the question were the stupidest one he'd ever heard. "Of course she wants to do Faire! Why else would she be here?"

I pointed down the aisle to Cait. "I'm really just the taxi."

Mitch peered at my niece, then turned back to me. "Oh, you're *Emily*. The aunt, right? Your sister's the one who was in the crash? How's she doing?"

I blinked. Goddamn small towns. "Good. She's . . . um . . . good." My sister hated gossip in all forms, so I made sure not to contribute any information that could get around.

"Good. Yeah, glad to hear it." He looked solemn for a moment

or two, then brushed it aside, jovial smile back on his face. "Anyway.
You should hang around, join the insanity. I mean, it's lots of work,
but it's fun. You'll love it." With that, he was gone, sauntering his
way down the aisle, fist-bumping kids as he went.

I watched him walk away for a second, because, damn, could he
fill out a pair of jeans, both front and back. Then what he said registered with me. "I'll love it?" I turned back to Stacey the volunteer.
"He doesn't know me. How does he know what I'll love?"

"If it helps . . ." She leaned forward conspiratorially, and I
couldn't help but respond with a lean of my own. "He carries a
pretty big sword during Faire. And wears a kilt."

"Sold." I dug in my purse for a pen. What was giving up my
weekends for the entire summer when it meant I could look at an ass
like that?

What the hell, right? It would be time with Caitlin. That was
what I was there for. Be the cool aunt. Do the fun stuff. Distract her
from the car accident that had left her with nightmares and weekly
therapy sessions, and left her mom with a shattered right leg. When
I'd arrived in Willow Creek, gloom had hung low over their household, like smoke in a crowded room. I'd come to throw open a window, let in the light again.

Besides, helping out my sister and her kid was the best way to
stop dwelling on my own shit. Focusing on someone else's problems
was always easier than my own.

Stacey grinned as I started filling out the form. "Give it to Simon
up at the front when you're finished. It's going to be great. Huzzah!"
This last was said as a cheer, and with that she was gone, probably
looking for other parental-type figures to snag into this whole gig.

Oh, God. Was I going to have to yell "huzzah" too? How much
did I love my niece?

The form was pretty basic, and soon I followed the stream of volunteers (mostly kids—where were all the adults?) to the front of the auditorium, where they handed the papers to the dark-haired man with the clipboard collecting them. Simon, I presumed. Thank God, another adult. More adultier than me, even. I'd rolled out of bed and thrown on leggings and a T-shirt, while he was immaculate in jeans and a perfectly ironed Oxford shirt, sleeves rolled halfway up his forearms, with a dark blue vest buttoned over it.

Despite his super-mature vibe, he didn't look that much older than me. Late twenties at the most. Slighter of build than Mitch, and probably not quite six feet tall. Well-groomed and clean-shaven with closely cut dark brown hair. He looked like he smelled clean, like laundry detergent and sharp soap. Mitch, for all his hotness, looked like he smelled like Axe body spray.

When it was my turn, I handed the form in and turned away, checking to see where Cait had wandered off to. I couldn't wait to tell her I was doing this whole thing with her. That kid was gonna owe me one.

"This isn't right."

I turned back around. "Excuse me?"

Simon, the form collector, brandished mine at me. "Your form. You didn't fill it out correctly."

"Um . . ." I walked back over to him and took the paper from his hand. "I think I know how to fill out a form."

"Right there." He tapped his pen in a *rat-a-tat-tat* on the page. "You didn't say what role you're trying out for."

"Role?" I squinted at it. "Oh, right." I handed the paper back to him. "I don't care. Whatever you need."

He didn't take it. "You have to specify a role."

"Really?" I looked behind me, searching for the desperate volunteer who had coerced me into this gig in the first place. But she was lost in a sea of auditionees. Of course.

"Yes, really." He pursed his lips, and his brows drew together over his eyes. Dark brown brows, muddy brown eyes. He'd be relatively attractive if he weren't looking at me like he'd caught me cheating on my chemistry final. "It's pretty simple," he continued. "Nobility, actors, dancers . . . you can audition for any of those. You could also try out for the combat stuff, if you have any experience. We do a human chess match and joust."

"I . . . I don't have any experience. Or, um, talent." The longer this conversation went on, the more my heart sank. Now I was supposed to have skills? Wasn't this a volunteer thing? Why was this guy making it so freaking hard?

He looked at me for a moment, a quick perusal up and down. Not so much checking me out as sizing me up. "Are you over twenty-one?"

Jesus. I knew I was on the short side, but . . . I drew myself up, as though looking a little taller would make me look older too. "Twenty-five, thank you very much." Well, twenty-five in July, but he didn't need to know that. It wasn't like he'd be celebrating my birthday with me.

"Hmmm. You have to be twenty-one to be a tavern wench. You could put that down if you want to help out in the tavern."

Now we were talking. Nothing wrong with hanging out in a bar for a few weekends in the summer. I'd worked in bars before; hell, I worked in two of them until just recently. This would be the same thing, but in a cuter costume.

Author photo by Morgan H. Lee

Jen DeLuca was born and raised near Richmond, Virginia, but now lives in Arizona with her husband and a houseful of rescue pets. She loves latte-flavored lattes, Hokies football, and the Oxford comma. Her novels, *Well Met*, *Well Played*, *Well Matched*, and *Well Traveled*, were inspired by her time volunteering as a pub wench with her local Renaissance Faire.

CONNECT ONLINE

JenDeLuca.com
JenDeLucaBooks
JenDeLucaWrites
Jaydee_Ell

Ready to find
your next great read?

Let us help.

Visit prh.com/nextread

Penguin
Random
House